SPIRIT VISION

Morgan Straughan Cormick

"Hold on to 'what if.'"

MORGAN STRAUGHAN COMNICK

First Paper Crane Books Paperback Edition December 2013

Printed and bound in the United States of America

ISBN: 9780615935461

For my family, friends, and teachers who cared enough to say, "You can do it."

1

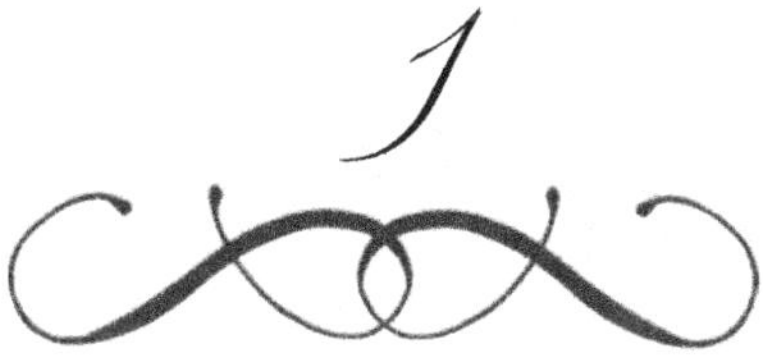

"CHOKE . . ."

The sharp, cool fog hit the back of my dry throat, filling it with dampness. It was harder to swallow with each sharp breath I took. It felt like a knife was being stabbed into my chest and letting all my air, my life, leak out. But I refused to stop breathing. I could not accept that the task that kept me alive was slowly dragging me to my end.

"*Go ahead and choke . . .*"

I held my chest tight, trying to keep this voice coming from inside my heart at bay. Clutching my hands, I saw how purple and shaky they were; it spiked my fear levels. It was becoming unbearable to breathe. My eyes found a dark skeleton of a serpent. It was wrapping around my neck like a fashion scarf. His beady eyes stared into my soul, gaining more control over me, his velvet voice hissing and commanding, "*Yes . . . time to end your life so dark hearts can thrive . . . Close your eyes as I stop your breath . . .*"

I gradually closed my eyes and felt my spirit lifting, my struggle to fight laughable. Heat crept into my face, making color flash before my eyelids. There it was; death was awaiting me.

My head fell back, forcing me to look at the ceiling. I sent up a silent message to the sky to the one who was watching over me and asked if they would care for my loved ones if I vanished. Suddenly, in a rush of speed, my hope dangling from a frayed thread, all of my life poured back into me, being carried into me by a blinding light. My eyes popped opened due to the power and love that radiated within me now. I scanned the room, noticing I was in science class and breathing like normal. The snake was nowhere in sight. No thoughts of him haunted me anymore. Only a scream and someone falling deep into a hollow hole that was invisible to me filled my head. Still, those thoughts were fuzzy and then it was stripped away from my mind . . .

I stared. Everything appeared stable, my choking experience only known to me. My classmates were pretending to write notes as they watched Mrs. Shell with bored eyes. I smiled from relief. It seemed like nothing had changed since the experience. My head was already pounding from trying to do conversion factors, but after my newest experience, my brain was on maximum overdrive and about to fry any second! I ignored the confusion and focused on trying to be normal.

"I want you all to add hertz to your list of standards, okay class?" Mrs. Shell announced.

I did as I was told and looked at the volt meter Mrs. Shell was holding. I halted when I heard a heavy sigh. I turned around swiftly to see Chloe frowning and tapping the band tune she had hummed in the hallway earlier with her pencil eraser.

I whispered with a grin, "Chloe . . . why aren't you taking notes?"

She jumped up, like I bombed her own little world she was consumed in, which was not surprising. Chloe leaned forward to my right ear with a big, weird smirk on her charming face.

"I don't need to write this junk down. When I get older, I'm going to marry Orlando Bloom and he can hire me and my best friend a person to write all these notes for us!" She winked at the end, referring to me. I had to snicker at "Chloe Bloom." I loved the way her dream name sounded!

Her face turned very strict and anxious. "Are you all right? I saw your hands shaking . . ."

A feeling of dread crashed the atmosphere into the day, as if being caught with the snake had set the world off-balance.

"Do you need to talk about something?"

I felt like my face was a blackboard and a teacher was erasing the smile off of it. My mind jumbled, I looked into her eyes to reply, "I'm fine Chloe. I just got a little sidetracked is all."

She squeezed my hand with sympathy, but we both knew her understanding was fake. Her eyes bugged out into the size of grapefruits, her head sinking down like a submarine. It wasn't like her to act so weird. My heart beat a message to me in Morse code: 'She knows something you don't. Run!' It raced faster, having the beat of a storm, the dread and anticipation too much for it.

She lifted her head up, jerked my hands firmly, and said, "Be careful. You are the only one that can open the gate for me . . . for all of us."

What? Open what gate?

I was petrified. I felt like I was looking at the eyes of a stranger, not my dearest friend. My hands throbbed under Chloe's strong grip. They became bruised. I tried to twist them away, but she grabbed them tighter, showing me a cruel smile that shattered my rationality. That look wasn't Chloe's usual angelic smile I adored, but a dark, sinister grin that ripped my soul into a black hole. A smile of humanity-shattering evil matched her new beady eyes . . .

I pulled and tugged with all my might to get away, but it was no use. Her nails dug deep into my flesh, piercing my body. I bit my lower lip, trying not to let the pain flood over me, but it was overwhelming, blocking my ability to think.

I was about to give up—death must have wanted to claim me—until I saw something . . . a mist of hazel smoke floating in Chloe's eyes. It was only there for a second, a split second, but I saw it. It seemed unnatural. What was happening with Chloe? Then, I realized it all at once: she wasn't with me anymore.

Using my last ounce of will, I ripped my hands out of its clutches and screamed, "Stop it! I know you're not Chloe. Leave me alone!"

Its face was taken aback; its eyes blackened darker than night. The smoke slithered out of my friend, shooting out of the tips of her blonde hair like gamma rays. Her panicked face was strained and terrified.

The energy that was released made the whole room become white and black, warped like a *Through the Looking Glass* checkerboard. Instead of a white rabbit, however, a shadow appeared, dancing in front of my eyes. It was spinning and twirling around me like a happy child. Leisurely, it went to my side. I couldn't see its figure, but I sure felt it and my heart yearned to love that shadow.

It whispered to me in its dance: "Remember the light. Remember my light. Remember your light. We are one."

I heard a snap. It echoed, ringing in my ears. I was dazed, trapped within its vibes. My legs felt rubbery, ready to fall to the core of my world. The shadow surrounded me, but a force pushed it back. It was close enough to protect me, but not touch me. I smiled and began to tear up at the same time from our situation and yet, I felt like I was drowning in an endless lake, about to faint. Too late, I realized I was—

I fluttered my eyes open, adjusting to the overbearing light of the light bulb above. All I could hear was Mrs. Shell talking about radios as everyone scratched down notes. I decided to look at Chloe, who still seemed out of it, but she appeared to be recovered. I glimpsed at her again and she glanced upward, giving me her angelic smile. Chloe was back! I shrugged off the vision of the shadow from my mind so I could continue on with the rest of my peers.

Mrs. Shell was showing us how to work a heart monitor before starting our new lab. The way it worked was so neat that I didn't mind writing notes. It was better than thinking about all the strange daydreams I was having, if that's what a sane person would call them.

With my head bent down to write, a glitter of golden dust entered my eye, making it watery. My poor eyes needed a break from all this pandemonium! While trying to get it from blocking my vision, I saw a little circle of sunlight on my paper. Where's that coming from? I touched it, oddly fearful of its power, at how it radiated warmth somehow on its own, but dazzled by its beauty. The warm glow was comforting. I figured it was from the window, but they were closed and covered by blinds. Strange—no! It was normal from what I had been thinking about all period!

It suddenly grew bigger and bigger, until I couldn't see my notes. Great! My mind drifted to Mark, who I imagined had it worse on his paper since he was closer to the window and all that jazz. I looked back at my beloved, short friend with his dark and lovely skin, rich brown eyes covered by cool glasses, and his sweet, but firm smile that made every girl go weak in the knees for an instant. However, his paper was ordinary, making my assumption incorrect. Weirder, Mark appeared to be moving slow, real slow.

I adjusted my head to see that Chloe, Rin, and Lauren were as well. Everyone was but me, the stupid girl with the dumb light on her paper, which was now swallowing up my personal bubble. Mrs. Shell became still, the heartbeat monitor attached to her showing a straight line. Nor did she breathe. Nothing but dead silence consumed me and the classroom. I was the only thing moving. Yet, a click entered my ears followed by a tick and then a tock. All I could hear was the school's cheap clock and it was like an omen for something approaching.

The glow was gone from my paper, but the heat from it that I had felt earlier turned into a blinding ray of white that shone only on me. It grew larger until I saw something flowing within it . . . Hair? Long and radiant hair at that! The beam began to take shape, a human form. It was so beautiful yet scary at the same time. What sort of CGI Hollywood movie scenes was I experiencing?

The light sat by me, touching my cheek fondly. I could feel the vivacity of the beam's finger as it brushed my skin and I could hear its melody like a heartbeat. Our heartbeats were then one, forming a stunning duet. That made me nervous, halting my ability to speak, breathe, and think. The enchanting song did not seem to belong to us to share, but it connected me to someone, like the ray of light was fusing me with the missing part of my soul through a song.

Finally, it spoke. "You are a special girl, miss. I know you will help us during this time of hardship."

I saw the lovely, but pained face of the divine creature. It was crying. It floated closer toward me, holding my hands as it began to continue its words, swirling me in a melancholic spell. "Yet, be careful pet. It will be dangerous for you to face your rival, but we will try our best to protect you." It smiled before going on with its speech. "I hope we both find what we are looking for . . ."

Looking for? What was I looking for? Who were the "we" it was referring to? Why did it mention an enemy? I wanted to know everything that very second, but mostly, I wanted the most obvious question answered: What was going on? All of this chaos was not ordinary! Sure, I had weird dreams, but never anything so real and upsetting . . . this involved . . .

Out of the blue, my legs began to move, but I knew it wasn't me doing it.

"Stary! Stary! Wake up now!"

That voice. It was faint, but heartwarming to hear something so familiar. However, I didn't want to follow its path just yet. The last thing I remembered before being tugged by invisible wires to the sound of my name was the light staring up at me with worried eyes. My heart felt cold and my spine tangled in knots, my body tingled. The reason was that . . . my soul was being ripped into two separate fragments.

"Stary! Stary! Honey, wake up!"

I leaped out of my bed, sweating like crazy to reply to the comforting sound. My chest was aching wildly and my throat burned.

"Stary, you were screaming in your sleep. Are you all right babe?"

I looked up slowly, absorbing the face of my father. I had no words; my lips were sealed tight.

I moved a loose hair from my face so it wouldn't be stuck in my nervous sweat before answering. "A dream? Are you sure?" My breath sounded like a fog.

He blinked at me in a funny way, like I had, without warning, put on a clown suit with stupid shoes to match. "Of course! What else could it be?"

What else? Life or death? Nothing or everything? Important or useless? Or maybe I was nuts. I wasn't sure what to believe, but I knew I was home and still, my mind was wandering to find its place where it belonged.

"I'm cool Daddy. Really," I answered in what I hoped would be a casual, chipper voice, but it sounded too forced to me.

He smiled with doubt in his aging eyes, but he let it go and hit my head playfully. "Good! Now get dressed and we'll have us some bacon and cheese sandwiches."

I grinned from ear to ear. Something soothing at last! "Sure thing Daddy."

He quietly left my room, allowing me to find some inner peace. I plopped on my bed, looking at the stars on my walls. They were glistening in the morning sun.

A dream? My brain could not focus on the beauty my life was built upon as these new dark visions consumed my usual peaceful world . It sure as heck didn't seem or feel like a dream! It felt real. It felt like I was being summoned, like I was—

A jolt of sensitivity zapped through my body. I thought I felt someone (or something) in the room. I looked in a rush, incapacitated by the energy. To my surprise, no one was there.

"Maybe I am nuts," I whispered, rolling my eyes. This is not something a fifteen-year old girl should be worried about! Oh well. I put on some outfit and ran downstairs, where to my surprise (again), I couldn't eat because I could have sworn someone was in my room, patiently observing me.

I gazed around the table to see my whole family there and nothing out of place occurred, but still . . . I felt like I didn't belong. I nudged away the thought, grabbed a piece of toast, and hopped in the car with my dad for school. My dad talked to me about the usual things: students, bills, and stupid stuff my brother did. But, my mind wasn't with him even if my body was in his old truck beside him. I was in my own little land, lost in the mysteries of my unconscious mind. All I could think about was the words I kept hearing, the meaning and images the dream showed me, and the beam of light. Who or what was waiting for me and if I faced it, would it show me rage or compassion?

2

SCHOOL WAS LIKE A SECOND HOME TO ME SINCE I WAS ALWAYS there for choir, school projects, or because my father had to stay for meetings or finalizing grades. I actually liked school. It was when I saw my friends and expanded my mind. I guess that makes me more nuts . . .

Dad had a meeting right away so I got to stay and play on the computer like I always did. He gave me two dollars for lunch and left; this was a daily routine. I normally looked up anime pictures on the web, but I decided to read a forum thread from people who had strange dreams. I just couldn't get my dream out of my head. I couldn't comprehend how a once in a lifetime dream was formed without it meaning something.

After reading a bit, I soon realized talking to real nuts wasn't going to get me anywhere. I then found an article about strange dream patterns, but all it told me was I needed more than a ninth-grade education to understand all of its golly goop! I sighed, defeated, and spun in the desk chair, spinning like the tea cups at Disney World, hoping my troubles would vanish from the velocity.

Then, it happened again. I was 110% sure I felt someone in the room. I didn't want to look because I was too frightened that I was correct about the odd yearning and too terrified of what I would find. So, I yelled, "I know you're in here . . . somewhere. So, please come and show yourself!"

No answer came, making my throat thicken with uneasiness. I swallowed hard and tried again, rephrasing as I stood. "If you need help, I can be of some use, but I don't do dishes."

I laughed to myself; I was willing to do anything to make the uneasiness go away. I began to breathe heavily and I felt light-headed due to the fact that there was another pulse in the room. The vibration of it was choking me like a noose.

I moved around the classroom like a zombie. Impulse seized me then, making me yell, "COME OUT!" My fear and frustration all rushed out at once and I wanted to apologize for my action. I usually overthink things.

"Shhhhh. My heavens! You do not have to shout so deafeningly. Do you want everyone to hear you, dear?" A voice that was as lovely as bells answered. It had a timid tone and a hint of irritation mixed into its bell-like speech. Regardless of the type of voice, I was still not prepared for *any* voice in the least bit.

My legs moved backward on their own, making me sit up in the computer chair. My mouth went dry and goose bumps were forming down my spine.

I had to answer. I might have been terrified, but I refused to be informal and rude. "I—"

A knock halted my courage. I looked up toward the ceiling, assuming the voice was from the Lord, but the voice was gone and no feelings were left in the room. I opened the door slowly to see Mr. Tin with a giddy smile.

Mr. Tin was a tall man at about six feet, always upbeat and ready to face the world. He was probably looking for my dad; he always forgot meetings and stuff like that. He, not embarrassed or scared at all, popped his head in the doorframe and asked, "Where's your old man at Stary?"

I shrugged, acting like I didn't care, and said casually, "At a meeting that all the freshmen teachers are required to be at, sir." I had to mess with him since he loved to pick on me. It was a never-ending war made up of friendly but tough battles.

He looked at me the way he did when he was impressed, arching one black eyebrow. "Nice try. I see I taught you well *Padawan*."

I wanted to scream in defeat since he didn't fall for it! I should have expected that for he was, as he said, "a role model for today's youth."

Mr. Tin winked at me, rewarding my efforts before turning his feet to search for my father, but he came back and asked, "I won't ask you what I probably should, which is 'why are you acting so weird,' but a question I have been wondering about for a while now. Have you ever not been a perfect student, Miss Moon?"

I stared at him, cocking my head, wondering how he could sense my nerve-wracking vibe. Was I that obvious or was he part bloodhound? With an evil little smile, I answered, burying my urge to burst open from the seams into a metaphorical dirt pile. "Define perfect Mr. Tin . . ."

He cracked up, tossing his bald head back. "Thanks Stary girl! You so kill me with your innocence and wit sometimes. See ya." He was gone in a flash. Sometimes I thought he had super powers since he was always gone in a blink of an eye. But I knew he was gone; I couldn't hear the clashing of the ice in his giant tea cup anymore.

With relief and concern, I looked around . . . no . . . more like felt around. No voices, no feelings, or anything of that nature. Everything was customary and peaceful. Wait . . . there was no such thing as normal from that moment on. That was one new thing I learned. I could sense it in my pounding gut.

An uncertainty ran though my veins, chilling my soul to the core with pain. My life was forever changed because of this feeling. So, what was it? And what did I do to deserve it? The ten minute bell rang, destroying my thoughts. I clenched my chest, hoping to keep the hissing voice that appeared out of thin air inside myself sealed; it was a fragment of the dream snake. I was scared to hold on to even a piece of him, and yet I was scared to let go. All of my fear might escape from my soul and right then, I needed that worry and unknown suffering to change my life and make sense of my mind's illusions. For one to have courage, one must also know how to fear and for one to feel joy, gratitude, and empathy, one must know suffering.

I slung my heavy purple backpack on my shoulders and exited my daddy's classroom, preparing myself for another average school day. I passed the math wing and skipped down the steps, my vision following the shiny tiles of the main hallway. Before I hopped the final two steps of the staircase and turned right to head into the lunchroom, I spotted a speck from the corner of my eye. It felt like time went into a slow state. Was it because of the speck or did the universe do it for the speck and myself to lock gazes? It stopped its hovering when I saw it . . . What was it?

It belonged to a far-off sliver of a line, a line of silver that flickered on and off, as if it did not know if it was supposed to exist yet. I was about to turn toward it when it disappeared before my mind could even consider blinking. That answered my question; this light was not meant to be seen yet. My gut was pounding these answers into my blood and I accepted them just as I accepted I heard a voice and was meant to know what sorrow was, the voice's sorrow, to improve myself.

The voice and dream were pushed to the back of my brain as I entered the lunchroom to talk to my friends before school. I had even forgotten all about the light by the time the bell rang for homeroom. I did not even think about that little sliver of line and light that was heading towards the main hallway's custodians' closet.

For my first class, I had reading so . . . I read! Big surprise! I became transported to a land of world travelers, a forgotten romance, a promise that could cost the young hero his life, and colorful costumes. I was getting to an intense battle scene in my manga when a balled piece of paper whacked my head. I straightened my back and glanced around the lunch room where my class was held. In the distance, I saw a group of boys in my homeroom class all wearing their Plantersville letterman jackets, waving like goofballs at me. This was going to end well . . .

I located the paper ball by my foot and picked it up. I flattened the wrinkles as I slowly opened the note. Not to my shock or joy, it read: "You know you're reading your book backwards, right Twinkle?"

I arched my eyebrows slightly and heard them snickering like they were Robin Williams's material. All I did was shake my head at them and place the note by my binder to be recycled later. I am not going to lie; it was tempting to reply back with an "At least I am reading" response, but it would do no good. One, these boys have been so kindly informing me all year that I have been "reading my book backwards." Last time I checked, not everyone in the world read left to right like we do in America. Two, although this group of boys were goobers, they weren't cruel and I had no vice towards them. Thirdly and last of all, it was not worth the time and risk of getting in trouble. Although the nickname Twinkle still bugs me after all of these years . . .

Although with this, I took a moment to be appreciative for the normality of my every day school day. Girls were gossiping about boys, half of them without their books even cracked. Boys were either copying someone's homework or seeing who could cram the most gummy worms into their mouth. Notes were being passed from table to table like a safe Pony Express. I smiled to myself at how simple everything was. It was almost laughable that I was hearing voices and being bothered by it.

I went back to my manga and was on the final chapter when our guidance counselor, Mrs. Timber, tapped me lightly on the shoulder and asked if I could help her sort some tutoring papers. My reading instructor, the '60s music king who loved to wear Hawaiian shirts, Mr. Ville, nodded to this request and went back to composing lyrics for a new song. As the clock informed me there were five minutes left in the period, I grabbed my binder and the note. Just as I turned my back away from the recycle bin, a loud crash filled the space.

Mrs. Timber and Mr. Ville went up the three long steps that led to the main hallway to investigate. Moments later, the husky voice of our custodian, Mr. Jerry, echoed into the cafeteria, "Everything's fine you guys. Somehow my tin trashcan slipped out of my hands as I was trying to put it in the closet and it hit the wall pretty hard. No one's hurt!"

A tin, wheeled trashcan smacking a wall would explain the booming sound. The teachers returned and Mr. Ville got everyone back into their seats as Mrs. Timber led me away. We walked down a small staircase to the counseling center. Right before I entered behind her, my ears detected a scream. It was low and muffled, but no one in the office moved a muscle. I tipped my head upward, trying to pick up a trace of it, but no sound came. With that, I shut the door with a click behind me, my insides shaking with premonition. The wheels were beginning to move.

The smell of freshly cut grass surrounded me as I jogged up the path to the tennis court where my gym class was. Inhaling the power of the natural Earth gave me the energy to sprint the last half of the way as the sweet-scented breeze skated across the flowers. The warmth of the blazing sun and dazzling sky appeared to put a spotlight for me to find my class.

I handed Coach my pass from Mrs. Timber. Instead of a snarky but good-natured comment as I would have expected from him, he grunted and merely pointed to my tennis partner. I cocked my head to look at him for a second; I noticed his eyes were dilated, as if he was waiting for something. I nodded to him, dismissing his look, and ran to my partner to begin our doubles match for the day.

I got in position and a shiver went down my spine. Everything was eerily quiet. Most days, when we were out on the tennis courts, someone would send the ball over the fence or people would make stupid faces at each other as they spin the racket on their middle finger. Today, the only sound I heard were balls going over the net with the lightest of taps, so soft I strained to hear my partner next to me practicing her serves. The conversations were spoken in whispered choir rounds; one pair would start a conversation and the pair next to them would start one almost in time and so forth. They whispered so softly that if their lips had not been moving, I would have sworn I had imagined it. It felt wrong somehow.

However, the oddest thing was everyone's eyes were darting around, their shoulders stiff as boards. Some girls were chewing on their lips until they became white and hugged their shoulders to warm up although the day was perfect for April.

I felt a smack on my forearm. My tennis partner gave me a small smile, admitting silently she was the culprit, and inclined her head to our opponents. It was time for our match. I apologized; I had no idea how long I had been staring so intently at the others, but I was ready to move on. I got in position to serve, the ball soaring above my head, absorbing the sun's rays and almost blinding me before it fell. I counted until it descended to the perfect angle. I hit it with my racket with as much strength and control as I could. The ball went flying over the net and barely landed over it, but the spot was so perfect that only a pro could have returned it in time. We had received the first point.

An overly happy grin stretched my face and I was about to cheer for my first amazing serve, when I paused mid-jump. My peers were shaking with fright, their bug eyes soaking in my image. My arm went limp, making my racket hit my thigh. Even my partner looked afraid. I spun a half circle to look at my coach; his mouth was agape and his eyes straight as arrows. My coach, who could wrestle a bear and win, looked terrified and protective. The courts seemed to be closing in on me. I did not understand what had caused everyone to become so alarmed.

The wind rolled my ball to me. It tapped my shoe. I glanced down at it, realization coming to me. The ball . . . I had smacked it with all my might and although I was not strong, all that energy made a loud sound like a firecracker going off. A firecracker no one expected, a firecracker that went off in a world where a butterfly's wings flapping caused yelps.

I picked up the ball and handed it to my partner to serve, getting in stance to continue the match. The taste in my mouth was sickening and my throat became parched. My lips were horrified of making a movement in fear of scaring someone else. I did not know why my classmates were on edge, but I refused to cause any more distress. I would contain my guilt inside.

With an aching head, but a sense of recovery, I went to my next hour. Third hour was my dad's freshman American history class. It was a neat class since I adored history and my daddy. I knew my dad would make me feel better. He always started the day by talking before we received our assignment or watched a video, connecting our world to our timeline as he sat on the desk like he was king of the world. Instead, all he did was smile weakly and said in a straining tone, "Please follow the directions on the worksheet. If you need help, you may come up to me and ask."

WHAT?! My dad never tried to do things the easy way! Never! Okay, my brain was going to explode. What in the world was going on? No one complained, no one fell asleep, or even talked. Again, everyone was looking around as if the pages of our history textbook would come to life and harm us. The most unsettling and confusing thing of all was that my dad was stationed by the closed door like a security guard, shifting his gaze from the door window to us. I ignored the sideways looks of determination and pain he was giving me every so often. He needed to be at his desk grading or at his podium lecturing, rambling about a section in the chapter or part of the video.

I needed to know what was going on immediately. If I didn't . . . if I had to keep looking into my father's glassy eyes . . . I knew my heart would break. The little voice inside my head was calling me a fool for ignoring what I should have known. But why it wasn't telling me the answer I wanted was another question. The word "time" kept echoing in my heart when I asked. I swatted the interrogations inside me away like a fly and decided, for the moment, to focus on behaving for my dad's and peers' sakes.

Fourth hour was Mrs. Shell's science class, the class my dream was set in. All the snapshots of the dream came unwillingly to me. I was too petrified to walk in the door after seeing the images once more. It felt as if invisible ice were covering my ankles. My feet refused to try to crack the icy spell that I placed on the floor. I felt someone gently push me and I flew forward, almost tripping in the doorway. Beyond afraid, I turned, getting my book ready to hit my attacker, but I ceased mid-blow. It was Rin who had pushed me.

She frowned, warning me to be more careful with her hazel eyes that reflected the spark of a personal fire. After she knew I got her message, she glided past me like a fairy on water. Seconds after following her motions, Chloe signaled me to my seat.

I sat there the whole class period ill and anxious. The surroundings were exactly like my dream. It was all there: the heart monitor, Mrs. Shell's lecture, and the silence of the room that made the clock sound like a bomb. A mad scientist must have brought it back to life from the dead memories of my mind.

I knew I was being as paranoid as my classmates. It did not get much better. Mark dropped his pencil once and the two rows by us all jumped out of their seats simultaneously, like we were all watching the scariest movie ever made. Mrs. Shell just gave us a look full of sympathy and continued to write in her grade book. Her calm grace allowed me to continue my work.

However, nothing weird happened. Thank goodness, I praised to the heavens! I sighed in relief when class was over, preparing myself for the final hour. I knew if I could handle the live-action version of my nightmare, I could face Mr. Tin.

Once the bell rang, Chloe and I walked upstairs to our fifth hour class, Mr. Tin's English class, but we had lunch first. We dropped off our backpacks in his room and talked about boys along the way (Chloe did most of the talking and I nodded and giggled). Chloe was chatting, but she still didn't seem like Chloe; no one seemed like themselves. I kept staring at her to make sure there was no smoke in her eyes, confusing her a bit by the way her cheeks flamed.

We walked slowly so we could talk more when I saw my dad and Mr. Tin whispering to one another with concerned and sad faces outside dad's door. Before Chloe and I could stop our steps, they saw us and became very still, not ready to adjust their gears. It was the eerie pause that made one feel that they were the center of harsh gossip.

Mr. Tin was the first to come up to us; he was the braver of the two. He cleared his throat, it making a strange sound, and swallowed hard. "Good afternoon ladies." He bowed and winked. He really was a funny man!

Chloe smiled awkwardly, trying not to be dismayed. "Hi there, Mr. Tin. Hi Mr. Moon."

My dad looked at her for a while like she was a stranger, not moving an inch, and refusing to say a word. Finally a "Hey Chloe" came out of his mouth, almost like it was something we had to imagine ourselves.

Chloe gave me a questionable gaze, but I couldn't take my eyes off my father. He seemed so depressed, so worried, so . . . not my father. I must have looked upset for he gave a sentimental smile; the same weak smile he gave in class! That made my heart sink and I felt worse inside, like I was being forced to watch a car wreck again and again in slow motion.

"Now, go and eat Stary and take Fluffy with you," my daddy said. Mr. Tin snickered at my dad's comment, covering his mouth like a child as my dad reflected some of his old light into his eyes. It seemed forced, but the effort was comforting.

Chloe was deeply insulted and showed my dad her feelings for him with a twist of her tongue. His nickname for her was Fluffy and she loathed it. "Well, fine then! Bye!" She grabbed my upper arm, dragging me away, but all I could do was say "bye" and give a shy wave.

What was wrong with my dad? I couldn't bear to look at him so frightened. Was this feeling of loss and sorrow supposed to help him or did

I have something else in store? The word "soon" was now pulsing through my body. Soon was not something I was looking forward to.

Mrs. Wave had me make up an assignment I missed for choir class, making me late for lunch. As I walked up the stairs to the lunch room and main hallway, I pondered the actions of my classmates and teachers today. It also seemed like I was being kept out of the loop on purpose, from my school and myself . . .

Before my foot landed on the tile of the main hall, a streak of sky blue zipped in front of me, blurring my vision for a heartbeat. I rubbed my eyes and regained my balance, following the blue streak. As it was getting closer to the lobby, it split into waves of blue. As I locked onto them, time slowed so much again that it appeared life had stopped other than me. My heart thumped the word "closer" over and over.

I tilted my head and followed the waves, each step dragging me down. I walked past the lunchroom and colors began to move, figures interacting, and voices hanging in the air; time had restarted, but I disobeyed my body telling me to stop and continued to follow the waves. I was so focused on the almost invisible blue waves that I didn't even see the crossing lines of yellow with black print ahead of me.

"STARY! Look out!"

As the yellow lines became clearer and my eyes could read some of the letters, my body jerked backwards and I crashed into a solid mass. I blinked repeatedly, trying to allow my mind to awaken. I turned to the call of my name and the chest I had landed on; it was Mark. He was panting slightly, his chocolate eyes large with worry. His hands were tightly around me and trembling. He appeared anxious to flee.

"Stary," he said, out of breath. "You shouldn't be over here. We need to go to lunch. Everyone is waiting. Come on." Without another word, he twisted my body forcefully forward, his arms around my shoulders and waist, and escorted me to the lunchroom, all the while speaking to me as if I were a child. He was ignoring the topic at hand; what I almost walked into as I followed the blue waves, which vanished at the sound of his voice.

In front of the janitors' closet and down the hall to the lobby, thick yellow tape was blocking it off. It was all over the place. I could see in the distance a few men in navy-colored uniforms standing by the main doors. I swore the yellow tape had black writing on it. My innocence or denial kept informing me the area was taped up from a spill or a science experiment gone wrong; it's happened in our school a few times before. My brain was telling me something different, that the word on the tape looked a lot like "police."

When I returned from the lunch line, I stopped hastily in front of our lunch table, expecting to hear the sound of laughter and talk of Mr. Tin, but the discussions at my table had taken a dramatic turn. My eyes paused their happy flicker from the food and fixated on the words being said.

"Do you think they will find out anything?" a female voice said.

"This is all so messed up! People are sick! No wonder they are searching all the lockers and classrooms," chimed an on-edge male voice.

"Can we think for a moment for the poor person? How tragic . . ." this came from Ami, whose heart was always so kind.

"The person had no family and no records in Plantersville. I don't understand any of this at all!" Allen said in a scared tone, biting his lips until they were white.

"The staff is supposed to talk to everyone officially tomorrow. Hopefully the officers will have something to report." This intellectual statement came from Lauren.

"I *hate* that we're all trapped here like animals at a zoo! What if the mad person behind this is here among us? I'm not going down without a fight!" Rin ranted.

"Rin, please control yourself. The school has to question everyone, which is why we're still here, just under full watch," Chloe squeaked.

"A girl is found buried dead behind a wall in one of our janitors' closets and no one knows her in the area . . . This all seems pretty twisted." Barbara made everyone quiet with her cold tone. She was holding something in her now shaking hands. It appeared to be a newspaper.

"What . . . ?" Was all I could utter; Mark had heard me and stood, placing his hands under my tray for support. He must have known I was about to drop it. Chloe, Rin, and Lauren, who were closest to me, jerked their heads up to give me a kind expression, an expression that shone light on my question: everything they said was true.

"What do you mean what? How can what I said be clearer to you Stary? It's been the talk of the school all day," Barbara barked. She shoved her chair away from her and slapped the newspaper into my hands.

"The school paper isn't supposed to come out for two more weeks," I informed her, my confusion controlling my logic that told me to never question Barbara.

Barbara was about to say something rude, but Mark butted in. He was always there to defend me. "It's a special edition. Please read it." He dragged over to me and gave me a big bear hug, almost knocking me down. Although I couldn't move, it felt like Mark was using me for support as his chest heaved. I gently returned his tenderness before he walked back to his seat.

I held the paper with a firm grip and opened to the first page and then . . . it all happened at once. I saw . . . *her*. I plopped hard on the floor in disbelief, tossing the paper to the ground, unable to direct my muscles. Mark ran to me, Chloe right behind him. They tried to get me on my feet, but my head was racing with a million questions, a million worries, and a million unwanted answers. The answers flowing through me stopped, as if we were disconnected.

Allen looked amazed and in a hyper, child-like voice, yelled, "You're a really fast reader!"

Barbara gave him a you're-so-stupid look. She gave me the article again with an angry stare plastered on her pasty face. I held my hand on my head, trembling with fear that I would explode due to unknown grief and confusion, unable to glance at the paper.

Chloe touched my forehead with her sweet, cool hand. Her touch made me realize I wasn't in a nightmare. "She's warm," Chloe told the audience of my pals behind her while giving me a panicked look . . . the same one from my dream before she got possessed!

That alarm made me stand up and violently grab the paper. I refused to allow any other part of my dream to come true, especially if it affected my friends or after what I had heard.

"I'm fine . . . A little shaky, but fine," I said in a voice that sounded like I was speaking a newly created foreign language.

Chloe looked a little less troubled, but still concerned. Moisture became trapped in her baby blue eyes. I sat by her, struggling, but patted her soothing hands as I stood up to thank her before I looked at the picture once more.

It was a picture of an extremely pretty young girl, about my age, maybe a little older. She had beautiful, wavy golden blonde hair to her upper back. Her skin was about as white as snow. Her eyes were sky blue and it was as if one could almost see through them. I knew they were a portal in a pure soul. A happy smile crossed her angelic face, a face that looked youthful and mature, graceful and cheerful all at once. In my heart, I knew the girl well, but I didn't remember her at all. Then, it hit me: she was the lovely light beam that took form, the girl of the maiden I talked to from my dream! No wonder my body was in complete shock!

"No one knows who this girl is, but she was found at our school," Lauren said. Found? I was unable to face anyone in the natural world surrounding me, forgetting that I belonged to it.

"The article tells all about it," Rin stated. I was frightened, but I began to read by instinct:

PHS Knights Page

Today is a sad day for our beloved high school. Sixteen-year-old Maren Crystal Rowe, daughter of Robert and Clara Rowe, was found dead in the supply closet in the northern business wing. Her body was buried deep in the back of a hidden wooden wall that no one had noticed before until a trashcan accidentally slammed it down.

> There is not much left of Maren, but she had an ID card near her, the only proof of who she was.
>
> Not much is known about Maren. When she was two, her mother, Clara Hombeck Rowe, died of breast cancer. Two years later, her father, Robert Rowe, was killed when one of his government machines blew up and the explosion destroyed his lab. His body was found in the Gate River, only half of a mile away from his home. Maren and her older brother, Elbert, went to live with their only family left: Professor Glen Rowe, a very famous inventor working for the nation's Department of Defense. His home and research center are still unknown.
>
> When Maren was ten, her seventeen-year-old brother left to follow his father's and grandfather's footsteps. Three years ago, when she was sixteen, Maren and her grandfather went missing. The professor's body was found right away, but young Maren was nowhere to be found until today.
>
> PHS has given her remains to the SRL in St. Louis to find the cause(s) of her death. Even though none of us knew Maren, PHS will wish her peace. Funeral service and burial will be at Holy Rest Church and Cemetery in Oldfield on Thursday, April the 16th. All are welcomed to come. More information will be given when known. All of this information was given to us by the Department of Defense and by Dr. Elbert Rowe.

I could not believe what I read! A poor girl that didn't even go to our school or even live in the area was found dead in our supply closet? How did I not know about this? Everyone seemed to assume I did or was hiding it from me. Wait. That crash during first hour. When Mr. Jerry knocked the trashcan into the wall of the closet, the closet that's now blocked off . . . That's when he screamed, that's when all of this must have happened. I never had to head in that direction until now and because I was with Mrs. Timber, I must've been overlooked for questioning.

This poor girl. Her life appeared lost, confusing, and heartbreaking. Yet in her photo, she looked happy, innocent, and carefree. I prayed to God, wishing for the sweet and wonderful child to find eternal bliss with Him in heaven.

I stood up slowly, careful not to lose my balance, and handed the article to Barbara, who looked at me, traumatized.

"How can you just walk away without wishing her peace? You . . . you . . . Oh! Stary Moon! Of all the people in this world, I thought you would never do something so inconsiderate!" she screamed as I walked away, not turning around.

Lauren gave Barbara an evil and long stare. Rin was about to raise her fist in my honor. Chloe was about to say something cruel back. I motioned to them to calm down, telling them I was not worth a fight.

"Well?" Barbara said, enraged. "What do you say, Moon?"

What could I say? That I felt like I knew the girl? The answers were back once more, and they gave me what I needed, however, this would be the last time. The rest of my answers, I would have to find on my own with whatever was waiting for me. I knew exactly what to say. It might have been considered mean to Barbara, but I knew it had to be said, for Maren could not herself. I didn't even turn to look at Barbara.

"Barbara . . . you're not a bad person. You're very affectionate and that's admirable. Please, let's not yell. How would Maren feel if she saw people fighting over her . . . ?"

Barbara, flabbergasted and ticked, replied, "Why . . . she'd feel happy because we—"

"Maren seemed like a very happy young woman who always lived life to the fullest and that's what she'll do now. If we fight over her, she'll worry, and then her afterlife won't be full of glorious and wonderful adventures. We'll wish her off as God protects her now." My hands began to shake and a lone tear dropped on my hand. "If we denied her of that gift, how evil would we become? Tell me Barbara . . . how evil would we become?!"

I choked the last part in between sobs. A stream of searing tears rolled down my cheeks. My heart was being shielded by an unknown emotion, making it difficult to breathe. It felt like . . . an understanding of sorrow. What was happening to me? I wasn't talking or acting like myself. I thought Maren's spirit had taken over my mind.

Chloe ran to me, touching my shoulder. She pushed my hair away from my stinging, wet eyes, whispering sweetly, "I'm glad you're helping her move on, but please don't make yourself sick. It'll . . . it would . . . that would make her unhappy as well." She showed me a delicate smile followed by a sigh.

I steadily got up, agreeing with her words of encouragement. I stood tall, facing Barbara, who could hardly move.

"Well, what do you say to that?" Rin said with gusto in Barbara's face.

Barbara spoke idiotically, "I . . . I guess you're right, but I don't completely understand . . ."

"Don't understand me. Trust me. That's all I ask." I smiled, my tears and sadness disappearing like the fading sun at twilight.

Mark said, "We'll trust you Stary, but it sounds like you actually knew Maren. Is this true?"

"Mark, let's just say my memory may not know her, but my heart says it does very well."

He looked puzzled, but gave me a smile as he walked to me, giving me his arm like a prince. "Can I help you with your tray, milady?"

I laughed, so lucky to have him as a friend and grabbed his arm. Together, we walked to the clean-up station. I wasn't hungry anymore and besides, I had only gotten a small bowl of cottage cheese anyway. As we walked away, I heard the buzz of my friends saying I was strange, kindhearted, gifted, or a combination of each. I wasn't sure what I was, but I was ready to make a difference by the answers I had to find; I was now on my own. My fate awaited me.

Mr. Tin's class was very quiet and simple, which was the opposite of normal. We read *To Kill a Mockingbird* by Harper Lee. To be honest, I really didn't care for it too much. I didn't hate it, but it was too deep for my current brain to understand! Maybe when I became older I would like it better or be capable to savor the lifelong lessons woven within the pages. Before I could finish my chapter, the bell rang and school was over.

Dad had another meeting after school until 4:00, most likely to discuss the handlings of tomorrow. He let me draw and go on the computer like I was a child. He barely looked at me when he talked so I knew the Maren issue was bothering him. I sighed when he left and decided to draw since I hadn't used my dad's ancient colored pencils in years and I was sick of the computer and its confusing internet sites about dream patterns that made me feel inferior or idiotic or both.

I loved to draw, so I decided to try to draw Maren as a beautiful angel, watching over Plantersville with the smile of Chloe, the safe hands of Rin, and the knowing eyes of Lauren. I gave her my favorite star diamond necklace in the drawing. It was all I had special about me. My illustration of her looked okay, but I couldn't capture her facial happiness like in her photograph from the newspaper. I frowned in disapproval and talked myself into taking a break and making a new one later to add to her grave as a gift.

With zilch to do, I went online to see if I could find anything extra about her. Nothing was there, although one website was fuzzy with static and the words "Angriff Squad" popped up. I tried to return to the page after refreshing it, hoping to clear the blurriness of the webpage, but the word vanished, a lost memory. There was plenty there, however, about her grandfather's achievement and kindness, but that was it. He seemed happy as well, like his granddaughter, both too wonderful for words.

I turned my head toward the cracking clock face; I only had eighteen minutes left. With this realization, I retried my drawing. The details of her gown, wings, and everything in my second attempt were better, but her facial expression was still wrong, ruining the whole feel of the picture. I banged my head on the table, furious with myself.

"Oh! I can't do anything right! I know something is waiting for me, that I'm meant to understand and help someone in sorrow, who's also afraid. I . . . I was just hoping it was you, Maren. I . . . I want to help you." I felt like crying, but I forced it inside. I didn't have time to focus on worrying because if I did—

A snap echoed across the room.

"Sweetie, please do not fret. I love your beautiful artwork. And . . . You are the one, the one who can help me."

The voice was the same one from this morning, but now I knew it was Maren. I wanted to turn and see the shining face of this lovely guardian up close, but I was still too frightened to move or even answer her. Silence filled the air. I heard her bell-like laughter from behind. I think she knew I was afraid.

"Oh dear child, I need to talk to you, now that we are alone. Please, I will not hurt you. Turn around."

My heart was about to burst. I wanted so badly to respond, yet I didn't and couldn't. What if the voice wasn't Maren or I was crazy? My heart was split in two and neither side was winning.

3

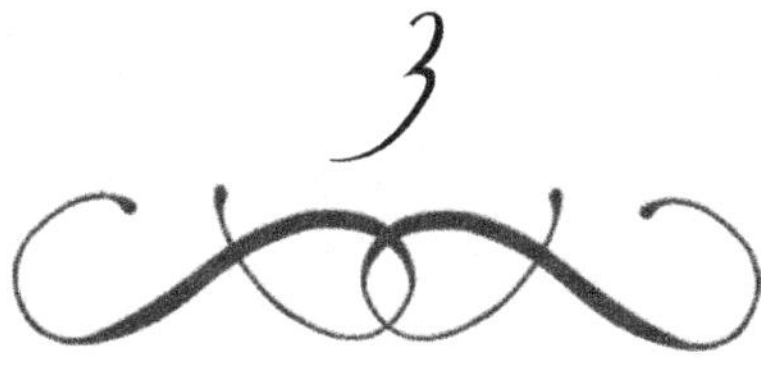

"ARE YOU NOT GOING TO ANSWER ME, HON? I REALLY NEED to talk to you."

I gasped, unable to make the slightest movement. I didn't want to upset her, but my body was stiff, my mouth broken, and my mind full of whirling thoughts. Time had frozen again and our eyes locked, our souls memorizing every detail about each other.

As she hovered there in her unworldly beauty, I noticed she was wearing the same outfit she had worn in the newspaper photo. She truly was a sight, almost divine in her expression, nothing what I thought a spirit would look like. I continued to search her with my eyes from her smile, her smooth skin, her bright eyes, and something that was flickering around her outline like candle fire. It was a dazzling blue, similar to—

"The . . . the blue rays of light . . . That . . . that was you . . . wasn't it?" I choked out. It felt like there was a ball in my throat and it was painful to swallow around it.

She looked more confident and gave me a slight frown before nodding. "Yes, it was. You saw me early this morning as well I believe."

I nodded, recalling the barely visible silver line I saw in front of the janitors' closet.

"You were starting to see me this morning, but the timing was not right, so that is why I only appeared to you as a light; you were seeing what was different from me to you. This, as you know, is the fact that I am a spirit and you are alive. The light that surrounds my body is a symbol of this and is now a part of me. Your eyes were adjusting to the unknown, the otherworld you are meant to be aware of."

I closed my eyes tight and then opened them again. Nope, the spirit was still there. I wasn't imagining things. I couldn't begin to tell her what was bottling up inside me.

I took a deep breath and tried to find a reply. "I . . . I'm not sure why my eyes are special or why I can see spirits, but I believe it because I see you and am talking to you now."

Maren's lips tilted upward a little bit.

I took another breath to collect my thoughts. "I . . . I dreamed of you this morning before I woke up. We talked . . . we talked about me helping you . . ."

Maren blinked rapidly, leaning her body away from me as if I had some sort of hidden ability that would hurt her if we were in close contact. "I thought I dreamt of you! I thought it was a symbolic dream from my Lord. This is why I was at your school; I was in Plantersville and was able to find you. You . . . I did find it odd you were calling me this morning, but I replied, hopeful you could see me. However, again, the timing was not right; we were interrupted and I knew you did not see me leave, so I vanished."

I wanted to ask how spirits slept, but I bit my tongue. She went on.

"When you saw me this morning going down the stairs, I looked at you once more, but I could tell we were not ready to meet yet due to the way you were squinting your eyes.

"However, before I was going to follow you, I was drawn to the supply closet of your custodian; it felt like something was calling me and I could not stop myself. My body was there and after it was found, I knew our time to meet was close at hand."

The proper time seemed to be pushing us away this morning, but was now pulling us together like magnets. Time must have given me the gut feelings and answers to be prepared and aid me until I saw Maren's picture. All this cosmos planning my life stuff was making my head ache.

"You didn't know where your body was?" This confused me. Wouldn't Maren know where she was buried? Were tombstones perhaps gateways for spirits to find their body? Since Maren did not have one, perhaps this explained her wandering soul.

Maren shook her head, her golden hair sashaying around her neck. "For people like me, that is all part of their mission in the afterlife."

I leaned forward, about to ask her what she meant, but in a flash, she was sitting next to me. My head spun, trying to figure out how she did that. Her answer to this was a pearly white smile that made her skin glow. It made her light shine brighter and it was so heartwarming that it made me feel too stupid and unworthy to be near her. My mind clicked off and the only thing my body could do automatically was bow to her, like she was the ruler of the skies. She looked at me, quite puzzled, but giggled.

Then, I was able to speak, her harmony breaking the ice block that my awkwardness caused. "I . . . I'm . . . Stary . . ."

She was still laughing. It was soft and graceful. She spoke in an enchanting voice. "I am glad you are not scared of me; that must have been a lot to take in and I apologize. I know who you are Stary Moon. I am Maren Rowe. Please stand up dear. I am not important enough for you to be bowing to. But, I am most flattered!"

I blushed deeply, so much that I felt the heat in my stomach. I stood up as my wide eyes tried to absorb our current situation, whatever it was.

"I'm terribly sorry. It's just . . . you're so formal and lovely, and well . . . a spirit! Oh gosh! Look at me go on and on! It's just . . . this is all . . . unbelievable! I'm sorry. I'm just not sure how to react!"

She laughed again, raising her pale hands to cease me. "Oh no, not at all."

I stood there for a second, trying to think of how to talk to her and ask her more questions. Quicker than lightning, she moved to the window on the other side of the room, my slow reflexes hardly able to keep up. She looked out at the trees, like they were her lost brothers. "I bet . . . Earth is so beautiful to touch . . . to experience."

My heart went to her longing tone. I would miss Earth too. I stood next to her, mustering all the compassion I could in my voice. "I am not sure I could leave such a world either at my age . . . I'm sorry you lost your home; it must've been hard to leave this planet."

She looked at me with sad puppy eyes. What did I say wrong? She looked like I stabbed her in the chest with a rusted knife!

She looked back out the window, sighing heavily and rested her head on her sculpted arms. "I would not know . . . I have not been to Earth since I was four."

"How can that be?" My brain registered my stupidity a few seconds after the words flew out of my mouth. I hung my head down, terrified I had hurt her.

She turned to me, forgiveness on her face. "Because, when my father died, I went to live with my grandfather. He lived in the Wonder Ship he created, which is in space, on the moon . . ."

I stared at her blankly. Living . . . in space? A normal family that did not work for a space station? Impossible! It was so science-fiction sounding that I had to chomp down on my cheek to not chuckle.

She frowned, her posture still poised. "You do not believe me?"

I answered as honestly as I could. "Well . . . I guess if you say it, it must be true, but it just sounds so out of this world." Sensing the awkward moment, I realized a way to change the subject, a light bulb flickering madly in a dark cave. "I bet your grandfather's inventions for the Angriff Squad—"

Maren jumped up so fast that if she had boots on, she'd have made scratches on the tile floor. She got right in my face, beating me down with cold looking eyes.

I stood there, not able to catch my breath.

"What do you mean? My grandfather made his inventions for passion, for love. The Angriff Squad tried to steal them, since he would not give his works to *them*! They are the ones that—"

She stopped, gasping, a look of shame on her face. I went to comfort her, but she turned away. I heard a low and sad sounding sorry under her breath. I knew she meant it.

Maren walked, or more like floated, around the room, as if pacing. She looked at the floor for a few minutes. All I could do was stand there and watch her graceful figure. When the silence got too heavy, she slowly brought her head up and looked at me. She smiled to herself and came to me, grabbing my hands. Same as the dream! Even though I couldn't feel her actual hands, I felt warm and safe.

"Let us not waste anymore of your precious life. To be truthful . . . I need your help Stary Moon. So I may rest in peace."

I looked up at her, wondering what I could do and what she meant. Words were floating in my head, but I was only focused on the connection I had with Maren through her touch. I nodded to her request, although it did not register. It didn't matter what she asked; I felt too safe with her to allow myself to fail her.

She beamed and let go of my hands, the sense of security dissipating with her touch. "I am so pleased! Thank you, Stary dear. You see, I need you to help find my murderer."

My comforting world I just adored a moment before was vaporized by her blunt approach to a touchy topic. I knew I should have felt alarmed, afraid, and protested. I was waiting for that electric zap to wake me from the dream and recharge my better judgment. The mission of finding a murderer . . . it was insane! It had to be dangerous and it would completely alter my life. However, instead of waiting for that electric shock to surge through my blood steam, I snapped off the invisible collar of doubt and exhaled my thoughts out, clearing my mind. I 100% believed Maren and was willing to aid her. My human instinct to flee must have vanished into an unseen pit.

I did feel a normal response as I sat down with a thud in my chair, totally bemused about everything. "Why me? How can *I* be of any use in tracking a killer? And why must you find your murderer before you can rest in peace? That's not fair at all!"

She smiled wryly, her tone informative. "It is a rule Stary. We must find our murderer so we can destroy the evil inside their heart and soul in order to save other people from becoming victims. And you have the power to destroy that evil and save us Stary."

Me? I had that kind of power? How? When? And what was with the "we" and "us"?

She looked like a child who broke their parent's prize possession and asked, "May I see the website you got the article information from?"

Still bewildered by the murderer concept, I bobbed my head, scared my voice would fail me and guided her to the computer. She tapped the monitor, her eyes wide with excitement. "It is so good to see one of these again!"

I guessed her grandfather used one a lot at his profession. The thought comforted me.

I rapidly began to type in the address, but it became a failed attempt. My computer froze the second after I hit the enter button. I clicked different buttons, the ctrl+alt+delete combo, and even hit the top of the monitor, but still nothing. I checked the system's hard drive, the disk and jump drives, backup files, all the folders I could recall and yet it said the computer was fit as a fiddle. What the heck?! And why did it have to act like this in front of Maren? I slapped it one more time, frustration fueled by my failure and embarrassment.

Maren was still smiling, almost like she was not sure to laugh or take pity on me. That's when the screen became hazy, blackish and gray, the color of smoke . . . and it was moving. A fire? No, not *inside* the computer! I stared at it long and hard, trying to classify the problem and then, something, a hand, came popping out of the screen. Another hand soon followed before I could react. Next was a head, a young man's head. It looked up at me meanly and, without warning, jumped on top of me, a lion playing with a mouse!

I shrieked and kicked fiercely in my chair as he piled on top of my limp body when he pounced on me. The scene created a world of noise. In a panic, I hit him with my notebook that was lying by the rusted little end desk, using it as a weapon. He cackled at the sight of me before hopping high above me, landing on top of the computer. His arms were crossed and he was still, eerily still, looking at me with cold eyes of ice.

He finally spoke. "Hmph, that's how you treat a guest?

I raised a fist, my body tingling with anger and fury. I began to get up to deck him one, but, of course, my klutziness *had* to kick in at that exact moment. I got my foot caught on the wheels of the chair, causing me to tip it over on top of myself. The impact was painful as my wheels spun along with the chair's. I gasped, but he laughed, which sounded as criminal as his glare.

Maren helped me up, looking at him disappointedly. He began to laugh even louder and after that sound, I was ready for the kill, sick of being the prey in this sudden twisted game.

"SHUT UP!" I yelled sharply.

He stopped in a blink of an eye, focused on my face, and then rolled his eyes in Maren's direction.

"That was very mean Umbra." Maren scowled, but her voice was still lighthearted.

Umbra? They knew each other? Was he part of the "we" Maren was referring to? I declared right then and there that there was no way I would accept this fact if it were true.

He turned to me with a dirty smile all over his incalculable face. "Oh Maren . . . I'm only having a bit of fun. It's not my fault this human is so weak."

That. Was. *It.* I pointed at him, begging the heavens to turn my finger into some sort of spirit gun to knock him out. My eyes were burning from the fury I was feeling, making my vision watery. I jerked my head to fully face him, my hair flying all over my face in the process. "I'll show you who's weak! COME ON!"

He laughed again: short, hard, and full of insult. "How cute."

I growled at him, clenching my fists against my jeans. I was about to snap back, but my mouth clamped shut. As my new red fury came to a halt, I took a better look at him. He had black, wavy hair that was mostly spiky, sticking out like quills. The spikes were embedded in a unique pattern against his natural curls. His eyes were dark brown, almost black with a hint of honey in the center, and they were cold and heartless looking. His features were as perfect as his lightly toasted colored skin and muscular body. He was wearing all black, but I could still see through him. He also had a blue glow around him like Maren.

I frowned, growling my rage out as I turned my head away from him. I could tell he was burned by my gesture because he did the same thing to me. It wasn't fair! He was a total cold and cruel jerk. I knew I couldn't stand him after one glance. And because of fate, I had to help him. It all sucked like a vacuum!

Maren giggled nervously. "Ummmmm . . . Umbra, this is Stary Moon. Stary, this is my dear friend Umbra."

Her friend?! I glared at him, sticking my lips out in protest. His head was still turned away from me like I was not worth looking at. I finally decided to at least say hi so I could make Maren happy; she looked so torn.

I forced *most* of my anger and scowls down into the tips of my toes, sending them to Antarctica. I held out my hand in front of him business-like. "It's nice to meet you Umbra."

It sounded cheesy and fake, but it was good enough. He turned around, puzzled and entertained. He gazed at me for a second, like he was shy, ordinary, and maybe pleasant. He paused, realizing what he was doing, catching himself in the act. He said, "Charmed . . . ," with a roll of his eyes. I lost all hope. What. A. Snob!

Maren decided to make the first move. "Umbra, this is the young lady that is going to help us, so please be nice. We will be with her for a while and she has kindly agreed to aid us."

Umbra looked at me from head to toe with laser-like eyes. I felt uncomfortable and wanted to cover myself with my arms, but then I would have looked even more foolish. Why was he cross-examining me?

He looked stunned at Maren and doubtfully at me. "Are you sure?" he moaned. "She looks like a skinny little brat to me. No thanks Maren. I can do this much easier and better than she could ever hope to!"

I stood there, hurt by his comment and feeling misplaced. All I could do was stare as Maren and Umbra fought over the abnormal issue.

After taking a cleansing breath, I built up the nerve to say, "Excuse me?"

They stopped mid-argument.

"Well, please tell me everything I have to do."

Umbra leaped down from the computer, scaring me half to death. He was in front of me in one motion, similar to how Maren moved earlier. His eyes were as black as coal now, the honey center gone. His fists shook and his mouth tried to move, but nothing came out.

I grinned. "Don't worry. I'll be fine. I want to do this."

Umbra backed off, but it still felt like he spat hot fire on my face with his tone. "You . . . you could never handle this. You'd—"

I gathered enough courage and created the right words to interrupt him. "Yes, I can! I promised Maren and that's what I'm going to do! I keep my promises!"

Umbra didn't say a word, looking like I slapped his pride with a metal glove. He turned his back to me, sighing. All I heard was a mumble, like he was talking with watermelon seeds in his mouth as my grandpa would have said. He started to speak up, staring at the wall and then back at me a couple times. "I guess I can't stop you. Stupid people make mistakes, too."

A laugh escaped my lips. I knew he was insulting me, but at least he was being honest, though it was cruel. He faced me, staring at me like I was a freak. All I could do was smile at him. "I guess you're not *too* much of a snob after all!"

He scowled. Maren came down to me, her expression relaxed.

I bowed to her benevolently. "What do I need to do for you first, miss?"

She giggled so sweetly that I was sure she was going to get cavities. "Thank you very much. We are both grateful, right Umbra?"

Umbra was leaning against the wall by the computer, his arms crossed. He opened one eye to scowl at us before turning to glance out the window for a second. Some birds were playing outside and for a moment, Umbra looked at them longingly, almost like he wanted to join them in their fun.

He shut his eyes and callously said, "We could do better, but if you want her, I guess she's decent . . . for now."

I felt something I never thought I would feel for him . . . sadness, pure sorrow. Maren looked at me, but I didn't ignore her contact. My glazed eyes were locked on Umbra.

He was staring at the window again, at those tiny, happy birds. His eyes were filled with a distress that appeared to be permanent and a look of longing was spread across his face as he leaned on the wall like he was trying to get support from it. Maren cleared her throat to get my attention. I slowly looked at her, but for some reason, I kept looking back to Umbra and those birds. He closed his eyes, a look of contentment on his face as the birds began to chirp. It seemed like the melody was washing over his mood.

Umbra opened his eyes suddenly and caught me staring at him. I tried with all my strength to look away, but couldn't. He was dumbstruck. "What?" he said, sounding stony as his face randomly turned a little peach tone, making him look like a prince from a story.

"Sorry! Oh my gosh! I'm so sorry. I . . . I didn't mean to stare. You and those birds and well . . ." I had to stop for a breath . . . or four. I was acting like a nervous child, no, right then, I was proving I knew I was still one.

I looked down and then up. Umbra was still staring at me. I ducked my head down again to collect my tiny mind's thoughts. "Sorry," I said bashfully.

He was silent for a moment, arching his dark eyebrow, and then closed his eyes and leaned against the wall, a pensive expression crossing his face. He spoke with an effortless shrug, "Whatever." Then he folded his arms across his chest once more, looking about ready to fall asleep or at least not talk for a while.

"Stary, love?" Maren said to motion me.

I stared at her wide-eyed, scared of what she thought. "I'm sorry Maren. I, well . . . I was . . . Ugh!"

She giggled. "It is fine. I understand everything. I think it is cute." She winked with her smile so ample that it had a bit of mischief mixed in, which surprised me even more than being caught. Did she think that I *liked* him? Don't think so!

"I don't . . . I mean. Oh, never mind!" I didn't want her to get any wrong ideas. I focused on getting her off track. "So, tell me everything I need to know."

She snickered again, probably since I changed the subject so quickly. "Well, first off, I am—"

Footsteps entered the hallway, coming from the right of the door. Afterward, I heard Mr. Tin's iced tea cup shaking. (He carried that thing everywhere and had about four to five big cupfuls in his huge Jets cup every day! No wonder he had so much energy.) I also heard a loud, hardy, but soothing laugh that I knew well. My daddy! I could feel my eyes getting bigger, so big that I bet they could have inhaled Saturn. What was I going to do?

"You two have got to get out of here. Please!" I screamed like a maniac, flinging my arms so hard that I swore I could have flown.

Maren nodded in agreement. "Let us go Umbra." Umbra didn't move; it was like he was made of stone. "Umbra!" Maren called more harshly. "Come on. We need to leave."

"What's the big fuss? Those pathetic humans can't see us."

Even if they couldn't, I knew I would act funny. This was going to be a secret that I knew I would have to cover up. Plus, I couldn't lie to my father or Mr. Tin, who had a built-in lie detector in his robotic eyes. I was so worried, but I felt calmer than I thought I would have in this situation. *That* shocked me more.

Maren spoke, her voice mimicking mine from earlier, "Umbra, I know it is unlikely they are able to see us. However, a Spirit Warrior such as Stary must treat everyone as a suspect in our murder. If they *are* the murderers, then they can see us too, the faces of the lives they have taken away. You know this! Now, let us go!"

A Spirit Warrior? What was that? And why was she accusing Mr. Tin and dad? "Maren, Mr. Tin or my father would never—"

She shushed me and winked devilishly. I got it then. She was trying to trick Umbra into leaving. How clever! I smiled back, since I couldn't wink, to thank the future angel for her overflowing kindness and sneaky mind.

Umbra stared at us. He looked at Maren first and then me. His eyes were on me mostly, studying me.

"Please?" I said to Umbra. He looked at my face for the longest time. I could hear my dad and Mr. Tin right outside the classroom now. The fear made my heart race and on reflex, I shut my eyes tight like I was getting shot at. There had to be a way to convince him . . . no; he seemed too stubborn. I had no choice. I opened my eyes.

I realized I couldn't force him. "I can't make you do this Umbra. Don't worry about it."

Maren looked shocked. "What?" her voice was a high-pitched shrill.

Umbra looked at me strangely. "You're not going to make me feel guilty . . . ?"

I made my smile wider. I really didn't want to ploy him; I was smiling because as I looked into his eyes, I saw his shields waver slightly, his anger a little less intense. It was reassuring.

"Honest Umbra, no tricks. Do what you want to do." I shrugged, acting like I didn't care.

He stared at me, looking for the lie with all his might. Finally, he got up from the wall and declared, "Fine, all right! Let's go Maren!"

She smiled at me and whispered, "Nice job!" good-humoredly.

I didn't do anything; Umbra did it all on his own. I smiled a little to myself. It was a relief Umbra had some good inside him

The door knob turned slowly and clicked. The sound made me jump higher than a frog on too much sugar. My dad was there, with his glasses on, and Mr. Tin, with his tea, right behind him. They looked at me mystified like they had never seen me before.

I chuckled nervously. "Hey . . . Hey there Dad, Mr. Tin . . . Have a good meeting?"

They looked at each other still puzzled, but Mr. Tin came to me first.

"It was a meeting, what do you expect? Anyway, we heard you talking to someone. Who was it Stary?"

They heard me, but not Maren or Umbra. Good! No . . . bad! How was I going to explain that to them? My facial muscles ached with pain from all the fake smiling I was doing as my mind formed a plan. "Well, Mr. Tin . . . I was . . . writing a story . . . for fun . . . Yeah! And I was acting as the main character to see if we were at all alike . . . all for comparison research."

"Was it about a bird girl? You keep flapping your arms there Stary. Maybe you'll fly!"

I mentally facepalmed myself. I really needed to learn how to control my hands when I was nervous! "I . . . I was trying to get fully into my character and yes, it's about a bird girl and some new, interesting friends she makes." Maybe Maren and Umbra could be the inspiration for this story!

Mr. Tin laughed hard. "So you're using one of my speaking training ideas, huh Stary? I'm real impressed! Of course, since you are such a good student and Mr. Moon's daughter, I *should* expect nothing less, right, Stary ol' girl?" He winked.

I could feel sweat forming, but nodded.

Dad smiled at me. "Yes, that's my girl! And I'm always proud of her."

I reddened again. Why did they have to praise me when I felt so bad?

Mr. Tin had to leave to go pick up his daughters from kindergarten so I was left to help Dad clean up the room before we went home. He stopped in front of my desk and picked up a piece of paper . . . my drawing! Next to it was the picture of Maren I got from the school paper. His face saddened while he looked at my drawing. I blinked, not knowing what to say.

"It's very good Stary," he finally said, his voice sounding as if he was lost in an endless tunnel. "I guess you know . . ." He paused to get the sweat off from around his nose. "I'm sorry I didn't tell you Stary, but honey, you're so gentle hearted and I wanted to tell you, but I also wanted you to learn about it on your own, like your classmates. I have to let you spread your wings and take flight on your own, like a bird."

A bird? Was that what Umbra was searching for? Freedom from his wandering spirit?

I patted my daddy on the shoulder. "It was hard, but I'll get through it. Don't worry."

He hugged me tight. "I know I can trust you. You're so grown up and mature now . . . mostly . . ." I smiled and hugged him back. I didn't want to let go. His familiar touch was as comforting and warm as Maren's.

He let go first and said, "Well, let's go get us some food. How does Mexican sound?

"Sounds great!" I said excitedly. So much for mature!

I grabbed my jacket and waited for Dad to lock up. I looked up at the ceiling. Maren and Umbra were sitting-floating, watching over for me. Maren pointed her finger out the door and nodded. I nodded back. I understood her.

In my heart, I knew she said: "We will meet you in your room to tell you what you need to know." How I knew, I wasn't sure, but I knew. Maren and Umbra faded away as my dad shouted my name. I left the room behind, but my destiny was right in front of me.

THE SMELL OF MELTING BUTTER HIT MY NOSE WHEN I FIRST stepped into the house. A pot of spaghetti was boiling on the stove. My vision caught up to my nose; I noticed my mom standing there, mixing the noodles. Her eyes looked tired but still perky, her ponytail was a little bit of a mess, and she was wearing an apron over her red Scottish dog pajamas. I had to chuckle. She turned around to face me, smiling with the mixing spoon in hand. I took a step back, bracing myself for either a hug that would take my breath away or a whack with the spoon.

"Welcome home sweetie," she said and ran to give me a hug, springing toward me like a mountain cat. I was not surprised that choice won, but surprised to see her.

"Mom, you don't get off work until 5:00. It's 4:33 now—"

She interrupted me, looking irritated. "I only worked until 3:00 today since our landlord is looking our shop over. I told you that at least fifty times."

I looked up at the ceiling. How could I remember when I had two spirits waiting for me in my bedroom? "Sorry Momma. I forgot," I said, giving her my best forgive-me smile.

She sighed in defeat and patted my head like a puppy bringing her a ball. "What am I going to do with you, Miss Stary Moon?"

I savored her touch for a moment. I knew all too soon that all the conversations I would be having would not be so pleasant.

Dad came in carrying our bags of Mexican food. When Mom saw him, she gave him a scary stare. This was my cue to leave and disappear to the playful comforts of Lancelot, Guinevere, and Gabriel, our three puppies, as they argued what to do about dinner, a battle I did not want to be caught in.

It was decided to have half of Mom's noodles and half of Dad's Mexican and the rest would be saved for leftovers. I really didn't care. I had to get upstairs to my room to talk to Maren and Umbra. If I was late, I knew Umbra would hate me even more. Not that I cared what Umbra thought. Goodness! But, I knew I needed to hurry up for Maren's sake.

I grabbed my half-and-half plate and sprinted upstairs to my bedroom, breaking the sound barrier. I could feel Momma and Daddy giving me strange looks from behind my back. They really didn't need to know about all my craziness, right? It's not like they would believe me anyway. Worst case: they'd send me to a mental hospital! I shouldn't have been worried since I knew my parents were not the murderers. I figured I was safe from being sent to an institution . . . for the time being.

It felt like it took me forever mixed with an eternity to get to my bedroom. I snuck a look around, fearing someone would assault me, but no Umbra or Maren were in sight and no feelings of their presence either. I placed my plate down on my white marble homework desk so I could see if I could sense a presence or two in my room. How I was able to feel Maren and Umbra already, I wasn't sure, but it was like they had their own unique pitch and warmth in the air. The room was silent and the temperature the same. There was nothing but uneasiness.

Then, a flash of blue fire light came from the ceiling beam above my bed followed by a pair of legs. It was Maren! She was making herself visible for me, but why was she hiding? As she descended slowly, she took a deep breath and smiled down at me, her face watchful.

"Sorry my pet," she said sympathetically. "A little boy was in here a little while ago and we cannot risk being seen yet."

A little boy? My brain was itching, trying to figure the meaning of her statement.

"Do not worry. In a couple of days, you will be able to see us as good as you see your family and friends."

Oh great! What if I went to talk to them and, knowing my luck, everyone would notice and see me as being weirder than normal?

But . . . stupid me! I was only thinking about myself. I was supposed to help Maren and Umbra. Well, I wanted to only help Maren and *not* Umbra because he was a mean, low-class jerk, and . . . yet . . . he seemed so heartrendingly helpless too and . . . and why in the world was I thinking about him like that? He didn't like me, so I shouldn't like him! Thinking of him made my body ache so badly that I swear my cells were moaning.

Maren looked at me funny like she swallowed a lemon. "Why is your face red, hon?"

I jumped and checked my forehead; my forehead was tepid. I was thinking too much! "Oh, nothing!" I snorted nervously, ready to switch gears. "Did you say a boy came in here? I bet it was—"

A knock, a rude one at that, blocked my thought. Maren disappeared again, almost terrified, but I could still feel her at least. I opened the door. In the frame was Link, my little brother.

I stared at him coldly and snipped, "What do you want?"

He gave me an evil look that could have knocked my jaw out by its force. "Nothing. But who are you talking to Freak? Your imaginary friends or your little gal pals about boys?"

I blushed a little, but I was more annoyed. He started pointing at me and making ghastly kissing noises. I frowned at his lack of maturity and patted his bleach blond mop-top head.

"Don't worry. In a year, you'll like girls and then I'll get my sweet payback!"

He stared at me like I was wearing a cheap alien costume one bought at a dollar store. "Me? Right! And I am the dark ruler of the world of toilets!"

I bit my tongue hard, trying not to laugh. He may have been infuriating, but he was really funny and *could* act charming if he tried!

I smiled cruelly at him. "I already know for a fact you rule toilets so don't worry about having to lose your kingdom. You're only ten now, but next year, I bet you'll have a girlfriend! I was eleven when I had my first boyfriend."

His eyes became the size of saucers. "I'm telling Dad!" he squawked.

I grabbed his shirt collar and glared him down. "He already knows who, when, what happened, what we did, and how long we lasted." My tone was sharp with thumping, truthful facts.

"Darn!" he yelled and threw his head down away from me.

I smirked because I knew I had won. "Go eat. I'm really busy!" And I pushed him away from my room.

Another evil look, "With what?" he said as he raised one eyebrow.

"None of your business," I stated, stomping my right foot down like a bull.

He walked away, whispering, "I'll find out." I knew he would try, which meant I would have to be on alert for that as well. Wonderful.

I came back and shut my door fast, leaning against it while holding the doorknob in place, and sighed. I really needed and wanted a lock for my door! Maren reappeared with a relieved look on her own face and gave me an envious smile as I moved toward my bed.

"You two have a special bond. It must be magnificent to have such a great little brother."

I looked at the floor, taken aback that I had not pictured my relationship with Link that way. It was nice how Maren saw the good in everything. "I guess, sometimes . . ."

She laughed like a fairy. "Do not act so tough. You do not have to be like Umbra to impress him."

I jumped five feet back, my face still red. "Why would I want to impress that loser?!"

"I heard that!"

I spun around. There was Umbra, leaning against my bed post. He must have been there the whole time! I was not sure how he hid his presence, but he seemed delighted with my surprise.

Maren tightened her lips into a line, her eyes darting between us nervously. It reminded me of the fairy tale where the maiden hiccupped jewels and she made that face to hide them in her mouth. Poor Maren was going to have sore cheeks if Umbra and I kept this stare down.

"That thing you call a little brother? He's not human. What is he?" he stated brusquely.

I was getting cross at his lack of social courtesy. "He may be different, but he has an imagination and character! Don't misjudge him!"

Umbra smirked. "No wonder he's weird. He's related to you."

What an utter a-hole! "Shut up!" I yelled to defend my relative.

Another twisted laugh came out of his mouth. "Is that the best you got, weak human?"

I didn't care if it wasn't ladylike; he was going down by my punches!

Maren sat on the bed, staring at us calmly despite the tension in the air. "Please, stop this! We must work together! Now, shake hands and let us start telling Stary what she needs to know Umbra!"

Umbra and I were surprised, our faces frozen, perfectly matching, as we interrupted our fight to consider what Maren had said. Maren wiped a bang away from her sky blue eyes, sitting there smugly with poise, waiting for us to shake hands. Umbra started coming toward me, getting really close, which made me strangely panicky.

He offered his hand and turned his head away from me, rushing, "Only for Maren."

I looked at him. His face was a little cherry. Nevertheless, I nodded, my mouth agape. We shook hands, but it was more like moving air. I could see I was shaking it, but couldn't physically feel it. Yet I felt some kind of warmth. Even more puzzling was the fact that I knew that warmth, but I couldn't place how. I bet it felt strange to him as well. I almost (big almost) felt bad for him.

We let go immediately, realizing what we were doing and refused to glance at each other. My face was hot again, and his was still ruby-colored. Maren patted my queen-sized bed. "I am so happy now!"

I sat next to Maren as Umbra leaned against my bed post again, trying to look hip.

"I guess I will tell the story Umbra. You add in anything you want, okay?" Maren sounded like she had been preparing for this moment her whole afterlife.

He bobbed his head. His face was covered in darkness, a shield, but his eyes were shining a bit. I bet he did really want my help, but when he turned his head away from me with a grimace, I began to think that maybe he didn't after all.

"You see Stary, as you know, I 'disappeared' three years ago, right? It said that in your newspaper's cover page article."

I nodded, my face searching Maren's for the answer.

"Well, I was actually killed," she said like she was reliving the pain, choking on the horror.

I interrupted, finally able to express my outrage from earlier in a violent, instant fume as I stood. "Who would do such a cruel and evil thing to you?! Don't worry. I'll do whatever I can to make them . . ."

Maren only bowed her head. Umbra came toward me, smiling a little, but it was not cruel or mocking. It was almost . . . kind.

"You don't even know the whole story yet and you're willing to help until the end? I sort of respect that. You may have guts after all, kid." He patted my cheek ever so slightly before walking back to his post. I was still, struggling to form words.

Maren lifted her head up like it was made of lead. It dawned on me why Umbra gave me that gesture. Maren was upset and Umbra was letting her have some time to recover since my loud mouth didn't help. No matter the motive, I was flattered and a little scared at his touch.

"Thank you Stary, but Umbra has a point. You do not know the whole story and you really need to."

I sat down and allowed her to start, giving her my full attention.

"Everything in that article was true, except my grandfather did not work for the Angriff Squad. They wanted him to, but he made his inventions for the love of making something and the thirst for knowledge, the good of science, not evil wars like they wanted to use them for."

Umbra's fists began to tighten up and his eyes blazed with emotion. I heard him mumble something like, "Why couldn't they just leave them alone?" His eyes then switched emotions and became sad and childlike. I had an urge to go to him, but Maren placed a hand over mine, forcing me to stay and listen.

"My grandfather was gifted in making world altering inventions that could benefit many out of simple objects one could never think of having benefits! He saw the purpose of everything. That was why he was so valuable since he was a young man."

My lips creased upward, imagining a young man happily making laser cannons out of tin cans and a flashlight. Maren went on.

"My grandfather worked for a secret unit of NASA, known as the Hoshi Project."

"Hoshi? Like Japanese for star?" I interrupted. Maren tugged at my hair playfully, smiling like she was proud I asked the right question.

Umbra blinked at me. "How'd you know that?"

"I'm a huge fan of Japanese culture," I replied. How ironic that not only was the secret unit using a Japanese word, but it meant star! Fate really was at work.

Maren smiled and cleared her throat to continue her captivating history lesson, her beauty radiating. "I thought that would make you happy to know. It had a Japanese name because the director of it was from Tokyo. There were only thirteen men total in the whole unit. The job of the HP was to see how far we are able to live in outer space."

Then, it clicked. All of what Maren was saying about living in space must have been true! Excitement bubbled inside me at the thought of living in space. I nodded for her to go on.

"My grandfather loved outer space so much and designed an amazing space mansion and laboratory. It had a pod gravity system where it could get and deliver items to Earth through a pull frequency. Once it was finished, he had to finish his mission by testing it out for twenty years to see if living in space was possible. If it worked, then HP could reveal it to the world through NASA."

"That crazy man always wanted to be one with the stars," Umbra chuckled good-humoredly.

Maren covered her mouth to laugh for a second with Umbra. "That is true . . ."

It was nice to see them smile in their situation.

Maren continued. "However, two weeks before he was scheduled to depart, my father died in the explosion from his machines your article talked about. My grandfather refused to leave his two grandchildren in an orphanage so he got special permission for my elder brother, Elbert, and me to live in space with him, becoming a part of the project. It would become a family living experiment instead of one person."

Maren looked at my disco beaded curtains when she said the word "family" before pulling us back in with her voice. "After my brother left when I was ten, my grandfather re-started working really hard on his greatest project, the world's most powerful living being that could blend into normal society and protect it at the same time. He had been working on it since I first arrived when he was not working on HP material. It took him six years to make the prototype, which looked like my grandfather's image of the sea legend Nessie. It was locked in the most guarded laboratory ever built! Even I was not allowed near there. The prototype's purpose was to see if a creation with machine-like qualities could handle human traits.

"Sorrowfully, it was too powerful and almost destroyed the moon because it was being unresponsive to the emotions and too focused on its power. My grandfather was able to lock it away in his moon base. It was near our home so it was easy to guard. It took him another year to complete his revised project, the one he dreamed of creating to help the world since a young child. The project appeared human and was able to choose 'his' own emotions, personality, and what 'he' wanted to do with his free will. 'He' also had many unique and powerful abilities, all anticipated to project what 'he' wanted by definition of 'his' free will. The press's title for 'him' was 'The Ultimate Being.'"

I leaned forward more with every word Maren spoke. I was truly fascinated by this part of the tale; how amazing it all seemed, like fiction. Although the way she flexed her tone and called the invention "him" baffled me. "That's great! I bet the Angriff Squad wanted it."

Maren smiled widely, making light dance in her pupils. "Why don't you ask 'him' . . . ?"

Ask the Ultimate Being? That would have been cool, but where was it? Could it even talk? I thought Maren was pulling my leg.

Maren laughed like a wind chime and Umbra's face became red to the hue of a rose starting to bloom. I must have looked really bewildered because Maren laughed even harder and Umbra got redder. Finally, Maren pointed to Umbra, who waved at me like an embarrassed guy in a swimsuit contest, but he was still trying to hide a creeping, cocky grin.

NO. WAY. I almost fell off my bed backwards.

"U-Um-bra! You're the 'Ultimate Being'? But . . . I thought you were . . . well . . . human . . . !"

He grunted as if he was upset by the truth. "I was created to look human, act human, and assist and live among humans. I'm almost human, but I have super speed, increased strength, unparalleled knowledge, and beyond natural memory storage along with free will and the ability to learn based on my surroundings. But, I guess I'm still only something created by genetics and science . . ."

"Not true!" I shouted, standing up. "You're special Umbra. And, if you can die, you have to be plenty human, right?" I wasn't sure why I said that or why I was so worried about Umbra bashing himself. Maybe because it seemed so out of character for him with his annoying confidence, but at that moment, I refused to let him say those words.

He turned his back away from me. It seemed like he was hiding himself from the world. "I was created to die by strange causes, like murders or battles, so I could blend into Earth's harsh culture, but I could never get sick. That's not human at all."

I didn't say anything else except, "Sorry, but I think you're still pretty special," before I sat back on the bed, knowing my words would never ring in his thick skull.

He stared at me for a second before acknowledging Maren to continue.

"My grandfather created Umbra to not only protect us and to live out his dream, but to make sure I was not lonely when he had to work. Umbra and I became the closest of friends! I even made Grandfather make Umbra younger than me since I wanted to be a big sister figure to him," she bellowed, making my walls bounce with the charming noise.

"We both dreamed of living on Earth someday like an average family. Umbra and I loved to look at it from the windows of our home. My grandfather promised me that on my eighteenth birthday, all three of us could live on Earth together for a while so he could record Umbra's existence in NASA's completed archives. However . . . it was not meant to be I suppose."

She swallowed hard and took a moment before talking again. "One night, I heard the sirens go off. Our house was incredibly advanced and ready for any attack. But, somehow . . . they got in. I heard running. I was too scared to move, but I got enough might to run to my grandfather's room. I saw some of the men in the hallway as I snuck that way. They were all wearing Angriff Squad uniforms! When I reached my destination, Grandfather was not in his bed. So, I crept around the corner and I found him in his bathroom with the phone in his hand. I bet he was going to call me, to warn me, but he . . ." Maren's voice broke into sobs.

I hugged her around the waist and Umbra patted her shoulder gently.

In between sobs, I heard Maren mutter, "After that, I ran back to the experiment room. I knew I was going to die, but I had one more thing I had to do . . . I had to . . ."

Umbra's eyes became extensive. I swore I could hear his nerves raging, his blood boiling. "STOP!" he shouted at the top of his lungs.

We both stared at him, frozen. His breathing was heavy and his eyes tar black.

"Then you did your duty and got stabbed in the back!" Although Umbra was standing tall, his voice was tight, as if he was trying not to break down.

Maren let go of me, sliding like butter out of my arms. She tiptoed over to hug Umbra, looking like she was trying to hold him together.

Maren was still crying a little. She wrapped her arms around him in a long embrace, squeezing Umbra firmly. "Please do not be upset. I had to do it . . . I *had* to . . ."

Umbra looked hurt by the truth before his face became unreadable. The level of sorrow they had was something I could not understand.

"But, why?" He was unexpectedly choking on his words.

I stood there lost, but I couldn't turn away. I realized that a part of Umbra was a good-hearted person; he only acted tough. I bet he was devastated by Maren's death, angry the rest of his life, which must have turned his heart to stone and become colder than the South Pole. Who could blame him?

Maren had a small smile, ready to answer his enraged question with a soft answer. "You are too important to me Umbra. I wanted one of us to live our dream . . . and I knew it had to be you. If you died, I would have never forgiven myself! I am so sorry I left you alone . . ." She was crying hard again, seeing how her good deed betrayed Umbra in some ways.

Umbra hugged her closer to his chest. "Shhhhhh. I know. I only felt terrible for you. You were all I had. I didn't want to live if you couldn't, but then you gave up your life to save me. So, I decided to avenge your death, and I thought that was by destroying the Earth since that's where the Angriff Squad lived. I could have done it! I thought that's what you wanted, but I was wrong. I almost destroyed the thing you wanted to see, wanted me to protect. I'm the one that's sorry . . ."

I had no idea what he meant by destroy, but my gut was in knots, conflicted by the possibilities.

Again, he held in his urge to snivel by the way he tightened his muscles. The way they were holding each other, looking deeply into the other's eyes, it looked like they were . . . in love?! They did give up their lives for each other. Yet, why did I feel so wounded when they had a long, loving history and I've only known them for a few hours?

I knew they had forgotten I was there, but that didn't bother me. When I saw Umbra hugging Maren that way, the way his face softened and the adoration he held for her that filled the room, it made me feel so . . . melancholy.

Umbra's eyes were closed and he was almost truly smiling. Then, for no reason, he looked up at me in a way that was apologetic. I blinked, surprised at his action. He lifted his head up, only staring at me. He gave me a sweet look with a shrug, like asking if I was all right with their loving reunion. His eyes started smiling . . . at me! I became flushed inside and out and turned my head to not look at their moment since I did not want to be rude in any dimension.

But when I turned back slightly, Umbra was still looking at me the same way. What was he thinking? Sensing the proper timing, Umbra patted Maren's back once he saw I was perplexed, giving her a caring smile to inform her I was still there, watching.

She looked at me and turned crimson. "Oh dear . . . I am sorry. I . . . Oh my . . ."

I grinned, uncomfortable, but trying not to show it. It felt like I was Maren's mom and I had walked in on her and Umbra. I wasn't sure if I wanted to roll my eyes or run away. "I know. You two needed to talk, to make amends. I bet Umbra's the best comforter in the world, right Maren?"

They both gulped at that, making me feel authoritative. Yet, man that came out stupid! My mouth needed to learn how to wait for my brain to process!

She nudged Umbra and he nodded back firmly but with easier eyes. I sat on the floor, adjusting myself once more for the story. Maren grabbed my arm, forcing me next to her on my bed, holding my hands like I was the lady-in-waiting seeking advice from her mistress.

Maren looked into my eyes. She appeared better. She took a big breath and said, "Umbra is right. You do not need to know how I died. I do not want to worry you."

But, not knowing made me worry more! However, I understood. It must have been too hard for her to talk about. But, from what I could pick up after Maren was killed . . . Umbra must have been so infuriated at the Angriff Squad that he used his powers to try to destroy the people on Earth. I bet Maren didn't get to make her final wish clear and that's what Umbra thought she had wanted. How he almost destroyed the Earth, I didn't know, but he must have gotten close according to the feeling in my stomach! I also guessed he realized the error that he made and tried to stop the damage somehow. However, again, I didn't know how he stopped it, but he must have died to save the people of Earth. If it wasn't for that, everyone, including me, would have been gone. Umbra really was a protector . . .

I supposed that was enough information. I could tell Umbra didn't want to talk about it anymore because his figure began blending into the darkness, his eyes timid and protective. I wanted to know how in the world I could help them.

Maren patted my hands, smiling sincerely, about to answer my silent questions. "Every forty years, someone is born with a gift to communicate to spirits and ghosts. Oh, there is a difference—"

I finished her sentence by impulse. "I know. Spirits are land angels that have to stay on Earth to finish something they left unfinished in their life before they can move on to rest their soul. Ghosts are jealous of the living and their hatred forces them to stay on Earth, so they haunt or scare the living for a type of cruel revenge. But most of them can't truly hurt a human."

Maren and Umbra looked impressed, almost bewildered, not speaking for a minute. I only sat there, my head held up high with confidence, an all-knowing grin on my face. I've always liked to read about the world of the non-living for some reason, which helped me here. I sat there, still as a statue, soaking in the amazement on their faces.

Maren finally spoke up. "Very good Stary . . . Anyhow . . . someone is born with a gift to talk, see, and help ghosts and spirits move on or stop them from interfering with human life. Many of the Spirit Warriors do not know they have this gift at all. We need someone to help us. We have tried to search on our own for two years, but to no avail. The Lord said we could ask you to help punish or save the murderer from their own evil, in any way. We are . . . genuinely ready to move on and rest in peace together in heaven. I also want to be with my family again. Sadly, we cannot find our murderer, even with our connection and powers. They must be full of too much malevolence. It may be too late to save them from themselves."

Too late? Like they couldn't be stopped? No, if that was the case, they wouldn't have asked for my help if that was true. Was it too late to save the murderer from their own evil? And God wanted me to do the mission? But I'm only fifteen! I can barely lean forward in a car without hitting my forehead on something!

"A Spirit Warrior, which is your official title, is the only one who can take the evil out of our murderer. It is a long and painful process, which will end up being their punishment. If they are lucky, they will live and have no urge to follow darkness again. Hon, if you can get the evil out, we are allowed entry into heaven's gate and can rest in peace forever and you can be allowed to live your normal life again with your spirit powers only if you are needed again. But Umbra and I have to find him or her on our own. You have to stop them and talk to them. Sometimes that method has worked. If the murderer finds out about you however . . . they will try to stop you at any cost I am afraid to say, love . . ." Maren gulped and stared at me with moisture in her eyes. It was similar to the look my momma gave me before I went into surgery when I was small—a fear of someone you care for being harmed.

Oh great! I hoped the killer wasn't too smart. MAN! This was a lot of information to take in. "Maren, why do you only say murderer?" I asked, the singular noun bugging me.

"Because, when one is killed by another human, that person's negative energy becomes a part of you until heaven's golden light shatters it. Every person has their own and different negative energy. Umbra and I have the same glow surrounding us."

I nodded to show I understood the sad reality; they were killed by the same person . . . "Wait Maren. Your grandfather was also . . . murdered, correct? But, you say he's already in heaven."

She bobbed her head, making her hair dance in a ballet of sorrow. "My grandfather was, yes, murdered before me and if he could not have moved on or did not know his murderer, I would have been drawn to him right away. However, since I have never felt him, that means he saw his murderer's face and accepted dying, gaining entry into heaven."

Umbra added, "When we first die, we go to a special portion of purgatory, telling us what we must do next. To enter it, we walk by the rest of purgatory and close to the gates of heaven. If Dr. Rowe was not able to move on, Maren would have felt him right away in one of the two places. Plus, a soul who does not know who or why another person took their life away can never rest in heaven. Questioning this for all eternity is more of a punishment."

This bit of knowledge opened my eyes a little. So Maren was being punished since she didn't see her murderer's face and her grandfather moved on because he did? That didn't seem fair!

"How will I know how to defeat the murderer after you guys find them?"

Maren answered warily, "It will come to you that moment, so do not worry about that. And Umbra and I will be with you until we find them, everywhere you go. Only they can see us, besides you of course, so you should be fine with your friends, loved ones, and professors."

Cool! I think . . .

Umbra stepped close to me and whispered in my ear, his breath tickling my skin like an ocean breeze. "Be careful. They'll feel your stupid energy soon and be near you."

I smiled at him to show how mature I was . . . or how mature I was pretending to be at that moment. "I'll be ready! I can do this. I want to do this. I have to."

He looked at me like I was a fool, but agreed. "Fine, but don't come crying to me when you change your mind!" He winked and gave me a dirty smirk.

I got a little red, maybe to the color of pink cotton candy. "OH . . . You . . . !" I wanted to smack my head with that one. What a dumb retort!

Umbra noticed it as well and laughed full of mean pleasure. Maren touched my arm. "We will see you in the morning. We must start looking. Goodbye my dear and thank you for your compassion and dedication."

I wanted to ask them a few more questions, but they were gone in a blink of an eye before I could insist they could stay or even thank them (at least Maren). I felt bare without them.

I stared at myself in the mirror again, flipping my long chestnut brown hair around. I was still me! I just couldn't believe that I, Stary Moon, was a Spirit Warrior! I looked the same and I bet I was the same person: same friends, family, hobbies, teachers . . . but I felt different. I felt shaken, nervous, worried, but, also a bit excited for some mystery. The bonus part: I had a new friend and even a . . . rival or unfortunate acquaintance, whatever Umbra was. How unbelievable it all was!

In one day, my life changed right in front of my eyes like a twisted dream. However, I was rickety about what was going to happen next in my life and how it would affect not only me, but others. I was doing a good deed, but I got a numbing feeling there was much more to it than I thought or hoped.

I jumped into bed, my thoughts tumbling in my mind. How I could complete this mission and help Maren swirled around me. Umbra's stupid face appeared like an implant in my brain. I groaned and rolled over. I closed my eyes and fell asleep, floating above the air like a feather diving into the descending pool of the unknown. The last thought I remembered was: What would my future be like, my destiny?

5

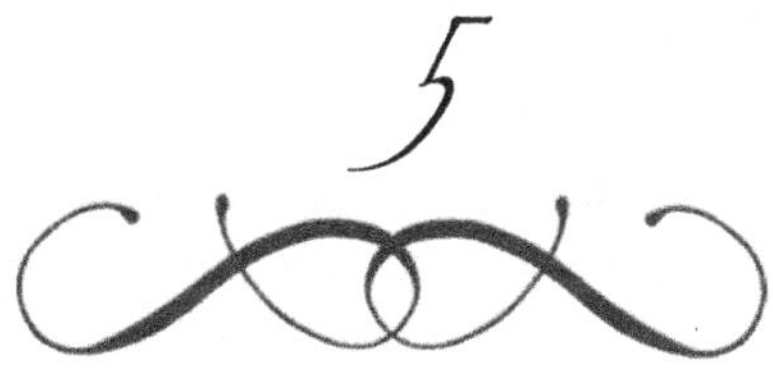

I WALKED DOWN THE HALL TO MY LOCKER, A DAILY ROUTINE THAT seemed so pointless now. I saw everyone chatting, talking, and having fun before the first bell rang. I always kind of felt different and lonely even though I had several great friends. But that day, I walked down the hall, looking, and wandering; everyone seemed to be moving slowly. They all sounded so happy when I looked at them . . . I felt like there was no place for me now that I was a Spirit Warrior.

I wasn't even thinking. It was like my body was moving me forward, but my mind wanted to turn back. If only I could stay in the present forever, I could stop the battle with myself. Of course, that would have me end at nowhere. That seemed like giving up, me allowing the small, bad things in life to consume me.

Everything seemed out of place . . . the lights were brighter, more piercing and burning. The shadows were darker like they had a mind of their own. Everything was blurry and unclear. I felt dizzy. And I knew it was all because of me meeting Maren and Umbra. Recalling I was a Spirit Warrior was like a strange dream where nothing happened, but still . . . the recent memory made me feel empty, lost, worried . . .

I was being too serious, but I couldn't help it. Was it all a dream? Maren . . . Spirit Warrior . . . Umbra . . . Umbra. OH! I hoped Umbra was only a nippy nightmare! But still, the way he held Maren with such tenderness. Come to think of it . . . I hadn't seen him since the previous night. I wondered where he was. That jerk was probably planning on ditching me the whole time! Why, I—

"STARY, LOOK OUT!"

What? I heard a voice but . . .

I screamed loudly when I felt a force collide with me.

All of my books went flying everywhere, looking like boulder-shaped confetti. My eyes closed from fear and my mind was in shock. My body was falling and I heard a crash as I hit the cold floor. Oh . . . I was the noise. How depressing . . .

Laughter and "Awwwww" were all around me, something else to make my day better! My knees were shaky, every fiber of me hurting and embarrassed.

Little by little, I opened my eyes, and there *he* was: Credence Horton, on his knees, leaning toward me with his hand stretched outward. His blue-gray eyes, his yummy pools to his soul, were forgiving and gentle, blending perfectly with his pale skin when he looked at me. His hair was a little messy, but it looked neat and shiny. He looked apprehensive, yet his face was still sincere. If I was dreaming, I begged no one wake me up from it. My heart was beating like rapids and in my mind I could have sworn I saw sparkles and bubbles of romance surrounding us at this small exchange.

"Stary, I'm really sorry! Are you all right?"

All I could do was stare at his beauty and nod. I grabbed his hand as he helped me up to my feet. His touch was so warm and inviting that I didn't want to let go nor did I care that I might have broken my tail bone . . . again.

He smiled like a young gentleman. "That's good. I was worried I hurt you."

I blushed, showing him a semi-smile. "It's my fault. I'm sorry. I wasn't paying attention! Sorry for being a moron." I bowed to him like he was my elder. What an *idiot* I was!

He smiled again, this time with more joy. "You're not. Everyone spaces out sometimes. Today was your day, Stary. Simple as that." He shrugged and winked. Gosh, he was *so* cute!

My face grew hotter. I was flattered. He bent down to the ground, back facing me. I was not sure what he was going to do. I had to be careful where I looked in case my dad stepped out into the hall. I closed my eyes, having to take in some breaths. I swept my left hand through my long hair to fix it and brushed my cheek, hoping to wipe the embarrassment away.

Credence then got up and in his arms were my books. I smiled, feeling shy. What a man! And like a magical-filled fairy tale, his sweet scent would be trapped on my books . . . a miracle if I had ever asked for one!

"I think you may need these." He gave them to me, our hands touching for a moment. He looked a little shocked when they did, but he didn't mind seem to mind by the look in his eyes. I put my text books into my backpack. None of his stuff was scattered on the floor much to my dismay. Darn! I was getting ready to thank him when my eyes noticed that his pants were ripped on one of his knees.

"Your leg!" I ran to him, bending down to his level. "I'm so sorry! Are you okay?" Not thinking, I touched it to make sure he wasn't bleeding. He looked at me confused, then at his leg. I guess he didn't notice. I felt like crying. What had I done? I felt a hand on my shoulder and looked up to see Credence.

"Don't worry. It doesn't hurt. It looks like it snagged on my keychain when we fell. This is an old pair of pants anyway." He leaned down to my ear, moving my long hair out of the way as he ever so lightly whispered, "I hope you figure out what's on your mind soon. You're a kind person. I don't want you to worry anymore, okay Stary?"

His voice was electric, his breath refreshing on my warm face. I thought my cheeks were going to explode from the reaction! My heart was so filled with elation that I felt like I could have done anything, even get an 'A' on one of Mr. Tin's pop quizzes.

I smiled a full smile, hugging my backpack and perkily saying, "Sure!"

He got up to dust his leg off. "I'm glad." He stared at me for a minute, which was fine because I *loved* staring at him.

"Yo! Creed!" An unknown voice echoed from my right, shattering our perfect moment together. He turned around, looking at two of his friends in Mr. Tin's doorway. "Come on Creed. We'll be late for class and you *know* how Mr. Tin is!"

His face twitched as if he was annoyed, but he didn't sound annoyed when he called, "I'm coming!" He then turned back to face me, still smiling the sweet smile he gave everyone. "We better get to class. I don't want your dad to yell at us for making a scene or hurt me for talking to his little girl, right?" I was then given a special wink and breathtaking grin. My day was turning lucky.

I laughed, trying to hide my embarrassment and disappointment. "Right Credence."

He laughed too, matching my tone a few notes lower. It was such a beautiful sound that I wanted it to ring in my ears forever. And I made him laugh? That fact was priceless. I felt my heart pounding in my chest. "No hard feelings about the bump, right Star?"

Star? No one had ever called me that, which always stunned me. I usually got the dreaded Twinkle, but *wow*! *He* gave me a nickname! I felt like I could have melted from happiness!

"No . . . None . . . at all! Sorry again." Talking was too difficult at that moment. I was feeling like a kindergartener with her first playground crush. Credence would have been the sweet boy who saved the little pig-tailed me after a mean boy kicked sand in my face.

"No problem! Hope you figure out what you need to Star." He dashed off to of his friends. His eyes were faultless, his face glowing, his look full of pride, and his bronze-brown hair was waving like a flag on a clear day.

He was a kind-hearted boy that any girl would want to hold. He turned around one last time and waved before he went into the classroom. "See you in homeroom Stary!" He gave me another of his smiles before disappearing, vanishing from my dreamy daze.

I was in paradise. I never wanted the feeling to go away. Then, I felt a gentle touch on my shoulder along with someone breathing on my neck. I turned my feet in a half circle, preparing to whack the attacker with my pointless algebra book. And there stood Chloe, giving me a you-evil-little-girl look, ignoring the fact that I was about to smack her with numbers.

I smiled, not wanting to move my gaze from where Credence stood moments before. "Hey Chloe. What's up, girl?"

She leaned her head on my shoulder, her arms dangling at my side. I looked at her because she broke my mood; but her cheeks looked puffy. "I . . . I was . . . trying . . . trying to catch . . . up with you so . . . you wouldn't run into . . . Credence . . . OH!" She moaned while panting like a dog on a hot day. She was such a drama queen.

I giggled at her antics; how sweet of her! She tilted her head up to stare at me.

"Are you laughing at my pain here, sister?" Her glare was accusing and her voice leaked with sarcastic judgment.

I shook my head no but had to fasten my hand to my mouth to suppress the laughter. I was laughing at her funny faces, although a tad of it came from her so-called "pain."

"I knew you'd be nervous and not know what to say," she continued. "I called you as loud as I could, but I guess I'm not as much of a big loud mouth as your dad says I am!"

I laughed harder, which made my sides hurt. "Sorry Chloe-chan! I'm not thinking today."

She looked up at me, her face telling me *duh*. "I noticed! You okay? You seem really upset . . ."

The look from my dream was back on her face! I could feel my face freeze and my lips twisting, reacting from the feeling of anguish that was dripping into my stomach. What was I going to tell her? Something was bothering me, but I didn't even know what. "I'm fine. Just one of those days I guess," I said as effortlessly as I could.

She shrugged. "I understand. I have those too. It sucks." She added a nod at the end.

She then hit my rib with her elbow with a playful jab and gave me a strange look. "I saw you talking to Credence without any help. You little devil, making us all think you're helpless!" She bowed to me with respecting eyes. "I am not worthy of your friendship, Mighty One!"

We passed a set of glass trophy cases where I got a view of myself; I looked like a cherry! I waved the embarrassment away with my hand and beamed to myself at the memory, wondering what Chloe was thinking while watching us.

"It . . . well, ah . . . It . . . wa . . . It was . . . was . . . noth-nothing!" I answered, stuttering. That was *so* not true, but if it got me off Chloe's intense interrogation, it would have to suffice! We linked our arms together, heading off like two best friends who could not be separated.

Thinking of Credence, the boy I liked very much, and walking to class with my best friend at my side made me realize I may have felt alone, but I never was. I was different. I always had been and known I was . . . but, at that moment, I knew *how* I was different. Umbra and Maren were my friends and I promised to help them no matter how frightening all the new information was. Despite that fear, I saw that even though my friends and family didn't know about all of my gifts, they gave me their love and support. Thanks to that thought, I knew I could do anything! I was ready. I was determined to save the murderer, help Umbra and Maren and also, hopefully, learn more about myself.

The day seemed typical enough. Mr. Galled's algebra B was normal. I was taking tons of notes, but I was not the greatest at math so I got uninterested. As Mr. Galled's voice became merely booming vibrations to my ears, I observed my classmates through fuzzy eyes. The edginess of the building decreased, the events a nightmare they could not shake. No one made any more acknowledgements of Maren and the police officers were gone, stating the school was clear. All the thoughts fogged my head and made the hour drag at a snail's pace. When we were dismissed, my legs were heavy and my body ached.

Lauren's next class was close to mine, so we walked together because our classes were down the "doomed wing." It was a tough battle to get through all the cheerleaders, popular kids, football players, and rich kids, standing there talking and being rude if you got near them. They assumed it was their hallway, which I'm sure is exactly what the architect had planned!

My feet felt like I was forced to walk in a sea of sand, my thoughts swirling and twirling around me at a force so strong, a vortex wouldn't have been able to contain them. Not knowing where Umbra and Maren were was disconcerting and then I had to be on alert for a killer I had no clue how to search for!

Before we reached the end of the dreaded hallway, I saw Credence and the sandstorm in my head stopped abruptly. He waved at me, a cute smile on his face, before jogging down the opposite hall. Although my head was clearer by seeing his presence, my nerves were shot at how drained I must have looked to him!

Lauren rolled her eyes in my direction, crudely asking, "Him *again*?" I stared self-consciously at the ground and for no reason, we both started cracking up. Although she was serious all the time, she still was an amazing friend. I could follow her calm example.

I walked into art with Mr. Sheep and grabbed my supplies for my realist shape drawings, which I was terrible at! I sat with a thud, intending to focus on my work. As I hatched a circle with my charcoal pencil, my table partner, Nikki, sat by me, her red hair as bright as the sun.

"I am totally rethinking the red and black color scheme for my wedding. It's a little too . . . Count Dracula, you think?" Nikki and I always talked about boys and wedding plans while we worked. She was two years older than me and it was wonderful to have a normal conversation with a *senpai.*

"I still liked the black and dodge blue idea. It's very unique and that magazine you brought in showed how many themes it could cover." I sharpened my pencil, the sound of it oddly loud and making my teeth hurt.

"You know I am all for traditional, modern, and elegance. It was a pretty scheme, but it screamed too *beachy* for me." She grabbed a red colored pencil from her can to start her apple.

"I liked it . . . ," I mumbled, ducking my head down. Nikki's well researched way of life always made me feel silly.

"You're still Japanese kimono all the way, right? I look forward to that! How fun the decorations will be and the beautiful patterns! And how many girls will have a real samurai waiting for them at the alter?" She sighed, full of wistfulness.

I laughed. I took a moment away from my shading to imagine a samurai, practicing his sword fighting under a large cherry blossom tree in full bloom. I knew the chances of finding a real fighter with attractive looks were slim . . .

The image in my mind shattered into a million pieces; the only picture left was a smirking Umbra with a katana in his hands. His eyes were glowing with hatred, but it seemed he was looking past my eyes and to something behind me. Was Umbra showing his powers as the Ultimate Weapon or was he seeking some sort of revenge? As I stared at the detailed image of him in my mind, he lunged at me, the tip of the sword coming into full view. A scream escaped my throat as Umbra lifted it above his head—

Pencils rained onto the floor. My eyes popped open in time to see that I knocked over my pencil cup and spilled all of my supplies. They were rolling away from my craziness. In a panic, I leaned down to grab them and my shoes caught on the legs of my chair, making me lose my balance. I landed on the cold floor with a smash and my chair followed beside me with a boom. I was getting sick of the close relationship I was now having with floors.

I sighed in defeat and rested my face on the floor as I heard my peers' chairs move to get a better look at me. Nikki became pale, her pencil in mid-air as she stared at me with worry. Everyone knew I was clumsy, but this was a little extreme.

"Stary, are you hurt honey?" Nikki asked, extending her hand to me. I took it, but stayed on the floor to grab my pencils. Since I was refusing to look at her, she spoke again. "Did you see something? You were screaming quite loudly."

I paused, my hands twitching. My face was blazing hot. I blinked and saw that everyone was staring at me. Oh Lord help me. I screamed out loud?! Crap sticks!

"Well . . . ," I began but Mr. Sheep snuck behind me, slapping my back immensely hard. It made a popping noise. I winced. A broken back is just what I needed.

I heard him chuckle deep in his stomach like he always did. "Oh, Moony! You're way too funny! Sweet little you crashing out of your chair, just to save some art supplies." A bigger, hardier laugh came out of his mouth. "That is the funniest thing I have seen in a while. Good work! Your drawing's not bad either." He walked off, exiting from his comedy routine. I just sat there flabbergasted. I supposed I lucked out by crashing in the room of the funny teacher.

I got off the floor, taking a quick gulp before continuing my work. Although my hand was filling in the white of my sphere, my mind was far away. What was that image? Was Umbra truly in my head or was my overthinking mind playing a trick on me? Did Umbra hate me or was there something behind me, causing the blackout in my brain? I knew Umbra was not fond of me, but those eyes were so soulless like a machine. I knew Umbra was not fully human, but he never once acted like a machine. Still, those glaring eyes . . . whatever it was, I knew now to never get on Umbra's bad side. I banged my head on my desk in rout.

Nikki patted my shoulder, smiling motherly with an array of concern. "Credence trouble?" Are boys the only reason girls get upset? I know hormones are everywhere, but I shook my head and apologized for my behavior, blaming it on lack of sleep. Nikki did not press it anymore and then chatted the rest of the hour about the test she had in my dad's class.

Nikki, as my *senpai*, told me she had to walk me to Spanish 1 across the hall. I didn't fight it. My legs had become Jell-O, numb and wobbly. I kept slamming them into each other, grateful when they tingled with feeling again. Nikki's brimming honeydew eyes informed me that I had lost my mind, but she waved me off, smiling all the same.

I was entering the basement room door when I slammed into Barbara, making her trip backwards. I was on a roll today. "Oh Barbara! I'm sorry! I hope I didn't hurt you!"

She stood tall, her brown eyes darting at me with a hue that now looked like oil. Her pupils were near invisible. I sucked in a breath, taken aback by her change and anger. Her voice came out at me like a slap in the face. "How idiotic are you? Don't ever bump into me again Moon Pie, or you don't want to know what I'll do to you!" She stomped off, almost shoving me to the side of the wall as she went to the restroom across the hall.

I began to shake. Barbara was often in a foul mood and became vicious, but to actually threaten me was new. She had also not called me Moon Pie since we were in the fourth grade. It stopped once we changed schools in fifth grade. And her eyes! It was like ink swimming. I hurried inside the room and prepared for class, sinking into my seat in fear of unleashing her wrath again. It was strange being scared of a classmate you have known for years.

I couldn't concentrate on my Spanish words. My mind was reeling the images of Umbra I had seen in art class and the fact that I had not seen

Maren or Umbra since they were in my room. I prayed that they didn't get harmed. Could spirits even get hurt? I wondered if they had found any clues about finding their murderer. What if—

Something shook my arm, cutting off my beyond terrifying suspicions. I turned quickly around in my chair, looping my legs over my book bag with great force as I held my pencil as a weapon. I was tired of being caught off-guard today. I'd be ready now!

I adjusted from my warrior stance when I saw Alden, looking surprised at me. "I was going to ask if you wanted to be speaking partners is all." He gave me the ultimate sad puppy look. Now I felt bad. I smiled, hoping to be forgiven and agreed. I placed the pencil on my desk. I needed to chill. I was so lost in thought that I hadn't even heard Señorita Orange state we were doing an assignment!

Alden was fairly good at Spanish, so we finished early. He kept touching my arm, but it was like he was checking something, either my pulse or how calm I was. I wasn't sure. In a way, I was glad he did for suddenly, I was having trouble breathing. It was getting hard to gasp for air. My lungs felt like I was a little, helpless gold fish that was thrown on a lab table, struggling to hold my own sanity and life. The realization hit me: someone was there, observing me . . .

My eyes were then locked to the first person in my row: Barbara. If wishing death on someone had a face, Barbara was perfecting it and it was aimed at me. As Alden rubbed my back as I gagged to get air into me, a pulse rang in my ears and my hands were glowing. I blinked a few times. My vision was blurred from lack of oxygen, but I saw it; my hands were glowing a dull pink as if something inside me was protecting me.

"Time is up!" Señorita Orange's voice must have broken Barbara's concentration on me because I was able to breathe again. Adrenaline rushed inside me, causing my heart to jerk. I inspected my hands and noticed the glow was gone, but they felt a comforting warmth. What was that? It felt like they were trying to protect me from Barbara. I thanked Alden for his kindness and then packed up slowly, scared to run into Barbara, but thankfully she had zoomed out the door like a jet.

As I walked in the white light of the fake illumination, I noticed Barbara was glaring me with her pebble-sized eyes at the corner, like she was looking for something ghastly and praying something was wrong with me to fuel her warped delight. I ignored it, refusing to let the carrying emotion consume me.

I was ready for a more peaceful afternoon. Having visions of being attacked with a sword, embarrassing myself, and choking because someone was looking at you was a bit too much to handle! I had homeroom next, which meant I would see Credence. I knew I would be fine with him there.

Homeroom was a haven! I read, did homework, played cards with friends, and stared at adorable Credence. Everything was perfect and before I could look at the clock, the hour and twenty minute period was over. The lunch bell rang and we all ran out swiftly to get in line, pushing like mad dogs trying to get the biggest helping of steak. It was as if nothing had changed.

However, as I was about to leave after allowing Credence to be in front of me so I had a nice view of all angles of him, I detected Barbara watching me. Why was she staring at me like I was a prize and yet she was disgusted by me? A black line around her neck caught my attention. It was thin, hard to see, but it was not a choker.

I was deciding if I should go up to Barbara to ask her if she had been burned when Chloe linked her arm through mine and led me away. As I looked back at her one last time, a lovely white flower fell from the apple tree in front of the window. It seemed like a sign that an end was coming.

"Stary! Why do you even go to the salad bar if all you get is cottage cheese?" Mark asked playfully as I sat down at our lunch table with my plate.

"It was healthier than some things and I don't like salads!" I defended my meal, scooping a large serving into my mouth. Mark chuckled.

The atmosphere felt much warmer and accepting than when the school learned of Maren's death. I was happy they weren't suffering anymore; they didn't need to be overly concerned because the connection to Maren was my duty. Talking casually, laughing, and eating with my buddies made me feel great and made me remember I was just an average teenager. Yet, why did that seem so wrong too?

I was eating a tomato slice Chloe stuck on my plate, stabbing it with my fork to allow the red juices to drip onto my food like blood when I felt a wind whistling inside my ear. I felt it inside my *mind* too. Beyond it being freaky, it was trying to say something . . .

"Star . . . y . . . ," it said ever so faintly.

That voice . . . it was Umbra! I didn't feel his presence or glowing force, but there was an eerie coil in my mind. I focused harder on trying to feel a presence in the air, the same way I felt them in my room yesterday, but I couldn't feel a thing. I couldn't whisper to answer him in front of my friends, but I certainly couldn't ignore him either. I feared Maren was in danger!

I whispered super softly, "Umbra?" I continued to say his name four more times, but still no reply. Oh heaven almighty . . . something was wrong!

I felt a chill down my spine, like a finger was writing messages on my back. I turned to my left shoulder as it began to feel like something was very slowly crawling up it, very sharply shooting pain into my flesh. Its movement was humanlike, making me question if the Greek west wind god,

Zephyr, was haunting me. I saw a hand that was quite hazy appear from the unseen mist, tracing my outline.

"Um . . . Umbra?" I whispered again, freaking out more and more with each second.

Out of nowhere, he made himself visible to me and almost shattered my ear drum with his yell. "You really think anyone is going to hear you when you talk like a sissy? Geez! Plus, I could have been an attacker. You're too trusting! You're such a vulnerable human."

I wasted my time worrying about someone like this all day? I was so blind! Newsflash: I already knew I was too trusting, I *was* human, and I was tired of randomly using my school supplies as weapons against my peers, such as the spoon I now had gripped between my knuckles. Why was Umbra acting like a slime ball now when I had not seen or heard or felt him all day? My glare towards him must have not projected my feelings for he continued to rant.

"I said your name with my head wind like five minutes ago, but you were staring off into la-la land. There's no way in hell, and yes, I get the irony, you're a Spirit Warrior! A true Spirit Warrior is meant to be tough, righteous, alert, and fearless, ready for anything at any time and let nothing get in the way of their obligations to the big guy. You are way too idiotic, unfocused, wimpy—"

I interrupted and whispered full of snip, having had enough, "You mean I need to be someone like you, except for the righteous part, in order to be a Spirit Warrior, a helper of God?"

His eyes were like bullets as a wicked smile crept on his lips. He said, too causally, "Exactly!"

With a vindictive look worse than mine, he threw in a little evil laugh on the side. He seemed to be absorbing my hatred like warm sunshine. He liked it? I gave him the meanest comeback I could ever think of on the spot, surrounded by my friends, ignoring the vile of guilt, and he *accepted* it?

He stared at me when his sour mood decreased, like he was testing me. "Oh Stary, don't give me such a dirty face." He pinched my cheek, talking in a baby voice. "I know you tried your very best and that makes me proud of you!" I received a pat on the head from his slimy hand. "You're too sweet to be mean. You'll never make it out there." He seemed serious. "Only . . . that was the worst comeback in history! An infant could make one a million times better than that!" His laugh was loud and full of contempt, stepping on my foot; I was an ant in his way.

That was the last straw! Walls were coming down and then I would be the one laughing . . . Ha-ha-ha-ha-*HA*!

"Umbra," I began. I was so annoyed that I could feel my eyebrows twitching with an uncommon form of fury. My fury, however, got in the way of my logic. My internal alarm knew I said his name out loud, but only loud enough so my friends could hear it.

"Umbra?" said Barbara. She blinked, looking lost by my blindsided action.

I felt my heartbeat increase as my face froze in its position. Oh fudge! "Oh, well, yeah! I meant my shadow. It's kind of . . . it looked weird . . . yeah! It just looked really weird. Sorry about that!"

They all blinked at me like I was stupid. Oh boy!

I heard Umbra laughing harder, but it sounded too strained to be considered enchanting. He was about to get Spirit Warrior smacked!

Barbara was not going to let it go, of course. "Why did you say umbra though? What in blazes does that mean?"

I gulped. Now I was going to sound weird and arrogant because I knew a word in a different tongue. "Well, you see, umbra means shadow or shade in Latin. I read it in a book the other day and it stuck . . ." My definition was followed by a beyond nervous laugh, preparing myself to block out the teacher's pet calling that was sure to follow.

Barbara crossed her tiny arms, gracing our table with laser eyes, targeted on me. She arched her eyebrows like she had a master plan. "That is the most—"

"Guess you didn't know that, did you Brainiac Baroness? Ha!" Rin declared. She leaned forward, her sandy hair framing her victorious face. Chloe and Lauren had their cheeks puffed out like a duo of blowfish. I could tell it took all their strength and oxygen not to laugh from their strained faces.

I sighed from relief, thanking Rin with a look. She gave me a wave and smacked the table with delight at shutting Barbara up for a second. Barbara turned her laser stare on full blast, locked now at Rin. Rin smirked, showing she accepted the challenge. When Rin didn't crack, Barbara's glare seemed to get deadlier, absorbing Rin's fire.

Mark spoke up. "I do have to agree with you Stary. It does look odd."

Umbra stopped dead and blinked; his laughter was transferred into me only at a higher octave. It was my turn to gloat at his burn. "It's an ugly shadow all right," I added.

Umbra looked at me kind of hurt after I said that. I stopped, shocked. Did I hurt his feelings? I'd feel bad if I did, but he vanished before I could wrap my head around the idea. Oh no . . .

"Whatever you say Stary," said Bret and everyone began to eat again.

"Umbra?" I whispered, trying to calm my guilty conscience down.

Nothing made a sound other than the popping of the air vents above and the clacking of lunch trays. No one acknowledged my voice. Oh rhino! I finally got the chance for a comeback, a really great one, and it bruised Umbra's feelings. I wouldn't have thought of Umbra having any feelings with the way he acted towards me.

Expect for the night before . . . the image of Umbra and Maren embracing, heart-to-heart, came to my mind again in a rush. Why was it so painful for me to think of that beautiful moment? The smile he gave me after I told him I accepted my destiny . . . His touch when he allowed Maren to cry alone . . . His suffering after losing all he had known and loved . . . It was like a film reel in my head where one is unexpectedly feeling sorry and supporting the villain because you forget they're a real person. Was I fearful of the vision I had in art class, the vision I didn't get to question or by his current meanness to me?

Umbra was real and he did have a heart and feelings. He hid them well, like he covered them in an unbreakable layer of shadow, his namesake. I really blew it. I was horrid. I really must have been a Spirit Warrior. If Spirit Warriors were supposed to be cold and heartless, then they got the wrong person because I didn't want to become that person. Umbra was right; maybe I couldn't do it.

Suddenly, my chair began to tip over backwards. I grabbed ahold of it before it got out of control. Was my chair rocking on its own? I started swinging forward and backwards and bouncing up and down. It made me nauseated. What in the world was going on? My legs weren't moving and it took all my energy to control the chair's legs. Out of nowhere, it slipped on the slick floor and I crashed on to the floor with a painful thud, my surroundings a blur. It seemed like chairs were out to get me!

Our whole area got an eerie feeling and snaps filled my eardrums. Chloe and Rin saw me slip. They didn't get up, but both gave me their hands and asked if I was all right. As I struggled to get up, making unattractive grunting sounds because my knees were banged up, everyone stared at me. I was getting a little tired of this permanent spotlight that shined on me during embarrassing moments!

All of my friends were waiting for an explanation. My mind was racing, trying to figure out how I was going to explain what had happened. All of a sudden, Umbra reappeared in the corner of my vision, striking the standard crossed-armed bad boy pose as he stared at me with emotionless, mocking eyes. I could see his foul smile and ill intentions. Looking at him made me feel lower than dirt. The only thing he said was, "Hmph . . . Worthless . . ." as he flipped his flawless bangs like a super model. He was so juvenile for a super being!

My legs were shaky as I stood tall. I may have hurt his feelings, but I could have been hurt! And he wounded my feelings first and didn't care at all. I took two giant steps towards the soon-to-be devil, my fists moving upwards to his face, flicking the impulses of my rage. My eyes were stinging with anger and my throat burned from heated passion as I stared at him as coldly as I could, but his face didn't change at all from before.

He gave me a wolf-like grin and said, rudely, "Oh! Are you mad?"

I began to breathe heavily. This meant war! I grabbed for his chest and to my surprise, Maren was right about how she and Umbra would be more real to me as the days went on. This meant I could now touch Umbra if I had a focal point, although it was like holding onto string. I yanked a piece of his tightly pressed black shirt, wrinkling the ghostly fabric in the process.

He gasped and held his hands in the air like I was the sheriff of the school and I caught him stealing a basket of ketchup packets.

I scowled, my voice screaming through clenched teeth. "Umbra! You *idiot*! You could have really—" The words flew out of me before I remembered only I could see Umbra. A dead silence filled the room. Everyone was looking at me and my invisible meltdown with Umbra.

It wasn't fair. Everything clicked. The chair event wasn't his true comeback. This was. I dropped my fists and my legs gave out as I realized that I had been played. Umbra gave me a calculating look from his hovered position in the air. I was tired, so tired all of a sudden. It was all I could do not to cry.

Why did he do that to me? I never did anything to injure him. I really did want to help him, despite my complaining. My internal questions consumed my heart and mind and they couldn't handle it anymore. Fine! He won! He wanted me miserable and for me to leave him alone during the entire mission then I would. I finally give up. I give up dang it! I. GIVE. UP!

My eyes became foggy, making it harder to see. I looked up at Umbra and for some reason, his mouth twitched. It wasn't his entire fault; he was unhappy and I was an easy target, a poor excuse for a savior. I could not understand his suffering, but I wished I could, only to make him less unhappy. He then met my gaze and his became lost and a tad apprehensive.

"Stary!" Chloe was at my side with Mark, Rin, and Lauren following. "You okay?" they all asked, but at different times.

I nodded indifferently. I forced myself to get up no matter how painful physically and mentally it was. My friends moved out of the way. They seemed to understand I needed some space. I stared into Umbra's dark eyes. He looked taken aback and bemused.

I whispered near him, "You get what you want. Me gone," and I stepped back to look at him with a merciful smile. I just had to let Umbra be Umbra. He took a step forward, then another, reaching for my arm, but stopped. His head was down, refusing to look at me.

I couldn't stop my tears from coming out any longer. The pressure was attacking my chest with violence. I ran to the bathroom, tears flowing down my eyes. Before I ran, I saw Umbra lift his head up. He looked like he was going to stop me, but his eyes looked too damaged, so damaged that he couldn't move his body. I thought I heard him say my name, but I bet it was a wish on my part.

I ran into the first open stall and began to sob, hard, my tears seeping into my shirt. My stomach hurt. I was close to getting sick. I was fortunate that no one else was in there.

My body was aching from confusion. I was worried about Umbra's whereabouts all morning, hurt by his actions and words, scared of the vision of him I had, nervous about the mission I had to assist him on, and embarrassed about breaking down in front of him. The emotions swirled inside, making me ill, my head about to split open.

"Why?" I choked between my tears. "I know . . . he hates me and all . . . but I didn't . . . think he'd . . . stoop . . . so low as to . . . hurt me . . ." I ran out of toilet paper so I wept into my hands, my hair brushing the dirty floor. I was a broken doll being used as a broom.

"I never said I hated you, did I? Please don't put words in my mouth."

I looked up, surprised. It was Umbra! It was really him! Why did that matter to me and make my heart swell? I flicked the thought away for the moment to focus on his appearance. He handed me a roll of toilet paper that he must have grabbed from another stall. "Here," he said, placing the roll into my hands. "You're going to need it." He winked afterwards.

I tried to make myself talk in a regular voice. "Why are . . . you in . . . here?" It was a failed attempt. I felt so pathetic, emotional, and so like a teenage girl. It was annoying.

He looked at me, puzzlement in his eyes. He appeared to be processing how to respond. "Well, they don't make spirit restrooms, you know?" He turned his head away.

I pulled my head closer to my body, wanting nothing more than to turn into a turtle to hide in my metal shell.

"Didn't work, huh?"

I refused to acknowledge him.

"That bad?"

Silence whirled throughout the air, creating a storm of tension.

"Ack! Come on!" he yelled, his tone sad and desperate. He groaned and I noticed the muscles in his face began to twist with guilt.

I lifted my head up to finally give him a break. "Now you know how I felt just then, but mine was ten times worse."

His stare was cute, but blank. He ducked his body down, popping his neck. A real faint whisper escaped his parted lips. It was barely noticeable. However . . . it sounded like a "sorry."

"What?"

"Sorry . . ." He was a little louder, straining to keep his pride.

"I'm telling the truth, I still can't hear you . . ."

"DAMMIT! I'M SORRY!" he screamed with his hands shaking like an earthquake. His eyes were intense as sounds radiated all out of his body. "Happy?!"

I grinned in approval. "Getting there."

He gave me a sweet smile, but it faded into space soon after it came. "Good! Because I'm tired of all this wimpy crying crap!"

I blinked and giggled. It came out of the blue from my lips. It was refreshing that he could be charismatic. He didn't agree and only blinked. Umbra was back and the Umbra in front of me was okay by my book.

"Why did you have to do that Umbra? I didn't mean to hurt your feelings and if so, I'm sorry, but what you did was a little extreme!" I rested my head on my knees, curling them up on the toilet seat. No one was in the bathroom so it was all right. If Umbra was visible, we would have some issues with screaming girls. I'm not sure if it would be from disgust or delight.

He looked at me with defensive eyes. "I wasn't going to let you get hurt moron. I had my other hand behind the chair . . . to catch you just in case . . ." He blushed a little. Thinking back, I didn't see his other hand. Maybe he was a knight after all.

"Sorry for assuming," I said, ashamed that I had accused him so hastily.

He tapped my shoulder to get my attention, stopping me from beating myself up. "It's okay. It's my fault too. I did start it . . . I guess . . . I'm not used to dealing with others or emotions." He got up to start walking away, his revelation sinking in to my being, but stopped. "Worthless humans have to learn somehow . . ."

I glared at him, not happy he ruined our sweet little moment. "Hey now!"

He turned to face me, smiling a bit. "Glad to see you're back, loser! Be careful and take care of what you got kid. Believe me . . . I know how hardships can change you . . ." His shadowed face was full of secret familiarity.

"Oh . . . Umbra . . ." My eyes were about to fill up with tears again but due to a new feeling Umbra caused.

He walked up to me, giving my cheek a little tap. "I said no more of your crying crap!" he demanded, but it sounded more playful than harsh that time.

I stopped, deciding to play his little game. "Fine!" I shouted heatedly back.

He paused, studying me to see if my yell was serious, but the light in his eyes showed he realized I was pretending. He growled then and ruffled my head like we were kindergarten boys. I hope he didn't do that to Maren, but it only made me laugh harder at the image, the sound bouncing off the walls.

He stopped and went back to his mocking Umbra face, turning around to exit. I had a few more bones to pick with him before he was gone from my sight!

"Umbra, can I ask you something?"

He turned his head only a little to face me. The way he did it . . . It made him look attractive. Although he looked irritated, his eyes and hair shined from the sunroof. I had to remember to breathe and shake my head to snap out of the state. "Is it something girly?" he asked, half annoyed.

I grinned, feeling coy. "Not really."

He stared into my eyes for a moment, almost looking like he took pleasure in my appearance before answering, "What?"

I smiled, overwhelmed by his acceptance. "Well, why did you come after me today?"

His eyes became huge as he looked at me funny, his dashing face quite red. He turned to his side, halfway facing me with his eyes shut, arms crossed. "Because," he yelled. He looked at me, upset, still keeping his cold pose. "Because . . . I was worried your crying would make Maren get upset at me and well . . ." His face turned a few shades deeper like he was a bomb about to explode and his breathing was slightly raspy. "I didn't want you mad at me, since we have to be allies and all . . ."

He was worried about me?! For some reason, my body felt as light as a kite. "How sweet!" I said as I leaned on his shoulder without thinking. It made *me* blush and I think I made his worse. I wasn't sure why he was blushing now, but I stopped, seeing the error of my actions. Moreover, I wanted to calm him down (and myself) before I got brave. I nudged my smooth cheek against his. This bathroom must have a virus in it that makes you loco!

This time I felt nothing but shaped air. I paused, looking into his eyes. "How come I could touch you back in the lunchroom, but it feels like air again now?"

Umbra gulped so loud that I could hear it. He grunted, upset I was still so close to his body. "I noticed that as well. We told you once you got more used to us, we would become like others in your life. That means seeing us, touching us, hearing us, and so forth. It's still new, so I suppose it's a little unstable. Within a day or two I bet it will feel more natural for you. Maren and I could touch and interact with you right away."

I nodded, remembering how Umbra touched me when Maren was crying and how Maren helped me up when I fell out of my dad's chair. Maybe anger gave me more control of my powers? Man, this was all going to be difficult to figure out. Still, I was curious.

I rubbed my cheek against his again; he shouted in protest. I wasn't sure why I was acting like an attention hog and flirting, but for some reason, it felt . . . right. No virus then. I hopped back to get a look at his reaction. Umbra was red, his breathing shallow, and he looked irritated.

"So, you were worried about me, huh Umbra?" I gave him a sneaky look. Did he ever turn to a tomato! Other than Maren, I guess he didn't have a lot of girl experience either.

He began to roar, his whole body shaking, becoming abnormally colored. "I never said—"

"I think you did. I think you *do* care . . . ," I interrupted slyly.

He flushed again, but it was more of an annoyed one. "Listen, I said we were allies. Don't give me all this loving stuff, okay? Or you'll make me regret it Moon!"

"It's okay," I said, satisfied. "I really like being allies with you." I smiled after whispering my truthful comment. I did my best to give an attractive look as I lightly turned my head like he did earlier. I think it worked because I felt him staring at me. The feeling I had at that moment wasn't the best. I still felt worried about what was yet to come, but this feeling . . . I liked and could handle. Umbra and I had a silent agreement; we were connected and willing to work together.

While we made our unvoiced pact, the vision from art class popped into my head. Although I was timid to ask, I wanted to make sure it wasn't another trick or something serious. I had learned from Umbra that speaking in my mind, his mind wind as he called it, spirits can apparently use the mind of humans. I also learned that his eyes changed colors due to his emotions. When he was insulted earlier, they were black. Now, they were the color of melting gold. I wanted to ponder more about these facts, but I had bigger fish to fry. Before I could get the sounds out, the bell rang. I made a mental note to ask him about it later.

I thought I would have wanted to leave, but I didn't. In fact, my heart felt like it was cracking. I laughed to myself. I wasn't sure why I was feeling that way, but it must have been because I ate too much cottage cheese. Still, looking at Umbra . . . Why was my stomach all in knots? I knew my friends were outside the bathroom for I could hear Lauren's fortune telling watch clicking, so I ignored my stomach.

Umbra gave a weak look like he was sick. He hurried me along out the door, almost pushing. "Can't worry them or be late. Maren will chew me out!"

I was unaware of what was happening, so I sadly answered, "Right."

He touched my back in a pat with a compassionate twinkle in his coal eyes. "You can be a Spirit Warrior. I know it."

An awkward pause fell and I felt my cheeks creep into a light pink heat.

He shook his head hard, trying to snap out of an evil spell before letting his face look normal and angry at the world again. "Don't tell Maren I was nice. I got a reputation to uphold."

I grinned, trying not to laugh inside. I didn't want to leave, but what could I do? Still . . . the mention of Maren made me queasy; something fretful was on my mind. "Oh, Umbra?" Fudge! The words came out of my mouth on their own, the wire connecting my mouth and mind was unplugged again. I really need to get that fixed!

He turned around, a 'hmmm' glance directed at me. Well, it was out so I had to pursue.

"Why did you come back here anyway? And where's Maren?" I sounded important.

He gave himself a stupid look. "She's fine. She told me to keep an eye on you. She has a lead, but it keeps getting closer to town. She wanted me to watch you and protect you while she was away. She'll be back at sunset. And besides, I wanted to see the learning process for this lazy, stupid species."

I glared at him and laughed in sad agreement.

"You're . . . laughing?"

"Well, yeah!" I said chipper-toned between laughs. "You're right. A lot of people are lazy and don't think. But, they have nothing to fight for."

He stared, like my words touched his soul, reforming him a little.

"But, not all of us are like that," I said with my arms behind my back. I had to defend us mortals for together, some of us could do the unthinkable.

He bowed his head down and whispered in the shadows, "I know . . ."

I wanted to thank him, but my heart was beating too heavily. I was scared it would echo out of my mouth.

When we were leaving to beat the bell, I felt something coming from the bathroom stall I was in with Umbra. My blood became ice cold and mad chills ran up and down my back. I felt like I was in my own little world of fear, pain, and confusion. It was only me and my guts that were trapped in the feeling of uneasiness.

"You coming Stary?"

I gasped at Umbra's call. He broke me from the short sinful pull that was radiating from the stall. How I knew it was sinful, I wasn't sure, but I knew it was the complete opposite feeling Maren and Umbra gave off when I felt them.

"Stary, you okay?"

I nodded. "I'm fine. I only . . . I thought I . . . only felt . . . something . . . Ah, never mind." I smiled to rub off the feeling. Umbra looked concerned, but believed me with a shrug and walked me to my friends. They all asked if I was okay. All I said was I was having a little teenage brain melt, which they said they understood and Chloe admitted to having some.

I felt Umbra watching me from the ceiling. I now had a protector and an ally. Maren had a lead as well. Surely, everything would be all right. But, what was waiting for me? Why did the feeling I felt in the bathroom make me feel so faint and unclear? What was I going to face? No, what were we going to face?

6

"TRAINING?" ONCE I WAS HOME THAT DAY, I WAS BOMBARDED with questions about how poor my sensing for evil souls was by Professor Umbra. His lecture was intense and I'm so glad Maren grabbed my ruler out of his hand during the climax of his speech. Man! He could scare the pee out of Chuck Norris!

"You heard me! You are so wrapped in fluffy clouds and too tense, getting ready to attack mortals with pencils if they're merely behind you. You have issues, sister, and no Spirit Warrior I have to work with is going to look pathetic."

I agreed that I needed to get better at sensing different types of souls other than Maren's and Umbra's, who were now natural to feel. Plus, I couldn't argue with the fact that I have been using my school supplies for weapons against my peers who made me feel jumpy. Still, Umbra didn't have to be so harsh and have my giant algebra book ready to throw at me. I supposed our moment earlier today was a figment of my imagination. Three hours sure change things!

Maren was wrestling Umbra, trying with all her might to get the deadly math book out of his firm hands. I doubted that would ever happen. She gave a cute grunt, looking so frail as he moved his pinky a millimeter to send her a foot back.

"All right. I'll train . . ." My voice was quiet, but it cracked the static in the air like an electric whip, freezing all the invisible atoms I knew were there. Umbra and Maren paused like I aimed my remote at them. They disentangled to investigate me.

"What? Really?" Umbra blinked, astounded.

I shrugged. Was it really that odd for me to think training to sense evil souls was normal? Wait, no one answer that. "Yes, I'm serious. I mean, it's not something I ever dreamed I'd have to do, but I think it's needed. I hate being more jumpy than usual and I'm sure the Lord will think it's needed as well. So, Umbra, I will train with you." I got up and bowed to my *sensei.* "Please teach me well. I'm in your capable hands."

Maren's mouth opened like a cave and her skin looked clammy. Umbra threw his arms dramatically outward, looking triumphant. "All right! That's the spirit! We'll start tomorrow after school."

I knew that would work since my dad had a meeting. "We can find an empty room to practice in."

Umbra went to the corner, talking to himself about his lesson as Maren moved her head back and forth between the two of us like a forced bobble head. I smiled at her to reassure her, but that only made her eyes wider. This . . . was all too much. I knew I was doing the right thing and I wanted to control my powers. However . . . having *Umbra* be my personal tutor . . . I silently prayed to my God: *I respect your choices sir, but maybe Chuck Norris would be a more suitable and safer choice. Keep me posted!*

"All right! Let's get started!" Umbra and I were in my dad's room, where, like magic, the furniture had been pushed back and the floor looked extra shiny. What did Umbra do, hire the Ghostbusters to be our personal movers?

I looked at him head-on, hiding my surprise. "You do realize you are going to have to move all this back, right?" I was also concerned with how he moved it, but my daddy was a scarier threat and I didn't want to make extra work for our kind custodians.

He fanned his hand in the air, rolling his eyes to the side. "Details, details. All right, class has begun Miss Moon."

I think this teacher thing was getting to his already huge ego. If he pulled a whistle out of his pocket, I swear—

Doot, doot!

I looked although I was afraid to. He had a whistle . . . Wow . . . Really . . . ?

"Okay Stary, let me ask you a question: How do you sense me and Maren?"

My back was away from him, but it shivered, reacting to find the right words for the answer. For some reason, it made me . . . sad to think about.

I inhaled, stalling for time. I hoped Umbra would not be upset with me or call me stupid. "You mean . . . what I feel when you and Maren are near me?" I hoped that was acceptable, because the *how* was still fuzzy to me.

I saw Umbra's shadow nod. He towered over me on the floor, making me feel small and useless, but I needed to answer. "It's . . . complicated. I know that sounds like a way to get out of an answer, but it's a feeling that I know, but I'm not sure words do it justice." I swallowed hard, my mouth tasting like cotton balls. I was expecting Umbra to explode, but he nodded to encourage me to continue.

"I feel for something that's completely the same as the rest of the world, but also completely different at the same time. If I had the honest skill to *see* the sense, I would say I'm looking for a glowing raindrop in the Atlantic Ocean on a cloudy day. It's small, near invisible, but its shine is beautiful and I notice it better when I'm not really looking for it. The feeling of you and Maren . . . it's chilling, but a comforting kind. It makes me confused and . . . happy."

I squished my eyes shut, hunching my back forward. I was ready for Umbra to yell at how corny I was sounding, at how I was making no sense, at how I was appearing to not take anything seriously. I braced myself for the blow, listening to Umbra's footsteps as he approached. I hoped he didn't believe in physical punishment like in convents.

"Stary, that's . . . you put that into almost poetic terms and I understand what you mean. I'm amazed you have that much ability to sense, and trust me, it's nearly impossible to shock me!" Umbra patted my shoulder, his touch tender. "Good job."

I blushed, my mouth struggling to take in little puffs of air. "Tha-Thanks . . ." I was so red that my reflection on the floor was hard to miss.

Umbra crossed his arms, pacing, appearing deep in thought. He took all of this so seriously that it made me want to chuckle. "Now that you understand the feelings of normal, non-living souls, let me expand to explain the feeling of an evil soul." He waved his pointer finger in the air, continuing to pace. His face was so serene and strong that I followed his words with an open mind.

"Evil souls, living or alive, are the same. The evil soul you will be dealing with is the murderer's. The murderer is dangerous because they can hide the glow and feelings that cling to their bodies. Maren and I can do this, but not as long, which is why we were always on the move, rather than tracking the murderer."

Umbra's words were as clear as mud. I felt like I was crunching on potato chips while someone was giving me a secret mission from the FBI. I knew it was important, but no matter how much I tried, I kept cramming those fattening chips into my mouth. The explanation was twisted, revolting, and I craved it, craved to learn more of the powers of the murderer.

Umbra went on, not giving me a chance to stop eating my metaphorical chips. "Don't worry Stary. If you train a little, you can be able to sense the murderer. You will be able to feel sparks of their misplaced aura that clings in the airspace where they have been. The feeling . . . it's a sickening warm heat, like all their pain and anger becomes lodged inside your chest."

By impulse, I grabbed my chest, squeezing it like a security blanket. My chest, which held my heart, the sacred organ that was filled with my emotions, the emotions that made me strong and delicate, had to experience such a sickening heat? To have it attacked with pain in order to feel a murderer made perfect sense, but I still didn't like it.

Umbra put his fist under his chin, looking like he was thinking strategically, his eyes big and bold. "You have the instinct to do it as a Spirit Warrior, but the problem is, you're so jumpy and get scared at everything.

We'll have to train you to be able to know the feelings enough so you won't attack your peers anymore." He glared at me then, lips pouted.

I really was a nervous wreck. I slapped my sides firmly, defeated. "Okay, I can see that. But how am I supposed to train 'feeling' the murderer when I haven't felt them before? I don't see any evil souls willing for me to sense them then stop them." I skewed my nose upward.

Umbra pointed his face harder at me, getting a tad closer, but a little sprinkle of delight twinkled in his honey-toned eyes. "Don't get sarcastic with me young lady or I will give you a month's worth of detention!" He swung his whistle in the air like a big shot.

"Sorry sir . . ."

"Now, before I was so rudely interrupted, I was about to explain. Since Maren and I are on assignment from the Lord, we can do small things to adjust ourselves if it's for the good of the task. I'll give you an example: we're able to track a little faster than most spirits, but our skills are sharper anyway due to all the experience."

I nodded, thanking the Lord for helping my friends out after all their struggles.

"So, since I dubbed myself your trainer, I will be able to modify my aura to that of an evil soul in order for you to sense it."

My mouth became a perfectly rounded circle. "That's outstanding, I mean, that you can do that Umbra."

Umbra shrugged his shoulders, acting casual. "It will only be for this session, so you will have to be able to master this in the twenty minutes we have left. Got it?"

I made my voice low and husky as I chewed my words like a lawn mower that ate a pebble. "Oh yeah . . . simple enough . . ." Maybe I can fly a spaceship while I'm at it.

Umbra threw his whistle on the slick floor. It bounced to the side and crashed into the wall. His eyes burned with rage, his face blank and mocking. His appearance made the hairs on my arms shoot straight up and made my stomach become an icy abyss. Umbra looked . . . murderous.

Before I could tell him I was ready, he disappeared into the floor. I turned rapidly in every direction, not able to feel his energy at all. My breathing became quick and I was about to throw up acidy bile. What . . . what was this feeling? My whole body shook madly as tears stung my eyes, piercing my vision. My chest *burned.* Not like after you eat spicy food burn, but like someone lit my heart on fire for pure spite burn. I felt hatred, I felt emptiness, I felt disgusting pleasure, and I felt pain . . . a lot of pain. It was like a knife was stabbed into my heart. I stared at the floor, but instead of my reflection, I saw a fogged figure. This feeling was unbearable. I had never been more scared in my life.

I wanted to say his name, to make sure something hadn't happened to him, but I slapped my mouth, tears cooling my enflamed skin. I had to be in training, yet . . . I never imagined that Umbra could feel so lethal. I felt for a pulse, a difference in the air, and even looked for a glimpse of a shadow, but Umbra was nowhere. *Click*. That sound, lighter than a silent breath . . . I had heard it before . . .

"AH!" In an instant, I was on the floor, my cheek taking the blow hard, a tiny piece of my flesh hung on to the rest of my cheek to stay attached. I felt a fist digging into my spine and another hand pulling my hair by its roots. My lungs were being strangled by my ribs, making me cough. I could have sworn I tasted blood. I was able to tilt my head upward to see that Umbra had pinned me down like I was an antelope with a broken leg and he was the king lion.

His breathing was heavy, his face clouded with darkness. It was like he was trying to regain something. "I gave you plenty of time to react and even a cleaned room so the airspace wouldn't be as built up. I didn't expect you to just stand there like a moron."

I grunted, spitting a drop of blood on the floor as I gave him a malicious grin. "I wasn't expecting you to full-on disappear Umbra . . ."

There was no kindness in his eyes, which were as black as the entryway of Hot Topic. "I wasn't Umbra then. I was the murderer. Of course my aura disappeared! But, I guess I should have warned you that you need to somewhat defend yourself." A flash of light went into his eyes, his pupils allowing me to see a reflection of myself. "Did you at least feel the aura?"

My face was frozen into a fake smile. "Sort of hard to miss, boss."

He snorted. "Well, at least those bruises weren't for nothing. Come on. Get up and let's try again."

Super . . . Umbra helped me up and for the next ten minutes, I was in my own personal montage of pain and fear. I had countless cuts, my hair was so tangled that I knew it would take me hours to brush it out, and Umbra threw me down on the ground so many times that it was a miracle the building didn't bust. After the fifth time my face and floor met, I sank to the ground, feeling like a statue.

Umbra joined me, handing me a bottle of ice cold water. I placed the bottle on my forehead, allowing the chill to freeze my brain into a normal state. Umbra watched me, puzzled; the coldness of the bottle was a relief to my overheated skin. "What? I'm more comfortable with cold. I get hot too easily."

Umbra nodded, curiosity making his face glow. "That explains why you are more comfortable near good souls than bad souls since good souls are chilly."

It was a strange realization, but one that confirmed I was a Spirit Warrior. Maybe all Spirit Warrior's preferred the cold like I did.

I took a nice gulp of freezing water, but the reaction to my overheated body made me want to gag again, so I sealed the lid tight and sat cross-legged on the floor like Umbra. I swayed to calm myself and our knees brushed, making my breath shaky. I had to break the silence; I didn't want

Umbra mad at me for doing such an awful job. "You were really convincing Umbra, I mean, as the murderer."

I saw in the corner of my eye that Umbra's back shot upward, like someone had shot him from behind, his eyes engulfing the room. I didn't get the nonverbal message and went on, twirling my water bottle in my hands with a small smile. "I expected the feeling and it was intense to the core, but you even looked like a murderer." I blushed when Umbra didn't respond. I ruffled my hair, plastering a huge grin on my face. "I'm sorry . . . I hope I didn't offend you."

Umbra's face was covered in a black overlay, his body leaning on his pulled up knees. His look hurt me and I could never describe it. "Well, there is a good reason for that. Although my soul is considered good, though I disagree, I am no foreigner to the feelings of a murderer. I suppose in some ways . . . I am one. That's why I can be so convincing."

I stopped cold, my water bottle slipping out of my hands, slippery as a fish. It rolled to the floor, banging against the wall. It escaped the situation, like my sanity. "Umbra . . . if . . . if your soul is good . . . then there must be a reason for it . . . right?" My voice was full of mucus; it was clogging not only throat but my thoughts and reason as well.

"I suppose I understand that and I am grateful the Lord thinks higher of me than I do myself. But, Stary . . ." He stared right into my eyes, reaching my soul. He looked caring and cruel, dainty and dangerous, like an angel and a devil. He tilted his head to the side, his eyes looking up at the ceiling with a faraway stare. "I've . . . I've hurt people, even killed a few times. I regret it every moment. It tears me apart, but I guess you have a right to understand why I was so easy to believe. I went tougher on you than I should have so the murderer might not shock you as much when the time came."

"I don't know if any of this will *not* surprise me . . ."

Umbra grinned. "I know, but I'm sorry again for scaring you and roughing you up so much. Although, it does look good on you." He toyed with my hair, unknotting it, making me flinch with shivers of fright and fantasy.

Shyly, I asked the dreaded question that hung between us, "Umbra . . . why did you kill?"

He stopped touching me, dropping his arm. His sigh told me it was a story he never wanted to share but knew he needed to. "It was in self-defense, which is why my soul is still good. You see, right after Maren sent me and my pod to Earth, I landed in the jungles of southern South America. I knew I messed up the route with all the banging I did trying to escape to go aid Maren and the professor. Well, it was raining hard and I landed in the mud. My mind, my heart . . . it went blank. All I could see or feel was Maren slipping away, suffering. I thought I was already dead."

Tears were building in my eyes again as Umbra transported me to his past.

"My back was turned, looking at my surroundings and my broken pod when I felt a sting go past my cheek. It hit a tree ten feet behind me, destroying the bark. It was a gun shot. I saw some men in dark green uniforms coming to attack me, running at gallant speed. They spoke in a different tongue, but I knew they were analyzing me and my pod by their reactions and gestures. That didn't stop them from shooting at me. I could have been a normal bystander who got stranded and they shot at me. I felt no anger, no rage . . . just myself changing at the loss of Maren."

Umbra twirled a loose hair from his bangs with his slender fingers before flicking it to the tile. He refused to look at me as he became lost in his own life story. "Those uniforms . . . I knew them well. They were similar to the ones of the men who killed Maren and Dr. Rowe, but theirs were the color to match the area. They worked for the USA unit though; I know we have secret locations worldwide. Anyway, they kept shooting at me and I lost it. I told them how sickening and unworthy of life they were. I blocked all their attacks without so much as breaking a sweat and . . . I suppose you get the rest. But, the only time I killed was to defend myself when blocking or running wouldn't work. I couldn't die. I had to avenge Maren."

The room was dead still, gravity pulling us back into our time, our place, our lives. I didn't know much about government or physically hurting people, but I knew that Umbra was confused and ashamed. It was hard to figure him out, but I was placed to work with him, which meant something. I trusted Umbra and I knew his soul was good without feeling it.

"I wish I knew what to say Umbra, but I think this is one of those situations where people can't understand what you went through and words only become reminders. I . . . I am glad you told me your story though. Thank you."

He studied me and a wave of understanding crossed between us.

"You are wise beyond my expectations Stary Moon. Now, enough about me. Let's try to get you to be able to defend yourself a little against an evil soul." He hopped upward onto his knees, staring at what must have been confusion plastered on my face with a mischievous grin all his own. Confident Professor Umbra was back. Send for the trumpets!

I adjusted myself to look at him more head on, uncertainty swirling inside my stomach. "I'm not sure I'm cruisn' for another bruisn' Umbra."

He hooted at my fake Southern talk. "What the heck was that? A way to charm the teacher? I could have you arrested for flirting."

I blushed, but it was one full of anger and guilt. "Pffft! Right! Like I would flirt with my teacher? My dad would know before I even thought about it at this school!"

"Agreed. But . . . seriously, what I meant was you need to get connected with your Spirit Warrior self. When that happens, your powers will evolve and change, making you stronger and more secure. Does that make sense?"

"You make me sound like a Pokémon . . ."

Umbra cocked his head, a glint in his eyes. "A what?"

I let out a sigh; the boy was deprived, not knowing a classic. "Never mind. I understand what you're saying. The 'knowledge is power' saying, right?"

He jammed his finger forward, almost poking me in the eye. "Exactly!"

Whatever kind of pill he was taking made me real tired and uneasy. I couldn't handle any more Umbra mood swings . . .

"Stary, can you think back for me? When you were little, did you ever see or feel anything odd? Something that made you feel . . . different?"

My eyes watered on impact, the power of his words smacking me across the face. I had to go back and relive a reality that I locked inside myself just from a stupid fear of not being accepted. I focused on breathing, but it made my throat ache. "You mean spirit stuff? Yeah . . . I . . . I think I have had a few experiences, but I was never sure if I really saw them or if I just imagined them up. I was a shy child and I had a very nice imagination."

Umbra looked at me almost with pity, but it was for a nanosecond, his face regaining its impassiveness I had memorized. "It probably was real and FYI, you're still shy! You see, your official Spirit Warrior powers may not have been activated until you were given a mission from the Lord to help Maren and me, but you have been the Spirit Warrior since you were born. God chose you then, so there might have been times your powers were trying to tell you something, because someone needed your power then. I'm talking in circles, huh?"

I shook my head in disagreement. "You're saying my powers are like a plant, right? It's been in the ground all this time, but you step over it, not seeing what's underneath. Then, on occasion, something will unknowingly help it grow, like the sun will shine on it or it will rain. Then, one day, when it's ready, it pops up for someone to notice then the rest of that plant's existence is in another's hands." Man, I was on a role with the analogies!

Umbra gave me a thumbs-up, although it had little emotion to it. "That's right. Can you recall any of those memories? Talking about them now can make you see things with your new Spirit Warrior knowledge."

I gulped, trying to rewind my mind in a hurry. The first one was easy to recall. "The first time, I was six years old, in first grade. I was picking up trash by the tree I used to play at all the time. I loved it and it was a great place to think and imagine things by myself. I even wrote messages in the sand! Well, my trash kept leaping out of the bag. By the fourth time, I knew I wasn't missing the trash bag, so I looked and saw an edged figure. It was like seeing a bold math line in the real world. I could see a face, one of a young boy, shimmering. He had nothing on his face; it was blank. I . . . I knew I felt scared, but I also felt sad. I left the trash there and walked away. I got in trouble for 'throwing' trash and my classmates were mad at me the whole year for being cruel to the environment, but I never saw the boy again." I traced the boy I knew was not there in the air, being careful and detailed, studying my slender fingers' movements.

"You helped him Stary. He was connected to the school somehow or maybe the trash, but you let him do what he needed to do to move on I bet." Umbra poked my nose.

It was hard to think about, but I never did regret leaving that trash that day. I smiled a little to myself, praying to God that the boy was able to move on.

Umbra nudged me in the ribs, making my body throb. "Continue . . ."

"The next year is vague, but I remember something, but I thought it was a mind trick. My mom went to an auction and got this antique wood and velvet chair with roses on the seat. She placed it by the corner table behind the couch. I was lying on the couch the next afternoon and I saw this old woman sitting in the chair. She just kept staring at me with mean, black eyes. I went to get my mom and I kept asking her, 'Why is there an old lady in the chair?' I asked her a dozen times, but my mom didn't see anything and the old woman went on glaring. Finally, she hissed a little and mouthed, 'I hate you because you live!' I cried like a maniac. Although the old woman only mouthed it, I could hear her voice clear as a bell in my head." I trembled, the thought still haunting.

Umbra seemed to be studying the story silently, allowing it to twirl in his head. "It is unusual for ghosts or spirits to possess an item, but if it has a strong connection to them or is a part of how they died, it can happen. Do you still have the chair and do you ever see her?"

"Yes, the chair hasn't moved from its spot, but I covered it in stuffed animals. It still scares the snot out of me and no, I haven't seen her since."

"Well, she must have been a ghost then. A spirit would have stayed until you helped and in most cases, wouldn't be that cruel. I suppose the old woman got bored of the chair or you and went to haunt something else."

My eyes wandered to the distant window. That was . . . sort of heartbreaking. I hoped that maybe the woman would stop hating the living and be able to allow me to help her in the future, so she can be in the beckoning light of heaven.

"Umbra, all you've been telling me is about murderers and souls and now you're telling me stuff about spirits and ghosts . . . I know I can see them both, but I thought my job was to only take the evil out of your murderer?"

"That is your first mission and it will be the closest to you and your strongest power. However, after this, you will be the official Spirit Warrior of the world until you're forty. I hope you notice why the number forty is important to the Lord. Anyway, you'll have to help all ghosts and spirits who need help, no matter what it is. God more than likely won't give you another real assignment after your first one."

My head was spinning. This was a lot of knowledge too fast. I needed Ghosts and Spirits 101.

Umbra's eyes studied my elbow, waiting for me to move on with my experiences with the supernatural world.

"When I was nine, when I was sick in bed, I . . . I felt this warm, dry blast of wind by my door and the door became much darker, like my eyes had been ripped out. Somehow, I opened them to look around the room and I saw a clouded figure. It reminded me of a clown drooling foam. My skin got prickly and the dark zoomed towards me. Then, I saw a faint light in the center. It was the most unique and beautiful blue I had ever seen. I opened my eyes again to see a teenage boy, perhaps about thirteen, sitting on the edge of my bed, watching me with the sweetest smile. He was in a baseball uniform and glowed in that blue tone. He was so bright! I was shaking, scared he was dangerous, but his eyes told me I was safe. He even patted my hand; it felt like tingling air. After awhile, I calmed down and fell asleep. I woke up to show him to my mom, but he had already vanished."

A little smile crept on Umbra's lips. "That sounds like Maren and I, the glow I mean. But, someone attacking you? It could be possible, but who could be able to tell you were the Spirit Warrior when your powers were premature? That's . . . strange. Did you ever see the boy later?"

That caring boy . . . his smile always made me want to smile. I never got to thank him . . . "No, I never did, as a spirit at least. I told my mom that story and she said she had met him once as well after she had a nightmare. She showed me a picture of the boy. He got ill and died right before my mom was born. His dream was to be a professional baseball player and his favorite team was the New York Dodgers, which probably explains the lovely blue I saw. I think they remodeled the neighborhood baseball field that year . . ."

I knew what Umbra was going to say by looking at his knowing smirk. "Ah. He still hadn't rested in peace and since something so close to him looked unfamiliar, it caused him to roam. He must have been a kind person to become visible to help your mother and later you or he was scared you would get as sick as he did."

All of the experiences of my childhood . . . all the times I had been alone, thinking I made up people or heard voices in the breeze . . . it was a sign. I was never alone. I had a gift and they were trying to tell me, help me. My eyes got misty, but only because my heart was overflowing with thanks. I grabbed my chest to contain the seeping warm feeling inside my soul; I wanted to remember it while going through all this hardship. "Thank you . . . thank you my friends . . ."

After the words escaped my lips, my legs began to shake a tad and the warmth in my chest expanded, growing warmer. It was an odd warmth, not painful like when one has heartburn. What was happening?

Umbra looked at me, his eyebrows arched. "Stary, I told you not to get emotional . . . holy crap! Star-Stary! Your . . . I mean! Hands . . . are . . . AH . . . ! Purple!"

Oh joy . . . my poor circulation had to kick in now? Last year, my hands turned blue and my homeroom teacher almost fainted! I was called Miss Smurf for a month! "Oh . . . it's okay. It happens to the women in my family as they mature . . . What?!"

I glanced down at my pale hands to see that they were a creamy, white chocolate tone. But attached around them was a swirling lilac-colored glow that tickled my hands, a tickle that made me feel thrilled and enlightened. Each speck of the glowing light looked like handcrafted lavender rose petals, all designed for me alone. It was stunning.

That tad uncomfortable warmness I felt a moment earlier in my chest was now expanding and traveling through my body. I giggled, feeling like a thousand butterflies were tickling me with kisses, ready to soar back to the sky to their father, my Lord. I traced the outline of my hand with my other and I smelled gardens and the cleanliness of a perfect beach. It was . . . pure.

My powers! They must have evolved since I accepted and understood the heart of my mission. My heart spoke this fact to me and I felt it was true. "Thank you," I whispered to the heavens, my breath traveling upward. With that realization, my glow sank into my skin, disappearing, but the magic was inside me. I felt calm and strong.

"Umbra! I'm no longer a caterpillar! I'm building my slimly cocoon for spirit training! Yeah!" I threw a power fist in the air like a cheerleader on sugar, pumped and excited.

Umbra shook his head so fast that I wasn't sure if he was proud, shocked, or trying not to cackle. "Stary Moon . . . you are by far the hardest human I have ever dealt with. I was proud of you, but now . . . How can I respond when you stupidly grin at empty space like that? Gosh! You're such an idiot!"

I fluttered my eyelashes cutely and smiled at him. "But . . . I'm your idiot, right?"

He flushed a color that reminded me of a red apple. I decided to bring my kite flying feeling down for a slow, gentle landing to give Umbra a break.

"I suppose by default, you have to claim me." I fluttered my eyelashes again and shrugged indifferently, giving him room to set the mood.

He nodded. "It's a sad fact but, yes, I do. Now . . . we only have three minutes according to that dinosaur of a clock before your dad comes back. Want to try once more to feel and defend against an evil soul?"

A burning desire filled my lungs and spread to my heart, my blood, my soul. I nodded with pride and tenderness, the spider-crawling feeling of my lilac light ringing just outside my body invisibly. Umbra did not reply, but went straight into practice mode, fading, blending, into the coil of the room.

My heartbeat echoed that of the silent airspace, becoming still. My breathing became one with my reeling mind. I closed my eyes, cutting off my human senses and in an instant, I gained the ones of a tracker. It was like I was in the center of the universe, the stars' pulses telling my long lost secrets in a liquid motion. Suddenly, in the distance of my dance, I felt a zap, a crack of lightning slapping the black chaos of space, all happening in a nanosecond. The stars were shrilling in madness, one at a time. The evil feeling crept closer and closer, a tiger on the prowl. I could almost count the beats before it ringed my neck . . . 5 . . . 4 . . . 3 . . . 2 . . .

Whack! Before reaching one, I extended my right hand to the side and grabbed the lightning by the tail, snaring it. I glared sideways, cool and agitated. My breath was trying to get used to human air pressure again and my heart was doing leaps to regain a healthy harmony. I heard a low chuckle and was able to focus my vision, like my eyes engulfed all the stars. There, in my hand, was Umbra's wrist, secure. His other hand was two inches from strangling my delicate neck from behind. His smile was a challenge but had spark and fun in it.

"Well done. You stopped yourself from getting attacked from behind by an evil soul and sensed almost right away. This teacher is impressed with his pupil." We just continued to stare, almost holding hands, our eyes meeting and challenging each other. It was like . . . a connection was born at that moment, but the sound of keys shattered it into oblivion.

I caught a peep at the clock and it was the exact time Dad said he would be back! I let go of Umbra's wrist with a slam like it was a poisonous spider that bit me. Umbra went at *extreme* speed and made the room spotless and flawless, like no one had ever touched it. It felt like my eyes went into the back of my skull trying to keep up!

Umbra then peeked through the window to be lookout, his face fogging the sheet of glass. "He's still down the hallway a ways, but I'll get going." He sounded so apathetic and business-like. I supposed my hand around his meant nothing, although his warmth brushed my fingertips almost to the same level as my purple light.

"Stary, you did good today, but remember, the real murderer will be different; I could never re-enact that or tell you how or when it will occur. But, you have the basic power and knowledge to at least sense it when it's near. Hopefully you won't attack your friends again . . . Shoot! He's about twenty feet away!"

Umbra was about to book it out the door, but for some reason, it twisted my chest in knots. "Wait! Umbra . . . I . . . I want to tell you something. It might be lame, but before this Spirit Warrior life I had, I always felt like I was a grain of sand."

Umbra turned in slow motion to look at me with faultless pools of honey. Our connection was back and I had his attention.

"You know how you can grab thousands of tiny grains of sand in your hands? Well, if you open up your fingers, most slip out. All you have left is like two or three tiny grains that are clinging to your skin. It's annoying and you can't flick them off. I felt like I was the one who got left in the hands of someone who didn't know what to think of me. But . . . because of you and Maren . . . I know why I was left there . . . Thank you!"

Umbra started to fade, meaning he was going to zoom out the door, but before he did, his mouth pleasured me with words so engaging, I felt like I was going to pass out. "You may be annoying, but it's those grains of sand that cling to me that I would've noticed and looked after. There has to be a reason they stayed and are special, right . . . ?"

His tone, his face, his words . . . it flooded over me like the waves crashing your tired feet.

Before I could thank him properly, Umbra fled the area and my eyes were replaced with my father, unlocking his door. Dad was stunned and delighted at how clean and bright the room was (thank the stars). As we were preparing to depart, I felt Umbra gaining distance from me, the gap widening out of my control. I felt our connection thinning like a rubber band that gets stretched. I prayed that it would not snap back and harm us both.

I got home and it was a 2,001 question session with Maren, her eyes flickering from fear to pleasure so fast that I doubted NASA could have tracked the speed. The poor dear looked exhausted, her shoulders drooped and her hands were wet from sweat. It took me awhile to get her breathing calm enough so she would not hiccup every time she spoke, although Umbra and I cracked up at how adorable it was.

Once we told her all we could, Umbra and I exhausted, I convinced her to lie down on my brother's sleeping bag that I "borrowed." I placed tons of hot pink fuzzy pillows on top and retrieved my old purple *Cardcaptor Sakura* blanket from my youth to make her be the sleeping princess she deserved to be. It was interesting to see Maren "sleep," but I think she was just shutting her hovering body down for a few hours to . . . recharge. I hated using that word because my mind went to the memory of Umbra being nothing more than a science project, but I knew he was much more.

He leaned against my wall, near my window, to keep a close, loving eye on Maren, but he nodded a few times during his shift. I yawned, noticing my digital clock was flashing 10:38 p.m. I never stay up that late so I decided to hit the hay. I just finished getting into my PJs and adjusted my comforter for the night when I heard a high-pitched whimper. It sounded lonely and fond, fueling my heart and then crushing it.

I bolted from my bed to check on Maren. I wanted Umbra to get some well-deserved rest. She was mouthing words, such as, "No . . . please stop . . .", "Grandfather . . .", and "Be safe . . ."I knew she was dreaming, reliving her agonizing past. Knowing spirits had to have nightmares of memories they didn't want to be reminded of every second dug deep into my bones. Her cheeks were glowing with dampness. I forgot about my bed and positioned myself to hug Maren from behind, comforting her like a child as I rubbed her hands with my softest and most meaningful touches. She moaned a little more, but caved her back into me, rubbing her hair into my nose. This made her breathe better and her mouth stopped quivering. It relieved me.

"You know, you didn't have to do that . . . It happens a lot."

I slanted my head upward to see Umbra, his body dazzling in the moonlight, his face wrapped in a type of mystery and enchantment that made his knowing eyes sing.

I sighed, not wanting sleep to get the better of me. "I understand that . . . but it's all right. I want to take care of Maren like she takes care of me. Now, you go back to bed. I don't want another grumpy Umbra to deal with!"

Umbra was silent for many minutes. I thought maybe he had fallen asleep or was sick of being in my presence. Then, a crisp frequency filled my ears from behind. "You know why Maren made me younger than her? It was so she could take care of someone. She told me she always had people take care of her and she wanted to prove that she could take care of herself and that she had enough love to give someone else . . ."

Although I couldn't see Umbra, I knew he was smiling and as my mind pieced together his memory, I had to share that smile. Maren made you smile . . . That angelic smile could do anything.

I chuckled, making my voice hum to soothe Maren as I kissed her pearl white cheek. "It is good to take care of someone, but it's so hard *not* to love and want to take care of Maren. I think she does an excellent job of both."

A bird joined our chorus, draping my room with the calls of the twinkling night.

"True."

"I always wanted a sister. If I could have one, I would want Maren." I smiled, sharing my expanding connection with Umbra, a moment only we would know. My body tingled with delight, ready to be placed under the spell of slumber.

"I think she already considers you her sister . . ." The air closed in on me, hugging Maren and I in serenity, my cells sighing their gratitude.

In a whisper so tiny I thought a molecule could not hear it, I called to him before I could not control my being. "Good night . . . Umbra . . ."

His sweet chocolate voice became one with the perfect night as he answered, "Good night Stary . . ."

7

MY TRAINING WITH GENERAL UMBRA BEING A SUCCESS, MAREN decided to be my academic tutor when it came to all things involving connections to my powers and the might of the Lord. I had my notebook placed on my lap and my pencil eagerly hovering over the paper, ready to record the knowledge for future reference. We had the perfect opportunity for it since my family was out getting ice cream and Umbra was in charge of following the murderer's trail for the time being. Maren was sitting at the edge of my bed, ready to lecture.

"I believe Umbra has told you about the types of spirits and ghosts and their reasons for staying connected or chained to this world."

I nodded, her voice pulling me in.

She pointed a dainty fingernail upward to the ceiling. "Reasons why ghosts and spirits stay on Earth is personal and to list them would be impossible. As your Spirit Warrior journey continues, you will meet and help many lost souls find their way to heaven's gate. Now, I will tell you about the basics of your connection to God."

I was scratching notes fiercely, quoting Maren word for word until she stopped out of the blue, a hint of a pale pink glow reflected off my paper. I glanced to look at her from my chair and saw she was blushing and had goose bumps on her slender arms. I was afraid she sensed something.

She threw her head upward and grunted so loudly, it bounced off my walls and rattled my bones! She looked into my eyes, her eyes looking like a shimmering lake. "Am I doing a decent job as your instructor Stary? I have never done this and to be frank, I am not sure what I am doing. I do not want to fail you and . . . and . . . ah! OH gosh! This pressure!" she yelled and shook her head fiercely at the last bit, her hair smacking her in the face.

It took all my will power not to giggle at how adorable she was! Maren continued to fret, her face reminding me of a china doll. I beamed at her and plopped my notebook and pencil on the desk. "No Maren. Honest, you're doing a great job, but just pretend we're talking for fun. That way, it'll seem less scary." I couldn't think of an example since she never had any other girls to hang with and we talked about Spirit Warrior stuff most of the time.

Maren let out a huge sigh and sat up straighter, ruffling a crease out of her blue dress. "That sounds much nicer. Thank you dear Stary."

I leaned my elbows on my knees and prepared to listen intently to Maren and her basket of tales. Maren went above and beyond of informing me about symbols in the bibles that I could use in my mission. She told me about how forty years for each Spirit Warrior represented the forty days of Lent and the great Flood and that the idea of the "magic" of each element had a background in the Holy Book. Water was to purify and reflect on discussion, such as when one gets baptized and how the Flood cleansed the Earth once from evil. Fire is to send messages, predict, and forewarn, such as the burning bush of Moses and how a flame of the candle is used to guide us. Earth, of course, is our birth place and final resting spot for the flesh. Wind is what gives us life and speaks to us, it is the Lord's voice guiding us and our world, like he led all his great prophets. I was told I may more than likely have dreams that are symbolic and mean something, but are not literal, such as Joseph when he warned the pharaoh. She also quickly mentioned there were seven great nations in the Bible that held special powers (seven for the days of creation) and that God had numerous helpers. It was all so amazing!

Before I could burst from the seams with a million and thirty-five questions, Maren did a one-eighty on connections to Bible stories. "To start, one thing that is comforting and marvelous after you receive your judgment to locate your murderer is you gain the knowledge of heaven and how it works in an instant along with your mission."

It was a little sad to me that she was thrilled about locating a murderer, but gaining all the knowledge of heaven and its components did at least make you like a firefly in a moonless, starless night.

"I'm sure heaven is a complex place."

Maren nodded. "It is very similar to the United States' system of government of what I can see. You do not get all of God's knowledge; that is just not right. But you at least have a comfort knowing once your mission is complete, you get to be a part of an organized eternal rest."

I snickered at how important that would be, but I would be confused if heaven was disorganized! "And is it like how the Bible and pictures describe? The golden gate at the top of the clouds and the angels?"

Maren grinned to show me the brightness of the rays of her desired location. "Yes. I did get an image of the outside of it when I was sent back, but not the inside. I do know also that angels are real and help the Lord extend his aid by going to Earth to help those in trouble. They are also, like the Lord, eternal."

Images of flying mysteries of beauty flying around us, as graceful as swans, yellow light reflecting off their halos and wings as they ascended to common good poured into my head.

"Since they are like the Lord, I assume they cannot have children together."

"Angels that are born as angels, no. I am not sure about people who have died and if they find their mate and want to have a child. Since they are inside the gate, I am not sure if that is possible. But the angels are kind and busy, each assigned to a certain area to protect."

I pondered what Plantersville's angel was like and knew we would be in good hands. But I knew an angel could not stop everything bad from happening. I recalled being told that the more light one produces, the larger the shadow it creates, which is why the battle of good and evil is never-ending . . . and then a zap shocked my face, realization attacking my brain.

"Maren . . . if . . . if angels who protect and serve heaven are real, then does that mean that . . . ummm . . . the story about the other place is also true . . . ?" My vision blurred trying to swallow the images I knew I would be forced to see.

Maren gulped and the shadow coming from my lamp appeared to cast over her. "Yes. The whole story of Lucifer falling and ruling hell along with the great battle where the angels fought against the devils who tried to take over heaven is, indeed, all true. Angels and devils are both still at large. Like God is eternal, so is Satan."

Satan is eternal . . . I mean, that made sense, but it was eerie to think about Satan lurking around in the darkness, waiting for his victim . . . Oh my . . . God! I launched forward, causing my hair to smack my cheek. My throat began to burn.

"Maren! Is Satan at all responsible for your murder?" Could we go up against complete, eternal darkness? Not to be a downer, but I highly doubted it!

Maren gave a reassuring lift of her smooth mouth, but it vanished a second after. "Directly, no, Satan has no power of his own to take a life. Satan's power is to influence someone who is weak and make them choose darkness, maybe someone who is saddened, confused, weak, and so forth. He has learned that once someone is devoted to darkness, it is very hard for them to go back to God's light. Unfortunately, Satanism is still worshipped today. That is what drives and delights the devil."

"Is there nothing God can do? I know He cannot destroy Satan, but I mean, God was here before Lucifer and Lucifer used to work side-by-side with God. Would that not have an influence . . . ?"

Maren shook her head, swaying her hair into her face. "That is not possible Stary, for God gave us free choice and he will not take that away. It was Lucifer's choice to claim to be as powerful as God and his actions cannot be controlled, but he also does not have the power to control anyone. He only enhances darkness that is already there. Do you understand what that means when involving our mission Stary?"

I nodded and my body became numb. I stared at my cupped hands. They looked like they were trying to capture and control invisible water, but it was free flowing, slipping through my fingers. A murderer, especially one with the skill ours had, already had darkness in their heart and chose to let

Satan influence them further until they were a monster in flesh form. I assumed every serial killer was like this, and I knew in my gut that is what we must have been dealing with due to Umbra and Maren not being able to locate them for two years. They almost gained an ability to leave no trail. I wondered what other supernatural traits they twisted to their will.

Maren took in a deep breath, stretching her arms outward. "I do not know everything about God's world, but I know he chooses a new Spirit Warrior every forty years who can help heal the scars of darkness inside a wounded soul and allow lost spirits to complete missions in order to go to heaven. You also have abilities similar to those of the angels and helpers of heaven, but other than shining light into souls and interacting with spirits I am not sure what else that entails."

I stood and shrugged, popping my back. "Well, I get super powers and at least I don't have the same gifts and level of power as God . . . That would be *too* much pressure!"

Maren cupped her mouth and giggled. I joined her, the tension of our needed discussion lifting. However, Maren's eyes became spooky serious and sent shivers of dread into my essence.

In a deep, serious tone, she said, "There is one more thing I must tell you . . .

"Stary, my dear," Maren said, holding my hands, making me feel safe once again. This was the end of our discussion, our talk becoming more dire. I could feel the fear radiating off her. Even though we were talking about something dangerous, we felt comfortable with each other like sisters or best friends.

"Stary, the evil is growing near and too fast, even too fast for Umbra to catch. And too clever as well! We can barely track them much anymore."

Does this mean the end of the quest? Are they giving up? What's going to happen to them?

Maren continued, her eyes seeming to understand my feelings of confusion and panic. "All this means is that you will have to be more alert and that Umbra and I must keep a close eye on you. It is likely that they know about you."

I held my star necklace tight, childishly hoping the diamonds would rain down like stardust, sprinkling into my praying hands to grant me a miracle. Maren's eyes became worried. They became a swirling gray, spinning and vibrating with despaired emotions like she failed.

I smiled at her, building my confidence since I had to be the brave one now. "Maren . . . you know what my grandpa used to tell me?"

She shook her head, looking eager to know the secret.

"He always told me, if I believed in myself, surely, everything will turn out to be all right. So, I believe and know it will turn out for the best, okay?" I giggled, recalling the feeling I got when he used to tell me that as I sat on his lap. I hoped he heard my plea to help Maren.

She smiled, but she still had doubt embedded on her face. She leaned close to me, looking like a perfect statue in a garden for the Greek goddesses. "Remember this Stary . . .

The sun means mystery and dependence
The moon pulls and is set on a path
The sun is powerful, alone, yet not
As the moon reflects the sun's wrath."

Squeak, squeak, squeak. The noise of my feet hitting the tiles of the hallway echoed in my ears, ringing, messing more with my head. My mind was roaming. It felt lost and empty.

"OH! What the heck could that mean?!" I stopped right in the middle of the hallway, holding my chin, thinking about the poem Maren gave me . . . Stupid mistake. I was so deep in thought that I didn't notice people were yelling at me to move, almost pushing me forward. I frowned, full of resentment.

"At least you all have time to yell at someone," I grumbled in my itchy throat to the irritated group. It felt like there was wind trying to pull me into a black pit of no return, but somehow, I moved forward and made it to communication arts.

The day dragged on with no sign of Maren or Umbra at all. When it was finally about time for fifth hour to begin, I walked into Mr. Tin's room when . . . *Snap!* Right when I stepped through the doorway, I felt it, a crackling in the air that made my eyes as big as the Lord could have made them. The speed of my heart and breathing became one. The whole room was red and a black line went past me by my cheek. I turned to look at it, the world moving much too fast. It zapped into a lightning bolt shape, vanishing out the window.

"*I finally found you, darling . . .*"

A message made of painful, inky energy pulsed inside my mind, each syllable cracking my bones, ripping my organs, eating away my soul. This feeling was like Umbra's when he attacked me and it was the same unidentified voice I heard in my first dream! I may not have been the next Mr. Einstein, but the puzzle pieces seemed to fit. Had . . . had the murderer found me?

"Stary . . ."

Another snap delayed my vocal chords from screaming. I had to fight back, to survive, and to do what Stary Moons were best at: panic. I turned and grabbed outward with a pincher-like grip, holding onto the wrist of the fowl monster that was . . . Rin?

I blinked, realizing I was in the doorway of the classroom, holding Rin's fist securely in midair! Her vein in her forehead began to pulse. Oh

Mylanta, I was *so* in for it! She got out of my lock and hit me on the shoulder.

She growled. "You idiot! I was only worried about you and here you go attacking me like you're flippin' She-ra! Did your mind turn into mashed potatoes?"

I bowed my head. "Oh . . . yeah . . . I'm really sorry, Rin-sama! I was . . . in another dazed spell and well . . . Hahaha, you know me!"

She smirked. "Well, I got to admit that you have a much better grip than I imagined. Not too bad if I do say so myself, Moon. But, you did learn from the best after all!" She jabbed her thumb into her chest, her chuckle that followed was short and confident.

I agreed, thankful for my magical once-in-a-lifetime physical strength and sat next to her at the table we shared with Chloe, waving to Lauren, Mark, and Allen at the corner table. I wondered what was wrong with me. My imagination seemed to be playing games on me . . . again. My training seemed wasteful. I failed Umbra and almost boxed Rin. Well, let's say I would have too many broken bones to do any missions if I would have succeeded in punching Rin! I gulped.

Class then began. Mr. Tin was deep in thought, rambling on as usual. "You know class, as a role model for today's youth, a father figure for many young girls, an inspiration to many boys with no tracking topic, I have to say that the people in here who don't do their work will all become worthless—"

A knock on the door halted Mr. Tin's sermon and there stood our vice principal, Mr. Limb, or as we were forced to call him from his former army days, Sgt. Limb, looking like he swallowed something bitter, but he always looked like that. "Mr. Tin, I need to speak with you out in the hallway for a moment please."

"Of course, sir. Class, please work on your mini templates and be the good kids I know you are." And he was gone before anyone could enjoy it. When a teacher left, most kids did the complete opposite of what the instructor said. But, I had too much to worry about, so I wanted to finish my homework right away in case I was needed for something greater.

I just started my second paragraph when Mr. Tin came in about five minutes later with Sgt. Limb right behind, staring all of us down. Mr. Tin rose up tall to make an important statement. "Class, we have a new student joining our little Jedi unit."

We all snickered. Mr. Tin thought he was the Jedi knight of English! *Right . . .*

"Anyway, please make her feel welcomed. Everyone, this is . . ." He paused abnormally, but was not ashamed; he always forgot names! Sgt. Limb whispered in his ear. "Oh yes! Everyone, this is Miss Cally Sun. Come on in now."

In stepped a young girl with hair to her upper back that was in a lovely sunshine orange tone and it was halfway curled in loose loops. She stood shyly, swaying her hips a tad to keep her posture proper and ladylike. Her head was down a little bit, embarrassed, her bangs brushing over her butterfly-like eyelids. In her hand was a Japanese-style briefcase book bag! Too *kawaii*! She looked around the room with a smile of pure incorruptibility. I could tell she was a girl of kindness and maturity. But, her grace was a little eerie . . .

She blushed as she scanned around the room with brown puppy eyes. Her eyes met mine. I smiled to welcome her; I bet it was hard to be new. She chose to sit at a table by herself, the vacant one next to Mr. Tin's desk. I felt sorry for her because everyone was profiling her like she was something to see at the zoo. Her face was red and she looked bemused, not sure what to think.

Mr. Tin instructed Cally on our "easy" papers. Rin shuddered and mouthed, "I'd hate to know that man's definition of a difficult paper," which made Chloe snicker until she hiccupped. After his speech, he left the room once again to follow Sgt. Limb. The second the door clicked, I saw Kevin Foils stand up and make his move. Kevin was your basic jerky, kiss-up to adults guy, the kind who loved to mess with women's minds as a cruel joke. However, I doubted he would try it on this girl's first five minutes of—

He had to do the hair flip before he spoke to the new girl . . . Gag me.

"Hey baby."

Oh horse mucus Batman. It had begun . . .

"My name's Kevin. Those losers at my table think you're ugly, but not me . . ." He proposed more sweet lies to her with his eyes, continuing to talk. It seemed like poor Cally was swallowing all of his twisted words like they were pure, delightful chocolate.

The pervert placed his arm around her shoulder. We were all paralyzed, watching the sad episode of an after school special; we knew the ending was coming, but . . . we could not find the strength to interfere . . . Her face became as red as a Valentine's rose and his idiotic skater friends were snickering at her from the back table.

He leaned in closer to her quivering lips, uttering in his sexiest voice, "Hey, baby doll. Is your name really Cally *SUN*?!"

She only reddened to an immeasurable scale. This episode was getting to be too much. It was more like bullying now than an after school drama.

He grinned his wolf-like teeth at her, seeing his chance for the kill. "Well, because . . ." He got closer to her ear with his lips puckered like a fish on a date. When we all thought he was going to kiss her, he roared with mockery, "Because that is the *stupidest* name in the world!" Foils cackled and his monkey gang joined in. The noise rebounded off the walls, sounding close to shots being fired. We all cringed.

By looking at her heart-shaped face, I could tell Cally's spirit was shattered. Her eyes were almost in the mist of tears, reddened from her mistake. The girl had been in class ten minutes and her first day was already beyond horrible! No one else in the room said a word. We stared anywhere but at them. The boys kept making rude comments about her name, becoming Foils's backup vocals. I also heard mean comments like those about my name, but mine were behind my back since I was their history teacher's little girl and they didn't want their grades to get any lower.

I had to shut them up. I had too much crap to deal with in my life. They picked a bad time to pick on a new girl. I was real grumpy and heart-crushing behavior just lit my fuse!

"Foils!" I yelled with intense breath. "Leave her alone! She did nothing to you."

He stopped like I slammed the car breaks on his joy ride and then his whole gang ceased their laughter a second after him. I swore he must have trained them on a leash, which was funny since he was a weak kid. Anyone could have taken him!

He sneered at me, trying to be tough, but I had no regrets. One of Foils's cronies copied what I said in a baby tone. Again, the group laughed. I stuck my tongue out.

"Real cute," I said full of fire, spice stinging my tongue like spiders.

Kevin walked to me with his sensual stride. "You're the last person I'd ever see talk back to any hot guy. But, I like it! Makes you much more . . . stimulating. I guess Daddy's little girl has some potential for being my toy."

Everyone gasped. I stood my ground, pretending not to be shaken up. Again, he got closer to me, the same as I had seen him do thousands of times. I pretended like I was buying it, hoping Mr. Tin would walk in; he would believe me in a heartbeat.

All at once, I felt a malevolence of cruel vigor. It was faint, but it sent chills up my back and made my hair stick straight up like I stuck my wet finger in a light socket. I even *felt* fried.

Then, the world took a deadly turn. From out of nowhere, Kevin's shirt turned into slashed up pieces of ash, his skin burned from nothing. His eyes bugged out and everyone stared at the sight. He was doing a Mexican hat dance motion, trying to make the flames stop that appeared on the floor by his feet at random. I had no idea where the fire came from, but it helped me. Determining he was busy, I turned to check on Cally. She kept her eyes locked onto her desk.

Before I could turn my head away from Cally, I felt someone squeeze my arm in a death grip. "You did this, you witch!" Kevin let out a hiss, his eyes smoldering and a strange warmth radiated as he breathed; you could almost see it. His hold really hurt. It was blocking the blood flow to my thin arm. I had to scream after a moment because the throbbing was too extreme. Annoyed, he cupped my mouth with his sweaty, disgusting hand so I couldn't breathe. I was losing my ability to see and my mind was clouded with haze. I had never seen Foils so upset, so focused, so . . . lethal.

Rin, Lauren, and Chloe ran to save me from my captivity, but Kevin's friends blocked them, standing like a sturdy moat surrounding the great

King Foils. Thank goodness a knight came to my aid. Mark slid under the biggest guys legs with style.

With his free hand, Kevin punched Mark in the face and a hard smack hit Mark's cheekbone. Mark fell to the floor, motionless, and he didn't get up. Chloe screamed in horror and I tried to screech as well, but Kevin held my ribs tighter, crushing my last few ounces of breath. What happened next was a maddening blur. I wasn't going to be able to contain my consciousness much longer . . . I needed Mr. Tin to come in or my daddy . . . I needed Credence . . . My savior . . . I needed . . . a hero . . .

"LET HER GO YOU PIECE OF TRASH!"

That voice . . . it was angry and comforting. It was . . . Umbra! I opened my eyes, but my vision was dark from the faintness Foils was causing me. I felt dizzy. I saw Umbra flying above us like he was a superhero. Kevin didn't see him, but I could tell he *heard* Umbra by the stupid turns his head was performing.

Umbra grabbed Kevin by the legs, making him fall to his knees and release me. I was like a panting mistreated dog on all fours. I had lost all my breath, wheezing, close to vomiting. I was almost choking just to get air into my lungs. Why is this so painful? The question reeled through my frail mind, but I ignored the chatter while I held my chest to contain my being. My eyes needed to search the air in front of me.

Soon enough, my breathing calmed down and I was able to see shapes and faces, objects and movements. That's when I felt a volt stab the back of my brain in a crackling current, like lightning being intensified by water. My eyes moved to see the fight. The area around Umbra, Kevin, and me was black. Why was black lining surrounding everything? I concluded it was an evil force field! Someone wanted to finish us off and they had to be among us . . .

Umbra grabbed me in his arms like a groom carrying his bride and set me in my chair next to the window, taking a pause to look into my eyes. It only lasted for a split moment. The air was so delicate around us that a ladybug would have broken the glass-like structure it held. I noticed nothing for that second, not even the chaos around me. All I felt was a hand cradling my heart. My blood started pumping a song into my veins that was beautiful, confusing, and scary all at once. Umbra gave me a small tilt of the corners of his mouth that made his eyes glisten to match the stars at night before he departed to finish off Foils.

The membrane around the classroom area was normal, clear, and white with unpolluted energy. A coating was around Foils and Umbra as well. It looked close to six feet long, but it was getting larger and engulfing them in a sinister fog. As I tried to blink my eyes to see images to match the punching and grunting I heard, my friends hovered around me as I stared off blankly towards the slowly coming-into-focus Umbra and Foils. At this point, Kevin's fan club was watching him beat himself up in midair, but they were still outside the membrane he was in.

Maren popped at my side to make sure I was all right, almost giving me a heart attack. I didn't care about myself then. A treacherous storm was forming in the classroom and I knew that more than rain would come out. I pointed to the force field around Umbra in silence, I wasn't sure how to react. The force field was turning crimson and harder to see through.

Maren's eyes grew big with fear. "The . . . the mur-murderer!" she told me, her voice quivering, almost lost in the vortex. I knew that and I felt sick by the fact.

I looked at Umbra kicking Kevin in the air, at how they were being swallowed up by the darkness, and realized it was coming closer to Maren and me. I grabbed her, leaning her on my chest to protect her with all my power. I guess the murderer didn't want us to know they were there yet for the red shield that once looked like lightning boiled into the floor and crept towards the panicked Maren and me like mutant magma with black chunks of darkness mixed in.

"Stary! Maren!" Umbra cried out with valiance. He flew as fast out of the bubble as he was able to before it was entirely red; I sighed in relief. He . . . he called my name first? And beat up a guy almost to death . . . for me?! I was locked onto him again that moment, my heart aching to that blinding new melody, but the red liquid still grew closer, so my mind focused on protecting Maren.

Umbra was there in no time, positioning his entire body as a shield in front of us but stood so we could see over his shoulder. The evil aura began to glow wildly, static popping everywhere. It was about to get us. I braced myself for the searing, painful impact . . .

Click . . . I heard a sound right before the red lights came toward us and the door flew open. Like a magic counter spell, the red wickedness vanished. Our "wizards" were Mr. Tin and Sgt. Limb, yelling, "What the heck happened?"

Everyone was so shocked that Kevin beat himself up that they didn't notice the evil lava charging throughout the whole room during the entire ordeal. *I* could not forget it.

Umbra was still in front of Maren and me, a protective screen. The actions and words that he did for me made me get such a wonderful feeling inside . . . I slapped that thought out of my head. No way was I thinking about Umbra as wonderful no matter how pretty that new song in my body was. Yet, I did owe him for his heroism.

"The feeling is gone Maren," Umbra said with dark circles in his gorgeous brown eyes, "for now." His voice was almost valiant. Maren was hidden behind me, her fair blonde hair spilling all over her shoulders as her hands clawed the back of her neck. She shook her head to Umbra's comment with fearful puppy eyes. Umbra looked at me all of a sudden with eyes full of loving kindness and focused on me. His hands shook like tremors. For a moment, I thought I saw a little smile trying to peek through, but he pushed it back to look more sharply, getting serious.

"Star?"

I looked at him, bewildered, as my mouth went wide open. Star? That was . . . that was what Credence called me! And the thought of Credence made me blush. Umbra seemed to know what I was thinking, since he frowned.

"Stary," he said again in a light tone.

I smiled, hopeful for some reason and whispered yes to him, getting closer. I was hoping with all my heart he was going to say something miraculous to me. I wasn't sure why I wanted him to say that to me, but the feeling was too strong to ignore, the song beating louder and louder in my ears.

"Don't let that asshole creep hurt you again, all right?"

I was glad to agree and smiled more, still getting ever closer to his face, which looked like it was made of pure ecstasy.

He began again. "Because I'm sick of rescuing you! If you're supposed to be this great Spirit Warrior, save yourself once in a while! Da—Dang it!"

My heart sank with a tug, yet it mended in a flash. That was the sort of thing one would expect from Umbra the Crud. My stupid emotions or whatever I was feeling when I was around the jerk would have to vanish, because I couldn't stand him for anything more than an ally.

"No one asked you to come! I could have saved myself if I wanted! You're a show-offing loser Umbra!" I shouted at him.

He gave a malicious laugh and a mysterious, but sexy, smile when he finished. Umbra grabbed Maren's scared hand in the process, ready to leave. Those two holding hands made me feel off, but I knew it was supposed to be. Poor Maren looked like a child whose parents left her in the rain all alone. She needed his peaceful touch more than she needed anything right now.

"Whatever you say, Moon!" he said with a nonchalant wave and vanished into the daylight rays. Maren only looked up at him with her bright eyes and sighed, allowing her alarm to be carried away into the forgiving wind. I had never seen her so sad and alone . . . even Umbra didn't help to weaken her fear. But their bond was close and seemed to make Maren less anxious.

My chest began to ache and burn all at once, thinking of all the painful memories they must have suffered through. Or, maybe, if I could bring my mind to think of it, it could have been something else . . . This was too much stress. Maybe I could see a school counselor to help me with all this goop!

Mr. Tin called the class to clean the room after he sent Foils to the nurse's office to get a new shirt and informed us we all would be questioned later. I was so not looking forward to that, but I was curious as to what everyone thought they saw. The classroom soon became diplomatic once again. Mr. Tin was typing, drinking some of his tea every two seconds as students pretended to work. It seemed like nothing ever changed . . .

I blinked to the snap of Mr. Tin's booming voice. He was going around and making comments about our papers: "The biggest change in your life." He only glanced at mine and said well done with a firm nod. He may have saw words, but all I saw was a blank page, like what my purpose of life was: a blur. My paper felt transparent with nothing meaningful on it. I kept thinking of that force field. Maybe Kevin was the murderer? He seemed to start the problem, but knowing that pervert, it was dumb and awful luck! I guessed I would have to let my mind wander until I got home.

A gentle wind filled the room and mystically only blew my hair. I stopped to feel the energy around my body. The evil was near, too near. With that sense of it, I got a raging feeling in my gut . . . I was going to save my new friends no matter what cost it took me. I doubted I would ever know where the evil hid. And if I found the murderer, it was something that everyone, including me, would have to witness and then and there, I somehow knew that's when I'd find out what I was made of.

8

IT WAS ALMOST THE END OF THE DAY FOR ME. I HAD TO STAY AFTER school with my daddy to help him file papers. I could feel a presence staring down upon my face. It was almost painful and felt like someone was trying to get inside my mind, my soul. However, I couldn't feel where the presence was coming from, but it seemed determined and cunning. I was walking up the stairs with some extra file folders for my daddy when I heard someone call my name.

I spun around and it wasn't a dream. I saw Credence running towards me! I could feel my cheeks flame and my heart was as high as a cloud, my smile moving even higher.

He stopped in front of me on the stairs, leaning one hand on the rail to act cool. "Hey, what are you still doing here?" he asked with a dazzling smile shining brighter than dew catching the light of the rising sun.

I grinned, shaking while I tried to make the words come out. "I . . . ummmmm . . . I'm . . . help . . . helping my . . . dad . . ." My laugh came out way too girly; I was so lame!

"You're so sweet, Stary."

I had never felt so happy in my life! I felt like I could have floated all the way to the stars from bliss. He walked up to the stair that I was on, getting closer to me with a sly grin on his face. My heart was about to pop out of my chest, beating much too loud. I prayed he was doing what I always dreamt of him doing.

He got a little closer, compassion sparkling in his blue eyes, when I saw something: a little, quick white cloud around his hand on the rail. Then, a second later, his hand slipped and he fell to the floor! I was in complete distress, my brain unable to process what I was seeing: Credence barrel rolling down the stairs!

I ran to see if he was all right, tossing my daddy's folders off the railing.

"Credence! Credence!" I shook him, holding on to him securely. "Credence, are you okay?"

He looked at me with a strained smile, confused. "We've both been pretty clumsy lately, huh?" He chuckled, pushing me back as he got up to dust himself off. "I'm great . . . now . . . Thank you so much," he reassured me while giving me his grin that made me melt. The way he looked at me with possessive eyes made me feel like I was his goal, his reason for going further in life. That thought made me tingle, like a billion spiders were crawling up and down the inside of my flesh.

The whistle called, ripping my fairy tale miracle away from my life's book. "Oh. Break's over!" he sounded a bit alarmed, like he was busted. "Gotta go practice golf. See you Star!" He ran off, waving and smiling at me until he was a speck in the hall, then out of my sight.

I sighed with pure delight. "Credence," I whispered into the air, hoping it would carry my feelings into his heart.

"You're so pitiful! You *like* that too skinny, half-minded boy? Of course, I guess an unaccomplished girl would want to date a loser like herself!"

I turned around, my bones popping. Umbra was sitting on the stair rail, his arms folded, looking smug.

"Umbra! You caused Credence to fall! That's really low!" I blew up. I knew I was right about his motive this time.

He turned his head away from me, looking disappointed. "I was making sure you didn't lose your focus for the mission. I don't trust that bastard anyway . . . Something's *off* about him."

I growled, my vision blurring from my anger.

"Besides, anytime I can make you mad, I'll gladly do it for the entertainment! It's just too much fun to toy with weak, stupid humans." He unfolded his arms and gave a tainted grin, adding a black glimmer in his left eye.

I stomped up the stairs, nose to nose with him, and yelled, "Why can't you stick to your part of the mission? I am doing just fine and I do *not* need any help from a low life scum like you!"

He glared, his eyes lethal, and got a little closer to my face, not scared by my challenge. "Don't you *ever* talk to me that way or I'll spin your little head so fast—"

I got one centimeter closer, on my tiptoes, interrupting his rebuttal. "Bring. It. On." I marched up to the top of the stairs, going completely around him, and grabbed the folders after giving him an angry *hmph* and pointed my nose upward to add flare.

I walked away, pacing myself, leaving him there before turning to give my final burn. "Why are you so worried with who I like anyway? Are you . . . jealous?" I acted like I didn't care, arching my eyebrow nastily as I kept my face still.

His face became red and he couldn't get any words out at all. Fire was raging in his eyes. "Me . . . jeal-jealous of him . . . for . . . you?! That's insane! Why would I like an imperfect moron like you? Don't flatter yourself with that idea!"

I sounded indifferent when I replied, "Only asking," before walking off. I leaned against the wall after turning the corner, hidden, to check on him. He was still there, sitting and fuming, a look of pondering and longing on the profile of him I could see.

"Attraction . . . How crazy!" I heard him say. He spit the words out like a virus. Yet, he looked over at my direction with apprehensive eyes . . .

Leaving Umbra alone made me feel heartless, but it was an honest reaction for hurting someone I cared about. I tried to shake the thought from my mind and continued to walk to my father's room. Outside of Mr. Tin's room was Cally, leaning against the wall, casting a small, lonely shadow on the blue block wall. Her eyes were locked on the floor and desolation poured from her. It seemed like she had an unknown purpose. In her eyes, I could see a little dark cloud swirling inside her pupil and it was pulling me in, making me feel dazed . . .

"Oh! Hello Stary!" I was startled by her voice and it made my heart jump up two feet. She flashed a sugary sweet smile at me to relieve my shock.

"Hi Cally. What are you doing here?"

"I was lost in deep thought. I suppose this is an odd place to do that, right?" She blushed and sighed.

I chuckled a little at her reaction. "Nah. It's not and you're not. There's no such thing as being normal because you can't group a single person. We're all unique."

She gave me the most warm, beautiful smile that captured her full refinement. "Thank you. Your words are so dear, Stary."

I smiled back. She reminded me so much of Maren. Her heart seemed delicate, but why did I doubt her words?

"Ah!" Huh? The next thing I saw was Barbara and Cally on the floor tangled in an almost pretzel-like formation. Out of nowhere, a jolt hit my chest, negative energy hitting my heart, a feeling stabbed throughout my body with black chaotic sparks. They were near—the murderer!

"Cally, Barbara, are you guys okay?" I said as the two struggled to get up. Looking at them made me feel dizzy as my breathing became heavy and my pulse's beat was at hyper speed. I couldn't focus. My eyes were blurry and my head felt too many unknown powers at once. Why was I feeling the evil rage in a hallway? Could it have meant that . . . ?

"Ouch! Be careful staring into space like that. You might catch flies, new girl," Barbara spat as she fought to get up from the slick floor.

Cally ducked her head after struggling to stand. Her blush was a bright red so bright that it blended with her orange hair. "I . . . I am . . . so . . . sorry. I . . . ummmmm . . ."

Annoyance surged through me at Barbara's insensitivity. "Barbara, it's my fault. I was talking to her, not paying attention to who was around. Besides, I didn't see you coming." My eyes darted to the hall behind Barbara and the one I had just came from. They were both free of people and I had not heard anyone come up the side stairs.

Barbara blocked my path to the side stairs, her face as still as stone and her eyes were mincing.

"Please don't be so cruel to Cally. Being new is hard."

Barbara glared at me in a way I had never seen before. It made my heart skip again and turned my resentment into pure trepidation. Barbara dusted herself off and stood tall. "Yeah, well, you have been acting weird Stary so do not question me." She walked off with her attitude high in the air, clouding my thoughts. Once she was gone, my head began to clear, but my body still felt burnt inside.

Cally beamed at me, her eyes bashful and her hair all in knots. "Thank you and I am sorry I was such a nuisance for you." She bowed to me and waved goodbye while going down the side stairs Barbara went down seconds before.

My heart ached with vagueness and a sickening piercing pain. My muscles were refusing to stop shaking. I had felt the murderer twice, but why was it only when I was near Cally or Barbara? My knees became weak at the thought. I knew I would meet the murderer one day to help Maren and Umbra, yet I never dreamed they would be so close to me or my emotions.

I saw Maren watching at me with strange sparkles in her lovely eyes as I walked back near the lunchroom. They were not the usual ones that glimmered like the morning sun, but like a forced shine that came when one makes themselves appear fine and happy when in reality, they have to perform a task they are dreading or that makes them sad. She noticed I saw her and plastered a real smile on her face.

"Hello Stary dear," she said in a whisper. I tried my best to not show her my worry.

We walked (well, she floated) together to get Umbra, who was still at the stairwell for some reason. Umbra also seemed distant. I didn't talk much about feeling the murderer earlier because I was sure Maren saw what happened. Then, I realized something with a jolt . . . The next day was Maren's funeral. My heart sank down into the Earth's core. I stopped in my tracks, trying to hold back tears.

Maren and Umbra looked back at me concerned. "Stary, are you all right hon?"

I swallowed hard, almost choking on my saliva and lie. "Nothing. I just stopped. Humans can be weird sometimes, right?" I smiled so hard that my insides shook.

Maren looked worried, but believed me. Umbra didn't say a word, but watched me with a look of unease and doubt. The next day was going to be a day of hard memories and for once, I think Umbra understood and thanked my feelings.

The morning came sooner than I thought. The sun's golden rays were reflected as sparkles against the fresh dew, reminding me of the previous night. I couldn't sleep at all because I was worrying about Maren. The only thing I could see was the moon gracefully shining silver beams through my window. The surface light, the outer ring, was bright and beautiful, yet the moon itself was dim. The moon reminded me of Maren; cheerful on the outside, lonely on the inside. That idea only made my soul drop faster, making the rays of the sun now a harsh reminder of my rough night.

Arriving at the funeral home made my heart miss a few beats. I walked to the courtyard, which was decorated with sky blue baby's breath and small yellow buttercups. My eyes scanned the area to see if I knew anyone, but no one seemed familiar. It was lonely and bare. The turnout was about twenty people, all socializing with cups of red punch. Watching the punch swirl in the cup trapped my eyes in a whirlpool of uneasiness; it was cruel irony to me that they chose that color!

My eyes caught sight of the white table cloth: the color of purity and Maren. I lost myself staring at it when suddenly goose bumps went up my arm and my hair stood up. I knew that fear, that reaction . . . The murderer! And at the funeral home? How revolting could someone be? I then felt a hand on my shoulder. My heart raced. I spun around, throwing my arm up in the air. I had enough force to stop my hand right before it met the person's flesh.

"Stary Moon, what in the Lord's name are you doing?" said a shrill, scratchy voice that my ears seemed to know. I opened my eyes that had been sealed tight from panic and examined the figure before me. It was Barbara, standing there with an arm full of white lilies and an old-fashioned camera with the Plantersville emblem around her milky swan-like neck.

"Oh!" I said, shocked and preparing to humiliate myself. "I'm sorry, Barbara. I was . . . well, I was . . ." I stopped to notice my hands were still raised, very close to her cheeks. I brought them down at my sides with a punishing slap as my eyes were stuck staring at the floor. "I thought you were trying to attack me . . ." I explained, lifting my head up, tilting towards my right shoulder with a cheesy, innocent grin to match. I hoped this made me look innocent. "You really startled me."

Barbara raised one eyebrow, looking at me like I was a complete moron (which I was to Umbra and myself now). I forced myself to stare at the floor again.

"I overreacted. I really am sorry . . ." My cheeks flushed as I continued to marvel at the off-white tile.

"Hey, no problem," Barbara said, adding some cheerfulness in her tone. I looked up at her, on guard. "Funerals make everyone crazy. Since you're already there, it must really make you nuts!"

Her words hurt me on the inside, but for Barbara, that was extreme sweet talk. I offered her my thanks and then remembered the camera looped around her neck. "I'm curious. Why do you have a school camera?"

She stopped her fake Miss Sunshine routine and looked straight down at the device. "I'm just taking some pictures for the school newspaper."

I felt uneasy at her false statement. I knew Barbara was not on the newspaper. She was too busy with band and the academic team; there was no way she had time!

"That's great," I said. As I looked back up at her, my long hair fell in front of my left eye. When I tried to brush it away, a jolt hit my body, snapping my neck in a position where I couldn't look at anything other than Barbara's bland face. Her eyes locked on me, glaring at me with polluted red eyes full of hatred. The room was still in view, yet it felt like we were in our own world, trapped in a binding field of iniquity and I was choking uncontrollably on its aura. Choking . . . fading . . . falling . . .

"Everyone, we are ready to begin. Please follow me to the gravesite." The tender voice of the minister awoke me from the spell of horror.

I stood up, shaking, to face Barbara. However, I only received a sly smile and a dismissive turn as she obeyed the priest's order. My veins felt chilled and my head was racing. I had only felt that gut-tightening feeling when I was near the murderer, but that was impossible, right? My head became dazed from all the thoughts and I decided to change my pace of deliberation and heart by following the others who were there to honor Maren.

As I stepped outside into God's creation, the blazing sun hit the top of my head, giving me absolute warmth, yet it did not thaw my frozen hands. My feet began to follow each other almost in a perfect line, making my walking pace odd. I passed a gorgeous elm tree with tiny leaf buds sprouting from its limber and elegant branches. My feet gained their own mind and refused to go any farther or join the others that were roughly thirty feet away. My soul was leading me towards the tree's base and telling me I needed to stay there. I hid my face in the gargantuan shadows of the tall tree, becoming half hidden, half lit like my feelings.

The wind blew a gentle breeze which made the trees whistle a song of discovery, informing me someone was coming. Almost after the wind's contact reached my back, a blue glow appeared beside me: Umbra. He stared directly at the funeral procession, his black and honey toned eyes rippling.

"Maren is above you," he said, not moving or changing his emotion at all. I looked at him with concern but gazed up to see Maren at the top of the elm tree holding on to the base itself, looking blank and distant from society. I frowned, feeling like an awful person, as if everything terrible that had ever happened or would happen was my fault.

"She just needed to see it for herself. Don't worry yourself." Umbra did a ninety degree turn, looking directly into my eyes. The redness inside his eyes had vanished and the black had softened into a rich, lovely dark brown. Even his face was lighter than usual. I could tell his heart was just as broken up as Maren's. I was trapped in the enchantment of his eyes and the sudden graceful nature of the music of the organ broke the mood and silence.

"'I am the resurrection and the life,' says the Lord. 'Those who believe in me, even though they die, will live, and everyone who lives and believes in me will never die,'" said the minister's caring tenor voice. His opening Bible words were standard for all funerals, yet they were so true and touching. I could tell Maren felt the same way because she touched her heart right after he uttered that quote.

He continued. "Welcome one and all: friends and family members, to the funeral for Maren Crystal Rowe. O God, whose beloved Son did take little children into his arms and bless them: Give us grace, we beseech thee, to entrust this child, Maren, to thy never-failing care and love, and bring us all to thy heavenly kingdom; through the same thy Son Jesus Christ our Lord, who liveth and reigneth with thee and the Holy Spirit, one God, now and forever . . . Amen."

My heart sank lower with every passing movement of the priest's mouth. He was kind and formal, but I couldn't help feeling appalled. Maren stared, seemingly brave, but I could tell she wanted to break down and scream at the cruel fate that took her life away. Her lifeless eyes looked at the funeral ground and her fading legs were quivering. I wanted to climb up to her, but Umbra grabbed my shoulder without moving his head.

"She'll be all right. She wants to do this alone. Please trust her Stary . . ."

I nodded and locked back into my previous position, trying with all my might to accept that the funeral would go on. The priest made a cross symbol with his right hand and motioned a man to come to the platform that was set up on the lawn of fresh green grass that sprouted rebirth.

"Now, for our elegy, Mr. Elbert Fillmore Rowe will tell us about his beloved sister."

From the small crowd of mourners stepped an extremely tall man that was well over six and a half feet. He had a pot belly that stuck out, but slim spaghetti legs that made him look like a preschooler's art project. His bald head reflected the sun's glory, yet he had a flaming red, bushy mustache that pointed violently at the crowd. He grabbed a folded piece of paper from his suit jacket pocket and unfolded it, squinting at his handwriting through cherry-colored glasses over his beady eyes. After a minute, he tossed the paper with flare over his shoulder and grinned at the crowd. This man was interesting to say the very least!

He had a deep, powerful, and almost villainous voice that boomed through the air like a knife. "I appreciate everyone taking time out of their busy schedules to come and honor the dignity of my younger sister, Maren. She was a happy child, always chipper and smiling as bright as the sun of the third solar system." He laughed heartily at his own intelligent joke; only the buzzing bugs responded. The odd way he talked about Maren made it sound like we were a PTA group of dead weight parents and citizens. I didn't like his tone at all; it gave me the creeps.

Elbert opened his mouth and went on. "I admit I did not know Maren as well as I should have and for that, I will forever be weighted with the burden of that guilt." He grabbed his heart and showed the people his fake teary eyes.

Umbra made a disbelieving sound with his mouth and whispered to me, "I have never liked the man. Yet, he *is* a good performer . . ." Umbra's head went immediately down, almost as if he had went down a dark pathway thanks to the mind controlling man. "He is a master mind in many things. He almost got domination of everything . . ." Umbra's eyes danced with smoldering flames after his statement. My heart went to him; Dr. Rowe must have been more than a talented actor.

"I pray that my darling little sea pearl will find peace in the sky and be welcomed by the people of the Lord with open arms." Elbert gave a wave to the people as they kept their heads downward in respect.

The minister helped lower the coffin into the rectangular pre-dug dirt grave in front of the gray garnet tombstone that stated to the world that Maren Crystal Rowe was no longer alive. The thought of a kindhearted person such as Maren no longer living because of a person who had darkness in their hearts made my blood race.

"It's not fair!" It came out of my mouth from my heart without warning. The snapping of my voice surprised Umbra. I felt his eyes gazing through my broken soul. "Maren . . . ," I said in between steady and agonizingly blurred sobs. "Maren . . . she is one of . . . the greatest people . . . I have . . . and will . . . ever know . . ." I stopped to take a cutting breath. "She is such a . . . good person. Why did she . . . have to die? Why did she . . . have to be . . . killed?"

My compassion turned into dark hatred toward the so-called murderer. "IT'S NOT RIGHT! IT'S NOT FAIR! WHY CAN'T I DO ANYTHING? WHY AM I SO USELESS? I just—"

Something tenderly grabbed my arm and I was being pulled into a bright white light from the sun. I landed into Umbra's chest. I could hear his heart racing like a rushing river. He was holding my arm and he was the one who pulled me into him! My mind was eased and my heart was melting from its frozen stage. Umbra held me in a loving embrace with his gorgeous honey eyes gazing at me with the most concern I had ever seen in them. His face was hurt and pained, almost as bad as mine. I noticed he was holding back streams of salty mist too.

"I know Stary. I know nothing is fair. Yet, justice will be made and we will save Maren together. I promise *we will* save her . . ."

I looked back into his eyes, the eyes I would trust with anything from that moment on. I grabbed Umbra's waist to reply because my mouth was disconnected from my spinning mind. It was thin, nothing but air, yet I felt his body heat and pure compassion from his ghostly light. The perfectly executed rhythm of the mysterious song I heard when Umbra saved me from Foils was playing again, but softer, like it was background music to my own personal movie. I never wanted to leave that feeling. I then understood *why* Maren loved to be hugged by him when she felt afraid.

The velvet voice of the priest rang above the sound of sadness as he recited the final prayer before dismissal. I turned to face the service but didn't let go of Umbra's waist. My head rested on his shoulder as I sobbed into it uncontrollably. His head brushed the top of my long hair, his right arm around my waist and his left tapping the crown of my head. I glanced up at Maren. She was staring at the end of the horrible event with utter dismay, standing as stiff as a statue.

Everyone began to leave the garden and enter the hall for refreshments. My body was quivering and my heart was shaken from the day. I couldn't imagine the terror inside Maren's gut right then. She sighed deeply and staggered like she was trying to break away her sorrow, but her ghostly form was still connected, preparing to release it. After that, she vanished out of sight, but I heard her light running steps. Maybe she was trying to hide the fact that she was running away. It didn't do much good; I could hear her sobs as she ran across the street. I ran with all my might to catch up to her pace with Umbra following close behind. I stopped, realizing it was hopeless. When we're scared, we run away from our fears instead of facing them and I didn't blame her. I had no right to stop her.

I yelled her name as loudly as I could, but it was no use. I began to tear up again. Umbra gently grabbed my shoulder, "Let her go for now."

I nodded, not wanting to agree with the fate of the morning, but I knew it was the only option. I began my steps towards my home when I felt an uneasy presence near me. My soul had felt it at the funeral grounds, but I was too concerned and destroyed inside to notice it. I ignored it and continued, alone, to my house when I noticed at the corner of my eye what looked like a ponytail disappearing behind the lamppost. It was gone in a flash like my imagination was tricking me with a mental magic trick.

My mind was reflecting images because my heart was in pieces. Yet, I was more determined than ever to build my heart back together and create the picture of the divine future everyone wanted, needed, and deserved.

9

FRIDAY WAS A USUAL DAY OF REJOICING FOR THE WELL-EARNED break known as the weekend. It was almost in sight for us students, yet the day dragged on to me. Sorrow, darkness, and dread stood in front of me and filled my soul like it did from the funeral the day before. My body seemed motionless and helpless wandering down the endless hallways and I swore I could taste moisture from the cracks of the doors.

I hadn't seen Maren or Umbra since the funeral. I tossed and turned all night thinking about them. It was hard being a Spirit Warrior. The powers were interesting, but at least the ones that never discovered their powers didn't have to deal with the painful relationships with the spirits they helped. I loved Maren and accepted Umbra (sometimes), but it was unbearable to see others suffer, but I guessed, sadly, I had to admit we all go through that path of truth.

I felt a gentle tap on my shoulder as I was going to keyboarding class. I spun around to look straight into Mark's honey eyes. He smiled, yet I saw sorrow flickering in his eyes. "Hey Stary. Can I talk to you for a minute on the bench?"

Lost, I stared at him for a second, but nodded. He grabbed my wrist, his slender fingers warm and loving. His touch made me think of Umbra's . . . I shook my head hard to get the image out of my mind. Mark sat on the bench and looked down at the tile that reflected his sadness and he began swinging his legs in a four-count rhythm.

"First off, I wanted to make sure you were all right. You've been acting far-off lately. I'm not saying you've been rude, not that at all, but you seem less 'here' is all. I'm sorry. I guess I'm being a worrywart!"

Guilt hit me. "Oh Mark. I'm so sorry I worried you. I do have a lot of things on my mind. Sometimes life doesn't happen the way you plan it . . . I guess I'll make the best with what I got!" I gave him a big smile and flexed my arms to prove I had the strength to get through this. At least, I *hoped* I did.

Mark laughed a little and patted my back. "I'm glad to hear that. You have such spirit and I envy that dearly in you Miss Stary."

I smiled bashfully at the ground. "You don't know how right you are . . . ," I said, my tone sarcastic. If he only knew!

Suddenly, he stopped smiling and stared at me with grief. His hand gestures told me he wanted to tell me something significant, but he seemed hesitant to speak. "My . . . ahhhh . . . my dad got a new job . . . ," he finally said in a muffled tone.

I jumped out of my seat and grinned at the wonderful news. Mark's father was a minister for the local Baptist church, which was small but proud and beautiful. "That's great! Your dad is a hard worker and deserves a new position in the church." I stopped, seeing Mark's head bent down and his glasses becoming fogged. "You're not happy . . ."

Mark looked deep into my eyes, making my knees go weak and my heart flutter. Even though he was the closest guy friend I had and we were only pals, he was still extremely handsome and sincere. "No, I'm happy. My dad deserves a job and he should get the position. The only thing is he wasn't offered the new position at our church. He was offered it at Conway Valley Baptist Church, which is forty-five minutes away. Stary, if he takes the job, I . . . .I . . . I have to move!" He almost shouted the last part. He dropped his head and grabbed the bench tight.

Move? The word sounded foreign, horrible, and the news jabbed me in the heart, stabbing me in an unthinkable daze. I was going to lose someone dear to me. "Oh Mark, I-I'm so sorry. I will miss you so much. When will you move?"

"At the end of the semester."

The end of the semester?! That was only six weeks away! Dread of school ending hit me hard on the face, leaving its scarring mark.

"My dad hasn't said yes, but I'm 99.9% sure he will. You're the first one I told since you're the closest friend I have ever had. I want you to know that."

My heart sank and moisture filled the ends of my eyes. I was about to wipe them away when I stopped and noticed Mark was about to breakdown, water about to stream down his face.

"Oh Mark . . ." I bent down and held his waist, digging my head into his chest. "I don't want you to go. I can't lose one of the most important friends in my life," I whispered into his heart, but I was not sure he heard me. My mind recalled the day I first met Mark and how we connected intensely, joking, laughing, and our morals were similar. He was like Chloe, Rin, and Lauren: a friend, a piece of my heart I wasn't sure I could lose.

Mark rubbed my back and hugged me as tightly as he could. I looked up at him; he had his eyes closed.

I tilted my head and noticed a gray cloud swirling slowly, running in an endless circle. Then, it took shape, human shape. Umbra emerged from the smoke and he stared at me with despair, his eyes dancing with surprise. Seeing him and thinking about me holding Mark made me think that soon, Maren and Umbra would be gone as well from my life . . . I would have to let them go. Scared at the thought, I squeezed Mark tighter. If I let go of him, I would lose him. That was the theory that had been buried into my mind anyway.

"You okay Stary?" Mark asked me, concerned. Darn, I worried him again!

I looked up at his face and loosened my grip. "Have you told Chloe yet?" I asked, changing the subject to stop my tears from coming out.

Mark blushed a bright red, which made his beautiful tan skin turn an odd color. "No. I-I'm scared of how she'll take it."

I grabbed his hands and gave them a light tug. "You need to tell her. I know it's hard, but she needs to hear it from *you*." He nodded and gave me a playful tap on the forehead.

"Oh, look at us! Here we still have a month together and we're acting like the world is ending!" I laughed and brushed my hair with my twisting fingers as I giggled at my stupidity.

Mark let go of my hands, stared at the tile and chuckled at our overdramatic reaction.

The warning bell sounded and Mark jumped up to his feet like he was just hit by lightning. He smiled his smile that always made me blush. "I'll walk you to class since this is my fault. Sorry for bothering you, babe." He bent his head down like a puppy that was in trouble.

I twirled in front of him with my hands behind my back and grinned. "Anything for you, buddy!"

He smiled with his eyes closed. "Thank you Stary." Mark linked his arm through mine and walked me to class like the gentleman he was. I turned my head to see if Umbra was still there. He was staring at me astounded. He turned and vanished into the sunlight streaming through the window; a mysterious phantom of the unknown world of God. Soon, he would be gone in the night and set free with his Maren. I felt twisted thinking this, but I didn't want to see that day come, the day I would lose them both in my life.

School passed by without a hitch and lunch was about to begin as usual. Umbra and Maren had been following me the rest of that day, yet both kept their distance. I supposed they were guarding me and searching for the murderer at the same time. Yet, I would only feel one of them each hour.

My table was talking about typical teenage things, giggling, smiling, slapping, and hitting each other. The only one that looked nervous was poor Mark, who stared at me and Chloe an uncountable amount of times. Whenever our eyes met, I smiled at him to reassure him that everything would be fine.

"Stary!"

My head shot up at the sound of my name. There I saw Maren running toward me with her compassionate and wide grin. Shocked, I blinked a few times to make sure it was her. It was. I stood up abruptly as my friends stared at me, bug-eyed with confusion.

"Ummmmm, I need to use the restroom for a minute guys. Be right back."

Mark looked scared, like a deer in headlights. I walked behind him as he was staring at the table, not making eye contact with a soul.

I patted his back, which made him jump. "Don't worry. You can do it," I whispered with cheeriness in my tone.

Maren grabbed my arm and led me behind the first brick pillar. "I feel the strong vibe of the murderer, but I cannot find the exact location. I have narrowed it down to be around here. Since you know the building better than I do, could you possibly help me, my sweet?" Her eyes sparkled in the lighting and her face glowed like a fairy princess. She looked better and my heart soared seeing that life changing, gorgeous smile.

"Of course Maren. It's my job to help my friends and do my duty as a Spirit Warrior. I guess I just need to focus?" I poked her nose like a little pixie after she nodded. Maren giggled and the elegant sound made me light up with delight.

I closed my eyes and tapped into my spirit powers, feeling the different auras in the lunchroom like Umbra trained me for. Thick designs of dull colors whirled beyond my closed eyelids in a slow forming cloud. I felt my pulse and the pulses of others around me. Subsequently, a strike of red lightning flashed in front of my eyes, making my heart rate shoot like a rocket.

I unconsciously pointed to my right, a flow of energy calling me. When I opened my eyes to allow the fading hues to vanish, Maren looked up, hope all over her face.

"That way, near the girl's restroom."

With caution, we took our first steps into the corridor of the bathroom and waited to see if my prediction was correct and what we would find if it was.

"Where's Umbra at?" I asked as we walked to the restroom.

Maren looked at the ground. "Oh, he is out searching. We have been taking turns looking at the area and then guarding you. It is simply my turn now." She paused and glanced at me full of concern. "I am sorry about yesterday. I, well . . ."

I stopped her with my hand. "Maren, you have nothing to apologize for! It's understandable seeing something so dramatic. I feel sorry you had to witness it."

"Thank you Stary. I will do my best to not let you or Umbra down. I know the murderer is in this area. We have to find them to save others . . ." She looked up at the lighting, which made her look like a beautiful, pure angel from a painting, a memory that would become forever unmoving in my mind. If there was such thing as a pure heart, Maren would have it. Here she was worried about letting Umbra and me down and was not one bit selfish since she only cared about the good of future victims, not her own fate. I admired her spirit, the physical one and her inner one.

We stopped in front of the bathroom, feeling the surroundings. Something was in the air; something sinister was filling the sky. I slowly stepped into the girl's restroom with Maren right behind, lightly holding on to the back of my t-shirt. The bathroom was old, from the '60s, so paint chips were everywhere and there was the stall that would flush at random with no one in it, making the situation appear even scarier than I had anticipated

My eyes scanned the room from left to right as my spirit detecting powers felt the air. Maren copied my path and tried to help. Something was there, but nothing jumped out at me. It was faint and I could not track the source. The suspect was long gone.

In the center of the restroom was the stall I was crying in the day Umbra tipped my chair. The thought seemed weird, however, it made me feel pleasant inside.

"Stary dear, are you all right? Your face looks flushed . . ." Maren's soft, soothing voice halted my train of thought.

"Oh . . . I'm sorry. I was only thinking about something that—"

I stopped. *Click!* The red pulse! I felt it staying still, almost hiding, trying to be nonexistent. I cautiously turned my head, scared to blink and too paralyzed to move forward. The pulse was racing and each second it quickened, it made my mouth go drier. A spirit was in that stall.

I had to be brave for Maren. I turned and tip-toed into it, cracking the half-opened door a little more. I looked around, scanned, did everything to find the unknown sensation. However, my efforts failed me. The aura . . . it was so off balance . . . Was it even real?

Tired of worrying myself over nothing, I put the seat down and sat, wiping the sweat off my forehead, panting. I looked in front of me at the blue door to notice something clear and different looking. It looked like some kind of writing and I felt a luring presence in every blurry letter. Confused, I stared at it, questioning what in the world it was.

Maren must have been worried because she came to the door and then screamed "Ouch!" out of nowhere. Startled, I got up from the seat and looked to see her on her back on the cold and dirty floor, dazed and rocking like a turtle swaying on its shell.

"Maren, are you okay? What happened?" I said, holding the door in place.

Shaking dust off her back with her left hand and rubbing her head with her right, a look of irritating pain crossing her face, she looked at me with utter bewilderment. "I am not really sure. I tried to phase through the door, but something is shielding the area . . ."

I did a double take at her and then the door. Could the writing have really been strong enough to stop Maren from phasing? Could spirits even phase through each other? I wasn't sure.

"Maybe try floating to the top and phasing on your stomach," I suggested. The writing was in the middle of the door, so maybe she could phase through it by floating. I figured that was better than crawling on her elbows on the nasty floor.

Maren stood up, grunting the whole time, and floated to the top of the gray and speckled ceiling, then went through the bathroom door. It worked! She floated right behind me, looking over my left shoulder before holding on to both of mine for support.

"Look at this. I'm not exactly sure what it is, but I think it's writing and it feels like the aura I was sensing earlier." Amazed, we both bent down to get a closer look at our mysterious clue. There were words, but I could not make them out entirely. I raised my right hand to touch it. Maybe I could feel the letters like braille . . .

"STOP!" Maren yelled.

I froze in my position, shocked by her reaction. She pointed to the writing and firmly placed my arm at my side.

"Mortals, even Spirit Warriors, cannot directly touch spirit writing. It is made with ectoplasm and can burn a mortal's skin when in contact with it. That is why you cannot phase through spirits. You bump into them and fall down."

I looked at the door, befuddled. A spirit wrote the letters with ectoplasm? "Maren, aren't spirits made out of ectoplasm? So, spirits write messages in their own 'blood'?"

"In a way, yes. We are made of ectoplasm. It replaces our blood because it is not only lighter, but can phase along with us, which is why we can phase through things without being detected." She seemed to be proud for teaching me something. I smiled.

Still, the *spirit* from the stall seemed off-balance. "Can you tell who wrote it, Maren?"

She bent close to it and looked serious and focused. After a few minutes, she blinked and shook her head, disappointed. "It is too off-balance. Maybe a spirit messenger wrote it. They can write in ectoplasm as well," she said with a shy intelligent look, wide-eyed, with her pointer finger in midair as she straightened herself into Ms. Rowe, the professor of the paranormal. Did it count as an unfair advantage that she *was* paranormal? HA!

"Spirit messengers? Can they see spirits like me?" Every day I learned something new. Could there be others like me? People who could relate to my powers and what I'm going through? The thought was reassuring and a little scary at the same time.

Maren beamed. "You are one. A spirit messenger is one that can communicate with us. They can be psychics, a few lucky people, or past or present Spirit Warriors. I doubt it is a Spirit Warrior since you are the only one who has knowledge of your powers. Someone could be here to help us indirectly . . ." Hope radiated from her.

I gave a wry smile. I wanted it to be someone who could help us, however, I felt uneasy and wasn't sure I should trust the message, whatever it was. I had to do something though. "Can I write back to them?" I asked Maren with my finger near the wall.

Surprised, she looked at me and said, "If you like, but what are you going to write hon?"

I thought for many seconds until I drew my calling with my finger onto the door. "How do I turn it into ectoplasm, if I can . . . ?" I looked away, self-conscious.

Maren giggled, her golden curls billowing from the air stream coming from the dusty vent above. "Focus your energy on what you want to write and trace it with your index finger on your dominate hand."

I did as I was told and my message was engraved into the spirit world. It was surreal. Maren spied to see what I had written. There, in the door, was a lonely question mark, aimed towards our mysterious author of the restroom.

Maren blinked three times fast, then patted my back in an understanding manner.

"We have to be cautious," I said in a monotone, lost in the spell of the spirit realm.

"Since we do not know if they are a friend or an enemy," she finished my sentence, copying my exact tone as we both seemed to become engulfed in the thrill of the unknown world, the world Maren wanted to be welcomed to. Only the future would tell how that expression would come into play in the ultimate battle, the fight I was destined to be a part of.

"WHAT DO MEAN YOU FOUND AN ECTOPLASM MESSAGE AT SCHOOL?!" Umbra screamed at me after Maren and I told him the news in my bedroom after school. I felt like I was being stabbed with ice shards from the look he gave me although his voice was brutally hot.

Dumbfounded by his reaction, I blinked and answered his simple question. "Yes, we did," was all I could say. What else was there to add?

Steam seemed to flow out of his ears. I timidly turned to Maren, who was sitting quiet and ladylike on my bed. I grinned nervously as she shrugged her shoulders. Her wide eyes told me she was as shocked by Umbra's blow up as much as I was.

His face inflated. "You idiot! It could be an enemy and you . . . Oh, heaven all mighty! How can you endanger Maren's soul like that?"

"You seem upset Umbra." My voice was gentle, hoping to calm him down.

"No dip Sherlock!" he snapped. Okay, that didn't work!

"Umbra, I'm sorry for making you angry, but Maren and I thought of that. I wrote something where we can get a real reply back without revealing ourselves . . ." I gulped as Umbra gave me the dirtiest look.

"I'm listening." He tapped his index finger on his crossed arms that squeezed his muscles over his well-built chest. Not that I was noticing . . .

Maren gave me a look of reassurance. Her angelic eyes were sparkling like wild fire, yet I could see on her face she wasn't sure what Umbra would say.

"I-I, well, I wrote a question mark . . ." I braced myself, too scared he would explode his fury toward me again.

Umbra was still for a few minutes, staring. I opened my eyes and lifted my head towards his face; his expression had not changed. The embers that were blazing in his eyes turned into daggers. "A question mark? Are you really that dumb? A stupid question mark?! How is that going to help us, you incapable, imbecile of epic—"

"Umbra, stop!" Maren's voice was soft, but sounded enraged. She stood strong and clenched her fists as they shook at her sides. "Stary was trying hard to protect me, because I wanted to add a nice comment . . ." Maren put her head down while some tears formed at the sides of her blue-topaz-toned eyes. "I am sorry Umbra . . ."

Umbra turned his head toward Maren, his eyes softer, but glowing with guilt. He grabbed his hair in his hand as he opened and closed his mouth a few times. After a few deep breaths, he placed one hand behind his back and the other pointed at her, Professor Umbra making another appearance. "Maren . . . you know better. You know you have to be careful or you could be spotted and then—" He paused. Although his heart couldn't say the words, they were all over his face: *You'll be gone from me again.*

Maren cupped her face and small sobs could be heard. "I know. I did not think. I am sorry."

Umbra gave an annoyed sigh, defeated. So much for his manly pride. "All right now. No more tears." He moved toward Maren, lifted her lovely face and wiped away her tears. "Just be careful next time, got it?" Umbra said, tilting his head with a small, kind smile.

Maren smiled, her face glowing more beautiful than the most precious spring day. She nodded happily and jumped up to give him a light hug. Surprised, Umbra stepped backwards a little but soon returned her tenderness. She opened her eyes to face me and gave me a thumbs-up behind Umbra's back, grinning like an imp and mouthing, "We are good now." Maren did that just to get Umbra off my back? I was thrown for a loop, but laughed at her caring, but sneaky, attitude. What a little prankster!

Umbra turned to face me, looking displeased. He stomped swiftly towards me, his arms and legs moving at the same time. Terrified, I stepped back wide-eyed until I hit my wall near my desk chair. I leaned my head against one of my several anime posters. I shut my eyes, digging my fingernails into the bumpy surface of my wall to save myself. Oh anime posters, please have the characters I love come out and save me from Umbra's wrath!

He grabbed my arm and forced me to look into his breathtaking eyes. "Look, I'm . . . sorry for yelling at you. But, you have to admit, a question mark is pretty stupid, even for a human."

I cracked a smile, mentally freaking out by the fact that he was saying sorry to me.

"Yeah, I agree. I . . . I didn't know exactly what to write," I said, trapped in his shadow.

"Well, if you need help thinking of something intelligent to say, tell me and I'll once again save your sorry little ass." Umbra gave a cocky grin.

I frowned at him, but brushed it off. "Fine," I agreed, pretending to be angry by his rudeness targeted at me when I wasn't. Tomorrow was another day to worry about, considering if the message writer was a friend or an enemy. However, right then, that moment was good with me because I got to hold on to the two of them for another day longer.

10

A SWIFT BREEZE HIT MY CHEEK AND LIGHTENED MY CHEST, allowing the warmth of relief to spread. I was nervous the night before, thinking of the murderer, the message in the bathroom, and worst off, the result. Yet, sitting next to the quiet window in my dad's class seemed to give me peace. Dad was discussing the reasons America went into the Korean War. I knew the information and tried to focus, yet my ears and eyes didn't seem connected.

As I began to start a new section of notes, I felt a chill behind me. I sneezed suddenly, but the eerie goose bump feeling was still there afterwards, hanging, clinging to my skin.

"Bless you," someone whispered. I turned to my left to see Allen, sitting in the seat next to me, taking notes.

"Thanks," I said with a sigh.

I felt something dark leaning over my right shoulder. It was getting closer, making my heart rate increase. The feeling was intense, making my face redden from heat. It got so close that I could see its black figure from the corner of my eye. Then, a hand touched my shoulder and a gentle breath went down my prickly neck.

"Boo!" mocked the voice.

I jumped out of my chair, startled, like I was bitten. When I did, Allen looked at me strangely and I heard an evil, yet familiar, chuckle. Umbra! I couldn't look at him for it would have appeared awkward. I hissed at him without turning or looking away from my notes. "You jerk! Why did you do that?"

Umbra cackled hard, but it was muffled as he tried to whisper. "I had to liven this place up and scaring you is just too fun." He slapped my back at the last statement, pushing me forward a bit. My eyebrow began to twitch with frustration, but I was going to prove to him that I was calm.

"Is that all you needed?" I said, my voice cool.

He moved up next to me. I could see he was frowning, which made me smile inside. "I checked the bathroom again and still no response. Lunchtime may be the best time to check. The murderer must go to this school," he said, switching gears.

"Or the note could be from someone who really wants to help us . . . ," I expressed.

He rolled his eyes and snorted at me. "Stary, please! I'm not Maren. You can't be so naïve to think that it's someone who wants to help us, right?"

I looked down at my notes, not making eye contact. "I will not take sides. The evidence will show up and right now, I'm ready to accept anything." My tone was dry and informative.

My father turned away from the blackboard and set his chalk down. He sat on his desk and began to ask questions, making commentary on his notes. The class hastily wrote down answers on their papers. Umbra began a fake coughing and hacking spell. I thought about stopping my writing for a second to check on him but decided to continue.

"You got that one wrong." He pointed to one of the questions, leaving his navy ghostly fingerprint on my smooth white paper. Well, that answered one of the four hundred and twenty thousand questions I had about spirits and my powers.

"I think I know what I'm doing," I shushed, somewhat looking up at him as I kept on writing.

My peripheral vision caught Umbra glaring at me. "I was programmed to know everything and can look up information in an interactional database that is programmed into my brain to discover things I do *not* know. I know I'm right and when you're wrong." His smile turned evil.

I looked at him, ramming my nose into his by accident as I said in a heated whisper, "Let me do it myself." The harshness in my voice felt sharp on my tongue, scaring myself a little as I stared at him. His eyes became enlarged the second I got close to him. Did he not like me next to him or did I hurt his nose by mistake? I heard him gulp as his face became red.

What am I doing? I turned back towards my paper, leaning my head on my left hand. "Forget it!" I said thickly before writing.

I noticed he went behind my back, but I pretended not to care. All of a sudden, I felt an energy go inside me. My eyes widened and my heart sprinted, terrified at what was happening. My right hand began to quiver insanely. It seemed to be trying to erase the wrong answer Umbra pointed out! I pulled myself back in my seat to stop the flow, to halt the sinking spell.

"The answer is wrong, stupid! You need to change it!" Umbra howled in an echo, but from where? I felt a pulse in my head and that breathing . . . Umbra was in my mind?! WHAT THE FUDGE!

"You went in my brain?" I shouted in my mind, using all my mental strength to push his presence out of the way long enough so I could control my hand to set my pencil away from me. My mind was swirling from arguing with Umbra. My heart was beating in pain and my head was splitting. I grabbed my head, hoping I could control Umbra or better yet, push him out completely.

"GET OUT!" I shrilled in my mind. Like magic, a blast of swirling colors zoomed past my eyes. I felt like I was traveling in a sci-fi movie, yet the beautiful and mysterious world disappeared and landed me in a place full of darkness with dull, gray clouds. That place . . . I felt like I was connected to it. The clouds wrapped themselves around me and before I knew it, I became weak and collapsed, accepting the burn of the hate-filled darkness.

My mind was racing, banging violently to the accursed rhythm the unknown fall caused me. I was aware of what was going on but too lightheaded to open my eyes, locked in fear of my mystifying surroundings. I fluttered my eyes slowly to view my landing spot. Spinning, I looked down to see nothing; a blank, pure black space of nothingness, scaring me, concerning me about my safety.

Turning my head to look above, I was hoping to find a source of light. I found one, however, it was an awful, dim red color. Somehow, it was being reflected off something I could not see, a thing that must have been amazingly bright. Ever so delicately, I stood up, shaking worse than Jell-O, still locked into the haze of clouded darkness. The fog was thick, yet transparent, a lot like . . . Umbra! Oh my gosh! What happened to him? Bent in fright, I grabbed my forehead to suppress the impulses attacking my brain. What if something happened to him? Did he even come with me into this forbidden wasteland?

There was no path and everything looked the same, no matter where I turned or what direction I faced. How was I ever going to get out? I kept looking and looking. My eyeballs were decoding every shape before me, wishing with all my heart to find any sign to help me break out of this hazy prison. It was dead quiet . . . wait. I didn't like that phrasing. It was completely, utterly silent, making my fears blossom into—

"Don't go that way. Head west! HURRY!"

I had no idea where that voice came from, who it was, or if it was even directed at me, but I ran with tears blurring in my eyes. With all my might, I jetted across the smooth, barren black arena. It was so chilly that I could feel the cold through my shoes and socks as my frantic feet ran.

I wasn't sure if I was in the right direction, but all of a sudden, I fell and my face felt the shivers that my feet had mere seconds before. I tapped my left shoe on the ground before trying to get up to feel a bump, a large smooth bump. That must have been what I tripped over. My right cheek throbbed, my teeth chattered, and my hands were dirty and sandy, making sitting up difficult.

I found the strength to get on my knees, sliding my feet with care behind me as I bent down with my tightening side. The process made my breathing stagger. I gulped and noticed a sickly potent odor dancing around my nose. It seemed to be in front of me. Curious, I opened my eyes to see a pond of strong, thick red liquid.

"It's blood." I heard Umbra's voice right behind me, his body freezing and warm behind my back, but my wide eyes were trapped on the motionlessness of the pond. Shaking, I could not look away from the pool of still, motionless blood, staring at me like common water.

"Where . . . is this place?" I asked in a quivering voice, frightened of knowing the answer, yet I had the sinking feeling Umbra knew.

"To be blunt Stary, we're inside my mind . . ."

Scared and not strong enough to argue, I nodded as slow as a turtle.

Umbra growled in disapproval, not believing my trust in him. "It's your fault! If you didn't fight me trying to help you, this reaction never would have happened. I'm shocked this did happen, but since you are the Spirit Warrior, I suppose messing with your mind would cause a reaction between us. But still! If you would have listened to me, you wouldn't have to see my inner thoughts, the world in my mind!" he huffed, trying to catch his breath.

So, I guessed then that all minds are decorated by a person's personality and memories. That was something that never left anyone; it's a part of all spirits, with a body or bodiless. I also assumed that Umbra had "influenced" humans' decisions before and never had a hitch, controlling everything like a master . . . until me and my spirit powers. Sharp butterflies hit my stomach to the core, the blades of their wings cutting my insides into tiny, unimportant pieces. All I wanted was to leave until Umbra was ready to tell me what he wanted.

"Come on, Stary. Get up before the smell makes you sick."

I felt his hand on my shoulder, firmly supporting me and gently letting me know he was there. I was aware of him and his touch, but I ignored it, not ready yet to stand on my own, not strong enough to either. He must have read my mind for he moved in front of me and I saw his annoyed face and he held his hand out right in front of my eyes, looking very welcoming although his eyes were still piercing.

Like a scared puppy, I locked eyes with his dark honey gaze and grabbed his hand as he lifted me up like I was nothing at all. When we touched, at first, all I felt was tingles of air supporting me like a hand. The sensation was similar to placing your hand above an area filled with static electricity that you can feel shapes and sometimes see sparks, but only for a moment. It was always like this with Umbra and Maren when I first touched them. However, they had a warm essence behind their fuzzy-feeling shapes, their souls. When I focused on this, they became mostly solid, human to me, occasionally flickering their physical form like a messed up light bulb.

In this hollow place, I focused hard on Umbra's essence to guide and calm me. When listening to it in this new way, a tune formed in my head. It was quieter than a dove's wings in flight, but it was natural. It spread tingling sensations into my body, warm sparks and cool crystals colliding inside, I the target. Umbra tugged me hard and the melody was lost, the concerns of our situation returning to my clearing head.

As I was getting up, I noticed huge rocks behind the pool, making a gate. The rocks were rigid, rough, and dark brown. At the far edge, dead center of the pool was a little island large enough for me to curl up in a ball and sleep on. Small plumes of steam rose from the rock island. High above that, again perfectly dead center, was a shield with skulls, actual 3D skulls on it. I guess Umbra didn't lie about hurting people in his past . . . I kept the thought to myself.

He let go of my hand, staring over his left shoulder. He looked hard, stern and unreadable. In an angry whisper, he told me while pointing, "There are bare trees and small cliffs all around the end. The closer we get to them, the whiter the fog will get and it will be easier to see our way. Bad luck for us, we landed in the middle, so finding the moving and only exit will be difficult. I do know it likes to hide south . . . *Where* is the question. Just stick by me."

Still startled over everything I had seen so far and scared of what was to come, the words struggled out of my dehydrated mouth. "But, is there . . . anything . . . I can . . . help . . . with—"

"NO! Just listen to me! It's dangerous here and you don't need to get lost in my past. *You got that Stary?!*" Umbra yelled so loudly that it echoed off the rocks. His whole body was vibrating so fast that I couldn't tell what color his eyes were. Despite his anger, he didn't look like he meant to get so mad.

I gave him a kind look to show I wasn't upset by his reaction, yet it didn't seem to help. He threw his head down toward the ground, veiled by the darkness, his breath near a standstill. He shut his eyes so hard that I thought, no, *knew* he regretted his tone, but not his words.

It was in that second I realized that Umbra was more delicate than I thought he was. He wasn't proud of his past and he was scared of what he would become. Umbra really wanted to change for the better, for the people in his life, but his past was so thick, like the fog, that he couldn't see through it well. He seemed to care about my safety and not because of what Maren thought or because he tried to change or to be a gentleman . . . He cared enough to let me see his emotions, the feelings that pained him, the feelings he tried with all his might to hide. I wanted to hug him, but I was so scared that his beautiful heart would melt in my hand like a lovely snowflake and he'd be lost in his own confusion.

There was at least one thing I could do for him. "Well, let's go," I said firmly, trying to hide my sadness from him and my utter fear of his world. This world was perfect and reflected his personality well—scary and in charge on the outside, but with some patience and searching, one could find a hidden gem. Granted, I haven't found the gem in his mind unless Umbra himself was it, which would not have surprised me.

I was so focused on walking and obeying Umbra, putting my fears behind me, I finally noticed his running footsteps sounded like an enchanted melody, catching up with the slight lead I had. I stopped until he was in front of me, huffing lightly, with big eyes that seemed to be saying, "*I cannot believe you left me and are really listening to me!*"

"I'm supposed to be the leader," Umbra confirmed as he tapped my head. A small wry smile crossed his face, a true smile that made his beautiful dark eyes light up.

I bowed like I was bending over for the Queen of England. "After you, sire," I said, showing off a cheesy grin.

He rolled his eyes and blew a loose piece of his curly and gorgeous black hair out of his eye before giving me a dazzling, breathless smile of his own that made him look beautiful. He turned his back away from me and inched forward. I followed with a paced jog until something enthralling caught my eye: a twinkle that was small, but promising. I stopped to look again to see the small yellow-and-white starlight, but it was gone. Whatever it was, it gave me a sense of hope. Umbra called for me then because I was lagging behind. For the time being, I ignored the possible make-believe light in Umbra's mind.

As I followed behind the echo of Umbra's footsteps, the area became more focused and deadly. The tip-tap of my sneakers boomed loudly for a mere breathless second before getting sucked into the blackness. My feet became heavy, disappearing into the eternal night. It was hard to contain my fear of the bareness that seemed so lonely somehow. Yet, it was Umbra's world, what was left of his being, and he continued forward with no emotion, never looking back.

"We're halfway there," his emotionless voice rang. His uncomfortable words were still captivating to me for it reminded me he was still there. Our footsteps blended into an odd, unique, stunning pattern, which made my body feel weightless compared to my dragging feet. My heartbeat increased, but not from fright or confusion, but from an overwhelming joy that I was with Umbra.

He could have left me. Although I still thought the entire situation was his fault, I was being stubborn before with his help. It was just the way he presented the fact I was wrong. I had no worries of being wrong; I was a lot. I always seemed to be pushing him away, hiding . . . hiding from something I didn't want to admit. I wasn't 100% sure what that was, but I had to work harder. I had to try for deep, deep down, I had to admit Umbra was a good person and I wanted him to know that, no matter how easy he let me push him or how exquisite that strange melody was that went off in my head whenever we were together—

Zip! A clouded white streak whizzed in front of Umbra and me. I gasped, confused as to why Umbra cringed and his fists tightened. I looked around to see if I could get a better glance at the cloud-like line. The streak zigzagged patterns all over the vastness of Umbra's mind and with each movement of its dance, the area became brighter and much easier to see through the fog, although it was still there. A rustle came from our right and zipped again, sneakier and quicker than before. I heard the patter of feet. Dust rose from the cold ground. Then, it appeared in front of Umbra.

"Get behind me Stary!" Umbra half-yelled, but it was in a deep and comforting protective tone that made my cheeks flush. He flung his left arm, straight as an arrow from his flawless chest for me to cover behind and his right hand became a fist, ready to attack. When the dust began to clear, the bright light was shining—the light I saw earlier!

It was whiter than ever with stunning rays shooting every which way. Even Umbra had to lower his gaze. All at once, the dust was gone like a bad plague and the light appeared to be something small but human-like. There, smiling at Umbra, standing at about two and a half feet tall, was a . . . gnome. I had to blink my eyes several times to make sure the universe was not playing a practical joke on me.

With a sweet, heart-shaped face and cheeks the loveliest shade of pink, he spoke to us in a high-pitched and pleasant voice. "Welcome my dear friends. I am so sorry for frightening you. Please accept my apology." He gave a lowly bow.

I gestured that it wasn't necessary with my hands, but I snapped upward with a kind grin. He looked just like the gnomes one sees in fairy tales as children: a long, white flow of fluffy hair came from his chin that almost reached the floor, a bright red cone hat hid more white hair, and he was wearing a gown I supposed, the most beautiful and perfect tone of sky blue I had ever seen, prettier than any amazing spring day. Of course, he had the reddest of red boots too, which matched his charming hat. I adored him right away.

I looked over at Umbra, who had the weirdest look on his face. His eyes darted with frustration toward the adorable little man, his face unimaginably tense, and his jaw clenched way too tight, but I saw no anger. It appeared he was . . . embarrassed? His whole body leaned back like he barely dodged a punch and was frozen in uncertainty.

"Who . . . or *what* are you?" Umbra struggled to say.

"Good Master, I am a part of your mind. I represent cheer, happiness, and light. I am surprised to see you here, especially with someone."

I bent down like the gnome was a preschool child. I placed my hands on my hurt knees and looked at him as level as my back could bend. "That explains why you shone so brightly. Since you represent all those wonderful traits, your heart blinded us with light, correct, good sir?"

I heard Umbra gasp in surprise from behind.

The gnome giggled and grabbed my right hand with tenderness before rubbing it against his old-looking, but surprisingly smooth, left cheek. "That is correct, my sweet girl. Master Umbra is really lucky to have you here with him." He paused to smile once more. I could feel the tension growing from Umbra behind me, but I didn't care because I liked my helpful, new friend.

He released my hand and continued. "You are Lady Stary I am guessing? I have seen a lot of pictures of you recently, like Miss Maren—"

"THAT'S IT!" Umbra thundered, shocking both of us. Charging like a mad man, he ran past me, almost pushing me out the way and raised a fist at the gnome's head. "I am going to destroy this accursed thing! There is no way in *hell* that this cheerful punk is a part of my emotions *or* me. I would never act like that, a weakling, like him. Time to die you waste of space!"

Umbra's hand suddenly began to glow emerald green, sizzling, making the hairs on my arms stand up straight. I was locked in panic by the image of Umbra as a monster, a killing machine like the vision of him striking me with the katana.

"NO!" I cried at the top of my lungs, becoming blurred by stinging moisture building in my eyes.

Umbra snapped in dismay, looking at me with silent disbelief and concern. Everything about him, from the way he looked at me to his pose, was all too perfect, all too precious to be real or to vanish forever. Although it seemed I was trying to beat the stream of time itself, I grabbed his arm as tight as I could to hold him back and not lose him.

"Umbra, please don't! He's a part of you and he's done nothing wrong. Please . . ." My voice was dying, sobs building in my throat. With all my might, I somehow held them in. I wasn't able to look into his dark eyes in fear I would snap and cry in front of him.

He brushed me off like I was weightless, making me fall on my knees hard. He aimed again, glaring once more at the little, fearless gnome, but his face and tone weren't as angry. "Stary, I have to. Someone like me having a pointless emotion like this . . . It's unnecessary and annoying."

"But, Umbra, you could hurt yourself. It's a part of your mind, your being." I grabbed on to him again, not as tight, but to confirm I was not going to give in.

He looked at me with rage, his dark honey brown eyes now bright amber red, almost blazing themselves. "Who cares? I don't. As long as he's gone, I'll suffer the pain and be more like the me I am meant to be according to society. Goodbye gnome man!" Umbra made the glow on his hand bigger and more dangerous-looking. He looked at me not with fury, but a look that I didn't understand before he ignored me for his battle position.

"I would!" I yelled, tears flowing like rainfall on the cold black abyss of Umbra's mind.

Umbra stopped in his tracks, staring vacantly at the world in front of him. Although his glowing fist was slowly fading, it was lighter around his body aura. I felt his muscles relax, but they began to form goose bumps and he shivered.

"Umbra, you're not a monster . . . you're not . . . and I don't want you to ever be one like you think you are. Don't destroy him! You have a good soul and light inside you. I'm the Spirit Warrior that's meant to save you, I know! Please . . . Um-Umbra . . ."

I looked up at him. His eyes flickered with confusion and his hands trembled.

I locked onto his haunting eyes as they somewhat looked into mine. "You can't destroy the goodness in you for you have always been good . . . You have free will. You *choose* to be good! Umbra . . . PLEASE!" I shrieked. The words were hard to come out of my mouth, but surprisingly, easily flowed out of my heart. My voice was half-destroyed due to shouting and swelled with pain, but I swallowed it down.

That was when Umbra looked directly at me, my cheeks damp with tears I could not control. He still looked distraught, but his eyes were so light that they reflected the color of mine—the dark blue of the stormy ocean, the eyes I knew I shouldn't have from my gene pool, but do. His mouth was slightly open, his breath huffy, short, smelling shockingly cool and sweet. Umbra's perfect face was graceful and his cheeks a medium shade of crimson, exquisite against his tan skin.

I lost myself in those ten seconds, that endless moment where Umbra and I were trapped in the swirl of each other for unknown reasons. I didn't remember what happened, couldn't see the place I was at or anything around me. All I wanted was to look at Umbra's priceless face forever.

The happy giggle of the gnome interrupted our moment, but we came back to reality as slow as we could, sliding our hands over the other's arm. His touch may have been tingling air, but the warmth, the chill, and the emotion was excruciatingly amazing to my heartbeat. Our eyes never left each other until the gnome stepped forward. That's when I noticed Umbra's left arm was normal again and dangled lifelessly at his side.

"I suppose you can live . . . for now, cretin. But, you are the least important thing here," Umbra affirmed.

"Oh, thank you my kind master!" The little gnome jumped up, trying to hug Umbra, but Umbra turned his head away, giving an annoyed sigh. The gnome couldn't reach Umbra's arms! I found it quite adorable. Umbra opened one eye directed at me and gave a playful and attractive half-smile.

Unable to stop it, fresh, but silent tears released from my reddened eyes. This time, they were from happiness and relief because the fight was over and Umbra's world was not as scary as when we entered it. Umbra looked at me concerned, his soft lips in a perfect line.

"Lady Stary . . ."

I looked to see my new friend in front of me, gesturing me to come down to his level. I gave a weak smile and did as I was told. With his pointer finger, he brushed my right cheek. Suddenly, the light we encountered earlier was glowing once more from his chest, but it was controlled this time and a small speckle of light came from his finger and a tiny, shocking sensation tapped my cheek. Like a rag doll brought to life, I rose up. Like magic, my tears evaporated into thin air and a wave of unfamiliar, warm, and amazing emotions flowed into my body and ended their journey into my heart.

I grabbed my chest, bending forward a little. My body tingled with affectionate bliss, my blue eyes sparkling as bright as God's sun in the reflective floor I could now see below me. A huge smile I could not control crossed my delicate face. "My heart . . . it's so nice and warm," I sighed happily before standing up and staring straight at Umbra with the same angelic smile.

He was caught off guard, but his puzzled look was mild and welcoming. He walked a few steps toward me when the gnome stopped him with a hand gesture. Stunned, we both blinked and looked down at him.

Umbra's light gnome pointed his finger up and smiled knowingly. "I did make your tears vanish, my dear, for your arm and knees were not feeling right, correct?" He winked as I blushed that he noticed. Then, he went on. "But, I am only half responsible for your happy heart . . ." The gnome then hooted as I gazed at him, perplexed.

Umbra caught his breath, his face puffed like a fish and a rosy patch colored his cheeks. Umbra was about to say something when from out of nowhere, the gnome laced his small hand through mine and dragged me forward, running and giggling with utter delight. "Come! I want to take you to my house." His joy of inviting me made me glad, so I looked back at Umbra, shrugged, and allowed myself to be pulled into another unknown world, but this time I wasn't scared.

"No thanks! Stary, get back here!" Umbra's yell echoed behind us.

I looked back to see him upset, his arms crossed around his strong chest. He reminded me of a sheriff who was mad his laws were not being enforced. Yet, I was too excited to pass the invitation up and Umbra had to come. From the look in his eyes, he had no idea about the gnome's home or what to expect either.

"Come on Umbra!" I returned his echoed call with cheer and signaled with my free hand for him to follow us. If he didn't, I was sure I would lose him. With a sigh, he mouthed, "Whatever," and slapped his arms against his sides as he followed us in a calm, swift walk.

For a few minutes, the mysterious road ahead of us looked the same as every inch of wasteland before it. However, with every foot, it got lighter, less foggy, and more alluring. Out of nowhere, appearing out of the fog, there was a circular pool of mystical clean water. White clouds clung to the airspace above the sparkling pond and huge, mossy rocks surrounded the background of the water, acting as a field of protection. Although it was not as vast as Umbra's pool of blood, it caught my eye; everything was so pure, enchanting, like in a fairy tale forest. As we walked towards it, the moss seemed to glow with a mixture of greens, greens so flawless they reminded me of a fresh box of crayons. The healthy looking water shimmered into ripples of beautiful dodge blue. I was expecting a unicorn to run through to get a drink, standing on the crescent-moon shaped opening of land to retrieve the sweet source of life.

So lost in all the unknown wonder, it took me awhile to notice I was being dragged behind the angelic pond and was stepping . . . down? Confused, I looked downward to see the gnome leading me down a speckled silver stepping stone path below the water, but a river of water was swirling around us with each step. Thin, cream clouds in an array of shapes followed us as well, completing the pretty, mysterious world. I could barely hear Umbra's feet for he was so gracefully fast and my mind wasn't paying attention on anything other than where I was going. Still, the ringing patter of Umbra's steps fitted into the world, no matter how little the sound was.

Then, I stopped, wide-eyed in fear that I did something wrong, but then I realized by looking at the gnome's expression that we had reached our destination. There, in a small area, surrounded by bright green grass, was the cutest little brown cottage with a white-trimmed roof and a red chimney with warm smoke coming out of it. That must be where the clouds came from! It was right out of a book, looking welcoming with its charm. It was simple with its own dull light source. Although Umbra's darkness was surrounding the exterior, it was light enough to see every little darling detail of my short friend's home.

"Welcome, my friends, to my cottage! Please, follow me and I will make us some berry tea," said our pleasant host.

I stood there, trying to soak in the new environment. It was hard to think that it was part of Umbra's mind! Umbra stood next to me, standing firm and alert, yet his face matched the same disbelieving emotion I felt, which I found amusing. His eyes were soft but his body rigid.

"Hard to believe this is a part of you?" I said jokingly, lowering my gaze.

"Uh-huh . . . ," Umbra said with his mouth open and slowly nodding. We looked at each other for a split second and shrugged. I gave a sarcastic grin and he replied by raising an eyebrow. When we noticed the gnome had left and the wooden door was opened, we carefully walked on the flattened grass path, our strides matching.

The door was only two inches above my head and Umbra had to duck a little, making him give a disapproving look in the gnome's direction. Inside, it was crowded with shelves of cute, colorful, and fun little trinkets. They were everywhere! Flowers of every shape were spread throughout the one room house. Yellow buttercups seemed to be the most common. Ladybugs lay sleeping on the brown walls, adding to the enchantment.

There was only one light source, which came from three small square windows at the top of the walls near the ceiling. A sweet odor of cinnamon filled the crisp air and tickled my nose. There was also a warm brick fireplace, a small and cozy black stove, a comfy looking bed on the opposite side of the house, and a sink next to the doorway.

A polished wooden table was by the stove with matching chairs and fluffy seat cushions in deep red. Our gnome friend signaled us to sit down as he prepared and poured our tea. Umbra refused the seat with a rolling of his eyes and went to a dark corner in the kitchen area, leaning against a semi-dusty open area where a broom was. With his arms crossed, Umbra adjusted his head to the left to get more comfortable and not hit it on the ceiling. The way the light hit him, the look on his face, the lean of his body made him look almost sexy. I mentally hit myself at the thought, but when I blinked and looked at Umbra again, the feeling was still there.

I sat down, lowering my head to not bump anything. Before I could really get settled, an adorable white cup with purple and yellow daisies and a matching plate were placed in front of me. Steam streamed from the light reddish-brown liquid in the cup and the smell of wild berries hit my senses in an instant, already soothing my throat. A sip and my body was once again warmed by the charm of this gnome's magic.

"I hope you like it, Lady Stary," the gnome said, smiling at me from across the table, his hands placed on his cheeks and elbows on the table. He looked at Umbra with delight. I could tell he was about to ask if he would like a taste of his proud creation, but Umbra shook his head once rudely before leaning his head against the wall and closing his eyes. Lines creased his forehead, making him look stressed.

"Delicious," I complimented my new friend with a grin before allowing the vapors to once more enter my soul to comfort me. I then took in the aroma, closing my eyes and sighing. For a few more moments, my troubles seemed to not exist.

Having some time, I looked around again, scanning the amiable surroundings. Then, I noticed behind the table, hidden in forest-looking plants, was a matching thin table with a lacy white tablecloth. But that was not what had grabbed my attention.

In the center of that table was a large and beautiful picture of Maren, her beauty and smile shining in the sun. However, this was a different pose from all the pictures that were in newspapers or online. She was facing the camera, looking over her shoulder, her body turned, only showing the upper part of her trademark blue party dress. Regardless, she looked as delicate and pretty as ever.

"Maren . . . ," I whispered. However, my surprise was discovered.

"Ah, yes! Miss Maren is important in this world. That is the table of all of Master Umbra's dearest thoughts."

Umbra opened his eyes, surprise all over his face. Was the surprise because I found out his secret or because he didn't even know about this table of treasures from his life? Well, I heard we only use 10% of our minds. Who knows what the rest of it hides?

"Oh!" I looked at the table. Beside Maren's darling picture was a small golden box that seemed to have eight shining and tiny gems around its lid that were shooting eight different colors toward the ceiling, a small machine-like square made of a hard silver metal that had a moon on top, a sky blue leather glove, and a golden wedding band with some rusty edges. All of the objects were pretty and must have been symbols of sweet moments in Umbra's life. The thought made me smile on the inside.

However, from the vibe he was giving, I knew I wasn't going to find out the meaning of the items for a long while, if ever. Then, the gnome snorted and nudged his head to the far left. Puzzled, I did as I was told and noticed, half-hidden in darkness and with a clear glare, was another picture about two-thirds the size of Maren's and I could just make out a human shape that was not Maren.

Interested and unable to control my curiosity, I strolled towards the image. When I did, I heard Umbra move, making a noise against the wall. I glanced over at him to see that his breath was caught in the back of his throat and his eyes were widened like he was about to be shot. Still, I ventured on, sliding my hand over the smooth tabletop for support.

I finally got in front of the picture, but it was still hard to make out. Scared to touch it, I narrowed my eyes and looked at it closer. The figure was a girl, with long semi-dark hair, straight as a board. She was in the same pose as Maren, but her head was cocked a tad to the left, making her look younger than Maren. She seemed too familiar . . . then, it hit me. But, it couldn't be true . . .

"I told you I saw your face lately, Lady Stary . . ." was all I heard from behind.

I gently picked up the photo by its wooden frame, tracing my fingers over the smooth surface. In the dim light, I could see it really was . . .

"It's me . . . ," my breathy voice trembled.

Umbra gasped. I turned, my whole body storming with several different emotions as I held the picture against my chest to control my increasing heartbeat. I had never seen him so nervous. His eyes moved everywhere with small dabs of moisture in them as he leaned forward, his hand trying to stop me from my deed, but it froze, seeing he was too late.

"Umbra . . . ," I said lightly and grinned, although I had no idea what was going on in his head even though I was in it. I learned that Umbra didn't hate me and for that, I respected him more and was thrilled to learn more about him. It even made me happier than I could ever remember being. Our eyes locked once again, almost like a cheesy romantic film and no matter how much I tried to focus, I couldn't and I didn't fight it. I wanted to stay like that until cruel fate made the moment end once again.

Umbra ducked his head in the darkness, hiding his attractive face. His breath was heavy and staggered, like he was trying to hold back words. I wanted to go and embrace him like he did Maren that afternoon in my room, but I knew I could never compare to her. That, for some reason, bothered me. Nevertheless, my heart floated. I went to him. It was a force too brilliant and powerful for me to control. However, I knew it wasn't coming from Umbra's tricks or his mind . . . it came from inside me.

With my left hand still pressing the picture against my chest, I freed my right hand and very carefully, brushed his right cheek. Although I could only feel air, I made out the shape of it and the sensation, the pulse coming from it flew inside me and made my blood race like a dam had burst. It was painful, scary, and incredible all at the same time. The sound of water gushing out flooded my ears and against its current was the melody I grew familiar with, the one that seemed to be part of the me that was with Umbra, as if he had awakened something inside me, something that craved only him.

Umbra was shocked, his eyes twinkling as he allowed me to lift his head to gaze into my eyes. He looked surprised but accepting. His liquid chocolate gaze trapped me in a spell. I saw my image absorbed in his eyes. Was it possible he was under the same spell I was?

"Thank you . . . ," I whispered honestly as we looked at each other, both standing still. Umbra's face grew redder, but relaxed, and was the gentlest I had ever seen it. Then, he lowered his gaze an inch to look at me more directly and he smiled the most gorgeous, no teeth showing smile I had ever seen on any guy. I was so lost in it and in his beauty that I was shocked to notice he was tracing his right hand over mine in a slow manner. Soon, but not soon enough, I felt his captivating fingers lace in between the gaps on my own hand, the one still on his cheek.

I inhaled, burning up from all the friction that was surging through my body. He started a pattern of backing off from touching me, but then tried to reach for me again, the seconds ticking away, killing me with yearning. He didn't squeeze my hand, but I felt his grip, his pleasing grip tightening around my small and shaking fingers.

Next, startling me, he leaned into my hand. He closed his eyes, still smiling lovingly and he whispered, "I'm honestly not sure why it's there . . ." His steamy breath hit my hand, making my insides melt. I forgot for a second he was a spirit; he felt so alive.

I was about to say, "I don't care. I'm just glad I am," when suddenly, he lowered his face so his nose was almost touching the palm of my hand. With his eyes closed and a smile still on his face, he inhaled my aroma. I thought I heard him purr as I watched his chest rise and fall, but I might have been dreaming that. I hope I was imagining that last part . . . I feared I was sweating!

He straightened, opened his eyes and started leaning closer and closer to my face until we were about two inches apart. By habit, I leaned back until I hit the stove, but then I gave in willingly. He looked playful and devious as a smirk curved on his lips, the sun shining on his bouncy, yet somewhat spiky, hair. I thought my body was going to die on me the way it was moving like an earthquake.

With his lean body straight and mine leaning back, both of us lost in the side trip to our spirit fighting cause, we failed to see the sun getting darker, but the source of light was coming down in green balls. Stunned, we both tilted up to look at the window, shocked by the new rays. We let go not as fast as we should have, but at the same time, making my heart sink lower than the Titanic. Still, I ran to follow Umbra outside with little footsteps behind me from our host. There, falling from the darkening sky were hundreds of beautiful, small balls of light, glowing like fireflies and bewitching the already fairy-tale-like region.

I "wowed" stupidly with a huge grin on my face. The light green fragments reflected in my eyes and spun around a few times, wanting to land in my outstretched arms. I bet I looked like a foolish child to Umbra. He only sighed and followed me with a causal walk, looking up to the heavens of his own world.

Our gnome friend was by the doorframe, beaming, and pointing up. "One is your way out Master Umbra. Look up, hold your hand out, and the right one will come to you."

Like trained animals, we did as we were told. Umbra lifted his palm out to catch our way home and like a magnet, the right one drifted down, humming as it stopped right above Umbra's right hand. The light was green like the others, but brighter, and had a circle of pure white around it. For a few seconds, all we could do was stare until it blinded us and grew about six and a half feet both ways in front of us.

Our gnome friend hopped to us cheerfully, his little hands behind his back. "Have a safe journey Master Umbra and thank you for sparing me. I will not fail you." He bowed.

I giggled and Umbra *hmph*ed. Our friend continued. "I am so lucky to have finally met you, Lady Stary. I can see why you are here."

I smiled sincerely and shook his hand before turning towards the light with Umbra. "Thank you so much for the tea. It was so yummy. And for everything else."

"Do not lose Lady Stary, Master Umbra. The light source is tricky . . ."

It seemed true for the light was getting smaller and floating toward the air.

"I won't," he answered with a slight edge. In a smooth motion, he rubbed his pointer finger over my right hand and shyly grabbed it. First our hands were cupped and then little-by-little, became laced. I grinned to myself, but hid it because I was frightened he would feel my heartbeat. A sense of panicked breathing made an embarrassing rhythm rise within me that went along with my blushing face too well. He was mostly air, but he was still a soul with warmth and feelings; that was a sensation I could not shake off no matter how many times he held my hand. I nodded at him, glancing to tell him I was ready to depart.

We walked into the light, absorbing the glow from its powers. With a loud boom, we rocketed upward, ascending into the space of Umbra's mind. After a few seconds, the ascent became a snail's pace. As we rose, glittering specks of silver and white circled us, full of dazzle, making me fly even higher inside. I looked down to get one last look of the amazing and unique place and, of course, my new gnome friend when I noticed him running towards us, half-startled.

"Lady Stary!" he hollered half-foolishly.

With his eyes large and a helpful small smile, he gave me a departing message: "Only a light that can accept the darkness will finish the quest of life, no matter how long it takes . . ."

"Wait!" I shouted, wide-eyed in dread and longing to know the meaning. In a blink of an eye and with a roar of thunder, I was back in my dad's classroom. My vision was clouded with swirling colors then rays of black destroyed them. Those soon evaporated to restore my natural sight. My head hurt and my body was full of aches and pains. Little by little, I lifted my head up from my desk, which felt like it weighed a thousand pounds. I shook it hard and blinked before getting comfortable back in the known world, but it was still too bright for my adjusting eyes to fully see my surroundings.

"Stary . . . ," a whisper echoed in my head.

Was it Umbra again?

"Stary!" it said even louder.

Finally, I snapped back into place to see my father, sitting on his desk, leaning toward me with confused and worried eyes. I slowly moved my head to see the whole class looking at me, awaiting my response.

"Stary . . . are you all right?"

"Ummmmm, yeah. I'm fine. I was just . . . a little lost in a thought. I'm sorry, sir . . ." I sounded tired, but tried to remain cheerful.

My dad nodded and continued his lesson.

I leaned over to ask Allen how long I was out and he said only a few seconds of blank staring. That comforted me; at least I wasn't that noticeable. Maybe mind time and real time were different. I would have to ask Umbra . . . Umbra! Where was he? I looked around behind me to see if he was there, but nothing. I exhaled, trying not to worry about it and restarted my notes.

Suddenly, my paper had a message in pencil on it that was not there a second before. I leaned over to see it read:

Sorry . . .

It was Umbra! Somehow, I knew it. I was happy because even if it was a scary quest at first, I learned more about him and knew he liked me as a person, even if our moment at the gnome's house twisted my heart still.

I wrote back, blushing a little.

It was practically my fault. I'm sorry for being so stubborn and next time you give advice, I'll consider it.

Soon, I got another message under mine in bold letters.

Have fun?!

I laughed quietly and responded to his message as honestly as possible.

Yeah. Your mind is interesting, but never again!

11

SWAYING TO THE MUSIC IN MY HEAD, I WAS COMFORTED THE REST of the day by the fact I was safely back at school. Giddy with joy, I did favors for everyone without a second thought. I wasn't 100% sure why I was so thrilled, but I was. My friends stared at me with dumbfounded faces, blinking numerous times, which made me laugh more. I didn't care; I was so happy to be back in the real world, my home front.

My stomach got all tied up in knots when I thought about where I went. I gave up trying to figure it out. In the blink of an eye, school was out and I was waiting to go home with Dad. Umbra and Maren decided to stay close to me and climbed in the back of the car. They both paled and looked nervous like they were just arrested. I kept turning around and chuckling, which made my dad check back there to ask what I was laughing at. This only made me laugh until my eyes were wet and my ribs ached.

Throwing off my backpack, I grinned to my mom and ran to my room and slammed the door, leaving a trail of wind. I wish I could have seen my mom's face! I flung on the bed, loving the temporary feeling of being weightless, deciding it was time.

"Maren! Umbra! You can come out now."

Maren and Umbra popped out of the wall and landed gently on the floor. I tilted my head up to look at them, smiling. Maren was between Umbra and me, confused as to why we were so excited.

She gulped to ask, "What is going on?"

I giggled a little bit and looked at Umbra. He actually gave me a handsome half-smile and winked behind Maren's back, making me snicker harder. Maren turned in circles, mystified, her poor hair becoming messier with every spin.

I decided to be nice and looked up at her, taking her hands. "Maren, Umbra and I went on a trip today."

She looked at me like a child being required to spell a college level word. "A trip?" she asked in a high-pitched voice full of puzzlement.

All I did was nod and pause to make her wonder where, trying not to laugh again. I saw Umbra bend over, holding his side as his hand covered his mouth. He made a "spa" sound, biting his lip hard after the sound came out. This instantly made me smile brighter as Maren twisted her body to gaze at him.

"Where did you go?" she demanded in a whisper. Her poor eyes were wide with nervousness. I couldn't be mean to her anymore.

"Umbra and I went inside his mind today," I said calmly and chipper.

Then, as stylishly as I could, I told my story about how Umbra went inside me to make me change my answer, the travel, meeting the gnome, and going to his house . . . the general stuff to make the quest seem more compelling. I left out things like how I was feeling when Umbra touched me, my picture on the special table, and what the gnome told me before I departed. I didn't need to worry Maren like that. Her eyes were huge the whole time with her mouth agape, nodding a few times. Umbra didn't say much, but he focused on her expressions. When I told her that was it, I shrugged and smiled at her, hoping to be forgiven for worrying her.

"Umbra! How dare you do that to Stary?" she said full of authority, her voice cracking and her face a little red from her trying to be tough. I found it adorable. "You could have hurt Stary, or something . . . something terrible could have happened. You . . . you were lucky to have that kind gnome help you . . ."

She looked away. I guess there were risks of us being trapped in there. I was aware of them at first, but before I realized it, I calmed down and was able to believe I would get out since Umbra was leading the way. I completely trusted his judgment.

Umbra lifted Maren's head up by cupping his fingers under her pale chin. His eyes were shining and he grinned tenderly, not showing his teeth. "I know Maren and I'm sorry. But, I didn't let anything happen to Stary . . . or myself. Please don't be angry. I'll be more careful, honest." He held his hand up to swear and patted her thin shoulders. "No more worrying, okay? It's bad for your skin." He winked at both of us. I chuckled in the back of my throat and Maren sighed, giving us a defeated smile.

"So, Stary?" She came running to me like a ballet dancer, bouncing on the bed next to me. I was startled that she looked so excited, like we were at a sleepover telling secrets. "Was the gnome's house really welcoming?"

I placed my index finger under my chin and thought, looking at the ceiling to contain myself before gleefully responding, "Oh yes. It was sweet and inviting. Although, I found the inside sort of girly looking." I said the last part with a hiss and winked at her like it was not meant for Umbra to hear, although he did. Maren laughed like a pixie and Umbra stood up straight to defend his supposed honor.

"Hey! That doesn't mean anything, Moon, and you know it!" He pointed back at me.

My finger challenged him and I pointed it even closer to him. "Whatever you say, Umbra. I know deep down you're a softie, like a melting chocolate chip cookie."

He stepped backward and flung his arms to hit the wall with a tap like he was disgusted. "I don't like chocolate. It's unhealthy and girly!"

Maren blinked with a blank expression on her face. "I like chocolate . . ."

"Oh, I do too!" I said almost too loudly and Maren and I started chatting about our favorite sweets, pretending to ignore Umbra. He didn't seem to like that too much and grunted loudly. I looked at him with a serious face. "Excuse you. Anyway . . ." and went on chatting with Maren about candy.

Umbra stepped forward and cleared his throat grossly by us. I moaned and gave up, acknowledging him. "Yes? You could have been in this conversation, but you don't eat chocolate because you are too concerned about your weight." I motioned at him smugly and smirked on the inside. I was having too much fun.

"*What*?!" he shouted. Maren whispered to me that Umbra worked really hard at being in shape and was not like a woman. I leaned in her ear to tell her I knew. Still confused, she only nodded and waited for a response.

"Well . . . ," Umbra said bent down to the side, his eyes shut and his eyebrows twitching in a funny dance. "At least I don't have to watch my weight . . ." He directed his mocking gaze at me.

I stood up and acted insulted. "How dare you? Girls are sensitive about that." With that, I nudged Maren to make him see he was outnumbered.

"See? I'm not sensitive therefore I'm not girly." He confirmed the fact with a hard nod.

"Vegetables don't help your soul!" I shouted at him.

He blinked at me, stupefied.

I wondered, horrified, where in hobgoblins did that come from.

Maren was resting her arms and head on the end of my bed, looking at us like she was observing animals at the zoo. "I think Stary means that chocolate is said to make one feel better when one is hurt emotionally, Umbra."

My life was over as I shook madly and my eyes began to sting when suddenly, I heard a hardy noise next to me. It was deep, but not bass deep. It had a supported breath that blended with the sound perfectly, making it sound even more wonderful.

I looked up to see Umbra covering his mouth, edges of a smile peeking out, and his shoulders were shaking like mad. Finally, he gave up. There, I heard it: a true, sincere laugh. This was Umbra's real laugh and it was the most beautiful sound that my ears had ever heard. I wanted to allow it to ring forever, imprint it like a footprint on my heart. If I could hold it in a bottle, I gladly would for eternity. I couldn't help staring; the sound had put me in a swirling spell.

He turned away from us a tad, again trying to cover his mouth, but failed epically. He accepted defeat. His mouth opened and laughter spilled out as he rocked back and forth, bending over and clutching his stomach. I thought I saw tears in the corner of his eyes, but his face was so red, it was hard to tell.

I heard Maren whisper that he has a nice laugh in a question form to me. Still hypnotized, I nodded and whispered, "Yeah," I think, and continued to watch the natural wonder. Soon, his laugh became softer, harder, and he began to cough as it subsided, heaving in between. By womanly instinct, I stepped forward to check on him, reaching my hands outward in a slow motion, but he halted me, waving his hand to inform me he was all right.

"Aha, ha, ha . . . Awwwww, whoa, okay . . . whew . . . ," Umbra said in between breathing, still bent down as he finished wiping the small amount of moisture in his sparkling eyes. Abruptly, he stopped and stood up straight to stare right into my face, which caught me off guard. Umbra smiled a huge smile, teeth sparkling more than the stars and it was as wide as his face, lighting it up completely in amazing splendor. His eyes reflected the same brightness and twinkled like diamonds. I gasped, my heart shaking against my ribcage. I thought I was going to die from a heart attack. All I wanted then was to take a picture of that smile and stare at it until it was my time to depart. Did spirits show up in pictures? I didn't care! I wanted to try.

Umbra spoke to me, his smile still staying. "Ah . . . God, Moon! You really are a riot . . ."

His words were sharp, but his tone was relaxed.

I tried to move the corner of my lips to agree, but couldn't. I was scared of the feelings surfacing inside me, taking over my body like an illness.

Nothing, nothing in this world had ever made me feel like that, not even Credence. I knew I cared for Credence, but other than him, no feeling was close. But . . . Umbra's laugh, his smile . . . it had nothing compared to Credence, which was remarkable.

I stepped backward as if controlled by a thread. My mind was dizzy and my face so red that I could see it clearly reflected on my white walls. Umbra looked worried and he leaned forward to check on me. I wanted to yell at him, "No! If you touch me, if you look at me like that again, like you actually care, I . . . I might die."

It was hard to imagine life without Maren and Umbra. I wanted to plead that they stay, but that would be cruel. I mean, when he was mean to me, yeah, I was hurt, but I would be sad when he left. I wish I had never heard that beautiful song, that chord of melancholic desire that played in my soul every time Umbra did something incredible, which seemed like it was more often. Once he was gone, I would never feel that misery again and that pain was the thing I would miss the most, for some abnormal reason. That was my mind talking. My heart . . . well, I won't go there. It was having a tug-of-war fight with my brain and my body was the battlefield.

I sat down on my bed, breathing deep, but signaled to them I was fine. Stress: it's a killer! Umbra still looked dazed, his magical expression all gone because of me and that made me feel like punishing myself. Maren patted my hand and she changed the subject.

"So, I was on Umbra's important table, you say? That makes me so happy!" She placed her smooth hand on her ivory cheek that hinted a pale rose pink.

"Well, of course Maren! You're my best friend and I would do anything for you, so why wouldn't you be there, dead center?" Umbra stated full of gallant pride, not one bit ashamed.

Maren ran to hug him zealously like their first afternoon with me. Their faces were both relaxed with slight and enthralling smiles as they embraced. I couldn't look at them. One, it would have been rude and they needed time together and two, well, I just couldn't without going bananas!

I guess I didn't have to worry about the weird stirrings inside me after witnessing their contact. Umbra was attractive after all and we were starting to get along. Maybe it was normal when one gets close to a member of the opposite sex; emotions come along with it to mix us up. Plus, Maren was the most remarkable thing ever, so he must . . . well, he must . . . oh! It was too hard to say, even in my own mind! He must have and still . . . love her. Yet, he did say "best friend" . . . but can you *fall in love* with your best friend? And how did Maren feel? I could never be mad at her. My brain was hurting and thinking like that was making my stomach ache worse!

Maren ran to me, scaring me and making me fly on my bedspring. She giggled as I rubbed my scalp, embarrassed. "Stary, is Umbra not wonderful?" Her smile was so pure. I had to answer her honestly, which I did, matching her expression to the letter.

She then jumped up and down on her knees. She reminded me of how my brother would find any excuse to come in my room to bounce on my springy bed. "I am so happy you and Umbra are friends now . . . I bet someday soon, you will be on that table as well Stary!"

"Wha—?!" Umbra and I said at the same time as we stared at her, both red. How were we going to answer that? A wide smile crossed Maren's face as she laughed without opening her mouth, waiting for one of us to answer. It seemed like behind that angelic face, she knew something . . . Umbra almost beat me to it.

"Maren . . . you shouldn't . . . say . . . ," then he trailed off, looking at the rug. He looked so uncomfortable. Maybe he was scared that Maren would think she would someday be replaced by me, someone they hadn't known long. But, maybe . . . he did . . .

I sat straight up on my bed, crossed my legs and grinned, showing the smile I practiced for hours before school picture day. "That would . . . I mean . . ." I became shy and had to tilt my head to the left to hide the rose creeping on my cheeks. I must have gotten Umbra's attention for he stared at me with wonder.

"I would be so honored if I got to be on that table . . . I would be, well . . . one of the luckiest girls ever born on God's glorious world . . ." My voice was quiet, but clear and candid. No one could charge me for lying. It was the truth, no matter how one viewed it.

Umbra was red all over, but it was an even and gorgeous tone to match his shocked face. "I . . ." He stopped when I looked at him from the corner of my eye. His mouth was somewhat opened and his hand reached toward me, but he was frozen in a sea of uncertainty.

Maren smiled once more and nudged me before stating it was time for them to go. "Come Umbra." She called him like a puppy, but Umbra was still stuck. Maren slapped her hand on his forehead to pull him back, but he didn't move much. "Stary needs her some good rest to get better." Maren looked at me over her thin shoulder, looking like a goddess.

"Uh . . . yeah . . . ," Umbra replied.

Maren grabbed his hand to drag his body away, but his face was trapped in the room, looking at mine until the last possible second.

When they left, I sighed, groaned loudly, and flung my body backwards to land on my comfortable *Lion King* pillow. My body had the worst goose bumps and I needed some high-quality sleep, even if it was only seven in the evening. Before I knew it, no matter how much I fought it, a blanket of darkness covered my eyes and I entered dreamland.

The world my mind creates when I sleep is always different. I have always had strange dreams, but usually, when I entered the world, I got a feeling about the dream's mood or subject. This dream was different and it felt so distant from myself, like only half of my being was in it and the other half watching . . .

My astro body was being flung backwards like I was falling. Wait . . . I was falling! And my feet refused to respond. The whole area was covered in a veil of darkness. A burning light hit my eyes as a large cloud. The cloud was so massive that it placed me in complete darkness for a few moments. Shards rained from the cloud, dimming my vision until I was forced to close my eyes. Once the darkness moved away, I tried to open them, but they wouldn't open. My heartbeat quickened in dire fear, but I was motionless.

Then, it happened . . . I just stopped and was suspended in the air, my back tilted at an angle. My head was jolted and blood rushed into it. The sensation was fast because the thing that was supporting me was gentle. The heels of my feet swiped the ground, but only by a scary hair. Whatever was helping me, it made the unknown surroundings around me not as frightening.

Like magic, the blackness covering my closed eyelids became a golden tint and it was the loveliest hue I had ever witnessed, even with my eyes closed! My face was still tight in alarm, but I didn't know how long I would be supported. With care, I opened my eyes to look into a face, the face of my rescuer, the face of a hidden . . . prince?

Perplexed, I blinked a few times to make sure I was not losing my dream mind. However, it was true; a handsome young man was holding me up from disaster. He was wearing a traditional classy tuxedo and a nice crisp one at that. I found it most appealing. To add to the charm, he had a long black cape like the Phantom of the Opera and his dress boots shined.

Yet, one thing was odd. His face was covered completely in darkness. All I could see was the outline of a dazzling smile and some coloring in his eyes, but he covered those in a thin white mask that looped around his curly black locks. His whole presence looked more splendid due to the fact he was gloried in a beautiful gold and white light as a background. I had to remember to breathe; looking at him made me feel fainter.

Suddenly, the hand that was arching my back, the hand he was somehow able to support my whole body weight with, lifted me to his chest with poise. I was spellbound not only by his looks, but also because my feet still weren't on the ground. I swallowed the last ounce of my panic to suck in his smell.

Before I knew it, I was looking at him face-to-face and our chests were only about two inches apart. His smile was so beautiful that I began to shake and I had trouble blinking. The prince grabbed my left hand and laid it softly on his waist, making my face apple red because *I* was making personal contact. He lifted my right hand up in the air and laced his right hand into it, bringing my chills back at full force. Yet, no matter how willing and prepared I was for anything, I didn't think he would literally sweep me off my feet. Shocked and wide-eyed as he beamed, we began to swirl around the area, ballroom dancing harmoniously as a couple. His air of mystery added to the charm of the moment.

Other than being caught off-guard, I got to see how beautiful the place was. The lights were the colors of the most beautiful sunset, pale pinks mixing with oranges and yellow as green and blue streaks danced across the dream's sky. It seemed to go on forever. I could not even see the ground because clouds, the fluffiest I had ever viewed, landed on the ground to stay and were dancing with us.

I was more amazed that I was ballroom dancing! I slow danced once at a middle school Halloween dance, but that was about it. I'm a terrible dancer! Yet, with this guy, my "prince" of sorts, I didn't care how dorky I looked. He looked happy to be with me.

He twirled me around and I did four big, graceful swirls on my own, left there to stare blankly at him. He positioned himself to beckon for me like Romeo did for Juliet outside her balcony, a part from the play I treasured. How I wish real guys would do that handsome pose for real! As I tried not to fall over, golden sparkles of dust rained down and covered me in fairy-like wonder, only making me love this dream world more. Soon, about an ounce worth landed on my head and my body was covered in golden waves, blinding my cerulean eyes.

When it cleared, my clothes had changed. I was wearing a fuzzy white tank top, the undershirt made of silk, with straps of gold. With it was a soft cloth skirt that was a little above my knees. It had a green lightning bolt pattern across the tan background. The bottom inch was covered in red and green diamonds with real yellow jewels in the center! To add to the charm, white fringe dangled from the skirt and sparkled dazzling silver.

My shoes were opened toe flats made of gold and had pink and green gems encrusted in them. My hair was in curls so perfect and lovely, they felt like waves, but the tips of my hair was crinkled in a zigzag style like I used a curling iron on them for too long. This all seemed odd to me since my hair cannot curl to save my life! I also had a headband that matched my skirt and the best part . . . a small and beautiful silver tiara. The outfit was cute, but wasn't really my style. For some reason, this outfit felt symbolic, like I had just come home after a long time. I knew I had worn it many times before somewhere . . .

The prince pointed to my crown as if indicating to mean I was a princess . . . I was a princess?! How cool would that really have been! Then, I saw him mouth "beautiful" and the motion rang in my ears, making my cheeks gain color. I looked around to make sure there were no other girls around before pointing to myself, dazed. He nodded and . . . wow! He was gorgeous! I couldn't control my body and I fell backwards and although I was scared, I was prepared to fall. Yet again and still surprising me, he somehow rushed over to me and caught me with one hand.

His smile was huge and good-natured, making me smile warmly at my savior. I thought Umbra and Credence were good-looking, but this guy would knock them out in two seconds flat! I apologized to them in my mind and heart. I was about to stand up to stop bothering him. However, he had something else in mind . . .

He leaned closer and kissed me with full-heated passion! My face was so hot I thought I was on fire and my shaking felt similar to a seismic activity. My eyes hurt; they were trapped, golf ball size, staring at the sky as I cherished his lips against mine. My body soon chilled into excited goose bumps and I accepted the warm tenderness of his being by shutting my eyes, the shock over and purity filling my veins.

The feeling was the most amazing thing I had ever felt. It was my first kiss . . . period! I felt longing, devotion, determination, compassion, caring, hope, tenderness, passion, endearment . . . and love from this masked man, his kiss revealing all his secrets to me, the secrets of his heart. As I melted, feeling the magic of those beautiful feelings inside my body, heart, soul, mind, and blood as well, I knew my feelings for this stranger. It was stronger than anything I had ever felt, real world or dream.

This dream was somehow telling me something and when dreams tell me something, I listen. I have learned it is unwise not to. I was given the gift to have dreams of important events and 90% of the time, they came true. We kissed for a long while and then he pulled away gradually as I smiled stupidly to look at his astonished and satisfied face.

He laughed intriguingly and whispered in my ear. His breath hit it, making me tip backwards a few inches from pleasure. "You are the most wonderful and beautiful thing ever created . . . I want to be with you forever . . . if I am worthy of you." I knew he meant it and I grinned to make myself as charming as I could, to tell him I felt the same way.

He seemed to understand. He lifted my arms like before in our dance pose. This time, I sighed, feeling like I was in heaven, light as a feather as he lifted my hands up. We took to the miraculous floor.

I'm not sure how long we danced: days, hours, seconds, but it was heart stopping and breathtaking. I felt incredible, like I had no troubles at all. All I needed was him with me; everything else was secondary. His eyes were my windows to the world, his smile my inspiration, his heart my heart. I know these are strong declarations for a dream guy I just met, but I knew it was true. I knew I had felt these feelings for him before.

He laced my hand with his in the air and we leaned into each other to feel the magic of our lips touching again, to express our love. What happened next, turned everything into an unexpected nightmare. A lightning bolt zapped in between us and with brutal force and threw us apart in different directions. As I screamed in terror, I saw fragments of earth and the hall flying towards me and before I knew it, I lost consciousness.

It was the same as the very beginning of my dream. I was falling the same way, having the same panic, and the world around me was clouded in darkness except for above, which was a dim yellow-and-white light. As I groaned to feel the pain at my sides, I felt a graceful tap on my shoulders . . . someone was helping me. It had to be him! I opened my eyes gingerly and tilted my head up to look and see him, but there was a wind pulling us down. We were both falling.

As I tried to wake up, he pushed my shoulders to let go, but I grabbed his wrists securely in fright. For a split second, I became aware of the sleeves from the pajamas I was wearing when I entered, which only made my fear become clearer. I knew what that meant; it meant goodbye and in this case, it was for eternity.

I began to cry hysterically, screaming at him, "Please! No! Don't leave me!"

All he did was smile forgivingly with misty, caring eyes before leaning down, his tone hushed: "I'm sorry darling, but I refuse to fail you this time . . ."

This time? What was he talking about? Wait . . . maybe this wasn't only a dream. I recognized the outfit I had on when we danced and I knew I loved him for a long time, even though I knew I had never seen him before. Was this more than a symbolic dream, but a memory from a past I had forgotten? I didn't know how that worked, but half of me knew it was true.

"I love you . . . ," he whispered into my ear before kissing me lightly but full of love on my shaking lips one last time. Accepting his answer with all my being, my grip must have loosened because he freed himself from me, smiling angelically one final time. He flew fast, high into the pink clouded sky until he was burned by the light.

Was . . . he . . . entering . . . heaven . . . ? *NO! NO! NO!*

"NO!" I yelled at the top of my lungs, startled to death that the one person I wanted to be with was gone. He saved me from death; the feeling was mind trembling. I had to try to get him to come back. Even if we had to be apart, I could not let him go.

"Come back please . . . I . . . I love you . . . ," I said too softly for him to hear. I really did, whoever he was, real or not. I knew he was my true love. He seemed familiar to me, although I didn't get to see his face. But, his eyes, his breathtaking, full of soul eyes! I knew them all too well.

I screamed with all my voice and cried so much that I felt like my body would drown itself with its own sad tears. "I LOVE YOU!" I wailed insanely, shattering my vocal chords. It must have triggered something because then, a light below me opened up, shaped as a pond. I tried to stop or delay myself from entering the world he made me fall to. I wanted to see if he was still there, but he vanished, only leaving me with a memory and a broken heart. My mouth was open in fear and all I could do was hold myself from losing my sanity as I sank into the light pool of the living.

I flung forward on my bed, sweating to no end, tears wetting my hot face, making me shiver from the reaction. I grabbed my heart. The rate it was beating hurt so much that I cried more. My breathing was short. My room was dark, too dark to comfort me.

"It . . . it wasn't a dream . . . ," I whispered, my timid voice lost in a world of despair. "It couldn't be . . . right?" I lifted my knees up under the covers on my bed and sobbed until my mind blacked out.

Getting the strength to go to school was difficult. My body had taken a serious toil due to my misery the night before. It was hard, but I somehow made my mind only think of the positive things of the dream, the charming face of my love the most apparent. My body absorbed my worries and made me look ill: my eyes stung, my skin sizzled like an oil lamp was trapped under it, and part of my sides were freezing with chills. My throat also burned, making singing in my beloved choir class impossible plus my nose refused to allow me to breathe through it. I felt miserable. I had no reason to make people worry over a complicated dream, right?

I knew Maren and Umbra would notice, so I hoped I didn't see them or I somehow got the skills of the best actress ever for the day; this thought made me snort to myself. Plus . . . the guy in my dream could have been Umbra. The more that I thought about it, I felt like I knew him from somewhere deep in my past, but if that was true, Umbra was in a different form . . . Son of a monkey fiddle! I sounded mental! I growled at myself and stomped on sluggishly.

To avoid an awkward talk with my dad twenty minutes before school started, I told him I wanted to talk to my friends, so he dropped me off at the front of the building. The second I flung open the glass doors and entered the building with its blinding white tiled floor, I felt like a runway model all of a sudden. Everyone was looking at me; not in a bad way, but like I stood out. For once, I liked all those faces on me. I felt normal. I felt better. I smiled halfway and my messy self stepped forward with a hint of pride. I was only five steps into the lobby when I picked up friendly voices and hastened footsteps.

"Stary!"

Turning my head slightly, I saw my friends, my dearest friends, running to me. Chloe waved like a maniac, her grin so large it was close to psychotic. Rin followed, giving me a smug smile and Lauren stepped from behind, the tips of her mouth sliding up to give me a warm greeting. As I looked at all of them in their different color choices, smiles, personalities, but same love for me, the tension in my body relaxed. With them in my life, how could I ever feel this depressed ever again?

I stopped in my tracks and gave a little smile. Chloe stopped right before she got to me and bent down to pant like a toy-sized dog for a few seconds, her lovely teal blue dress top swirling around her waist. Lauren and Rin laughed unkindly under their breath at her rushing.

Chloe than sprang up so fast that I had to jump back, scared, which only made her huge smile larger. "I . . . we-we're so . . . glad you're . . . here," she said genially, but she was still trying to get some breath into her lungs.

Like a fixed jack-in-the-box, she hopped up, making me squeal for being caught off-guard. She grabbed my hands in a friendly and tight grip. "We have some wonderful news to tell you Stary and I could *not* wait! Although . . ." She bit her lips, assessing my wardrobe. "You really may not look . . . good enough for this amazing news . . ." She lifted up the ends of my lazy ponytail and then dropped it like it was disgusting.

Rin grunted, her eyes focused on my oversized army coat and faded jeans. "Yeah Moon. You look like a train wreck. I even put effort on my appearance today." I noticed, looking at her red polo shirt, which was unusual since her mother made her wear pastel colors that she hated. She crossed her arms with a firm nod while Lauren shook her head, her ponytail hitting her athletic arms and mint green shirt. If it was at Rin or me, I was not sure.

Chloe's eyes sparkled so intensely that the sickening feeling in my stomach vanished. I gazed at Rin and Lauren, who were patient with Chloe and only raised their eyebrows in a comforting way, making their faces light up with excitement as well, although they didn't smile. They were both not real emotional, at least with their expressions, so this gesture was enough to tell me something; the excitement was about a boy . . . And for too-tough-for- men Rin and boys-are-undeveloped-apes-and-a-waste-of-time Lauren to be excited about this news and smiling for me, it must have been big!

I smirked at Chloe. "I guess you saw my dad drop me off here, right?" Almost every day, I was in his classroom until the warning bell, stealing a donut from the teacher's lounge. I was curious how they knew I'd be here.

Chloe grinned. "No, we didn't see him or your truck . . . ," she said in a monotone, but it was on the edge of being chipper. I blinked while looking at my three friends, their expressions the same as before. I was getting ready to ask "how" when Chloe interrupted. "Just a feeling . . ." She winked.

Still puzzled, I looked at Rin and Lauren for a straight answer. Lauren nodded and Rin confirmed, "Right, just a good feeling . . . ," with a sly grin. I ducked my head down to hide the fact I was lost but understood Rin's meaning. Although she didn't have spirit powers, she was intoned with the elemental worlds and presences. She was right about many things.

Chloe nudged me along to the lunchroom and grabbed my hands as if leading me to a surprise haunted house. Still, she looked so enthusiastic. It was a slow walk to the lunchroom when it was really only twenty-five feet. I finally got the voice to ask her when she was going to tell me what she was so giddy about, but all Chloe did was smile and softly say, "Soon, but now . . . we rarely get to see you in the morning. So for the next twenty minutes before the bell, we're going to gossip!" I gave her a mocking face, but accepted it because I did miss seeing my friends in the morning.

Everyone was shocked to see me, so much so that I felt famous. Mark ran to embrace me close. He was as affectionate as always, but still, feeling his muscles cradling me wasn't as fulfilling as before. I hadn't really talked to him in a few days, so I whispered in his ear, "How are things going with moving?" I rubbed my face against his smooth cheek so he was forced to look at Chloe.

Mark blushed like a laser beam was set off in his cheeks and whispered back, "It won't happen, Stary. I know we're good friends now, but . . . I was so mean to her at the beginning of the year. She would never believe me. I'm really not sure *how* to feel . . ."

I had to laugh at the memory of how unkind Mark was to Chloe to the point she would cry. She had no idea why some random guy that I only knew for a year and the rest of them did not know at all was so mean to her. So, Chloe made me ask him why face-to-face one day; that's what best girlfriends do for each other. Mark bluntly, with no hint of embarrassment, said to me: "Because I like her." Yet he made me promise not to tell her.

I smiled at him evilly back in the present because I knew the whole time, no matter how elementary he was being. It's strange how it's so easy to read other people's feelings but not your own.

Chloe was looking at us, a little hurt. She never directly admitted to me that she *liked* Mark, yet, as her best friend, it was pretty much a *duh* situation. I told her a million times Mark and I were just friends, but I guess we did get a little too romantic sometimes. I would have to be more careful with that I supposed from now on.

Chloe then looked up at Mark, who struggled to give her a smile. His jaw tightened then grinned way too big. He looked like of those people who get their faces frozen! If he wasn't a nervous wreck, we would have laughed at how dumb he looked!

Chloe blushed redder than a cherry and turned away fast to talk to Rin. Mark was upset and gave me a "you see?" gesture with his hands. I patted his hand lightly and had to laugh harder; boys are *so* clueless!

We all decided to sit at a table near us. It was fun to feel ordinary for a change and only focus on my wonderful friends. I rarely thought about my dream in those fifteen minutes, well, until Chloe opened her mouth. "OH! We haven't talked about our dream journals in forever! Stary, what kind of dreams have you had lately? Anything . . . juicy?" I loved Chloe, but she was so nosey!

My face got ruby-toned as I thought of my handsome dream guy. I couldn't hide it from them, so I thought I might as well spill but lower the drama. "Well, last night, I had a dream about this guy . . . I couldn't see his face, but I knew he was special. He was dressed like a prince . . ."

"A prince?" Lauren said baffled in appearance, but calm in voice. Rin smiled callously and rolled her eyes. Chloe then nudged me to go on with a devilish grin and inquisitive eyes.

To support myself, I leaned my elbows on the table and placed my head delicately on my too pale hands. I gazed up at the ceiling light, focusing on how bright and tepid it was like in my dream. "He was real handsome. I felt like I've met him before, but . . . in a different form. He was very kind to me and we danced like something out of *Beauty and the Beast*. He really was . . . the most wonderful boy I have ever met . . ."

Chloe sighed romantically while Rin and Lauren watched me with wonder, because I meant what I said. Chloe grabbed my shoulder and she looked like she had just woken up from the enchanted dream herself. "That sounds so sweet Stary . . ." Then she leaned in a little with a toothy grin. "I bet it was Credence. Was it Credence?"

Somehow, a rage of burning fury engulfed my entire body. The thought of this prince, this man who gave up his *life* for me, to be compared to some other guy . . . the thought was betraying, sinful, and wrong. Anger rushed into me like a dam that burst, too fast to control, and it hit my mouth before I could react. "It wasn't Credence, okay?! Never!" I yelled full of intensity, it echoing back at me.

Chloe looked shaken, hurt. Lauren gazed from Chloe to me, bewildered at my reaction and that my voice *could* yell. Rin looked disturbed and gave Chloe a stare, as if telling her that she pushed me too far. I bet I yelled so loud China heard me. Maybe even heaven and the spirits of . . . Oh no . . .

I began to quiver. I couldn't believe I blew up at the world. No one knew my dream and made me lose my caring protector. I slapped myself mentally to focus on the problem in front of me first: my wounded best friend. "I mean, I like Credence, but it just . . . didn't *feel* like Credence and his hair was different . . . so, uh . . ." I gulped, blushing pink as I stared at the floor.

Chloe nodded to end the conversation and grinned before lifting my face down to look into hers. "I'm glad you still like Credence. That's what I need to talk to you about . . ."

The bell then rang. Chloe didn't let go of me and Rin stood up to block my back while Lauren grabbed my backpack to carry. In no hurry, they led me down the hall. I got a little nervous like someone was planning to attack me and they were my secret service team.

Chloe linked her arms through mine before telling me this "great" news. "Credence has been talking to Barbara and me about you lately in homeroom . . . and with interest!" Her smile was so genuine that I knew it was true, but what bugged me was I was right next to them. How couldn't I have known? Am I that dense?

Chloe giggled. "You may be easy to distract when you're doing homework, but when you read, it's a lot harder, especially with manga."

"Ah . . ." Not only did she answer my unspoken question, but I agreed that when I was reading a manga, I was in another world. I have been doing a lot of "world" travelling . . .

Chloe laughed once more before pumping me with more rumored knowledge, the fuel for high school teens.

"I also know that he wants to ask you something . . ."

I drew a blank. By Chloe's taunting tone, I knew it was something romantic in her mind. That made my body heat rise fast and my words began to shake inside my throat. Lauren and Rin smiled halfway as well. They knew! Oh tuna crackers! Why am I always the last to know?

Getting excited, I began to think maybe . . . maybe Credence was . . . he was . . . I was so floaty that I couldn't say it! I grabbed Chloe's arms tight, drawing designs with my finger. "What, what, what?!" My eyes and voice grew more intense with every word.

Chloe poked my nose and pressed the same finger she used to poke me against her lips, sealing the secret. "He has to ask you himself, his own way at his own time. We just wanted to warn you of something so you won't have an emotional overload or heat stroke!" Chloe winked.

I looked back at Rin and Lauren, still acting like body guards, and they pointed to themselves to tell me that they suggested I'd be told. I sighed and thanked them. I figured they would; Chloe loved to see my reactions, no matter how stressful they were on me.

Credence . . . Credence Horton . . . his name still sounded amazing. And he was asking about me? I was so surprised! Maybe Credence was my prince after all! My mind stopped dead in its tracks then, making my heart feel guilty for even considering that. I felt like I was cheating . . . however, I was still glad. Would my prince want that? ALACK! Mental attack!

Lauren and Rin had to go to their lockers and left early, leaving Chloe and me alone. Chloe asked if I was mad about being nagged about Credence. I told her not to worry and tapped her cheek. "I'm not the only one that needs to be thrilled about love that is so near me . . ." and I partly winked, leaving her there for a few seconds dumbfounded.

As usual, she shook it off and ran to catch me. But when she grabbed my arm, she tugged me too hard, making my body and heavy backpack fling backwards. I was barely able to regain my balance as I tried to not land on top of *her*! We both blinked at each other and at our near clownish collision and chuckled before grabbing arms to walk to class once more.

Her smile was so sweet that sugar would have been jealous. "You are so lucky. You'll have a boyfriend real soon!" she told me. Like she could see the future?

I sniggered and surprisingly, I didn't blush; I guess the dream seemed too insane. I was also tired of her being so blonde, literally and figuratively, to not notice the greatness she had waiting for her. Well, Mark was at fault, too, for being too chicken!

"Yep, soon we both will!" I told her, beaming. She only paused before we had to go our separate ways.

Lunch: a unique frontier with more chaos and yelling than a battlefield and that was where I felt the most relaxed . . . strange. Chatting like cheerful blue jays, our table never felt livelier. My breakfast club from that morning was still teasing me with poking and playful words about Credence. I was so nervous all of homeroom, blocking everyone away with my elbows. Credence glanced at me quite a few times and grinned, but he didn't speak to me. His group did their normal routine of playing violent card games and slapping each other's backs as hard as they could before Mrs. Nodean saw. As I watched him, I noticed that he wasn't as fast at Egyptian Rat Screw as he usually was. Oh well. I was gliding on a cloud just being a normal girl again.

In fact, I hadn't seen Umbra or Maren all day. I felt Maren's presence a few times, but it was distant. I guess she was doing research or hunting . . . And Umbra . . . maybe he was keeping his distance because of yesterday.

We both did act kind of abnormal or he may have been scared that I'd freak out about him taking control of me again. Thinking of the way we acted, the childish fools we became over gentle words made my heart race. Chloe noticed and asked if I was okay or in a lovey mood. All I did was nod by holding my cheeks, hoping to control the heat and tried not to roll my eyes and smack her.

Then, a gut feeling hit me inside, like I had forgotten something I had needed. No, not lost . . . something I forgot to do. A real faint feeling, so faint that it felt like someone was lightly painting the air a few feet from me and I was expected to feel it, came from the girl's restroom. I sharpened the tips of my eyes to glare from the side. The aura was faint, barely a breeze, but it still bugged me, sending small chills through my arms.

I must have had my mouth open for Rin pushed my chin up hard and my teeth clacked together. I snapped out of my focused state and looked at her grayish eyes. "Stop staring, stupid. People will think you're dumb and attack you!"

I sighed internally. Another good sentence of advice from Rin . . .

I rubbed the back of my neck timidly and made my head drop before looking at her. "Right, sorry . . ." I had to go check the restroom. Maybe there was a message there, a friendly note to help us or . . . a threat of our enemy, the concept that still felt too fantasy-like to be real.

I flung up like a soldier saluting and slammed my hands on the table top, making it shake and my peers look up. With those eyes looking at mine blankly, I got nervous and felt dumb. "I have to go to the restroom!" I announced, squeezing my eyes shut to not see their laughing expressions.

"Why do you always tell us your gross personal business, Moon? It's quite pathetic." I heard a choking and cold voice behind me. I spun around to see Barbara, glaring at me as she floated to her seat in the center of the table. The sight of her current state made me fall backwards a foot and gasp, unable to control it. I covered my mouth to hide my shame.

Barbara's eyes were black, not medium brown like usual, but a dark and swirling black. She looked thinner, sickly thinner. She was all bones, her elbows so pointy that she could poke someone's eye with them. Her legs shook like crazy like she hadn't eaten anything in three days or she was doing drugs. I had such a bad feeling from her, like I was allergic to her chi. The air was tight and polluted. What was going on?

"Did you enjoy the bathroom?" Mandy said to her, smiling widely as she always did at her best friend. And, as usual, Barbara glared at her like she was stupid.

"What kind of an imprudent question is that?" Her tone was so snippy, even more than usual. Everyone leaned back and an awkward, dead silence filled our area.

I wasn't surprised that Mark was the one that wasn't affected. He spoke to Barbara and put his arm around her small shoulder, giving her a cocky yet breathtaking, knees-weak smile with a full set of white pearls. "How was the bathroom, Barbara?"

I smiled a little; it was quite a riot!

A hint of red appeared in her eyes, spreading until her irises looked like a fire was lighting her up from the inside out. I blinked and rubbed my own eyes, trying to clean my vision, but the fire tone in her eyes was still there. I must have been the only one to see it for no one else gave her a strange glance.

She flung across the table to Mark, her hair dangling prettily as she smiled like a model. "Mark! I love when you ask me things like that!" and she laughed exaggeratedly loud to make a point. It was *so* fake. All she wanted was attention. She seemed and to me, *felt* normal, still . . . I wanted to check the bathroom . . . What if she was . . . ?

Poor Chloe looked so upset at the sight of Barbara nudging Mark's shoulder. He was smiling like it was nothing, which I knew was how Mark felt. I rubbed Chloe's back lightly and gave her my most reassuring smile and tone. "She has nothing on you babe, trust me." And I waved, slowly walking towards the restroom.

Chloe asked before I got too far to shout if I wanted her to come with me. I shook my head no, still maintaining my positive smile. I told her I was a tough girl. She sighed and told me I was weird since girls always go together. Yet, I pointed to Mark and winked, making her flush. She had something to keep an eye on like I did.

The old restroom had such a painful hollow aura. My thoughts could be heard, ringing through my ears. Against the odds, I set my mind on the task to see if there was a message. The stall felt cold, distant, and vacant. The writer was long gone, their trail practically worthless.

I bent down on my knees to look for a message. I saw the first one Maren and I discovered. I guess there was nothing . . . Then, in the upper corner of my left eye, I saw an ectoplasmic 'e' that I didn't notice before. The aura was trembling, like the writer was not well. There also appeared to be some sort of grainy substance on top of them, but it was also made of ectoplasm. Treating it like dust on an old book, I blew on it to reveal a response:

I am here.

12

I STUDIED THE MESSAGE FOR ONLY A FEW MOMENTS, BUT IT FELT like an era into eternity. It didn't really explain anything to help us uncover who the messenger was or what side he or she was on. Still, I got quite nervous that this person, the closest to my spirit abilities I was going to find around here, was at my school. Were they watching me? Do they know who I am? I couldn't feel them in a crowd, so maybe I was safe.

And then, the whole thing with Barbara only made me sink lower to the tile. The way she had been acting wasn't comforting. True, Barbara was really moody in general. One day she could bring you a flower with a sweet smile and the next she would come charging at you to eat your head off with unjust words. It was either agree and accept her emotions or get devoured. She had been like that since elementary school. Yet, I had never seen her act so cruel and how sickly she looked sent my nerves in roller coaster knots.

Barbara was also known to get sick a lot more than most people, which caused her mood swings half the time, yet she looked so pale, like she was . . . dead! I sadly knew what that color of white looked like. It yanked my heart down like it was attached to a rusted chain. Maren and Umbra look the way they were when they had been alive to me with the exception of the blue glow around them. But when I first met them and when the light hit them head on, one could see they were the sickly color of a dead person. I never gave it much thought until that second. I admit, it did scare me. Seeing Umbra and Maren by the window the first day I felt them and that awful color shining through their arms . . . Looking through them made them like imaginary friends one has as a child, only better, and more horrible. Yet, I ignored the thought.

I looked up at the ceiling, hoping to get something else on my mind. A haunting, non-living presence that Umbra told me a little about was hanging over the air space I was in, almost bumping the ceiling. It was a slow moving swirl. The beautiful sapphire blue swirl had crystals on it and caught my eye; it moved gingerly like it was blind. Shards carefully floated down, looking like diamond ice debris. I knew it was left over from the power of the messenger. But why didn't I see it the last time? One of the shards landed close to me. With caution, I lifted my finger up to tap it. Dumb move.

It landed on my finger, barely touching my creamy skin. When it stopped, it began to spin and release white light through its crystal coating. I was fascinated by its graceful movements, trapped in a spell of being content with watching it dance forever. Although it was pretty, the back of my mind was telling me something didn't feel right about it . . .

It stopped spinning and the light grew blood red and began to shoot sharp pains into my finger. I screamed. The pain was too much, so much so that I couldn't move my finger. It felt like a thousand needles were stabbed into me, destroying the inside of my skin. My blood was on fire.

With the rest of my strength, I flipped the shard up into the air and moved back an inch so it would land on the floor. Then I stomped on it with all my might, allowing red liquid to escape on the floor. Once the light hit it, the glow became blue and vanished, seeping into the floor, the movement of the liquid like blood soaking into soil.

Panting, my eyes stung with teardrops. I threw open the door and ran to the sink to wash my finger. I had to hold my wrist with my left hand to make the quaking settle down enough to see my right hand. There was a cut, but it was shaped oddly. It was a detailed, charcoal-colored crescent moon that was broken in half by a lightning bolt, the picturesque moon on my finger crumbling into debris. To make it worse, my cut was steaming! I gasped loudly at the symbol. It meant that this person must be against us, ready to destroy the moon, which in this case, was me, Stary Moon.

I knew this truth would break Maren's heart, that the messenger was not our ally. I was pretty sure Umbra would agree and go into revenge mode for this person tricking Maren . . . I almost didn't want to tell him, but I had to tell him first. Although tough, he would know how to break it to Maren then figure out the best course of action.

After a few minutes of heaving, I was finally calm enough to stir a plan and turn on the cold water full blast to rinse my damaged finger. The pain was unbearable, but I had to do it. I added soap as well, hoping it would clean any infection out of my poisoned mark that was still steaming a tad. My scar began to foam from the soap, but I scrubbed it harder and soon, it was gone. All I had left was the pain, a moon-shape cut, and the misfortune of living through the event.

I left the restroom quickly and quietly, holding my finger to my chest to cuddle it, to protect it from any more discomfort. I glanced back once, making sure I was not being watched. I had to go and find Umbra right away. I still had thirteen minutes until lunch was over. I bet Chloe was worried, but she had to wait. Looking ahead to make sure no one was on lunch guard duty, I hopped down the stairs and ran with all my might. The threat had been made and I wasn't yet ready for the battle.

I got tired too fast, running and hiding around half of our huge school. I couldn't feel Umbra at all, which was strange and it frightened me. Umbra always let me detect him in case of an emergency; he and Maren had both promised to do that. I didn't feel her either, but she left a small trail for me by the history wing door, meaning she was out hunting. I thought of all the possible places I hadn't looked.

Sore, confused, and feeling sick, I had to lean on the wall to rest.

The floor was cold, but in a good way. I leaned my head on the wall, thinking of happier things. The first item was my prince. The thought left me tingling with delight yet cold and empty from longing. I had to stop thinking of him though for if I thought about how we were forced apart, how he no longer existed . . . I would rather take my chances with the poison.

Dizzily, I stood up, my hair sticking to the wall from static, and began to walk toward the music hall. It always made me happy to be in there plus it was small with only two rooms. Too bad I didn't have the delicate and spellbinding melody that had become a part of my weak heart since Umbra and I had accepted each other at the moment. It constantly gave me a soft warm feeling in my chest, but hopefully music would aid me once more.

I struggled to open the heavy swinging doors to the wing, but I was already feeling better by merely being there. I sighed and peeked through the window on the band room door. Rats! Someone was in there . . . Wait! I did a double take to get a closer look to see. It was Umbra! He had his back turned, staring at the drum set intensely. The door was cracked, which allowed me to slide in and hide behind the pillar in front of the room. Umbra looked lost in thought and I could tell he didn't detect me in the room with him. What was he doing?

I heard him sigh, facing the instruments, and say pleadingly, "I know it's pointless and foolish, but I need you now. I've been thinking too much lately, too much about strange things, things that are not related to my mission. Please, comfort me . . ."

Was he talking to the drums? Did objects have spirits too? Ah, those thoughts made my concentration hurt worse!

Suddenly, he moved up to get something from the supply closet. I had to duck down in the darkness to make sure he didn't see me spying on him. He came out soon with a microphone and an adaptor. Umbra was going to record something? Or sing? Umbra singing?!

That fact made me blush because I love guys that sing. It was a dream of mine to marry a choir guy. I sighed helplessly. Even if Umbra was one . . . that would never happen between us for many reasons. The main one being I *don't* like him! I kept reminding my silly mind. The poison must have affected my thinking.

Umbra set the microphone down flippantly and went to the drum set again, picking up the sticks. He then hit them to get a beat, the ringing echoing inside my body. I was a little nervous since the band kids were at lunch and if they heard him . . . boy, that would have been disastrous! He strutted to the center of the blue-and-white room, holding the mic with a tense, but protective, grip and turned the machine on.

Abruptly, he looked serious, bestial like as he moved the palm of his hand toward the drum set. Energy formed in a flicker of static, looking like a mini tornado coming out of his hand. Magically, the drum sticks lifted up and began to play on their own! It took my entire will not to gasp. Playing the set was a pair of hands that were clear like . . . ectoplasm! Did Umbra rub some of his ectoplasm on the sticks, meaning he could control their movement like a puppet master? If this was so, spirits could really do some incredible things. He then did the same routine with the gorgeous deep red electric guitar.

It hit me like a bullet train rammed me. The melody he was playing . . . it was lingering. I liked the tune a lot, but it was sort of . . . dark . . . but it did explain Umbra poetically. Still, the beat was foreign . . . maybe Umbra wrote it himself. It appeared he could do anything. Engrossed, I perked my ears up and prepared to get swept away to a mystifying world . . .

I'm hollow, inside and out.
I'm numb without my spirit.

I stopped to listen to Umbra's song, the smooth texture of his voice engulfing my flesh. He was really singing! His voice was . . . breathtaking. As I watched him move with an array of emotions while swinging his mic around, I was lost in his spell. My world was a line of nothingness, my body became numbed, and my ears and eyes got the pleasure of a lifetime. I couldn't see Umbra performing in front of people, so I got to witness a rare show.

I'm dizzy, confused without her wit
I'm lost without her heart to aid my lift
I'm bare, all over my soul
I'm beaten, no strength to fight
I'm trapped, never tasting true sadness
I'm wounded, by the scar her vanishing caused.

Listening to him, I heard how vindictive and heart squeezing the words of the song were and Umbra was singing them with perfect intensity, making them stunningly believable. I knew how he felt and he made me see how thrilling the power of a song was, causing emotion so thick in my throat that it hurt.

Umbra was really perfect, created to do anything like Maren said. Still, a part of me didn't think Umbra was programmed for all that creative wonder. He was made to do inhuman and human things, but he grew on his own, created his own personality and emotions. That astounded me and made my breath shorter.

I'm empty, my emotions only specks
I'm scared that her voice will never return
I'm sick without her curable laugh
I'm weak, my heart looking like a burn
I'm void, a black hole controlling me
I'm depressed, no arms to embrace
I'm injured, deeply leaving its mark
I'm restless waiting for the big chase
I'm nothing . . . I'm nothing without her.

I'm nothing . . . I'm nothing without her. At that line, my heart sank. The hidden meaning of his lyrics and the message of his song rushed into my mind: Umbra was singing the song for Maren. After Maren died and Umbra was all alone on Earth for those two years, he had to think of ways to control his anger, to not go insane. It appeared to me that he must have written a song that suited him well and with it, he mastered how to console his broken heart.

Although Umbra seemed to want to be tainted in darkness forever due to rage, the spirit of Maren haunted his heart; it was a light that he was forced to face again and again. I thought it was genuinely sweet that those two could influence each other after being separated by worlds. Still . . . I felt like I was about to be submerged into the floor from sorrow and no one would save me.

But . . .
I'm hopeful that she will come smiling
I'm praying she will always care for me
I'm dreaming for her to say my name
I'm knowing . . . she will always be my—

"NO! NO! Why does this keep happening?"

He slammed the microphone on the carpet and bent down. He was red in the face, his eyes shut. His fists were so tight that I bet no air could have escaped through them. Umbra looked like he was in so much pain that I, unknowingly, stepped forward to soothe him, but my hand slid on the pillar, making me snap back to reality. The real world texture reminded me that I was in hiding.

Strange to say, Umbra looked attractive being weakened by emotions, looking so human that my stomach did flips and my legs shook from loss of fluids, my body heating up. I swallowed hard in fear of realizing what was happening to me. I stopped being selfish and stared at Umbra, curious as to why he was so upset by his enchanting melody.

"Why . . . ?" His back was turned toward me, shaking madly, and his voice was choked. It almost sounded like he had tears built up in his throat. "I don't . . . get it. I, before, have always seen her, the one who has always been with me . . . Yet, lately . . . I've been seeing . . . her . . . *her* . . . in my mind`. . . for that part of the song . . . Her freakin' shining face with that stupid ass smile . . ."

I backed up to support myself. Umbra sounded like he was having an emotional crisis. Maybe he didn't love Maren anymore and was in love with someone else. Or he didn't *love* Maren until recently? I looked at the floor to relax my upset heart. Although Umbra and I were getting along, I knew it wasn't me he loved. No matter . . . or even, if maybe I . . . wanted him to . . . I sighed heavily, my chest tighter than the inside of a clock; I couldn't deny it any longer.

Umbra let out a loud and distressed grunt before flinging his arms up in the air toward the light peeking through the high window. "God! What's happening to me?!" he screamed.

All I could do was watch in wonder and let my feelings go toward him with my energy, my will, my personal desire to be with him. I wanted to do something.

Umbra groaned and hung his head, like maybe my thoughts reached him and calmed his spirit or maybe our gnome friend helped him out. Either way, he seemed to relax his rippling muscles.

Suddenly, I heard a creak from the wing doors. Umbra must have heard it too because his head jolted in the direction like lightning flashing across the midnight sky. Still, he didn't see me since I was well hidden behind the fat pillar and in a hefty blanket of darkness.

I heard whistling and the jingle of keys . . . oh no! Mr. Wave was back and outside the hallway doors! He was my choir director's husband and he ran the marching band and special bands at our high school like jazz and drum. He must have come back to his room early before lunch was over! Umbra sucked in his ectoplasm from the instruments like a vacuum, but the drumsticks hit the metal rim of the drums and made a noise. Umbra's eyes got wider as I saw Mr. Wave through the door window stop to listen, his face twisting upward, looking a tad distraught.

While Umbra was moving the equipment, I was able to sneak out of the band room door before Umbra could see or feel me. He would have been mad if he knew I heard his secret comfort song. Plus, with my new confession for him to myself, it would be readable all over my face! Now I had three guys wrestling in my heart! Bloody codfish, this was mental!

My whole body was jumpy. Mr. Wave was nice, but I knew the rule that no one was allowed in the room without him to watch since the instruments cost a lot of money for the school. It must have been my lucky day for my timing was perfect and I was skinny enough to hide behind the water fountain between the band and choir room.

Mr. Wave opened the hallway door to look in, his face ready to bellow at someone. I noticed he paused and looked towards the fountain. Did I make a sound? Worried, I covered my mouth and, in the panicked process, my leg hit the metal underneath with a loud ram. I knew that was going to leave a bruise later. Let's just also make this If-you're-name-is-Stary-idiotically-keep-injuring-yourself Day! Now my cute glitter tennis shoe was exposed.

Halfway in the room, Mr. Wave stopped and looked at me oddly. "Stary? What in the world are you doing over there?" His voice was part firm. I peeked to look at him and tried to get up, dusting myself off without making my leg throb. Heck on wheels, this was *not* my day, dear Lord . . .

"Oh. Hello Mr. Wave. I was . . . ah . . . looking for Mrs. Wave to get my choir music to practice on extra at home and . . . well, I . . . ah . . ." I was a terrible liar, but I was so well behaved that teachers seemed to believe whatever I said. Today was the day to put that power to the test.

I needed a way to explain why I was on the floor. I rubbed my head and giggled toward Mr. Wave a little, looking down to see a wet mechanical pencil in the corner against the drinking fountain. I snatched it and showed it to Mr. Wave so he could behold its plastic, but disgusting feeling glory.

"I then . . . noticed Mrs. Wave was out to lunch, so . . . I, ah . . . went to get a drink, but I dropped the pencil I was holding to mark my music with in the water fountain and it fell on the floor when you came in, sir . . ."

He looked at me with one eyebrow lifted. I wasn't sure he was buying it.

I held up the pencil again and laughed stupidly. "It's . . . slippery. See?" I let it slide through the gaps between my fingers where it fell into the palms of my hands and bounced it a few times before I caught the devil. I laughed nervously again. I wanted to scream, "Boy, I'm an idiot!" skyward.

His mouth formed an 'O' shape and his eyes softened as he rubbed his neck. "That makes sense . . . ," he announced as he turned toward the classroom.

I held my chest, wrinkling my shirt and sighed. What a relief! I apologized to God for lying.

I decided to make a smooth break for it when he caught me by the wing doors with his booming voice. "Stary?"

I cringed with one leg up. So close! I turned to face him like a soldier as he motioned me into the entrance of the band room with his powerful index finger. I did as I was told, feeling like a puppy in trouble and being pulled by an unbreakable leash.

"Did you hear a drum being played?"

Ouch! Busted! What was I going to say, no? It was loud although quick. I had to think of something to protect innocent students from being accused.

"Ummmmm, yes . . . yes I did, sir. But, no one has been in there since I entered, so I think it was the wind." I waved my arms frantically like a maniac.

Mr. Wave glanced at me like I was stupid, showing disbelief in my story.

His voice was cold when he asked, "You think the wind can play a drum? It's not that strong . . ."

His eyes were so intense that I had to duck. What was I going to say? It did sound ridiculous, but I'm bad at lying! I noticed the little window was open, the one Umbra had been staring at. It was never open before according to my knowledge, but this was my chance.

I ran over to the drums to show him. "Because . . . the window is open and at the direction the wind is going, it would hit the drumsticks." I had no idea what I was saying, but it sounded smart.

Mr. Wave looked up at the window amazed. He seemed to be wondering how it got opened since it was always closed. He then asked me to prove it. I froze and told him we had to wait for some wind. The two of us waited for a minute; not even a breeze. Mr. Wave began to tap his foot, making me more nervous.

"I'll show you!" I said, bending down to the drum set and blowing on the sticks to see if they would roll.

Nothing. Mr. Wave didn't look too pleased. I shrugged with a giggle and blew harder, my cheeks puffed. At random, the sticks placed on the drum rolled to the side and hit the metal coating, forming the exact sound we had heard!

I leaned on the cool metal, once again relieved. Mr. Wave looked at them, stunned and while he was in his spell, I ran off and out of the wing, heading toward the lunchroom. That was too close! I must have had an angel with me.

Out of breath, I huffed for some cool air to heal my aching lungs as I made it to the entrance of the lunchroom. I really hoped Mr. Wave didn't tell his wife how weird I was. If he did, I might have been in trouble in choir, my most beloved class! But I would deal with it to protect Umbra.

As I slowly stood up, I recalled how the window was open. Was it before Umbra sang? I couldn't recollect, but I knew it had never been opened before! Ever! Could Umbra have been there to bail me out? Then he would have known I was spying . . . Ah, my nerves were so edgy that they made my teeth chatter.

I had to ignore it for now. My pals must have sent a search party for me. I looked at the old wall clock; only four minutes left until lunch was over. That whole ordeal of running away from pain to covering for Umbra's secret song only took nine minutes? Dang! It felt like an eternity!

All of a sudden, I sneezed loudly, my eyes stinging. I looked at the floor embarrassed, blinking a few times. Was someone talking about me? Like a call, I got the chill of a presence coming from behind me . . . it was Umbra! Crap! And I could sense he was upset. I must have been discovered. I began to laugh insanely in order to cool myself down, but that only made Umbra accept my challenge more and we came face to face, him glaring, me shaking.

"Hi . . . Heya Umbra . . . How are you . . . ?" I said low and frightened to death, yet somehow I remained cheerful in tone. Umbra only looked at me with deadly eyes, eyes that could literally kill. His face was all creased in the center, making his eyebrows lower and him look scarier. He backed away and his face lightened up into a dazzling look of relief, making my insides melt like butter.

"How dare you!" he yelled, changing his attitude to match his first awful face. I held my hands against my chest, timid with fear. I felt like I was in *Dr. Jekyll and Mr. Hyde* and Umbra was winning the actor's award of the year. Again, his anger vanished as fast as it had reappeared and a beautiful small smile made his slightly tanned skin glow. And like before, I was a victim to his magic charm . . . and so very confused.

He patted my shoulders and sighed. "I can't believe you're smiling and being so pleasant to me after I left you all day to do . . . personal things. You really are something else . . ." His tone was so honest and pure that I blushed madly, not caring. Then it struck me . . .

"You didn't see me all day?"

My reaction must have caught him off guard because he flung himself backwards. His face was a little red with a questioning look. He had enough sense to shake his head, still locked in alarm and puzzlement. I jumped up and gave a huge grin. Umbra didn't see me! I was in the clear! No criminal record for me!

I began to twirl around like a ballerina, forgetting I was in public. I bet I looked like a dumb child to Umbra, but I didn't mind. I felt a little bad that I felt no guilt at all, but I'd live with that sin. As I stopped to look at Umbra, his eyes were smiling although he looked just as baffled. His face was also an attractive tone of pink, making it hard for me not to blush.

Then, it dawned on me: I was dancing around in the entrance of the lunchroom and I was the only one who could see Umbra. Wow . . . I was an idiot! The teacher on duty looked at me incongruously, making me wobble sideways from embarrassment. Umbra looked at me funny as his aura turned bluer to protect himself. Aura . . . blue . . . ectoplasm . . . Oh Snapple! I couldn't believe I forgot! I bowed to the teacher and sprinted, grabbing Umbra's wrist on the way.

I sneaked into the lunchroom, unnoticed by any of my friends, and hid behind the pillar Maren showed me after we read the first message. I had to lean on the pillar for support. I knew my lungs would forever hate me after all this running!

Umbra popped up from out of nowhere next to me. I gave myself a minute to collect my thoughts and took a deep breath before telling Umbra everything about the message, Barbara's strange behavior, and the shard.

"You got hit by leftover ectoplasm energy?!" Umbra yelled at my face, but he didn't sound angry. I felt shy all of a sudden and hid my finger behind my back as I nodded.

"It's leftover ectoplasm energy? Is it like when humans get a cut and they lose blood?" I asked, remembering what Maren told me about ectoplasm.

"No, not really like *losing* blood . . ." He leaned on the pillar, looking cool as he crossed his arms, thinking, similar to the first time we met three weeks ago. Three weeks I would never forget. "You see, when spirits perform any kind of major action, such as writing to the outside world, they must use some of their ectoplasm. In that sense, it's like writing in blood for a mortal. However . . . we leave behind a small trail of ectoplasm after we perform the task. It's sort of like when your blood doesn't clot right, but only for a few seconds . . ."

I nodded, narrowing my eyes to focus on how intense the situation could be. I knew what that was like because my mom's blood didn't clot well, making it dangerous. A few seconds' worth of blood would be a few drops, so I guessed that amount of ectoplasm would be around there. Still, there was a great deal more in the airspace than a few seconds worth!

"There was a whole heap more than that above the stall."

Umbra continued being the professor. I wondered if Dr. Rowe just programmed him with a teaching degree. "Hmmmmm . . . that means the spirit isn't feeling well, like they're sick . . ."

I blinked a few times questionably at the fact spirits could get sick.

Umbra studied the blankness on my face and sneered. "I don't mean like catch a stupid cold and whine for a week like you weak humans. Maybe they had to use too much of their ectoplasm for some reason, to defend themselves from being seriously harmed . . ."

My eyes locked onto his calm face. "Harm?" I mouthed, in fear of those harsh words. Spirits could get hurt? I guess I knew it was possible, but seeing how strong and special Maren and Umbra were, I didn't want to believe it. Plus, if someone attacked the other spirit messenger, then . . . they could soon come for us.

Umbra must have seen how troubled I was, soaking in the information. "But, it's really hard to do."

I looked up to see his face was half hidden, but his smile was comforting. I smiled hesitantly back. He then winked at me, a wink that said I-can-rule-the-world-so-fast-that-you-little-humans-wouldn't-have-time-to-breathe. My worries evaporated. I felt sorry for anything that messed with Umbra!

"I guess ectoplasm is also your source of energy?"

Umbra nodded at my question.

"Wow. It really is astounding . . ." It really was like how blood is important to us. "Wait, there's something I don't get. All spirits release leftover ectoplasm when they do a deed right? Then why was it floating in the air instead of being by the door, the thing the messenger touched?"

"Usually, that's how it works. Although you're human, you were able to use powers, in the easiest to explain sense, to turn a message into ectoplasm. This makes your energy rare and threatening. So, your ectoplasm energy blocked theirs from settling on the door. The leftover just floated to the air above the energy flow. It's all about the blend of substances. But, normally, spirits' excess ectoplasm is left on the items they messed with. Humans can feel it a little, but they don't know what it is."

"So, you mean someone will feel the energy you left on the d—" I paused and covered my mouth. I was about to give it away!

Umbra stared at me oddly, one eyebrow slightly up.

I had to cover myself. ". . . stuff . . . ," I said with a cheesy grin.

Umbra let it go and continued to answer my questions. "Yeah, but only for a little while. It just feels sticky, like a small covering of honey is on it." I giggled at that, seeing the drummer with his sticky sticks in my mind's eyes.

"Yet, something bothers me . . . ," Umbra said, his face looking down at the tiles. "If the ectoplasm had shards in it, that means the creator of the message created them on their own. Ectoplasm doesn't have those, especially kinds that can affect humans, no matter how much power you have with our world. So, that leaves two things: one, this messenger is really powerful, more so than me even, and two . . ." He looked at me worried, like someone was going to take me in front of his eyes. He sighed while looking at my worried face before he turned his head to continue. "They didn't want you knowing about the message. It is possible they could be . . ."

"The murderer," I whispered in horror.

"I'm sorry you got hurt . . ." Umbra looked so pained, taking in the fault for him not being there. That was just ludicrous! I wanted to scream at him and hug him, destroying the guilty face.

"No! It's my fault Umbra! I . . . I shouldn't have touched the thing. It was stupid . . ."

"Yes, yes it was," Umbra said bluntly, nodding smugly to himself a few times.

I was thrown backward by the surprise turn of the conversation.

"It was stupid, but I understand. I don't expect anything less from an impractical human . . ."

I laughed nervously. Umbra's verbal insults really burned. But, Umbra interrupted my moment, changing his tone again to serious and lonely. "Stary, this really is bad. Our enemy is not only close, but more powerful than I ever hoped this early in the game. I need to see your cut."

Startled, I hid my finger and folded it against my chest. All I told Umbra was it was an odd shape, so if he saw the broken moon . . . "Umbra, really, it's okay. I would rather not have you worry over nothing."

"Stary, it was smoking! Damn right I'm going to worry about you!" He yelled at my face so intensely that I began to shake. I knew he was trying to be nice, but for some reason I felt self-conscious about my scar. Lucifer could have used me as a pawn to get his point across to Umbra: *evil will prevail through my minion.* It was my action that marked me; I refused to get Umbra or Maren involved in more concern!

"Umbra, please . . . it's not necessary." My voice sounded mousey.

All the light in Umbra's eyes had turned dark, his voice losing all kindness. "Stary, let me see your finger."

I stepped back a little more, out of the pillar's shadow, but still hidden a tiny bit. All I could do was quiver. My mind was a blur, like viewing a highway when you're half-asleep.

Umbra didn't care about my personal space anymore and got in my face, his palm under my chin. "Let me see your finger now!" His shout was more vicious than before.

"No . . . ," I said scared, but I stood tall as I took another small step back.

"God, Stary! Let me see your finger now! Stop acting like a baby!" His voice was so booming and aggravated that my heart echoed it into a black vibe, washing my once happy soul with dark energy. I knew I was acting childish, but I was not letting Umbra look at my finger. It looked awful and I would have rather had him angry at my sudden dedication to the sin of too much pride than to attack him with a picture of guilt.

"NO!" I screamed with my eyes shut and tears trying to escape. The rest was a haze. Umbra began to wrestle with me to see my finger: grabbing my shoulder, then hips, and then arms tight. I was determined not to let him see my mark of shame. Plus, I knew he really wouldn't hurt me so I fought back. In the procedure, I guess we slipped backwards and away from the pillar, but it wasn't a huge change for us to notice it.

Once I saw a little light peek through the streams of our tango, I began to kick him in the stomach, but not too hard; I just needed him off me. He kept yelling at me to see my finger and I would always reply "no" at full volume, without looking at him. I couldn't believe I was fighting Umbra in public! I am not sure what our dear Lord was thinking of it!

"That's it . . . ," Umbra growled low, his voice filled with intensity. I feared he was about to do something undignified. Umbra stepped back a foot and with amazing speed, scooped me up in his arms like he was carrying a bride effortlessly.

"Calm down!" he roared, looking directly into my eyes, staring me down; even my bones bent to submit.

I could see he didn't want us fighting and I knew he was concerned about me, but I just didn't want him looking at my scar. The pain was gone and I wanted that to be a symbol to bury the memory deep, to only let me suffer through the physical reminder. That was irritating; he most likely wouldn't listen anyway.

His breath came out jagged. If I gave him a work out, good!

Our faces were so close and being cuddled in his arms like that . . . it made me blush as bright as ninety-nine red balloons. I had to use sad human tactics. I kicked my feet in midair, making him struggle to not drop me. His eyes were vast and fiery as I tried to escape his grasp.

"No Umbra!" I screamed, unable to control it or look at his handsome face. He was having trouble and looked at me with mystification and pure resentment. He wasn't giving in the slightest. I forgot; he was programmed for super strength and he was waiting for me to back down.

I stopped for a second, realizing what was going on then I got mad at him and myself. So what does stupid me do? I began to punch his chest, his iron chest, with all my might as I kept repeating "no," stressing the word more each time I said it.

Umbra exhaled hatefully and began to shout at me again. "Stary, stop it! You're making me really mad."

I knew he was sugar coating his amount of anger towards me, but I was in too deep now and I wasn't going to give in; a rare stubborn streak was in control now.

"Why can't you just leave it alone Umbra?" I screeched, still hitting him.

He then threw me in the air a foot, scaring me to death, but he caught me before giving me a piercing, wicked stare. "I don't listen to idiots," he told me dryly.

First off, I *hate* heights and he knew it. How dare he pick me up in the first place and then scare me like that? And that idiot comment . . . OH, it was on! "How dare you?" I shouted, full of rage myself, punching his unbreakable right shoulder hard, making it pop. I hurt my fist, but I didn't care. It was worth it.

"How dare I? How dare *I*?! You're the one being unreasonable!" I almost saw fire come out of his mouth and smoke out of his ears.

"Because you won't listen to my request!" I informed him, my voice like ice.

The battle began; a battle of hurtful words, insults, and fury. I still kicked him, trying to escape, but there was no hope. His face was against my blazing cheek, shouting in my ear cruel phrases. I pushed his cheek away with both of my hands, hiding my finger still. This was insane. I was not even sure what was happening anymore!

In the background, I heard my name in a breathless and mousey tone. "Stary?"

Shocked, I turned my head, eyes wide, to see Rin, Lauren, and Chloe staring at me, white and pale in alarm. I looked at the tile and realized to them, I was floating in midair.

Umbra and I paused at the same time, both with huge deer-in-the-headlights type eyes. I jumped out of his now frozen arms and gazed at my friends' blank expressions. My mouth was opened, shuddering, trying to think of an excuse, but that was impossibly difficult. What was I going to say that sounded like it made sense? I had to think of something . . .

"Well, ah . . . ha, ha, you see, ummmmm, well . . . I, ummmmm . . ." It *was* impossible! I laughed nervously, looking towards their faces, but not into their judgmental eyes.

Their mouths were now opened in little 'O's like mine. I rubbed the back of my head with my palm, still fake laughing to keep myself from weeping. We only had about one minute until lunch was over. *Ring darn bell! RING!* My mind raced to think of an un-lame and un-dismissive answer.

Then, I thought of something in the middle. I was about ready to say it when I noticed Chloe was tipping over to the left and her eyes looked foggy. All of a sudden, she fell backward. Thank heaven Rin was able to catch her!

Lauren and I ran over to her. "Chloe!" Sprinting by impulse, I slid roughly on the tile floor to her right. She fainted! I made my best friend faint! "Chloe! Chloe! Please wake up!" I screamed, holding her hand, looking directly at her pained, but sleeping face.

"Hey, Chloe . . . wake up! I can't hold you forever and I *know* I can't carry you!" Rin yelled too, partly in personal discomfort, before she flicked Chloe on the cheeks to get her attention. Tears began to well up in my eyes. I felt appalling: spying on Umbra, being stupid by touching the unknown light, physically hurting Umbra when he was trying to help me, allowing myself to be exposed, lying to my dearest friends, and now, making my most treasured friend faint. I'm the worst kind of person.

It took all my might not to sob on Chloe's soft hand. Lauren was strong, so she helped prop Chloe up on Rin and then ran to get the nearest teacher. I wrapped my arm around Chloe's waist to help Rin support her until we could get her somewhere comfortable. While Rin still tapped her, I looked up at our table to see that hardly anyone was in the lunchroom. Did the bell ring or did I miss something?

Rin must have read my thoughts because she answered me, "The bells are off a few seconds, so everyone was scared Mr. Tin would get mad and they lined up early. Chloe was worried about you and begged us to stay and wait . . ."

I pouted in shame. Chloe, a true angel on Earth . . . She was good to me and I worried her.

"I'm sorry Rin. Something happened and . . ." I broke off, squeezing Chloe's hand in my own to tell her how sorry I was. I had to hide my face in fear of crying in front of tough Rin.

I heard a sigh and felt a light but quick tap on my right shoulder. Surprised, I popped up with puffy eyes and gazed at Rin, who had an understanding smile on her face. "Don't worry yourself about it; I trust you had a good reason."

I forced a smile and refused to be sad anymore. I had to focus on getting Chloe safe again. I was glad Rin was in tune with the unnatural because she would understand if she knew the true reason, but I also knew she didn't have strong enough powers to be my enemy. She was an incredible friend and maybe an ally in a sense.

Lauren sprinted towards us and then crawled by me, squeezing my wrists painfully tight, sliding them out from Chloe while throwing them on the ground. I was about to protest when I looked to see she was helping Rin lift Chloe to a chair. I gazed up at her in shock.

Lauren looked down at me, her eyes smiling a little. "You're too weak Stary. I got it."

I colored a little and nodded. Lauren was also a great friend. I heard her tell Rin that the teacher was on his way after she told Mr. Tin what had happened.

I sighed, jabbing my guts, able to catch myself when I remembered the pillar. Nervous, I turned to look at it, but Umbra was gone. My chest got stiff and my heart began to hammer. It broke my insides more seeing he was gone in a second, even though I needed to watch Chloe. I was scared: fearful of losing him and terrified of getting too close to him. Umbra really was a good guy. I gazed down at my scarred finger. The scar was hardly visible and the moon pieces almost blended together to look normal, humanly normal. Why was darkness mocking me?

"I'm here. How is she?" I heard a kind and half-panicked male voice behind me. I raised my neck upward to see a young teacher on his knees looking at Chloe. I'd never seen him before in class, until I remembered he was the teacher on duty that caught my funny dance with Umbra! Wow, that seemed so long ago! I was trapped in my position, unable to move. I felt like I was watching someone else's horrible dream.

"Chloe!" Rin screamed, almost excitedly, and I heard Lauren exhale. In amazement, I saw Chloe flutter her eyes a little and heard a steady groan of confusion.

I ran to her, faster than I could have wished, landing on the floor in front of her. With a relieved smile, I rubbed her forearms and looked up into her half-opened eyes. Full of hope, I bawled. "Chloe! Thank gosh you're awake! Are you okay?"

Chloe, looking dopey, gawked down at me, and extremely tired, said, "Stary . . . ?" Then, her eyes flew open and she clawed my wrists with her nails to make sure I was real.

Warning alarms were buzzing in my cerebral. Oh no . . . she remembers!

"Stary . . . you're here! But, how . . . I mean . . . you were . . . up . . ." and like that, her head fell backward, her eyes became as clear as glass, and she was out like a light.

Lauren nudged her shoulders a little and the teacher rubbed her sides. I got a small glare from Rin that told me to let Chloe wake up before talking to her. I was a little hurt, but I was madder at myself for rushing. Scared I would be caught in a wildfire, I tiptoed backward until I was close to the pillar again, awaiting my chance to embrace my best friend once more.

I sighed deeply with my eyes closed, feeling dizzy myself, trying to get comfortable when I heard my name being called in a rush of panic, a ring of angelic harmony. "Stary!"

Befuddled, I looked to my left to see Maren, beautiful Maren, with her hair a mess, her face flushed and paler than usual, and her eyes dancing a spell to escape some sort of unknown hell.

I walked a few steps to save her some breath. She sounded sickly and short of breath.

She met me, half-jumping into my arms. I grabbed her delicate wrists, dragged her behind the nearest pillar, and brought her a few inches closer to me to calm her with my warmth. "Maren . . . what happened? What's wrong? Are you—"

Breathless, she stopped my questions with one of her own. "Where is Umbra? I need to talk to Umbra, now!"

13

SCARED, I SCANNED MAREN OVER TO BETTER SEE IF I COULD HELP her. The proper young woman I knew and adored was no longer there. Her curtsy was listless and her eyes had an almost psychotic look about them like they were about to explode. I caught my breath and held her shoulders to support her frozen balance. "Maren, please tell me what's wrong." My voice was as kind and gentle as I could make it, but Maren only looked worse.

"Stary . . . I . . . it's just . . . I really need Umbra . . ."

I felt horrible that Umbra might not want to come since I was there. Yet, Maren looked like she was about to faint, looking paler every time she took an uneven breath.

"Maren . . . I . . ." I sighed in defeat and shame, not sure to tell her that I made Umbra extremely upset over my own foolish pride and instinct. "I'm not sure where Umbra is right now . . . ," I stated.

Maren's eyes began to look puffy and pink, but no tears were coming out. The situation was all so bad! Even I knew that if you can't produce tears, something was really wrong. I shook her hard. "Maren, please calm down."

Her body was still frozen. Her frightened lips began to move as if she was going to speak, but all I heard was silence. My heart began to beat so loudly that I could hear it through my clothes. I got in Maren's face, staring into her crystal glass eyes, praying life would come back into them. I rubbed her shoulders to loosen her stance and soothe her.

I faked a smile to hide my fear and made my aura sparkle with a beaming glow to snap her back to reality. "Hey, Maren . . . it will be all right . . . Umbra will be back soon, I'm sure." I had to stop; my voice was failing to sound hopeful.

It all happened too fast. Maren began to fall forward. I was able to turn around and grab her waist, then spin her around to lift her up into a straight position. Her eyes were shut, yet I knew she was conscious. Goose bumps formed all over her frail body and something tingled my hand, the one that was supporting her back. It was cold and slimy and sent an electric shock through my hand that made it feel like it was on fire. Her back, something was literally going up her spine, but the evil feeling was in a shape like a snake! A poison-filled, no good snake! It seeped into my core, shattering my strength from the inside.

It made her back make a disgusting cracking noise and I could have sworn it sent me a silent message: "*You're almost too late . . .*" My eyes lifted up from the floor to see a pitch black shadow form around her slippers.

In a terror-filled state, both for her aura and my sanity, I almost clawed her shoulders and screamed with all my might while shaking her like a tree you want an apple from. "MAREN! God . . . please . . . PLEASE WAKE MAREN UP!"

Tears were streaming down my face. I couldn't lose someone else, not in one five minute block. I pushed the toxic thoughts out of my system. I refused to let Lucifer or his followers defeat me!

God must have heard my prayers, for ever so delicately, Maren fluttered her eyelashes like a beautiful butterfly and she allowed the sun to enter her eyes. She still looked weak and pale, but some lovely peach tones hit her rosy cheeks and she was able to somewhat stand, but I still held on to her just in case. Like an illusion, the poison invisibly poured out of my fingertips, the poison I didn't know I ever absorbed. Perhaps my powers absorbed the evil and released it when I touched her? Still, it was gone now, as if it never existed and the cold reptile was nowhere to be found. The only sensation left was the traces of the poison my Spirit Warrior powers sensed as it left Maren and me.

She rocked a little and looked at me, seeming misplaced. Suddenly, she let out a huge breath with an agonizing sound. Maren was awake now, coughing and choking to get clean air into her lungs.

I stared, wide-eyed, allowing her a few moments to recover. Her coughing, the chill in the air . . . it was like what happened to me in my dream the night before I met Maren and Umbra! But how did it—

"Stary," Maren interrupted my thinking, but I didn't care; she seemed better, although still frantic.

I had new tears welling up in my eyes, but not from sadness or fear. I smiled and gave her a small, light hug before I let go of her hands.

Maren blinked rapidly and then she gasped, looking like a light bulb just flickered on in her head. "Stary! Do you know where Umbra is?"

"I'm right here."

I heard the voice, but it seemed to be coming from underneath me? Maren and I, both puzzled, looked down at the ground to see a small black dot, yet it didn't stay that way for long. Umbra jumped out of the circle in between Maren and me. Startled, I screamed and jumped back. Maren only shook her head with a small, disapproving frown.

Umbra looked back at me sideways, pleased by my reaction. I must have look confused for he bumped me with his butt, making me lose my balance and having to grab a trashcan lid for support. I growled, but he winked with a deliciously, devilish smile before turning away. I blushed and had to take a few long breaths prior to sliding upward to hear what Maren had to say. I wasn't sure if I was supposed to, but I cared for her too much not to try.

"I saw . . ." Maren's voice was so low and husky, I had to rub my eyes to make sure it was her. Her eyes were clearer than usual, almost cold looking and they appeared to be looking through me. Umbra nodded hard, pausing to make his shoulders move up tight like a wall shielding me from Maren's words. I didn't care about Umbra blocking me! After her attack, I was not taking chances. I had to know what was going on and Umbra's "wall" was about to come down like the one in Berlin! Maren stopped in her tracks and gazed at me, her blue eyes ample with an unknown emotion to me.

Umbra half-tilted toward me, leaning close to my ear as I leaned on his muscular shoulder for support. I halted, in fear of becoming red since his lips were so close to my ear; I could almost feel when they moved to form words. His cool breath tickled my skin and gave me goose bumps. We were both hidden completely in the darkness of the pillar, but I bet my face could have lit the whole lunchroom.

Umbra took in a deep breath before speaking, "Give Maren a little space. It's not that she doesn't trust you, but let her do things in her own delicate way. Okay, Stary?"

I looked at his priceless face. I wanted to be nice to Maren and respect her wishes, but I also wanted to be let in on the situation, especially after seeing her almost collapse on me. Yet Umbra's eyes were so hypnotizing that I had to remember to breathe no matter how much my ribs ached or how many butterflies my stomach had.

I nodded like a puppy in trouble again, allowing the melody of my unknown song pound life back into my overworked chest and then I leaned on his back to hide from Maren. This made him chuckle. Umbra was warm through his clothes, but soon, all I heard were mumbles between Maren and him. My mind and ears did as obeyed, but my heart and eyes were trapped into wanting to embrace Umbra's warmth for a long time. I felt like I was the one who was dead to the living world.

Umbra must not have felt the same way for he gestured with his arms to state emphasis for me to go away, physically blocking me more from the conversation. It made me sad to be shut out, but I ignored the feeling because I heard Umbra's voice incline, the shock making me lose my balance and bump my head into his shoulder blade.

As I rubbed my head from the throbbing pain, the thrill of touching him was little by little leaving me and I felt all right then. I groaned from the slowly subsiding pain and stood up a tad straighter. Umbra and Maren blinked at the noise I made and stared at me. I blushed timidly and giggled, sounding more like an idiot.

Maren heaved a sigh but smiled, her blue eyes shining again. "It is all right Stary. You do not have to hide behind Umbra unless you want to of course."

Umbra and I stared at each other at the same time with big eyes, red faces, and tight lips. I let go of his shirt like it was a hot pot and rubbed my arms to cool my body temperature down.

After I felt like me again, I placed my arms behind me and gave Maren a playful look as Umbra stared at me with a dazed, stupid expression. I beamed and rubbed Maren's little wrist with my palm.

"Maren . . ." I bent my knees down four inches so she would be taller. "I want to be there for you. I understand you're scared to tell me, but I can handle it. I'll do anything I can as a Spirit Warrior and as a friend. So, please tell me, what's wrong?"

She raised her shoulders up and gave me a small hug. "I . . . well, I . . . I feel the trace of the murderer and it is very near . . ." Her adorable voice was flat, but she was shaking like an earthquake. My mouth dropped. I knew the day would come, but I really wasn't sure when and being told like that felt so bizarre . . .

"EH?!" Umbra yelped. I blinked, surprised at him and Maren looked just as confused, I guess because Umbra made the Japanese noise for shock. It would have been funny if it wasn't a serious time. Umbra gasped and slapped his mouth fast; like doing that would make us forget!

"You mean, you didn't know?" I asked, confused.

Umbra struggled to get his plastered hand off his mouth. He gasped for some air before saying, "NO! All Maren told me was there was evil energy nearby!"

I looked at Maren, then back at Umbra a few times; they were having a personal conversation with glances and I didn't want to interrupt anymore. Once I thought they were finished, I mustered up all my courage to bend on my knees to look into Maren's eyes once more and ask her a tough and fearful question: "Where or who do you feel the energy from Maren?"

With her index finger shaking like a seizure, I followed the path. There, behind Chloe, Rin, Lauren, and the teacher, was a familiar face hiding in the shadows and slowly turning to leave the lunchroom. My insides blazed, but my outsides froze. I couldn't locate my lungs. Umbra patted my shoulder, but his hand was shaking too. There, walking slowly away from my life, yet soon, I would be confronting her . . . was Barbara.

I swallowed hard, but my mouth was dry. I was numb to the core. I studied Barbara's retreating figure, hidden behind my dear friends still trying to wake up Chloe. How long had she been there with those devious black eyes, chilling my bones to a rotting state with one quick glance? Did she see me talk to Maren and Umbra or, more importantly, could she *see* them?

I began to tip over and had to grab the pillar for support. Umbra leaned on the wall behind me, stern and silent. Maren was still frozen in her pointing pose, but now her lovely eyes were full of concern for us.

"I . . . I can't believe it . . . Barbara . . . is . . . I mean . . . I've known her since elementary school . . ." I was on my knees, my flaming hands pressed painfully against the cool floor. Barbara and I have never been best friends and I knew she had been acting strange lately, plus the whole energy thing, but still . . . maybe my heart didn't want to believe someone so close to me and my friends, who was an avid member of her church . . . was a mad killer. Who would?

Umbra *hmph*ed and straightened up before talking; I knew he thought the same way I did. "I have felt a similar connection with that girl and the murderer. However, the evil energy is starting to turn in the air space, making everyone get a little on them."

"So, energy is like cobwebs? It's hard to see them sometimes, but when you walk through one, you flip out?"

Umbra nodded.

I propped myself upward as straight as I could and gazed at Umbra's wisdom with moist eyes, my hair smacking my face in the process. His words were truthful, but it sounded like he was trying to sugarcoat the situation for me, making me feel better. He paused to look at me and turned away with a funny look on his face like a child getting in trouble. I guess I looked terrible for him to do that.

He continued: "She has been acting very dark lately, more than normal I'm guessing by what you've told me about her and how everyone around her is on edge."

Could Umbra read minds?!

He corrected my thinking. "I can tell by their expressions!" His voice cracked as he shouted, sounding nervous at the same time. I sighed from relief before standing up to face them.

Maren cocked her head sideways, making her once worried face look gray.

I sighed and had to confirm the realization, pointblank. "So, you have a lock on the murderer's vibes in Barbara and she is the main suspect to being the murderer?"

Maren smiled before correcting me. "If the energy was inside Barbara, that would mean she *is* the murderer. However . . . I only feel it on her, more than anyone else here. So, it probably means the murderer is around her a lot . . ."

I took such a large breath from relief that I began to cough. So, Barbara may not be the murderer after all. Thank heaven! It was really scary to think someone you played Candy Land with would try to kill you someday!

I suddenly felt a sense of pride in my mission as I addressed my spirit friends. "Regardless, we have to examine her and who she's with. It . . . sad to say, may be possible that she's hiding her vibe, making her stronger than we thought . . ."

Umbra stared at me. Looking at him sideways, I narrowed my eyes and gave a nod of confidence. Umbra, surprise still in his dazzling eyes, closed his lips together and nodded in agreement. Umbra's information about the blue shard that hurt my finger meant the murderer could be that capable and I was not risking anyone else's life.

"There she goes!" Maren shouted, snapping me out of my conversation with myself, but my leadership skills were still burning inside my chest.

"Let's go . . . ," I commanded full of power. I ran with Maren and Umbra behind me. My mind was so focused at that point that nothing in the world could have stopped me. I zipped past my friends, not even sure they saw me leave. I made a silent promise that I'd come back soon to Chloe as I ran by her.

Inhaling deeply, I continued my focal point and ran faster with Umbra on my tail. Barbara was heading for the lobby . . . but, she had Mr. Tin's class with me, so why? My vision became blurry and my hair was slapping back like a whip, but I didn't care; it only made me run harder and try to be stronger. My target was in sight, about fifteen feet away. Barbara was walking slow and normal, yet seemed to get farther ahead of me as Umbra and I were both running insanely. Her walk was so calm, almost inhuman . . .

"Stary!" Something grabbed my left arm and for a brief second, I was frozen in an unmovable position, dazed and confused. Then, quickly, I was flung backward in a painful jerk, but landed on something semi-hard, yet soft. Shaking, I opened my eyes to see a hand was around my waist and I had landed on a chest, a boy's chest to be more exact. It smelled amazing like the ocean breeze, and the blurred colors that were once mixed in my eyes became a clear bright red and white stripe. Gazing up, bewildered, I looked into the gentle eyes and smiling face of Credence.

Realizing who was holding me, my face turned blood red and I lost my ability to speak like an intelligent person. "Oh . . . ah . . . Credence! What . . . I mean, are . . . um, well . . . Hi . . ." I sounded like a mouse, a stupid mouse who wanted to hit herself with a baseball bat.

I felt the vibrations of his enchanting laughter moving up and down his chest. My stomach began to do flip-flops as my cheeks heated like a stove. "Hi yourself."

Credence really was adorable and handsome all at the same time and his laugh was really . . . special. Still, it didn't echo like someone else's I recalled. Then I remembered: Barbara, Umbra, Maren, evil energy, deadly . . .

"I guess I should let you go," he teased.

"Oh . . . uh, yeah . . ." I hopped down and dusted my legs off, hiding my embarrassed face by fixing my hair. I really didn't want to be let down. Still . . . my mind was focused and won the match against my heart's wishes, although it was still fighting strong.

"I guess I'll see you later . . ." I waved, walking away slowly, but he grabbed my arm again, dragging me close, almost into an embrace. His eyes were as focused as my mind! What could he want?

"Stary, there's been something I've really been wanting to tell you all week, but I've been too nervous in seminar with all those people . . ."

I gazed into his dull eyes that were telling me his tone was serious. How did he know I would be here alone? I really wanted to hug him and tell him my dearest thoughts right that second, but it was not the time or place, here in his affectionate arms, locking into his tranquil, breathtaking eyes, with that priceless face and . . . I had to get out of there fast before I forgot my mission! I sighed in defeat and utter disappointment. The murderer would pay for this later!

I gave him what I thought to be my most attractive and warmest smile. He slid back an inch and blushed a little with mystified eyes. His reaction made me blush harder and I had to gulp to get back on track. "Credence, I'm really happy you want to tell me something and it seems important and hard for you, but I really need to go. Please, can it wait until tomorrow? I promise I'll make sure we're alone. Still, thank you for being so sweet." The last sentence came out in a Southern belle-like drawl like from *Gone with the Wind*. Man, I really needed to leave before I was too tempted to have him whisk me away! I waved and once more, turned to leave, the yearning to stay with him *very* strong.

"Stary, please wait . . . It will only take a minute!" Credence grabbed my wrist again, a little tighter this time. My face was flushed, forced to look at him closer. He looked so sad. Gosh . . . I had been praying for months that he would act that way with me and, of course, the one time I couldn't stay . . . Someone in the universe must have disliked me! I wish I could have told him that a minute may have made everything too late.

"Credence . . . I really want to, but there's something—"

"*PLEASE!*" he screamed with tears almost in his eyes, his grip around me almost hurting. My legs kept trying to move forward, but I was trapped under his spell. His hurt face was so close that I felt his minty breath and my impulses wanted to kiss him, although my legs still kept trying to go.

"She said let go, buddy boy!" I heard an intense and low threat by Credence's ear. Umbra! I forgot that they were there. The next thing I knew, Umbra flung his body forward, ramming into Credence's lower chest (making sure not to hit me), and Credence fell down to the ground on his knees, body shaking and eyes sealed shut.

Umbra made a disapproving noise aimed at Credence and stood up high and proud before popping his collar up like a bad boy. I glared at him in disbelief that he was that rough, but he only shrugged me off with his jerky attitude. I guess some things will never change.

I ran to Credence, scared Umbra might have aimed in the wrong place. Bent on my knees and my arms supporting him with maximum comfort, I asked him the obvious question: "Credence, are you okay?"

He smiled a slight bit, making his hurt face look a little lighter. After a few seconds of struggling, he opened his eyes halfway to look at me. "Yeah . . . I wonder what that was," he said while rubbing his hair.

I laughed nervously and jumped up to lend him a hand, giving a small grin. Getting to hold Credence's hand for a few seconds was nice and doing it that way didn't make me get nervous since I was doing a good deed. Credence looked a little taken aback, smiling at me just as big and somehow, I pulled him up.

I fixed his collar and smiled sweetly like I was his wife. He blinked and looked stunned, but it made him look so adorable that I had about a million butterflies taking flight in my stomach.

However, I stayed focused. I tucked my hands behind my back and stared at his picture perfect face one last time. "Credence, I really am sorry for all the trouble, but I really need to find Barbara. It's urgent."

"Barbara?" He placed his finger under his chin and tilted his head a little like a puppy. Lord, he's too cute! I wanted to scream that to the clouds, but I took a breath and nodded at him calmly. Credence pointed towards the main lobby. "I saw her pass that way a few seconds before I saw you actually. She had her stuff with her, so maybe she's going home."

Credence really was amazing! "Thank you so much Credence!" I said full of too much cheerleader-like energy.

He blushed cherry red and smiled like a beam of new born sunshine. Gradually, with that look plastered on his flawless face, he walked towards me and grabbed my hand. I had to remember how to inhale and think to control my heartbeat. I thought I heard a giggle and a groan from behind me, but I didn't care.

"I understand, but I'll get you next time Stary Moon and tell you what I really want to tell you, okay?" It was a threat, but a sexy, to-die-for threat. I nodded and began to run. I looked back at his expressionless face for a few seconds before strutting forward to continue my task at hand. I heard Umbra right beside me mumble something fowl in an anger-filled tone under his tongue, but I couldn't clearly tell what it was. He did, however, look back at Credence longer than I did.

Getting to the lobby seemed like an endless journey, but we made it to the open area. The white tile reflected the noon sun, making the room eerie. It was hard to see anything for a few moments, my eyes adjusting to the brightness. Once I could see, there wasn't a soul around.

Crap! We were too late. Barbara was nowhere to be found and the energy was nearly eaten up by the normal atmosphere. I hit my leg hard, angry at myself. I wanted to sink to the floor. If my stupid emotions didn't get in the way, maybe we could have caught Barbara and interrogate her.

I heard Umbra grunt, looking toward the clear doors. I bet it was Credence's fault to him. I was still a little miffed of how hard he tackled my poor Credence. Maren heaved a sigh, almost whining a little, but then, I felt her fingers brush my shoulder in a supporting fashion. I thanked her without words by leaning my head closer to hers; she must have understood how difficult it was for me to leave Credence like that.

I heard a moan then that evaporated my thoughts, but it was in front of me, not behind me. Shocked, I saw a sore sight: Cally Sun was bent down, shaking like a seismic activity was planted into her frail bones. She was on the cold floor, her head under the bench, and her legs dangled by the short heater attached to the window's edge. I ran to her as fast as I could, almost tripping along the way. She was shivering, looking like she was terrified of something. There, by her right elbow, was a normal bruise, but looking at it gave me the worst feeling in the world. My suspicions about Barbara were beginning to dawn on me and it was a cruel slap in the face from reality.

"Cally. Cally . . . Hey, Cally! Wake up! Are you okay? Cally?" I was shaking her shoulder with all my might. I was tired of people fainting in front of my eyes, seeing them in such terminal discomfort. It broke my heart and made my blood boil.

Ever so carefully, I rolled her on her back, away from the bench so she would not bump her head. Maren somehow managed to get Cally's feet off the heater without burning her ankles. Together, we propped her up by the legs of the bench, making her head lean on my shoulder. As Maren checked her for more marks, I heaved for a moment; being a weakling sucked!

Cally's poor little face was like a glass doll that had just been dumped on the side of the road by her beloved owner. It was filthy from the floor and her stylish red-framed glasses had marks across them.

Again, she groaned, but I felt her move a bit up and down my shoulder blade. With a smile, I gazed down to see her pale face fill with rosy luster. I decided to sit her up so she would be looking at me, hoping it'd make her less confused, yet I supported her weight by holding her shoulders tight.

"Huh?" I heard her whisper as she moved her head back and forth, ruffling her shoulder length hair. Watching her wake up, looking so innocent, somehow sent a sharp blade of rage in my body and its sharpness was more painful than a foil through the chest. I inspected myself to make sure I wasn't hit, but the pain vanished as fast as it came. Forgetting the sensation, my reactions led me to Cally's now opened amber eyes.

"Oh . . . Stary . . . ! OH! Miss Stary!" I groaned to myself: *Miss Stary*? I really didn't do anything special. I heard Umbra snicker as Maren's shy giggle blended perfectly with his, forcing me to give them a be-silent-now face.

Cally flipped her hair from side to side, looking lost and dazed. She placed her hand where her heart was and held on to her shirt. Her poor eyes were teary and devoted to looking only at me. "I do not remember what happened, but thank you so much Miss Stary. You really are a truly wonderful and blessed person. I wish I can someday be like you and have the honor of calling you a friend . . ."

What was this, the colonial period? Umbra lost it and laughed so low and hardy that I thought he was going to explode. He was bent down on his knees, moisture forming in his eyes. I gave him my most annoyed face, but then I saw Maren holding her pale hand against her lips and her chest was moving like crazy as her cheeks became super red. I guess she was trying to hold it in for my sake.

I moaned, ready to set Cally straight. "Hmmm, I really didn't do anything Cally . . ."

She interrupted me. "Miss Stary, that is not true! Your heart is so light that it warms my soul and amazes me to no end." Her face was red and she looked away. More chuckles from my lovely audience. I sighed hard; the adoring fan routine was getting old fast.

I gave her my hand to help her up. Like a child with a crush for the first time, she looked at my hand with a brighter than day smile and allowed me to pull her up. She didn't let go and only gazed at me more longingly. I hoped she hadn't fallen in love with me!

"Thank you so much Miss Stary. I do not deserve such an honor." She bowed her head in respect and then leaned forward, inches from my face. I gulped, scared and lost for words. The fall must have made her loopy.

I shook my hand and looked at her firmly to tell her my standing. "All right, all right, it really was nothing. You do not have to call me Miss Stary. In fact, *please* don't! Stary is fine."

Cally nodded, embarrassed. "I apologize if I made you uncomfortable. Extreme politeness was something my parents beat into me." She smirked for a millisecond but replaced it with a full smile before I could blink.

I shook off the image. "So, what happened? Why were you halfway out cold under the bench?"

Cally snapped out of her freaky state and then cocked her head, confused.

I sighed and asked, trying to sound a little less annoyed this time. "Do you remember anything that happened?"

She giggled and rubbed her hair, turning ninety degrees away from me. I guessed she was uncomfortable since she couldn't recollect the event. "Well, ah, I do actually remember . . ."

I looked at her attentively. Umbra and Maren also finally stopped laughing.

"I was sitting down resting, waiting for my mother to pick me up for a doctor's appointment. I saw Barbara, walking really fast towards the door. I stood up to say a quick hello to her. Suddenly, well . . ." Cally paused, sounding petrified, and refused to look at me.

"Her eyes were so dark, almost pitch black, with what looked like some blood in the center. I asked her if she was okay, but she approached me and, well . . . pushed me into the wall, telling me to stop looking at her. I remember being awake, but I could not open my eyes longer than a second and my body was throbbing. The next thing I knew, I was with you."

I was lost for feelings, lost for emotions, and my heart was scared and angry, all at the same time. Barbara had no right to do that to Cally! But, now . . . Barbara may be fading to the abyss of despair and she was planning on taking others with her.

Maren said others' presences could land on us, so maybe Cally had some of mine on her. I know the murderer was after me, but what was Barbara after? If they were not the same person, maybe they were working together? I needed to see Barbara for myself, to look into those deadly eyes no matter what happened to me. Umbra and Maren nodded, agreeing they were both with me.

Yet, I had no idea what traits the true murderer had or where to find them. The murderer was so powerful, according to Umbra's fears of the power of the shard that marked my finger. And sweet Maren . . . she worked so hard, but the trail had always turned so faint in an instant. I had to finish the mission as soon as possible.

"Cally!" I grabbed her shoulders a little too intensely. "Do you have any idea where Barbara went?"

Cally's eyes became huge, puzzlement filling them. She took in a small breath to answer. "I am afraid I do not."

I sighed with my head down in deep defeat.

Cally added, "I did notice the van she got in had tons of white roses in the back. I saw it before I passed out. She glared at me before getting into the van through the back way."

White roses? Why would Barbara have white roses? Wait! Her mom owned a flower shop, so maybe she was helping her mom take them to their new owner. Who would get that many white roses? I looked at Umbra leaning on the cool window, looking extremely handsome with the white light shining through his dark hair. White . . . the color of a pure maiden . . . A pure maiden is her loveliest when she is in love . . . That's it! The roses were for a wedding!

"Thank you so much Cally!" I hugged her shoulders, leaping in the air as I ran toward the lunchroom with Umbra and Maren following my trail. I knew I left Cally there confused, but she would be all right with that kind smile of hers. I smiled for the pieces, no matter how scary the puzzle was, were finally fitting together.

I stopped gradually to catch my breath, remembering who I was and what I was. Although I had this unusual gift, I was mortal and had to rest. For a few minutes, I had forgotten that. Umbra stopped as well, looking at me oddly and Maren placed her pale hand on her chest, looking at me with eyes of worry. Tears were forming in my eyes and my throat was on fire, the pain tickling my mouth.

I was able to get enough air into me to give a hard sigh and stand up a little. As I was catching my breath, I looked down to see the lunchroom and there, still where I left them, was Chloe and the others. My body became numb with concern. I had to check on her before anything else.

"Stary, you okay? What are you staring at?" Umbra asked annoyingly. He was on the edge, in the zone, ready to settle the score with the murderer; that was easy to see.

I turned to look at him and continued to breathe little by little, sounding weaker than I really was, sweat forming on my forehead. "I . . . I have . . . to . . . check . . . on Chloe . . . first . . ."

Umbra glanced down at Chloe and then at me puzzled. I guess he didn't understand why I would lose my focus on the murderer's trail for another human. He informed me with a snippy voice, "She's moving her head up and she's fine. We have more important things to worry about. Let's go now!" He already had his back turned toward me before finishing his last sentence.

I didn't move; I only watched him. This made him stop to give me a cruel look, but in front of him, Maren didn't move an inch either, throwing him off guard. She looked weary and tedious.

"I can't just leave Umbra!" My breathing was fine now, but I was so stunned by Umbra thinking I could walk out of school with no one noticing when my father worked here!

Umbra growled at me like a German shepherd on duty, his eyes narrowed, glaring red as he clenched his teeth so tightly together, I thought they would break. I took a step back, almost bumping into the window. Umbra was really determined. I understood, but I just couldn't face danger right that second. Maybe I'd never truly be ready. The cruel thought dawned on me, piercing me like the fangs of the serpent I encountered earlier in my vision.

"Umbra . . ." Maren's voice was faint, but so crisp and beautiful sounding as it traveled in the air to our ears. Umbra turned his head to look at her, only softening his hard look a hair. Maren looked timid as well, staring at his beastly face, but she swallowed her fear away and stood tall, her hand still resting on her chest. "Stary cannot leave school now . . . and we do not know where Barbara is . . ." I wasn't sure Maren's words were comforting Umbra, but her smooth voice made my skin tingle and my racing heart feel at ease. Umbra must have felt it too for he hid his head in the shadows, still growling.

When he spoke, his back was turned away from me. Standing tall, not ashamed of his actions, he told me, "Fine. Hurry up."

I sprinted down the stairs to see Chloe, my thoughts swirling. It was almost farfetched to think that the chance meeting with Credence and Cally occurred in only three or four minutes.

There, sitting like a queen, was Chloe with Rin and Lauren at her feet, gazing at her, her loyal guard protecting her in my absence. Our mysterious teacher was holding her back for support. A smile escaped my lips and tears built up in my eyes. I knew she would be okay, but I was just so relieved. After everything with Barbara, I was terrified for their safety.

Chloe looked up to see me, her blue eyes sparkling like the stars that surround the angels. I couldn't control myself any longer. I ran to her, yelled her name with pure joy, and threw my arms around her waist, pulling her into an embrace. I didn't care if everyone stared. I didn't care that I hurt my knees again. My best friend was well!

After a minute, I loosened my grip a little and gazed up into her face, which still looked confused, but she smiled warmly at me. I was all antsy, making my words sound rushed. "Chloe, thank goodness! Are you all right? I mean, *really* all right?"

She kept that fond smile on her face and bobbed her head. "Yeah, I'm fine. I'm still a little dizzy and tired, but I'm okay . . ."

I sighed, closing my eyes; Chloe snickered. Rin and Lauren came behind me, smiling as well. The teacher patted Chloe's back and told us to go to class in a minute. Chloe agreed and thanked him with grateful eyes.

Lauren looked down at Chloe and me with a shimmer of a smile. "We're glad you're okay Chloe . . ."

Rin added, "Yeah, we're glad you're okay Clo . . . ," but then she hit me hard on top of the head.

"Ouch!" I held my head and looked at Rin questioningly. Her eyes told me Chloe didn't know why she fainted. I was happy for that, but it wasn't necessary to punish me . . . Okay, so maybe it *was*.

With her hands on her hips, Rin bent down to look at me and yelled, "Stary, let go of Chloe! You're embarrassing us all!"

I moaned, agreed, and placed my hands in my lap, pouting like a puppy. Lauren shrugged at us and Chloe grinned in approval. But she didn't obey Rin. Chloe took my hands into hers and placed them on her lap.

Chloe and I stared at each other, proving to the world how close to sisters we were. She rubbed her fingers over my hands, telling me not to worry anymore. I giggled to myself since Chloe knew I was the biggest worrywart in the world! "I'm sorry about all of this," she said to me, but then looked up at Lauren and Rin before ducking her head down with gloom. "I wish I remembered why I fainted . . ."

The three of us laughed nervously and worked hard to change the subject. Rin pushed me out of the way and grabbed Chloe's hand, pulling her up out of the chair slowly. "Come on. We better get to Mr. Tin's! I don't need that loser picking on me anymore," and Rin gave a grossed out face. We all cackled thinking of how bummed Rin got when Mr. Tin called on her.

Lauren nodded and walked to Chloe in an anxious stride, letting Chloe lean her other hand on Lauren's strong shoulder. I felt bad, standing there as they helped Chloe, but I really was a burden.

Once Chloe was standing on her feeble legs, she looked at me with need. "Oh, Stary?"

I snapped out of my sorry state and stood tall, a soldier in attention, before yelling back, "Yes?"

"I left my purse in the bathroom. I was looking for you . . ."

I bowed my head down. I made Chloe worry because I had to touch that stupid, painful shard. Rin scowled at me and Lauren looked at the crown of Chloe's head worried. That explained why they were walking past our pillar and they, so to speak, saw me flying, thanks to Umbra.

Chloe coughed and continued, "Would you get it for me please?"

"Of course!" I said, forcing a way too big smile. I ran into the bathroom, scared of finding something new and fearful. There, by the sink was Chloe's little black purse with the silver buckle. I checked to see that everything was in it and to my luck and knowledge of how often we shared items, it was. I held it tight to my chest and began to leave when I paused in the doorway, feeling guilty for forgetting something.

Scared to admit what it was, I turned around slowly to look at the stall with the messages. I gulped and tiptoed to it, cringing with every small step. I knew that more than likely, the messenger was not on our side, but still . . . it was rude not to respond, right?

Acting hastily, I scribbled a message, neither helpful nor hurtful and then gazed at it for a second before slamming the door and running away, turning my back once again from my fear of a dark tomorrow. There, I left the words:

Why are you here?

I ran with all my might and stopped right by the pillar, about ten feet from my friends. Chloe was now sitting back in the chair, resting I supposed. Her poor legs were shaking and she looked exhausted. Then, something hit me, something from my hidden life that I needed to know.

Again, out of my control, I jogged toward Chloe and threw her purse on the table she was leaning on. I grabbed her wrists full of energy, staring at her face. "Chloe, do you have any idea where Barbara went?" I screamed it on accident, cringing with guilt again, but my deed had already been performed.

She was surprised, that was sure, but gave me a little smile and answered, "Yeah. Her mom was hired to do a whole bunch of arrangements for a wedding. They're dropping them off at the practice, which is at four this afternoon. The wedding is tomorrow at two I think . . ."

Although they were not best friends anymore, I was glad Chloe could connect to Barbara better than any of us could. She was really helping me and the world out. I got on my knees again, giving her a kind look to apologize for scaring her. "Do you know what church it is?"

"Yeah, it's the Catholic church on Mary Street. They have a gym, which is where the reception is being held, so they're having the rehearsal dinner in there, too."

With my warmest smile, I thanked her and helped her stand while Rin and Lauren supported her. They told me to walk behind her in case she fell and to hold her purse. At least I could do something right!

I then glanced up at Umbra and Maren, who were at the window watching me the whole time. Maren gave us a beautiful smile, telling me she was glad Chloe was all right. Umbra, on the other hand, looked dead serious, his eyes dark and soulless, a purpose full of revenge radiating inside his eyes. He gave a curt nod, ready to go see Barbara after school. I equaled his motion and walked with my friends, trying to think of how I was going to get there.

There were three problems with this mission: I had to get there, I only had an hour to find a ride while I was in class, and the biggest problem was my father letting me go to something on real short notice. I couldn't focus on English at all.

I had to break the plan up into pieces, worrying about one problem first. If only Chloe was a month older, then she could have driven me! I had to know someone older who would . . . Wait . . . this was a wedding. I needed someone who loved weddings, a girl like Nikki! We *always* talked about our dream weddings in art class. I knew she worked sometimes . . . no, she wasn't working. In fact, she told me she was *in* a wedding. Maybe it was the same one! That would be great. I sent a silent prayer that that would work.

Now, how to convince my dad to let me go since I wasn't invited and I wasn't really going *in* the church. It would be nice if I could say: "Dad, I think Barbara is connected to the evil murderer of my two spirit friends and I'm going to spy on her." Even better if he smiled and said: "Sure honey. Here's $10. Be back by eight and have fun." Boy, I was living in a dream world!

Oh well, I had to face him real soon. The second class was over, I threw my books on the back table in my dad's room and ran like lightning to grab Nikki before she got to the junior parking lot. I told her I needed to go to the church (which was the wedding she was the candle lighter in) with her for something important. She joked and assumed it was boy stuff. I exhaled and gave in, pretending it was. Nikki only giggled and told me she would gladly, but I had to meet her by her car in ten minutes.

All right! Two problems down. The next was the tricky part: asking the father. I stood in the doorway of the classroom, feeling like one of the boys from *The Brady Bunch* when they broke their mom's favorite vase. I rubbed my arms nervously. He was erasing his blackboard with easy strides. I had to hurry and be strong. If I couldn't ask my dad something, then I was going to be a lousy Spirit Warrior. "Um . . . Dad?"

He turned and gave me a strange look. I always called him Daddy or sir in class or if I was in trouble. He knew I wanted something by me calling him Dad. "Hey Stary. Man, you made a breeze running out that door! Did you need something?"

"Yeah . . . well . . . ahhhhh . . . I wanted to know if I could go hang out with Nikki today, like right now . . ."

He moved his glasses, surprised I would ask. "Why didn't I know about this until now?"

Man! It was way too hard; he knew me too well! I lowered my head, scared to look at his cold eyes that he used to crack information out of students. "Um, well, it was a last minute thing." I groaned in a small voice, "Believe me." I added in a normal voice, "She wants me to help her pick out clothes tomorrow. She's going to a wedding and you know how much Nikki and I love weddings!"

Dad looked at me, not really believing me, his cold, but beautiful blue eyes glaring at me from head to toe. I shook a bit. Nikki and I were good friends, but since she was two years older, we never really *hung out* other than at school. It did seem weird, but it was the only thing I could think of. "You'll be at Nikki's right?" he boomed suddenly, making me jump.

"Yeah . . . ," I said, pondering the truth of my statement. Nikki did say she had to get her clothes at her house before we went, so that was true.

"And you're staying with Nikki the whole time?"

"Yep!" That one I knew was true. We would both be at the church, only her on the inside and me on the outside accompanied by two spirits. Loopholes were so handy.

Dad gave a long sigh, but waved me away and said, "All right, all right, you can. I'll take your stuff home with me. You stay with Nikki and be home before seven. Got that?"

I hopped up, almost bumping my head on the door frame. I hoped the practice would be over by seven, but I would work around it. "Thanks Daddy! You're the best!"

He took off his glasses to wipe his eyes and hide his face; he knew I was sucking up. "Yeah, yeah, yeah. Your mother's not going to be happy with this, so next time, tell me earlier."

"I will! Bye!" and I zoomed out the door after blowing him a kiss, which he ignored. He always said I was too old to do that. With all my might and in perfect time with my heartbeat, I ran to meet Nikki who would take me to Barbara. I was afraid, but also willing to accept anything. This one close-up stare into Barbara's eyes, one meeting, could help me find the murderer and save Maren and Umbra.

"YOU WANT ME TO DROP YOU OFF *HERE*?" NIKKI ASKED ME, stunned.

I nodded to her with a little smile before skipping out of her ruby red car. When I turned to thank her, her mouth hung open and she could only blink.

"Yep, this is it. Thanks so much Nikki. I'll wait for you in the church lobby at 6:45." I tried to look innocent to hide my guilt. I hoped the Lord would make an exception for lying.

Nikki finally shook her head, making her pretty red hair swing to her neck. "All right, sounds good hon. I'll see you then," and she quickly drove up the street to turn into the church parking lot.

I sighed deeply and turned to stare at my odd choice of a drop off point: a small, dirty alley with an uncountable number of trash cans. I made a face at the sight, understanding why Nikki was so appalled. I told her on the car ride here that I wanted to see Credence. I guess it did look a little extreme! However, it was the best spot. Since I was not actually invited to the wedding or practice, the alley that led to the back door of the reception room was the best place.

Umbra and Maren popped in, standing on either side of me; I felt like a sad excuse for a leader." They were as blank and serious looking as I was.

"Ready?" I asked, looking at both of them. They both gave me a nod and slowly, but in perfect sync, we crept from trashcan to trashcan down the long alleyway until we were as close to the door as possible.

Plastering against the wall at first, I tilted my head to see where the window was located and what angle I had to move. It hurt my neck, but I finally found the window and practically crawled like a mountain lion to get behind three tin trashcans that were almost nudging the doorframe. I felt dirty, for many reasons, but had to remember to breathe and always keep my guard up.

Umbra and Maren hid behind me. Umbra leaned his sculpted chest on my back once on accident. I gulped and we looked at each other at the same time, large eyed and embarrassed. In a blink, we both turned away and continued our duty as my heartbeat seemed like it was echoing off the metal.

My hearing picked up on some yelling, a familiar voice ringing in my ears. "Barbara," I whispered to my team. Maren slid her feet a little closer to Umbra, but Umbra pushed me forward, making me stumble. I glared at him, but he ignored it and motioned me to go near the window.

It took me a few seconds to get there and find a safe area for peeking. Looking through the half-fogged window, I saw Barbara with her hands on her hips and snapping like Hitler about the flower arrangements to a numerous number of guys. "You! Move that over there now! No you idiot, over there! Let's move it you waste of human skin!" Hearing her insults didn't make me feel better about spying. I glanced at Maren and Umbra who seemed astounded at her dictator-like outrage.

"OH! You ruined it, you clod! It's no good! Give it and let me do it!" My neck cracked back to the window and I noticed Barbara, her face twisted in a scowl, had a vase of bent flowers and was heading my way!

My heart was racing and my mind became a blur. I started to panic. Umbra and Maren signaled me to hide behind the trashcans, but it took my body a lot longer than I hoped to respond. Seeing Barbara so close, I gasped, ducked under the window, and crawled as fast as I was able, somehow avoiding making noise. I hid in between two trashcans on the opposite side of the door, Umbra and Maren still farther down the alleyway.

She clicked open the door. Her skin seemed darker as her hatred permeated the darkened alley. She paused, scanned the area in such perfect motions that it made her look part robot. Maybe she could feel me or Umbra and Maren. If so, we were in trouble. With fearful eyes, I leaned closer to the trashcan.

Barbara gave up her task and hurled the flowers into the garbage can by me, the glass vase shattering on contact. My ear was on the trashcan and the noise pierced my eardrum, making me throw myself backwards right before Barbara. She was almost completely inside the building.

"Moon Pie? What the hell are you doing here?" Barbara sounded boiling angry. I cleaned off my shirt, willing myself not to cry. I was able to stand about an inch from the doorway although my legs ached. I sighed, taking in some short breaths before looking into Barbara's eyes, the eyes that would tell me my next step in my destiny.

"I'm sorry Barbara. You see . . . I was looking for something and the sound of the vase hitting the bottom of the trashcan just hurt my ears and . . ." I stopped, huffing madly, my lungs shrieking, and my ribs abruptly crushing my heart. I had to break free from the fear and look into Barbara's eyes. All at once, I loosened the chains and snapped to look at Barbara. Her eyes were pure black, darker than a starless and moonless night. In the middle, her pupils were red, deep red, the color of blood. There were some black specks in the corners of the red circles, but no white, none at all!

The sky began to change color, a navy blue, then stormy dark, swirling only over my head like a personal tornado. Barbara glared at me and with each second the world began to fade and the clouds closed in on me, the static coming out of the swirling sky shocking my skin.

Barbara finally spoke. It was her voice, but the tone and cruelness behind it felt like another. A voice tainted by a lifetime of evil.

"What is with you Stary? You have been a freak as of late, an insensible freak that worries her so called loved ones and lies. Oh, the sinful lies! How can you be so selfish? You are nothing to anyone, just a lifeless tool that will be broken and die soon. Your existence is not needed . . ."

I whimpered, shutting my eyes tight and shaking my head, whispering to myself that it wasn't true. Everything was painful. My stomach felt like it was actually being twisted by cruel hands, claws, and gunk. My heart was getting softer, weaker, vanishing. My body was refusing to listen to anyone but the malice around me. I was able to break free for a moment to see that the clouds were still above me, but the alleyway around me was burning red now like fire and blood mixed, getting ever closer to me. A face was imprinted in the sky. It was beautiful, eternal, and the most horrifying thing I had ever seen. It smirked with cruelty at me—the fallen one himself.

Barbara pointed at me and my knees buckled, making me drop and ache more. The air was suffocating me, the glow of the alley staining me in crimson. The face of Lucifer was now gone, but his mission was far from over. In his game, the murderer must have been the knight and I a pawn. Barbara continued, her voice now thunderous.

"Why a human like you was ever created and why you think you deserve happiness is unknown. It will not be much longer . . . Something as pathetic as you living is laughable . . ."

Her cackle echoed off the burning walls, blocking all my will and thought. There was no use denying it; Barbara *was* the murderer. Umbra and Maren were gone and I was now being choked by invisible strings, only allowed to scream in horror for a few moments before the strings crushed my windpipes. I was sinking, my body falling downward to death.

"You are useless Stary! You are pathetic Stary! You are weak, a mistake, and a waste! You are nothing Stary, you hear me Stary Moon? *Nothing!*"

I screamed. My knees hit the ground, but instead of concrete under my flesh, a dark, liquid pool was under my knees, my body beginning to sink deep into the earth. I was going to lose to death. I held my ears and began to shake like I was in a blizzard, trapped in ice, slowly fading away into the black pool, being covered in bloodstained snow. I didn't want to believe any of her comments or listen to her, but maybe I had to accept my failing fate . . .

"Stop!" I heard a voice and an echo began to ring in my ears, reflecting circular waves in my mind, all across the area. It was like my first dream and the time I met Maren. But who? I carefully opened my eyes to see that Barbara was scowling steely over her shoulder at Credence! I was so weak that I needed to catch my breath and let my heartbeat stabilize. It was nice to hit ground even if it was rough. Credence's voice must have made Barbara lose her hold on me; the alley was now normal instead of a deadly snow globe.

Credence glowered at Barbara. I couldn't believe he saved me like a hero from a story book! Did he know about Barbara's darkness, too? Did he know I was close to dying? Or was that all in my mind?

"Credence . . ." Barbara's attitude was colder than ever, acid dripping off her tongue. I wasn't sure what mode she was in.

Credence matched her hard, stern face, making him look scary for a moment.

"Go away, Credence. This doesn't concern you."

"No one talks to Stary that way, especially you," Credence said full of heart, but his voice was hard. It made me blush a little that he cared and was, unknowingly, facing a murderer for me.

"How dare you! Stary has no right to be here."

I could tell she was flustered at Credence, but she redirected her rage at me. Terrified, I stepped back, holding my shaking hands on my chest to calm my heart. I didn't want to knock on death's door again.

"GET OUT!" She screamed at me so spitefully that it bounced off every trashcan, making the alley hollow and deafening. While covering my ears, I noticed her eyes were no longer black, but her normal dark chocolate brown. However, her eyes were sunken in and she had huge bags under her eyelids. Did her black eyes have to do with the darkness from earlier?

Credence slapped his hand hard on her shoulder, his eyes leveling into a glare. "Watch it Barbara! I'm tired of this attitude of yours. Besides," his voice got softer as he gazed at me devotedly. "Stary's with me. I invited her, so back off and deal with it!"

My heart was hammering now, but for two reasons. In the last part of his speech, he got face-to-face with her, his voice tight, almost spitting on her for emphasis.

"You are both idiots and I refuse to be near you!" She slammed Credence into the doorframe and stomped off, breathing dragon fire. I wasn't sure what to think. Even Umbra and Maren, who had not left their spots from down the alleyway, looked amazed that Credence got tough for me and went against a minion of Lucifer.

With a poison-filled heart and a tapping pressure in my forehead, I leaned on the wall, waiting for calmness to surround me in its grace. I wasn't sure if what had happened was a bloody nightmare or not, but the murderer was too near me and powerful enough to call on Lucifer for a moment. My head was fuzzy and my body ached all over. I felt like Barbara controlled my mind and scrambled my insides.

As I fluttered tears away from my eyes, I managed to get the courage to smile at Credence, my savior. I saw my reflection in the window by the door and fixed my messy, wind-folded hair first.

"Thank you . . . thank . . . you so . . . much Credence . . . I'm really . . . Sorry to cause you so much . . . trouble . . ." Talking was still difficult. I gazed at him with praise, making him slightly turn red.

"No, really, it's okay Star. I'm really sorry that Barbara has been so mean to you. I mean, someone as compassionate and cute as you . . . She must be a devil or jealous of your loving nature." A curl was on his yummy lips that matched his now wild eyes.

Did he really care for me? I mean, he was saying some very nice things about me in front of me, things he had never said before. Oh, could I be so hopeful?

I felt darts behind me, stabbing me chillingly in the back, but my warm spirit melted them away. I was grateful for being alive!

I showed Credence my dazzling smile I practiced in the mirror before picture day. "Thank you Credence," I whispered. He blushed.

"You . . . ah, worry too much . . . It's . . . no . . . problem . . ." Now the smooth Credence Horton was stuttering like I did. I let out a giggle, covering my mouth to stop it. Credence gave me his lovely smile and it made me stop focusing on everything except him.

With a light heart, I grinned again and decided to find a way to slip out of the alleyway (although Credence was blocking the backdoor that Barbara dramatically left from). Umbra and Maren needed to check her energies and I knew I had to look into her eyes again. Those black eyes were haunting my thoughts . . .

Rocking on my heels with my hands nervously behind my back, I looked up into Credence's crystal pools to ask him a question: "So, you heard that I was here. Can I ask why you're here Credence?"

My voice lost all flirtation as I waited for his answer. Before my weak heart could react, Credence, with even, perfect strides, walked up to me, leaning down into my face like Umbra and I had at the gnome's cottage. My heart was hammering and my seriousness was sinking fast into the pavement.

With twinkling and playful eyes that matched his new mocking grin, he whispered, "I can't tell you that. You might leave again."

Scared and not sure what to think, I stepped too far back and rammed into the wall. Credence seized his chance. With lightning speed, he grabbed my arm and pinned me to the wall. I was terrified and hoped he was joking. Something felt . . . off.

My eyes were locked onto his, forced to only see his priceless face three inches from mine, looking so desirable despite my rising fears. I swallowed hard, trying not to let tears of uncertainty fall. I could feel Umbra and Maren's eyes on me, but I couldn't see them. Why was I so frightened by this new form of Credence and his touch?

Leaning into my ear, Credence whispered, his breath tickling my ear, "I won't let you escape me this time Stary. There's something I have to tell you. I'll tell you why I'm here, but only if you stay."

By impulse, I nodded gradually. He then transformed back to the shy Credence I knew and beamed and the world made sense again. "Good!" he said with much glee. With my agreement, my body relaxed.

I turned to see Umbra and Maren stunned as well. I was scared Umbra would tackle Credence again except harder and use his combat skills. Umbra, like an enraged puma, narrowed his eyes and leaned forward, but Maren elbowed his ribs. He made a face at her. Maren shrugged at me, not sure what to do.

I motioned under my hips for her and Umbra to go on. She nodded and grabbed Umbra's hand, but he refused to move. His honey brown eyes looked pained, like I was shooting an arrow into his chest and watching him suffer. I felt a tingle of guilt like the one I felt when I was with the man I loved from my dream. I shook it off and moved inside so Credence wouldn't get suspicious.

Maren got enough strength to get behind Umbra after she failed at pulling him away a few times. She was able to push Umbra into the hall Barbara went into, which was amazing. Sadness overwhelmed me as Umbra gazed at me, biting his lower lip. Then, he vanished down the hall and it felt like he took half of my heart with him; my other half was right next to me. Why did I have doubts?

Credence grinned and motioned me into the reception room. It was huge and decorated in pretty blues and whites with dazzling swans all around. I *ooh*ed and *ahh*ed over the soon-to-be wedding. Credence was ahead of me and turned stylishly on his heels to glance at me. I smiled at his gesture until a unique wave of sound splashed an enchanting, slow melody into my ears, leading my heart. This song was a mystery and it was not my usual one inside me, but it was beautiful, losing me to the spell of my own living world. To find the source, I turned to see a man in the corner with large headphones on at a turntable.

Credence chuckled with delight. "I guess even DJs have to practice!" I giggled at his comment, lost in the lights reflecting in his striking eyes. It was nice to be calm and not relive my encounter with Barbara. Out of nowhere, Credence placed the palm of his smooth hand in front of me and asked me in an embarrassed tone, "Stary . . . would you like to dance?"

I looked around for a moment, my mind trying to figure out what was happening. Was he really asking me? I nodded, my heart soaring to the clouds. When I touched his hand, electricity surged through my soul, giving me a strange thrill that I would never have given up. Although we mostly rocked back and forth, his arms wrapped around my waist and mine around his neck. Twirling with Credence was so wonderful just like dancing with my dream prince.

"To answer your question," Credence started, making me look at him, "I'm here helping my neighbor. She's in charge of all the food for the wedding tomorrow and was short on waiters today, so I offered to help."

It amazed me how sweet Credence was and it was then I knew that this wasn't just a large crush that I had been hiding in the holes of my heart. I wanted to be with Credence, even for just a moment. I wanted to be held like God's child on a pile of clouds. I leaned down to lay my head gently on his chest. I heard him gulp and felt him tense.

"Stary . . . ?" Credence asked me nervously.

I looked up, wanting to hear his voice again. "Yes?"

"I . . . well, I have been . . . wanting to . . . ask you something . . . for a while now, but I've been too scared . . . so . . . don't laugh for I have to do this now before I faint or there isn't even time . . ."

I giggled and asked, my voice coming out breathy, "Yes, Credence?"

"Well, ah . . . Stary . . . Will you go to the spring dance with me?" With a start, my heart jumped into my ears and twenty feet higher, probably making the whole earth shake from my excitement. It happened. My dream guy, my sweet hero, Credence Horton, had asked me to the dance! This must have been what he wanted to tell me when I found Cally and why he had been pumping my friends for information.

With all my being containing my girlish joy, I smiled and with all the truth and proof in my heart, I answered: "I would love to Credence."

Credence smiled wide, from ear to ear and so bright, the room seemed to glow. "I'm so glad. I was really uneasy plus with your dad . . ."

I chuckled again. My dad isn't mean, but he is real protective of me, especially with boys and since Credence was his student, it was understandable. Even Mr. Tin was overprotective of me, calling me his daughter-in-training. I would have been nervous as well.

"Don't worry. I'll make him accept you!" I promised, giving him a thumbs-up.

With a musical laugh, Credence nodded as well and said, "Good," full of poise. But, the dream didn't last forever because our song ended. As it stopped, Credence lowered my hands into his and swung them back and forth between us like a child playing Ring Around the Rosie. My face was burning so much that I could have roasted a bag of marshmallows in a second! I was holding hands with Credence!

Still, although my world seemed endless and perfect, I felt wrong. I felt like being with Credence was a horrible sin, his touch was nice, but a little wrong, no matter how much I cared for him. I wanted him to be my true love, the prince from my dream. They did have a lot of the same traits, inner and outer, but my heart was vibrating louder for something else . . . something buried in my soul. But, for now, Credence was the one who I allowed to look after my heart.

Things faded and I heard a call for Credence in the distance, the hall where Barbara, Umbra, and Maren had headed earlier. Credence continued to swing my hands and with a light smile, but saddened eyes, told me, "I have to get back to serving."

I nodded and beamed, full of cheer for seeing him again. "Good luck!"

He gave me a fast laugh and bent a little closer to me, looking splendid. "Thanks, I'll need it. I'll talk to you in homeroom tomorrow about the details."

"All right. I can't wait . . ." I said the last part in a playful tone.

"See you!" He let go of our laced hands and ran fast, almost tripping when he rounded the corner, nearly bumping into Maren. She was so cute; she looked shocked and blushed a little before looking ahead to come to me. Umbra only glared at the doorway for many seconds before stomping behind Maren.

"Stary, dear, did something happen? You have this pretty and big smile on your face . . ."

I laughed nervously, trying hard to rub off my happy mode, replacing it with focus for our operation. "Oh, nothing. Did you find out anything?"

Maren shook her head in defeat. "No, nothing other than Barbara's usual, ummm . . . rude behavior . . ." Maren blushed madly. I laughed, unable to control it. I would have called her a flat out jerk, but Maren was much more worthy of being an angel than I was.

Umbra folded his arms, his face sour and eyes wicked. "Humph! It was horrible how that Credence bas—brat forced you to stay. He'll surely be arrested for his cruel ways with women . . ."

Some of the guilt I had felt about liking Credence vanished as I stared at Umbra. I had no idea what he was getting at. All I could do was sigh; he didn't understand.

I mustered a serious front and turned to face both of them. "But, something is coming fast and at us. I feel a dark sharpness in the air. A spark is forming above." Memories of the storm Barbara created, her pitch eyes, and the face of Lucifer in the clouds told me this.

Umbra confirmed my analysis. "There is something extremely sinister in the air and it's after us."

Together, in perfect step formation, we walked out, ready to face the unknown heading our way. Evil was giving us a warning, telling us: "*I'm coming after you.*" I was going to try to get ready to receive its call. The end of the mission was too near.

15

THE DAY WAS ALL A BLUR, A MESS OF COLORS FLYING IN FRONT OF my face, which felt like it was covered in spider web-like mazes meant to mock me. My heart was light, ignoring the sharp pain each breath gave me. I had to wait awhile for my dad since he had to grade the last few big worksheets so we could use them on our next test. Bored and not wanting to get him tenser, I decided to stroll down to the front lobby and maybe find someone to talk to.

It was pretty cleared out by the time I got there, but I caught Allen in the corner. A warmth was on his usual overstressed face. Seeing his smile made me feel at ease and my feet led me to him.

"Hey Allen. Mind if I sit here with you? My daddy's grading papers."

With much enthusiasm, he leaned forward and exclaimed, "Your father is an amazing man. Such power, poise, and an inspiration! I want to learn everything from him and be half as intelligent and worldly as he is." The glitter in Allen's eyes was as scary as usual. He always talked about my father like he was God himself. Admittedly, it gave me the creeps, but I giggled at his honest good humor and nodded in approval.

The glaring sun forced me to move my head. I noticed Allen's crisp white shoes with a line of black and a cherry red pinstripe.

"Nice shoes Allen!" I said, trying not to be jealous. I wasn't really a shoe person, but those athletic shoes looked stunning.

He grinned from ear to ear, making his small oval face the normal tone of red I knew. "Thanks. They're Nike and I got them up in the big city."

"Nikes? Those are expensive!"

He ducked his head a little. "I got them at a tent sale."

I knew those well with going to those evil clothes shopping events with my mom. I flipped my hair out of the way to get a better look. "That's good. How much did they cost?"

"Hmmmmm, well . . . $80 . . ."

My mouth dropped. $80 for a pair of shoes that were on sale was madness to my lower middle-class family! If a pair of shoes was more than $20, I flipped out and rarely bought them. However, Allen's family was pretty well off with a beautiful home, a swimming pool, and other nice things. Wait . . . I remembered something from English class. "Is this what the other kids were teasing you about today?" I said in a monotone and full of regret for my reaction.

Sinking lower, he nodded and smoothed his golden blond hair with the palm of his hand. He rested his foot on top of the heater. Poor Allen . . . he was so smart, nice, and a cute guy, but he had so much pressure on him to be an 'A' student like his dad and a musical legend like his mom. Our peers were always mocking him, calling him "little rich boy." Still, I liked Allen for his goofy, stressed-all-the-time self, not his money.

"I still dig the shoes!" I said with a grin. He laughed, looking carefree for a moment.

As we were engaging in a light conversation and laughter, a unique smell floated through the air. It was warm, crisp, and sharp and too near to be comfortable. I knew that smell . . . it was like smoke . . . It *was* smoke!

"Allen! Your shoe!" I screamed as large puffs of gray smoke escaped from his clean shoe that rested on top of the heater.

Allen hollered as he grunted with difficulty as he tried to get his shoe off the heater. After a few failed attempts, he pulled his shoe off the dragon's fire. It was sticky. The rubber bottom looked like glue. Panic was all over his face and he fell backwards, landing on the wooden bench where I found Cally the other day.

With a nest of nerves, I ran to Allen to check on him. "Allen, are you all right?"

He took in a deep breath and then began to choke, hacking. With the whitest, biggest eyes I'd ever seen and a pure red face, he gulped and looked at me, nodding and shouting, "What in the world just happened?"

Curious by the heater's sudden attack, I went to feel the air. It was warm like it had always been until that point. Seeing the white rubber stuck on the coils of the black heater and watching it bubble and stir black waves into the atmosphere made me feel queasy.

"I guess these shoes weren't meant to work out, no matter how cool they are—were." Allen coughed. Tears built in Allen's eyes, but he soon replaced them with a small smile. "I see why they were on sale. Because they cause crazy chemical reactions with heat!"

I nodded to reassure him while he was checking for damage on his foot. I didn't think it was caused by science, although it did look believable. Watching the white material drip to the sides of the heater, clinging, drying to become forever molded with it made my heart feel like it was getting stabbed, because I felt Allen being hurt was my fault and more was yet to come.

Walking up to my father's room after Allen's mother picked him up, my mind began to throb, racing and spinning arrows across my brain. None of this was right. It had been a week since Maren, Umbra, and I had decided Barbara was more than likely the murderer. Since the stirring we felt (and I experienced alone) at the wedding practice hall, strange, and I mean *strange* for me, things have occurred . . .

Two days earlier, I was lost again in fear that the murderer was going to strike at me or worse, observe me for my weaknesses. I was out of it playing Ping-Pong with Rin, so I asked her to play volleyball across the court so I wouldn't make her lose points. Upset at myself for hurting my friends, I tapped the Ping-Pong ball over the net, or so I planned. There was a force. It made rings on the table below and ate the world away in a red blaze. It was humming a terrible echo from the ball's outer shell.

My tap turned into a twenty foot zoom of lightning that whammed into Credence's eye, who was across the volleyball court. As he held it in pain, blood seeping through his fingers, the volleyball from the other side of the net whacked Credence in the head and he was out cold. Luckily, Rin caught him two inches off the hard tile. As everyone crowded around my in dire pain Credence, I snuck into the locker room and cried because I caused such an awful thing to happen to my dream guy. The fact that the murderer was so close to me that they were hurting my loved ones without a second thought made my body become engulfed in violent tremors.

Sliding my feet to the beat of the D-chord chorus the lights always performed with their buzzing sound, I was also worried about Rin. Earlier in morning PE, I was still engrossed with concern, but was in a lighter, more focused mood for our four-on-four basketball game. As the fun progressed, I felt like nothing was going to happen. I jinxed myself. Soon, I felt a dark shadow hiding, craftily watching our play by the large wooden doors. All I remembered seeing was the glare of glasses and my heart jumped out of my chest knowing it was Barbara.

Out of the blue, one of the boys got real aggressive getting the ball away from Rin, having black, heartless eyes, and a wicked smile. He almost foamed at the mouth and growled like a hungry wolf! The worst thing was that I could tell everyone was seeing him the way I was because they froze, staring at him. Rin ignored this change and fought back well, thinking he was only playing rough. He pushed her hard on the floor and she received a broken ankle for it, which she was extremely angry about.

I had never seen her in so much pain, no matter how hard she tried to hide her discomfort with snippy words toward the boy. He didn't remember anything later and was concerned about Rin. I knew he was telling the truth for normally he was a nice guy and the chill in the air that swirled around him vanished into the astral space as soon as the gym doors were opened.

And now, Allen's shoe had caught on fire, almost burning his foot. Glaring eyes of pure hatred were looking up at me wherever I went. I could hear the calls from the lockers, the inner souls of their history warning to me: "*Run, run Stary, for you will die . . .*"

No matter how light it was, the hallways were gray and lifeless, trying to crush me before untimely fate was supposed to take me away. I had to stay calm and not listen to the truthful advice, even if my skin was literally crawling and my heart was freezing over, destroying my smooth skin.

I locked my hands around my shirt good and tight, trying to calm my heart down as I forced my salty tears away, whispering a mantra that my grandpa always told me: "Surely, everything will be all right . . ." I had to stay positive and think of something to warm my heart and let hope flow into me like sunrays. Credence . . . he was a ray of new beautiful sunshine smiling rainbows around me. But I was too concerned about his injury to make him my positive thought . . . so, I thought of the moon, shining, always there watching out for me. I warmed up in a snap. Scared, but ready to stand on my own, I headed to my father's room.

To list all the various emotions I was feeling that week would have taken a century without a problem: nervous of being hated, fearing death, no confidence in my powers, guilt for causing my loved ones pain, scared of even standing, sick to be on my own; the list never ended. The people who didn't know they were Spirit Warriors were lucky because they never had to deal with all the crazy feelings.

Umbra and Maren had been MIA for a while, searching for vibes similar to Barbara's, so I was all alone in the messed up mortal realm I caused. But things were starting to turn. Credence and I talked about our dance plans in homeroom (and he had no idea I hurt his eye). Still, the guilt killed me inside so, the night before, I made Credence some fudge and placed it in a cute little silver star tin. I had plenty to give out, but I made it special, placing my own feelings in there for Credence Horton.

My mom and I were in such a rush to wrap the frozen fudge that morning that I didn't get to taste it. Food was tasting funny to me anyway since my emotions were on high.

My dad and I got to school early as usual the next day. As I placed my school items at my "locker" in the corner of his room (mine was stolen by a senior), I began to worry about my food not tasting well. I needed the power of the Garbage Disposal! "Daddy . . . Could you taste my fudge please?" He thought it was for a choir party.

He turned from writing the day's assignments on the board, grinning from ear-to-ear. He tapped my cheek with affection. "You know it's bad for me, but if my little girl insists . . ."

I giggled as he popped the chocolate into his mouth. He made a noise, saying he approved, but I was still nervous.

"How is it Daddy?" I asked nervously.

He swallowed the remainder and answered, "It's really good honey, but a little warm and melty. How long did you put it in the freezer?"

"What?!" I remembered I had placed the fudge and the tin in the freezer for about twelve hours and it wasn't that warm outside, so it should have been fine for a few more hours. My dad must have lost it because the tin was still ice cold . . . Wait . . . I focused on the feeling in my fingers as they circled my tin and noticed they were quickly getting warm. I could now smell the chocolate evaporating as the heat on my hands became more unbearable. At the same time, my daddy and I opened the tin and peeked inside. The whole container of fudge was completely melted and hot, bubbling into a fudge soup with the sole purpose of laughing at me.

"My fudge . . . All my hard work . . . gone . . ." Tears blended into my cheeks.

Dad ran to look at the heater. "Honey . . . I'm so sorry. I have no idea what's going on, but it'll be all right." He lifted my chin to make me stare into his smiling blue eyes. I let my tears vanish, but didn't smile.

Just as I was about to thank him, something crawled down my fingernails, making me feel dirty to the core.

"HONEY! The tin!"

Confused, I gazed down to see the beautiful star tin was melting in my hands, dripping dark waves of chocolate and silver as my palms began to smolder. I didn't even feel the heat! I let out a small ear-piercing shriek and threw it on the ground between my daddy and me just in time before I was burned. There, a brown and silver swirling puddle steamed on the floor, bubbling into a faded and silent state of sickness.

"Stay here, Stary. I'll get someone to clean that up. Don't touch it, okay? What in heaven's name . . ." My daddy was off, running like wildfire. Heaven . . . this was my fault again. The murderer felt my heart go out to Credence and destroyed the labor of my mom and me. Like the chocolate and lovely tin, I sank to the floor, allowing my soul to melt away for a moment.

I didn't have much time during the day to worry about the melting fudge since the school was starting to go mad. Going into third hour with Chloe, I entered my dad's room, listening to her endless boy talk when I saw my dad looking terrified on the floor behind his large wooden desk, his head making snapping motions.

"DADDY?!" I screamed, throwing my books on the floor by Chloe's feet and running to him without thinking.

"Stary, halt! Look behind me!" he barked.

Dazed, I glanced up at the blackboard. Black and white fragments were dripping to the floor, uniting in the middle with metal. The blackboard was melting?! The room was about 68 degrees according to the system and it felt nice. How could this be?

Startled, I tilted my head around to see the rims of his bulletin boards beginning to dissolve into the wall, fusing into the clipboards. "What's happening Daddy?" I squawked again with uncertainty.

"I honestly have no idea. It's only my room, but Mr. Tin told me things are disappearing from his room that were just there in front of his eyes. I'm on the ground because . . . well, look behind me, but be careful, dear."

Scared, but obeying his command, I moved my body in a slant to see that my daddy's old chair had melted into a silver puddle as well, it's metallic texture looking like my tin that just melted that morning in this same room. Wait . . . my tin . . . The murderer was targeting my daddy!

I gulped and tried everything in my power to sound calm, but some squeakiness escaped out of my mouth. "Daddy, do you need some help getting up?" I asked, extending my hand out to his.

He brushed his palm over mine gently but got up on his own. "Thank you, honey. Please excuse me. I need to find an empty room and inform the principal. Stary, will you watch the class for a few moments since you and Chloe are the first ones here? Get Mark to help you once he shows up. He can be scary for a little guy!"

I smiled a little. My heart dreaded him not to leave the safety of my sight. I replied, "Sure . . ." Before he left, he rubbed the top of my head like a dog and jetted off through the sea of his students that started staring inside the room, off on a quest to find a new learning spot.

All I could do was sigh at the melted blackboard, which had stopped. This frightened me because Barbara was in my class. The thought sent chills up my spine.

"Stary? What happened?" Lauren sounded frightened, which was unusual because she never seemed to be scared of anything. Turning to see my dear friend huffing, her long ponytail flying around her neck, I had to be honest, especially since she pushed Chloe out of the doorway.

"I'm really not sure, but all the stuff just started to . . . melt . . ." Even halfway lying made me feel awful.

"Oh that's so . . . AH!" Lauren screamed as her notebook flew open and all her pages of history notes ripped out on their own, flying skyward to the ceiling, creating a mighty wind. They all banded together and circled Lauren at an unrated speed that trapped her in a paper tornado. As she yelled, some of the papers broke temporarily from the chain and would cut Lauren with their sharp, crisp edges. Thank goodness she was wearing her hoodie, so most of the attacks didn't seriously harm her.

The storm was raging, making the area gray and clouded. My hair was blowing harshly, slapping my back. All I could do was look back and forth at my surroundings, uncertain of my abilities. The wind, the emotions, the pain, Lauren's scream, and feeling Barbara's evil glare hiding behind the group of my peers . . . I couldn't take it anymore.

I stepped forward, as close to the tornado as I could physically get although Barbara did a great job pushing me back, making me shield myself with my arms as I gritted my teeth together. I stared at Lauren for a moment to compose my anger. Her glasses were getting twisted into her face, creating a dark crescent scar which only added a heavy weight on my heart.

"Stop this," I whispered, timid by the twister. "Please, stop," I said a little louder but still timid. Nothing. I had to be strong; I had to prove I was the Spirit Warrior.

"STOP IT!" I yelled, hurting my voice, trying to activate my powers and show my intense disapproval. Steadily, the storm ceased and Lauren was revealed as her papers floated down like graceful angel feathers to the floor. I wasn't sure if I did it with my spirit powers or if Barbara just got bored of our torment, but regardless, it took a toll on me, inside and out. Lauren and I panted together in unison.

Lauren dropped to her knees on the floor, wheezing. Chloe ran to her and wrapped her arm around her for support. Lauren was so weak, she ignored the fact someone was touching her, something she did not like. I had to take many deep breaths to steady my nerves. My chest was weighed down in pain.

Before aiding Lauren, I looked to see the unknowing faces of my fellow students outside the classroom, who were blinking rapidly like they had just woken up from a spell. It appeared that only Chloe, Lauren, and I, the three in the classroom itself, truly saw what had happened. Shelving that mystery in my mind for later, I continued to scope for Barbara. I saw her dark shadow from behind the crowd, but when I blinked, she had already disappeared.

In science class, it was electron lab day, which depressed me more because I hate labs! I was partnered with Lauren and Barbara. However, Barbara seemed real ill and begged Mrs. Shell to let her rest with a snippy attitude. Lauren, a trooper who refused to miss class and ruin her perfect attendance, was upset that she had to do more work. I worked hard, but I wasn't nearly as good as she was. I was just happy I could watch Barbara from behind and not have her staring into my deathly-afraid-of-her eyes.

Lauren and I were waiting for the beaker to warm up, which would take about five minutes, when I heard a noise from my right. "Pssst . . . Stary . . ."

I turned, confused. Moving to the pulling sound of the voice as Lauren was triple checking our starting directions, I saw Mark smiling in my direction, signaling me to go over to him. I gazed at him nervously. I didn't want Lauren mad at me for leaving her, not after what the poor thing went through.

"Go on!" Lauren urged, not even looking at me. I looked down at her, anxious, but she tapped her stirring stick and pointed to Mark with a wink. I nodded and tiptoed over there, not wanting to get caught.

Mark was with a group of three other squirrelly guys, all talking about a rock band while Mark was half leaning on the table with his movie star grin, waiting for me to approach him. The only bad thing was I had to walk past Mandy, Rin, and Chloe's lab table to get there. I felt bad for Chloe, although I had a good guess on what Mark wanted to talk about.

"You called for me, sire?" I said in a low voice, bowing my head. I was rewarded a chuckle.

He cleared his throat before looking serious, playing along. "Why yes, milady. I wish to have enlightening conversations with you on a certain matter and drink up the beauty of your company." Mark lifted my fingers with his own, playing along, and led me to two stools hidden in the back of the corner. However, they were full of dust, so we leaned proper-like on the edges of his science lab table.

I wasn't worried about his group: one boy was sitting on top of the table, one making rubber bands fly and bounce off the wall, and Foils was burping to entertain his followers. How Mark got stuck with this group was way beyond my scale of knowledge.

I whispered, cupping my mouth, "What's up?"

He sighed and in his low, smooth baritone voice, he answered, "The move is becoming more and more for sure . . ."

I nodded slowly, not wanting to show the sadness in my heart caused by my best guy friend in the world leaving. Still, he needed help to confess his feelings to Chloe, no matter how in denial they both acted. I smirked and, feeling bold, asked, "What's your take on Chloe then?"

Mark just stared at the ground with gaunt and hurt eyes. "She's wonderful Stary, really wonderful. Yet, after the way I treated her at the beginning of the year, I can't believe she's still so . . . so . . ."

"Wonderful?" I finished the line, mocking his breathy, romantic voice as I fluttered my eyelashes towards him.

"Don't get sassy with me!" Mark whispered sharply, but his face was glowing, so I knew he wasn't angry.

"Sorry pal. Continue."

"Stary . . . I want her to be happy and if it's with me . . . that would be wonder—amazing! But, I have little hope I will ever be coming back before we—you guys graduate. I don't want to confuse her and tell her when she could be with someone else, someone here . . ."

"But Mark! She wants you! Can't you see that?" I was heartbroken for both of them. I saw his point, but not telling someone you loved them when the emotion was pulling you like an invisible thread, controlling your every choice was unbearable. Mark's dark chocolate eyes looked dazed. I could tell he was trying to take my advice to heart. Chloe might be lovesick and Mark stubborn, but those two lit up the room with their hidden feelings. I knew they would make it work somehow.

"Thank you Stary, but I don't know if she feels the same. You can tell me that and my heart will want to believe you, but I won't unless she tells me. Sorry . . ."

I gulped, trying not to get flustered. I guess to a sweet, not super confident boy that did make sense. Girls are scared all the time to confess their love, but their nature and romantic hearts made it a little easier to admit when they were in love in my eyes. "Still, Mark, you should tell her. I mean . . . do you really want to live your life thinking 'what if?"

What if . . . those words echoed inside me, making me analyze my feelings, wanting to tell the world life was too short to not take chances with the heart or to be too scared to feel anything. But, keeping feelings bottled inside . . . maybe I should have taken my own advice then and there.

"I'm not really sure what to do Stary, but I love talking to you. It makes things easier for me. I hope I'm not bothering you by all this."

"Of course not! Mark, we're best friends and we promised to always be there for one another. You always help me out when I'm too shy to defend myself. Now, it's my turn." I hopped off the edge of the table and faced him, smiling.

Mark chuckled a little and stepped toward me, a few inches from my face, warming my shoulders with his touch. "You are one of the things I will miss most of all. I love you, Stary." His smile was sweet and a little bashful, but he locked his gaze to the ground.

I guess some people would be terrified by that, but I knew Mark loved me like a sister and a friend, which was how my heart placed him. I replied back, full of heart, "I love you, too!"

The room was then engulfed with the sound of a small clatter from the middle of the room. Mark and I turned around to see Chloe with her hands placed over her mouth and the meter stick on the floor, ringing still from the metal frame. With wide eyes of fear, Mark and I glanced at each other, thinking the same thing: *Chloe heard us and misinterpreted.* A gentleman, Mark ran to the table and picked up the stick, placing most of it on the lab table with some hanging off.

"There you go Chloe," he said angelically, but laughed nervously between the words, waiting for her response.

With a face as red as the dot on Japan's flag, Chloe hid her face. With her mouth still covered, she whispered timidly, "Thank you . . ."

I grinned as Mark let his hand linger on hers for just a few seconds longer than it needed to as he helped her up. Chloe gasped, showing him her baby blue eyes. I was thrilled to see such romance in a small exchange.

Walking smoothly with an in love as a dove grin on his face back to his lab table, I greeted him with a high five and pat on the arm. I slid past him because I saw Lauren signaling to me that it was time for the next phase of our experiment. Mark turned to see all his lab partners, if one could call them that, were gone, sitting at the desk area, playing guitar around Barbara who was sleeping. Mark groaned, meaning he would have to do it all alone, but his positive attitude melted away the bad situation and he continued to work.

Feeling gentle hearted for my two dearest friends, I only glided a few feet towards my lab area when I got a feeling of deadly nervousness pumping into my veins. As the trigger point lifted into my heart cavities, I had to glance around to find the source of the feeling of rage that was now making my head pound and blood cells boil. As I looked behind me, I saw Mark with a red aura around him. Although I was the only one capable of seeing it, I knew the events that were about to follow.

Mark turned away from me, figuring calculations on his paper, when a howling and unthinkably loud ringing entered my ears. I bent down to cover them, but it had little effect. With one eye opened, I had to find the cause, where the wail was stirring from.

As if the world heard my thoughts, the item causing the noise revealed itself—the beaker next to Mark on the lab table. Vibrating and creating splashing noises with no liquid inside it, I viewed it lift an inch off the surface, slide perfectly forward, and with a slam, it shattered into several tiny pieces on the floor.

Startled, the entire class turned around in harmony as Mark snapped his head to look at the mysterious damage, his eyes flickering with stunning curiosity. He sighed and gave a small smile, knowing he would have to clean it up. The split second he took his eyes off the shards, the pieces took their chance and began to shake again, humming and making ripples like before. I guess, again, I was the only one who could see it, but a rush of time hit me from behind, seeing the next few seconds in my mind.

"Mark!" I screamed with my hands still around my ears, but it was too late. The biggest, most jagged shard turned, flew upward, and slashed Mark's beatific face. Thank goodness he moved in time or it could have done scarring damage.

He stood up, groaning in pain with closed eyes for a moment, shaking like the ground in a seismic activity. His breath was short but calm and he looked cross-eyed at his cheek, trying to see the five-inch long glass stuck in it. Blood dripped down his face like rain water. All Mark and I could do was stare blankly in terror.

I was able to make myself glance at Barbara, who had her face tilted to gaze at Mark with black as coal eyes and a smirk. However, once our eyes locked, she smiled more cruelly and laid her head back on her desk. I began to get dizzy and tipsy; it was my fault again. I was helping Mark with love advice for Chloe, and Barbara, who I was pretty sure liked Mark, got jealous. With a rampaging murdering spirit inside her . . . I began to shake at the thoughts of truth haunting me.

"Are you okay, Mark?" I heard a whisper in the wind, high and mousy, but very caring and adorable sounding. I spun to see Chloe wiping the blood off Mark's cheek with her lace handkerchief. I knew that this was a huge deal for blood makes Chloe ill. Mark looked shy but precious, and they both gave each other little heartwarming smiles; their cheeks warmed with a blush. It was a pretty sight, the kind that makes girls confident and I wanted to watch forever to be inspired.

Mark leaned his head down to almost brush her forehead and in a breathy, smooth voice, he placed his confession of true love in the tone of his voice. "Thank you . . ."

Chloe gasped, but gave him a dazzling smile, whiter than a thousand stars shining on a pitch black night. I smiled, feeling my soul warm up like a flare. I snorted to myself, gazing at Barbara and challenging her silently: *Looks like you didn't win after all.*

As I walked away with my soaring heart and devilish grin, my mind told me a secret: *Maybe you should follow that advice . . .*

We freshmen had a meeting to go to about making good choices for the future. Imagining all those teens in one room with the old bleachers . . . I shook at what the murderer could do! All the signs were there, that Barbara was the murderer, but my heart was not completely embracing the idea. I mean, I had known Barbara for so long. When could she have done all that killing, had that type of connection or training with the Angriff Squad? I was overthinking. It was just . . . knowing anyone near me who could be a killer was a hard thought to accept.

"Did you see the way he looked at me . . . Stary, are you listening?"

I snapped my head out of my current fog, feeling like a puppet being pulled by a string too hard. Nervously, I looked into Chloe's blue eyes that were blinding my dull ones with their luminescence.

Grinning widely to hide my inner discomfort as I rubbed my head, I thought of an answer. "Huh? Oh, well, yeah, of course I am. It was about boys, right?

Chloe sighed and gave me a little side hug while giggling, the type that made me happy to be alive. "You are so lucky that I'm guy crazy enough to accept such a general answer!" Together in a splendid melody, we laughed and linked arms, getting ready to go down the stairs to the gym with our classmates.

As if good cheer was forbidden in this twisted place, a black flash, straight as far as I could see, zoomed past my eyes and created a crackling friction at everything near us. So engrossed in the mystery, I didn't think to notice that it was not aimed at me but the innocent victim I called my best friend. Gasping, I was able to see Chloe slide on her black Converses, rolling down half the flight of stairs, trembling to hold on to the middle step.

"CHLOE!" I yelled in the highest voice I had ever made, throwing all my books behind me as I raced against the evil to get to her on time. "Chloe, Chloe! Did you get hit anywhere?" I had to shake her a few times before she was able to look at me.

Cradled in my arms, I moved her hair, scanned her skin for any marks, and felt her bones for any separation. The whole area of about a hundred kids stopped, circling the bottom of the stairwell, gazing at us with wonder and concern. Finally, Chloe pushed me back a little with her hand and with a murmur, she leaned to sit up and face me with the help of her elbows.

"Are you all right?" I asked again, the words strained.

Chloe nodded with her eyes closed and then grinded her teeth while propping her left elbow, looking at it in pain. Curious, I looped my vision around her body to see her elbow was stuck in a black liquid that looked like ink. "Gosh, it really hurts and I can't move it!"

Aiding her, I was able to lift her elbow out of the substance from underneath, but the damaging results had been done. Together, we gasped in astonishment; her skin had peeled off with only a small piece dangling, mocking her. Steam was coming from a large and almost seamlessly round opened cut, leaving a large dent in her arm. It was so big I was scared to look too closely in case I saw her bone. However, her blood was not dripping like normal, but jiggling in place like trapped cherry Jell-O and the scarring cut had burnt black edges around it!

When the cool air hit the exposed cut, Chloe bawled and held her elbow to her chest with tears building in her eyes and steam leaked through the gaps of her fingers. I was helpless with my mouth rounded as my eyes flashed with apprehension, my hand gently placed on her back.

"Could someone please get a teacher?" I pleaded, looking at the crowd of faces staring blindly and wide-eyed like fish out of water. A few smaller boys in the back ran toward the direction of the nurse's office. I sat down against the wall under the stair rail, Chloe almost falling on top of me, unable to support herself. She was clinging to my shirt and lying on my chest, her pale face scrunched in pain.

My thoughts traced back to the inky liquid, settling still with no movement at all. Freeing my hand from Chloe's back and allowing the other one to support her against my chest, I gazed down at the substance. I had to see if it could affect me. If so, that meant the murderer placed it there and that would be the final straw.

Chloe stopped me for a moment, dragging herself to the other side of the stair to lie on the cool wall, panting. Sweat was dripping down her face at an alarming rate as her body started to shake. Her glassy eyes stared at the ceiling, her face paling closer to Maren's ghostly shade with each passing minute. She didn't respond to my touch and presence. With caution, I moved my hand above the liquid, almost touching the material.

My palm was about four inches above when the blob began to sizzle and so many lightning bolts zapped out that Jupiter would have been overjoyed. My hand was the connecter, taking every blow. It felt almost exactly like the ecto shard I foolishly touched. Boy, I was on a roll with touching things I shouldn't! Stupid Stary!

A sharp pain hit my body and slithered up my arm like an electric whip. Steam emitted from it as well, but soon, the signs vanished and fortunate for me, there was no cut, probably because I hadn't touched it.

My heart was aching, beating like a current through my ears; the murderer was way too strong.

"Miss Stary!" Like a puppy hearing the call of its beloved master, my head shot up and my ears became perked in attention. Miss Stary? I knew that pet name and that sweet voice . . . Cally.

Jolting my head in her direction, I saw her emerge from the crowd in a bright yellow sweater, making her reddened hair look inflamed. In fright, her delicate face became the color of ripe strawberries, her mouth larger than a cave, and her arms were out in a shocked gesture.

"Miss Stary, what happened?" she wailed, straining her small voice.

I knew her intentions were good, but I was not in the mood. The murderer was upon us, hurting all people who had a connection with me, and I wasn't going to let another person get hurt from my vain. Chloe moaned, rolling her sickened head from side-to-side. Quickly and with a stressed heart, I flung my body over to her at full force to support her and allow her to use my flesh as a cushion.

I caught my breath after the second impact of pain on my lungs, sighing in relief I received some pain and not Chloe. I had to make Cally leave, deciding to glare to do so. "Cally, please! You need to leave. Someone's already getting help. Don't come any closer."

My voice was firm and cracking, trying to peek out its utter concern and guilt for what happened to Chloe. I supposed Cally's kind heart saw my outrage as a cry for help. "Please Miss Stary, I want to help . . ."

She took one step forward toward us. As my worst fears became realized, the ceiling began to ring a black aura, shaking a little to increase my blood flow. It was strange how all those staring eyes didn't move or blink, but only looked mindless, gazing at the show on the stairs and no one had come near the stairwell from behind. Maybe it was the murderer playing with me again, but the course of time needn't worry. I had to stop Cally now.

"Cally, stop! Don't get any closer."

"Miss Stary, I am glad you are worried about me, but please let me assist you." She took another small step, the sound amplified in my ears. The ringing sounded like a cell phone sending a stress call at the bottom of a lake, causing a reaction with the ceiling. The tile began to make louder vibrations, losing its bond with the exterior of the man-built sky, spreading the evil aura farther.

"Cally, get the heck away from me! Don't get near me: I don't need you!"

"It's fine . . . I do not mind aiding you." She took another step, making dust fall from the heavens. That dust was like fuel that increased the devil's power.

"Please Cally!" I screamed at the top of my lungs, tears in my eyes, begging, while embracing Chloe.

"Miss Stary, what is the matter?" She took a baby step but it was enough to release the malevolence.

In a second, the ceiling tile right above Cally's head broke off and with it was a damaged solar light. "CALLY!" I screamed to get her attention. By luck or impulse, she paused and saw the light about to crush her. Although the damage only took a few mere moments, time slowed down, engulfing me once again in remorse as I saw all the possibilities one had to do to save another but failed to perform.

I was lost in a dark world of loud and terrible noises, only feeling Chloe's light breathing and dread within myself. By the time the world had light again, I was shaking insanely and saw Cally on the ground, her face away from the fallen tile. Ever so gently, she was able to lean up on her elbows and stare at me with deer-in-the-headlights eyes but with a thankful smile. Other than some floor burns and marks on her face, she seemed fine. Then, I noticed Cally couldn't get up with all her strength; her body had missed the light, but her leg took the impact.

Soon, the nurse came to get Chloe and Cally, making the next twenty-four hours a blur. Time laughed at my existence as I held my head for hours, locking my soul from sound and screaming in terror of all the hurt I had caused.

By the time I semi knew I was alive and walking in the world of God's children, it was 12:30 in homeroom, about twenty-two and a half hours after Cally and Chloe received their mark. The talk of the whole day was all the events happening, but of course, my emotions absorbed the words to heart, each word attacking my insides. My body's painful dismay was my just punishment. Scared of harming anyone who talked to me, I sat alone in the row by the door in homeroom, staring out and not really seeing my surroundings.

I don't recall much. I remember Credence talked to me about plans for the dance the next week and me smiling the best I could. His eye was better and he said it would be okay in a few days so he wouldn't get blood on me when we danced. I said "That's great" or something like it.

I saw and heard Chloe and June gossiping about all the strange things happening and how scared they were. Chloe had a wrap cuddling her arm to cover the gross mark, but there seemed to be no more pain. However, her body was shaking from fear ever since, waiting for the aftershock. I do recall her asking me if I was okay since I never sat by myself. I lied with a fake grin and told her I was sick to my stomach and I didn't want to infect anyone.

The truth was in Chloe's words; it *was* all my fault. Those four haunting words kept echoing in my mind, bouncing like heated electrons, sending my soul to a downward spiral. *'It's all my fault. It's all my fault!'* I wanted to scream and cry bloody murder to be forgiven of my sins, if that was possible. Sins caused by a supposed good deed. It was too much for me to take.

Gasping wildly and trying to calm myself to not draw more attention, I noticed Barbara out of the corner of my eye. She was sitting behind Chloe and June's circle, looking gravely ill as darkness swirled around her eyelids. A frown was stuck on her shadowed head. Maybe she felt guilty or was plotting her next motive, but whatever it was, it made me crawl in my seat. I focused on the other area of the room, where the window was opened, allowing the chilled wind to enter through.

There, in the large tree outside our room was Umbra, sitting coyly and leaning his weight on his arms. His face was concerned, informative, and serious, making my mind unfasten to give him full attention, to let him evaporate my fears and doubts.

Magically, a list appeared in Umbra's hand in a lovely penmanship. My eyes were not that good to read the tiny print on the piece of paper, but Umbra gave me a nod with a straight face. Somehow, my body knew what to do: I closed my eyes, took a deep breath, and focused on the words on the paper, allowing myself to see them. My wish was granted and my sight zoomed forward, making everything crisp and clear.

The list was entitled **Injured People**. Maybe this was why Umbra and Maren were gone for so long because they were researching about all the strange events at the school. All the people who had been injured were connected to me. All the names on the list were crossed out, but the top one. I focused on the circled name: mine.

I was surprised, and yet I was not. I knew this was coming, with the murderer close enough for me to touch her. It was terrifying. However, Barbara seemed to get weaker with each passing day and much snippier. It was odd she didn't notice Umbra at all. Still, I turned once more to look at him and watch his tender lips mouth to me, "We have a plan," pointing to himself. All I was able to do was wait until directions came later in the day.

16

HOPPING DOWN THE STAIRS WHERE CHLOE WAS INJURED, I hurried to the lobby as fast as my aching legs could carry me. I was being forced to leave the area while Maren and Umbra left a message in the restroom for Barbara/the murderer. For some reason, I was forbidden to view it, even by Maren, so I did as told. By the frantic hand gestures Umbra was performing when telling me this, it was for my own protection. I hated not knowing what was going on, but my sinking heart raised above the icy waves enough for me to accept their duty.

At home, I tried to act like everything was normal, but all the painful feelings, stressful images and such made my task near impossible. I hated acting like that in front of my parents and lying, but worrying them would only bring more heartache for me. My poor mother looked so concerned and even my brother was surprised that I didn't yell at him after he insulted me at dinner. I wasn't very hungry and my body had little rashes, more than likely from stress my mom told me in her loving, but professional nurse tone.

I excused myself due to being sleepy and told them my teenage changes were just real strong lately. My father took it as my menstrual cycle, which did make me laugh a little. I knew they were whispering about me in the dining room, but I vanished into the shadows, allowing myself to be gone, stopping any more pain to fall upon my family. How could I tell them or even explain all the feelings I had? None of it was normal for a fifteen year old!

Giving up, I put on one of my favorite pairs of PJs on with stars, moons, and clouds on them, hoping it would improve my mood. I threw myself on my bed, face down on the pillow, and allowed my mind to ease as I tossed and turned with no sleep, trying to let the warmth of my body heat soothe me. But nothing was working. I whimpered in distress, ready to let tears free fall from my eyes. I felt like a small child all alone and unable to do anything. I just wanted to be with someone, someone wonderful who would get the evil plots of the murderer out of my mind . . .

"Ha, *ha*!" I heard a dramatically sounding boom from my wall. It was loud and sounded like Prince Charming was fighting a dragon inside my wall and winning. In full attention, I raised my head up and wrapped my navy star and moon comforter around me, curious of what the noise was. Suddenly, Umbra jumped out of the wall with a large childish grin on his face. His sneakers landed on my floor and he stared at me with a stern face and darting honey eyes. His muscled arms crossed for a moment before placing his hands on his hips.

Playfully, he said to me, sounding like a parent, "Little girls should be in bed resting." My whole body felt inflamed looking at his dazzling eyes and desirable smile.

"Umbra, what are you doing here?" I sounded groggy and felt dizzy as my head tilted from the heat, my heart and head pounding as one.

"Just following orders, miss!" he said in a low, mocking military voice as he gave a salute. I let out a small giggle, but it choked me and echoed inside my hollow chest, buzzing in my ears. Why does he have to be so painfully charming and adorable tonight? My mind was pleading for control of my emotions.

"From Maren?" I asked, my tone calm, finding it odd that he would leave her alone in the darkness with a murderer's trail.

"Yep. It was all her idea."

"What?! How could you leave her like that? All alone, following the trail of a dangerous person that killed her once? What if something happens to her? We—I . . . couldn't bear it . . ."

I looked away for a moment, trying to keep myself together, heaving. I shook, my face feeling feverish, and my stomach began to quake. Umbra may have listed everyone in the mortal world who had received pain from the murderer, but he did not include Maren or himself. The realization broke my heart.

"Because although I'm more powerful, she was killed two years before I was, making her able to track the trail better . . ." His voice was a whisper, light and delicate, about to break. He bowed his head down. "Maren's so worried about you getting harmed and she insisted with those eyes and that mousy voice . . . What was I supposed to do?" He didn't want to leave her either, but Umbra looked torn, like he also wanted to be with me. Regardless, I had to play along and be a good girl.

I looked at him with narrowed eyes before placing my cupped hand under my chin as I stared at the ceiling, tracing the white bumps that looked like jouncing stars with my eyes. Talking to myself, I said, "I'll have to thank her . . ."

Again, saluting like a tin solider, Umbra informed me of the task for the night in his mocking military voice: "My mission is to guard Miss Stary tonight while Major Maren follows the murderer's trail."

I cocked my head like a cute puppy when their master puzzles them. What was he talking about?

As if in my mind, he zoomed past me in a blinking second, giving me a heart attack. "I am going to protect you. So be a good little girl for me, okay?" He gave an attractive grin and tapped my nose. We were only inches apart and I forgot how to swallow, my chest hammering as my whole body trembled, waiting for my volcanic heart to pop. I thought my lungs were melting into my socks.

Umbra hopped backwards to give me some room and looked at me bemused. Umbra and I would be alone . . . together . . . all night? I was about to hyperventilate and I covered myself up with my hot comforter, completely embarrassed.

Umbra tipped backward on his heels with a sour face and blushing cheeks. "I . . . I was never . . . I mean . . . I would . . . I was never going to do that Stary!" he yelled back at me with his eyes shut tight and hands pounded in a ball.

"I . . . I'm . . . I'm sorry . . . I didn't . . . mean to accuse . . . I mean, you and me . . . AH! Never mind! I'm sorry!" I squeaked, sounding awkward as I embarrassed myself even further. Umbra seemed to understand and sighed.

"You are one interesting creature, you know that Stary Moon?" His voice was stern, but each word trailed off his tender lips and sounded more meaningful and sweet. I was shuddering too much to remove the covers off my body. I needed an escape.

Umbra tiptoed to me, pushing my body backward by tapping my shoulder with his pinky, showing how weak I was. "You need to go to sleep. Nothing is going to happen. That's why I'm here."

"Yeah . . . *you're* part of the problem," I wanted to say sarcastically. His eyes were so brilliant that I took a deep breath and turned to my side, facing the window. I tried hard to catch the clouded path to dreamland, but I couldn't grasp the road.

For half an hour, I tossed and turned, adjusting my head, unable to get comfortable no matter how much I needed sleep. I peeked over the covers, scanning the room. My eyes focused to see Umbra leaning on the wall with his head down, arms folded across his chest, eyes shut, his eyelashes brushing his handsome face. He looked like he was sleeping. I wasn't sure if spirits went to sleep like I did, but he looked too relaxed, calm, and peaceful; nothing like what I normally saw with Umbra. I smiled underneath my blanket. It was amazing how angelic he looked . . . Wait . . . that was a bad choice of words. I found it also funny that if he was sleeping, he was failing his job of guarding me miserably.

I had to stop focusing on Umbra or I would never get to sleep. Even if he wasn't there, I felt like it was one of those nights where I would be restless and uneasy, unable to find the magical dream world's comforts. I tossed about five more times, back and forth, flattening my pillow at a rapid pace before I groaned. Being extremely tired and unable to sleep hurt my eyes something fierce.

Umbra popped his right eye open after I made a noise. I felt hot, like I was burning in the underworld . . . again! My mind was all blurry. I had to get to sleep, but my body was becoming utterly useless.

I heard a slight rough sound by the wall. I looked and saw it was Umbra straightening his back by sliding up the wall. I pulled my covers over my head, trying to burn out my fever, but with the feeling of Umbra's sharp glare on me, I cracked. I propped myself up so fast, the covers fell off my head and to the middle of my back. My hair was most likely a mess.

"I can't sleep," I said crisp and clear to Umbra, but reserved, because I felt blameworthy for the awkwardness in the room.

His eyes were strained. He pushed himself off the wall and stepped a few inches closer to me. I could see how radiant he looked in the moonlight. "Maybe we can do something else to make you sleepy or at least make the night seem shorter."

I gulped, more awake now, thinking of something we could do that didn't sound like an . . . invitation. I closed my eyes, thinking, until I realized this was my chance to learn more about Umbra! "Mind if I ask you some questions?"

Umbra glared at me with one eye. "Did you plan this?"

I shook my head, embarrassed, if it looked that way.

He sighed like he was losing a game and shut his eyes for a moment, turning away from me before answering me, annoyed, "Go ahead, but I get to counter."

I smiled and let out a small giggle, which made Umbra focus on me, his body open towards me as his face lit up with amazement. I wasn't sure why he was looking at me like that, but I was happy. "Do you know why Dr. Rowe created you?"

"Some of it was motivation on his part, to see if he could make a creature capable of real feelings. He also created me to use as a defensive weapon and retriever to get his stolen machines. The human format itself was so I could play with Maren when he went on to his next crazy idea."

I sighed, feeling bad for asking. Maybe something a little easier. "What did you and Maren play together?"

"Whatever she wanted."

"What did you guys study?"

"Everything."

"Do you eat?"

"I can, but it doesn't give me extra energy or anything. I get energy through working."

"Do you sleep?"

"Back then, I recharged in my room at night. Now, I'm eternally sleeping."

"Did you ever play tag?"

"No."

"Hide-and-seek?"

"No."

"Did you ever swim?"

"No."

I yawned wide. My quiz show wasn't going very well. Umbra was answering trivial things. I wanted to know more and make him want to tell me, but I guess I couldn't do that. The deafening, swallowing silence scared me and I leaned on my knees, whispering to myself, "I wonder what your home was like . . ."

Umbra gazed at me considerately. With some childish eyes, a sparkle formed and his grin was sly but gorgeous when he told me, "I can show you."

My heart hammered at the wheels that were turning in his head. His eyes, staring straight into mine, were glowing intensely like fireflies dancing in a foggy night. A cat-like grin spread across his face, one of a cat ready to pounce on its prey.

Out of the blue, Umbra pinned my body down, holding my hips. His muscular legs became a barricade I couldn't escape from. I was too shocked to move. With an evil smile and a twinkle in his eyes, he stared at me with only three inches between our faces. My body craved to embrace his. His expression became hidden in the shadows as the moonlight spilled behind his head and onto my face.

Umbra leaned to my right ear as he held my face lightly with his smooth hands. He whispered so near my ear, I could almost feel his gorgeous lips forming the words before he spoke them. "I can show you with your astral body."

No matter how nice Umbra smelled or how nice his lips felt almost touching my flesh, my eyes widened. Astral body? I knew what that meant from reading books about the other world; my eternal spirit was released from its earthly body for a set amount of time. It was like something out of *A Christmas Carol.* I looked away from the light, my eyes blinking to stop tears, fearful of the worst case possibility.

He slid his head to look at me with questioning eyes. "What's wrong?"

A few tears escaped from the corner of my eyes. "What if I don't come back?" I whispered.

He sighed, almost sounding relieved. He allowed a small laugh to flee from his artistically-shaped lips. I liked this Umbra compared to Mr. Grumpy-All-the-Time Umbra. "As long as we get back before sunrise at six, you will be fine and your body will accept you. We have five hours until then, so we'll be fine."

It seemed like he was trying to show me he was willing to protect me. It would be neat to see his home plus there was no way I could sleep. Maren told me it was in space. I honestly wasn't sure if I believed that, but I bet it was unique. I gulped my fear away which made my eyes real watery and nodded, agreeing I would go as long as we were back before six.

He narrowed the space between us, our foreheads a hair from touching. A squeal left my quivering lips even though I was trying to be calm. He wasn't even looking at me, but down at the mattress, focusing hard on something, but that didn't matter. I could feel his warm breath and it smelled like the salty sea, cooling the fire on my cheeks.

I was choking on my own air supply, trying to keep myself from exploding or dying from a thinking fever. My heart was ramming against my ribs, wanting to break free and be given to Umbra. My heart was trying to get its secret message across to him, one my soul was not ready to believe. I wished I could sink away into the floor, away from my guilt of caring for two people, especially one who had an angel waiting for him.

What was taking him so long? I wasn't sure what he was doing, but having his protective hands pinning me down made each second more awkward and unbearable to stand.

"Stary, you okay?" Umbra was gazing right into my eyes then. They were gleaming and reflected the moonbeams streaming from my window. His face had a unique expression, filled with concern, confusion, kindness, and something else I couldn't pinpoint. Umbra's cheeks were a light pink, making him look innocent and vulnerable for a change. "Sorry it took so long. I was collecting my thoughts before doing the action . . ."

Collecting his thoughts? Was he worried about something involving me? He gave me a wry smile that made my knees weak, so weak that I had to turn my head away for a minute. It was then that I noticed Umbra was breathing raggedly like me. I looked at him surprised, holding back the urge to touch his cheek.

"Ready?" he asked, more serious and in control of his breath.

I nodded slowly to not make my head spin more. With a warm grin, he leaned down to my left ear, his cheek almost rubbing against mine, the friction hotter than summer time. He whispered in his beautiful voice, "Hold on okay? It won't take long . . ." Before I had a chance to respond, he closed the little space we had between us and embraced me tight.

The world spun and all I could see was Umbra and darkness clouding him. My head felt like it weighed two tons and my neck was forced backwards, making my mind black out for a few seconds. Then, I felt like a feather floating to the top of a clear pool, but something was holding me when I opened my eyes. I groaned and looked into Umbra's face, which didn't have the blue light around it like normal.

He beamed and allowed me to lean back in his arms to look at his beloved face, brighter than any star. "You did it and a good job at that. How do you feel?"

"I'm really not sure how to feel . . . ," I said with a little giggle at the end.

Umbra smiled again and scooped me up like a princess. Actually, he was more mischievous than a knight in dark armor. He stood on my bed and opened the window with his plasma ray, allowing the crisp night wind to refresh us before our unknown journey. "Ready?" he said full of energy as he began to jump up in the air.

My stomach dropped in nervousness. "Wait a minute! We have to fly in the *sky*? I hate heights Umbra!" I shut my eyes tight in fear of falling thousands of feet and also because I didn't want to look down to see my motionless human body on my bed, staring at me like an abused Barbie doll.

"How else are we going to get to outer space silly? Suck it up and hold on to me tight."

I was fine with the holding on part for a few reasons, but I still hated heights and flying. Maybe there was another way. "Umb—"

"HOLD ON!" he battle cried and we zoomed out the window at lightning speed, like we were a bolt ourselves, traveling onward to the starry skies.

I screamed, my form feeling like Jell-O. I could feel Umbra adjusting us to go faster, faster than I wanted to go. He was doing it on purpose! "Umbra! I thought you told me you'd be nice to me!" I shouted, tears stinging my eyes.

He gave a short, breathy, cruel laugh before answering, "I didn't say for how long . . ."

I wasn't sure if he was serious or having too much fun messing with me, but I wasn't happy at all. I felt my tangle hair behind me. I puffed up like a puffer fish. "This is so mean!" I was able to open my eyes to glare at his profile. I didn't care how adorable he was or if he was the only thing from me and the ground . . . I was upset!

He groaned, annoyed. "I have to go fast to be able to get out of the atmosphere Stary and I have extra weight with me. You do the math!" I hope he wasn't calling me fat, but he did pick me up easily, so it was okay. I guess ectoplasm had weight as well. I still didn't like the idea, but I sighed and rested my shoulders on Umbra's to try to enjoy the rest of the roller coaster. I was defeated, stuck in the flashing sky.

"Don't worry. Once we reach the night sky, it'll be worth it. It really is beautiful and our home had a nice view of everything."

I guess he was trying to cheer me up because him saying "beautiful" in that smooth, almost romantic voice was not Umbra's style, plus he looked sick after he said it. I let out a snicker. Umbra shot me a puzzled look. I snuggled closer to his body to help me ignore my fears. It was slowly melting away the farther from home I was. I felt as if Umbra's heartbeat was destroying my dread.

"Look up Stary. Those are the border clouds of the sky, which means we're almost there. Hang on to me. There are a lot of those clouds and they're super thick, so things will get messy."

The clouds were as white as purity. They were sparkling with loveliness, looking like silver stardust had landed on them to whisper stories of enchantment to its travelers. I did as Umbra had told me and got ready to embrace for fluffy impact. That was no joke; it was like cotton was trying to go through you. I supposed in my living body, I would feel nothing at all.

It only took a few minutes of rough riding before I saw a clear black sheet of wonder with dazzling red and blue stars shining, twirling, glowing, and shooting across it. It looked like my blanket had come to life in front of my eyes. I could then see that being named Stary was a compliment, being compared to such God-created beauties. Umbra slowed down to allow me to view a dreamlike world.

My eyes were honored with beholding the glory of the night, the ancient sparkles that had guided the leaders of our living Earth for ages. Their beauty would forever be timeless, inspiring the creative souls of all the worlds, and protecting all who gazed at their splendor. I was always curious what stars were other than shining space gas in scientific terms: souls, living forms, an accessory to make the universe beautiful, a symbol . . . There had to be more to them.

Umbra zoomed forward, the speed he was creating making a blinding white comet tail. We continued to speed to a destiny, maybe one where we were intertwined. The black blanket of God's filled sky hummed every time a burning ball of light released a small amount of glowing power. It seemed that Umbra was gliding in the airless amount of space with ease like His son walked on water: weightless, lifeless. I supposed that was what astronauts felt like, but Umbra was still somehow flying, hovering in the emptiness; the exquisite, mesmerizing emptiness with its lights I was named after.

Being cuddled in his arms, floating to an area that only few were allowed to be part of, flying through outer space, before entering the golden gates of heaven . . . it made me feel like a loved girl. If only Umbra wasn't doing it to please Maren . . . no. I shook that thought right out of my head. I could never hate Maren in any manner. Even thinking about hating Maren made me feel like I would break her frail bones. Was I really supposed to know all these secrets, see all these wonders not meant to be seen by man? I felt one of Umbra's curly bangs drop and poke my exposed forehead. A ticklish sensation made my spine tingle and my heart vibrated with a unique beat. This moment being held by him, my forbidden moment, was perfect.

Umbra amorously smiled at me, allowing his pearly teeth to shine brighter than the stars. Butterflies fluttered in my chest, making me flustered for no reason. Cold chills hit my arms stronger than a hurricane. My cheeks were hotter than the blazing sun, all due to a true, gorgeous smile. I smiled back, responding to his kindness for forcing me to come. It turned him off like a light switch. His mouth puckered up like a sour grape and he turned away, almost looking embarrassed. I bet that last part was my imagination, but he did act funny and his strong arms felt warmer to the touch even in the extreme chilled environment.

"What do you think?" he asked quietly, without looking at me.

I gawked with my mouth agape, almost able to taste the warmth of the spherical beauties enchanting us with their firefly-like glow. "It's so beautiful here! I really am lucky to be named after something I can never be compared to . . ."

The granite-like leftover bits of asteroids and space rocks floated around us, landing on my skin like a protective shield, bringing a freezing movement with it that made my body shake. "Thank you Umbra," I said in my kindest and most honest voice as my hair flapped in front of me like angels were lifting it like a bride's veil although there was no air in space. My eyes were half shut for my smile was too wide and happy to control. I hoped Umbra could see the joy he created in me.

Umbra was vibrating so much that I thought maybe I was getting too heavy for him, but his entire body was smoking hot, leaving a mark when I rubbed it. I traced his forehead lightly with my fingers, checking for a fever and to make sure he was all right. He made a heaving sound and squinted his eyes as his mouth shook like an animal scared of the vet. Yet, the haunting thing was . . . half of his noises made it seem like he enjoyed me doing that! Weird . . .

I was only worried about him. The idea of him liking me stroking his skin made me blush and stopped me dead in my tracks. I felt like I was committing a crime. I folded my hands in my lap and refused to look up.

"It'll be a little longer. Rest for now," Umbra said softly, reassuringly.

I nodded and cradled myself against Umbra's supportive chest. How peculiar. I was finally sleepy despite me being in a spirit form, seeing the night sky and its lights blur into an unforgettable image. Maybe I could fall asleep because I was still human with a breathing body. I grinned, tilting my head back at my beloved stars before closing my eyes to enter the magic dream world, one that would be safe because Umbra was in my mind.

The world was so warm but entirely black. I felt like I was falling into a hole created to ease my mind and erase all confusion. I knew I was there, at the bottom, but I couldn't see myself and the area began to twirl. The circular shape soon began to dissolve its eternal state and separate in the middle, allowing orange and yellow enchanting lights to heat up my heart and give my mind peace: "*You are no comparison to beauty; it needs to learn to be more like you . . . The stars are honored to share their lovely name with an equal.*"

I fluttered my eyes open a little in my dreamland, wanting to hear that low, affectionate voice again, hear it echoing in my hollow heart. It sounded so familiar and filled my veins with pure bouncing life. The right side of my face suddenly felt something breathtaking, something slightly moist. It almost felt like someone, on the outside world, was trying to show their love to my half-aware body. It traced my cheek, not exactly landing on it, but it was heading for my lips that craved that love . . .

Zoom! A yellow and white blaze flashed in front of my eyes, shocking my dream body, and snapping my eyes open. My hair roots felt like they were being tugged, then tugged harder until it was almost painful. Dazed, I woke up from my short rest, but I had to take it slowly so I wouldn't get dizzy in my new form and place.

I heard a small, fun-loving giggle in front of me, but I was too dazed to pinpoint where it was coming from or figure out what was going on.

"STOP!" Umbra yelled.

Confused, I glanced around to look at Umbra and see he was staring at me, with anxious, saucer-shaped eyes that told me one thing: busted! He was so close to my face, about an inch or two that it took me a little longer to get my heart to restart. Umbra gulped. Did he steal my favorite stuffed animal or something?

I then heard the giggle again that seemed to only move a few inches closer. Like a psychic, I stopped time in my head to see a small, shining star bouncing up and down in happy strides, its light so gorgeous and adorable. It was almost as if it was smiling and alive, twirling between Umbra and myself.

"Why, hello there little one," I said, smiling warmly to match its shine and shifted my eyes so I wasn't looking directly at my new little friend. I wasn't sure if staring at it would make me go blind.

The star must have enjoyed my greeting for it made a pinging sound and spun dizzily around in at least five perfect circles. I chuckled to match its charming pitch because it was too darling. Umbra mumbled something like, "stupid particle." So Umbra!

It began to make noises again and mess with my hair: hiding in it, spinning it, and trying to get Umbra to watch its splendid dance. I laughed hard at how amazing those simple, small gestures made me feel. I could have never imagined I would be with a spirit and a star! The star zapped stunning sparkling dust behind, making a trail. My friend then tapped my nose before it went to Umbra's ear and made more pinging noises.

Umbra's face became bright and he stuttered. It seemed like they were having a conversation. "What? I know . . . I mean . . . well . . . ummmmm . . ."

The star whizzed one last time past me and seemed to give me a peck on my cheek. I chuckled and thanked it for making my space experience even grander. It whistled rudely at Umbra and paused at me before leaving into the vast twinkling sky, making Umbra blush a little redder. I had to ask. "What did the star say to you?"

Umbra looked like I hit him in the head with a one hundred pound hammer, wanting to dodge the question, but he sighed and looked at me. "He . . . he said . . . you're beautiful . . ."

I felt my cheeks warm, wishing I had thanked the sweet star. Seeing Umbra so embarrassed about it made me feel hopeful, my insides melting into a warm glow. I smiled shyly at him as he continued. "He also told me to be good . . ."

"Be good?" I said, dazed.

He blushed so red then that I thought he was a lost ray of the scorching sun. The way he said it made it sound like he did something bad or almost did already. Was my dream . . . ?

"There, over the blue area, is the moon. That's our home, my home . . ."

With wide-eyed excitement, I was ready to gaze at the wonder and supposed thrill of this moon base. Although my heart was ready to leave its dock, the sight made my boat sink, sink into the dark swirls of despair. There, I surely did see the moon shining an off cream color with dents molding its unique shape. However, this moon base was a long row of complex, rusted silver metals with holes of sorrow and missing pieces, keeping its secret destruction hidden from human eyes. It floated, forced by the pull of unwanted gravity, making it look more eerie.

As I was able to get a clearer glance, I saw their home, the warm working center Maren referred to, was meant to be an advanced circular shape that one might see on the SyFy network, but it was forever a modern set of ruins. Tears welled in my eyes, wanting to break free of my self-control. This place, this sight, the memories . . . I felt them and they, against my will, stabbed my heart, making me feel lost in soul and dead of mind. Poor Umbra . . . Poor Maren . . .

Umbra gently set us on a smooth surface on the moon, one near an edge, facing the point of our quest. I sighed low and deep, allowing the breath to push up against my throat and swell my face with stings. That was where Maren had lived, where she grew up, where her grandfather had raised her and made wonderful machines, where Umbra was created, where they unknowingly fell in love, where Maren and Dr. Rowe were murdered, and Umbra's life was sent into chaos before his life was taken. My whole chest ached and my hands began to sweat. They turned into fists, fists that were hiding my anger, fists controlling my pain, fists hiding my pain from Umbra.

"I'm sorry that this is hard on you. You really shouldn't feel bad for something that didn't involve you in our living days . . ." Umbra's voice made me jump, my brain protest, my soul scream in confusion, but my body stayed perfectly still, numb from the power of my emotions. I was able to slowly turn my head to face his focused face, darkened with rage.

"This is where Maren lived after her father was killed by his own machine. It was a difficult move, but Maren did it with a smile. At least, that is what my master told me . . ." Umbra had a small smile and his eyes twinkled with amusement. I knew he was trying to make things easier for me. I nodded and allowed that sweet thought to permeate through me.

"It was modern and very big, with lots of wires, but Maren made it her home and brought life into it. Dr. Rowe made sure she was happy and had rooms just for her, adding cute things. It made the place more homey and warm." Umbra breathed, trying to blow the negative energies of the story away.

"Maren meant everything to my master. Not that he didn't love Elbert, but he was too much like his father to try to better himself for the world or worry about others. Maren was pure love, joy, and compassion. She reminded me of sunshine. Deep down, she wanted to be normal and go to Earth, but she never pushed it for the sake of her grandfather. I was the only one who knew her dream for a while. It always hurts me knowing that Maren died when her dream, the only thing she wanted in life, was within her reach."

My fists tightened again, my nails digging into my hand and leaving a mark even in my astral form.

Umbra drew in a staggered breath and continued, this time his eyes darker than our present night. "You already know how she died, all for the love of others, never caring about herself. I guess there's nothing that can be done now about that, but we need to try to make this eternal choice easier on her. I hate that I caused her early death as I got saved. It's not fair at all!" His velvet voice shook all the beings along the horizon.

I was aggrieved hearing Umbra scream something so untrue. I had no oomph or spirit to disagree however.

I had to ask Umbra the question then, the most painful one. I never felt so timid or scared in my life. "Did you die there too, Umbra?"

He looked a little surprised, but then exhaled noisily with a shy smile and shake of his head. Umbra pointed to the most brilliant heavenly object known to all mankind: the sun. He turned and pointed at it, his face masked.

I gasped loudly, allowing the rays to blind me, to shock me, and to boil my heated ectoplasm. "YOU DIED IN . . . THE SUN?!" I regretted saying it as soon as the words left my mouth. I studied his face, wishing he was lying about such a cruel fate.

He lowered his arm and shook his head, forcing his eyes on the dark beams of the moon's surface his shadows created. To my surprise, he smiled at me. Not the hiding-his-feelings type, but an honest-to-goodness smile. Maybe he was happy I was there to learn more about him.

"It's all right, Stary. It came out of nowhere, but I have no regrets because I was able to correct all the harm I almost caused due to my anger at humans for killing Maren. It's scary since we were murdered by the same person and I still don't know how they got to me, but I got to be with Maren again and keep my promise, her true promise for a moment. It's all right."

"No!" I cried, allowing tears to run down my face. They stung, clashing with my burning with anger body. I allowed my fingers to cut my palms so badly that I'm sure my human body at home was bleeding. I didn't care. Umbra was accepting it willingly. He was never upset about it; he thought he deserved it due to Maren's choice. Neither of them deserved it! No one ever does! I felt like all the angry thoughts I bottled up since I was born were released and the power was incredible, surging like a flood through my muscles.

"All innocent people who get killed for no reason, all who have their precious lives cut short by someone disgraceful—It's not fair! I swear, I will stop this murderer to not only avenge you and Maren but to save others, and I will do whatever God tells me in a second of my beating heart to stop all people like that." I had never felt such determination. I wanted to protect everyone with my life. At first, I only did this because God told me to and I wanted to be loyal to him. At that moment, I saw all the innocent faces and wanted to do it for them.

Umbra looked stunned, but then nodded firmly with a powerful smile to match. He had his arms crossed, and approached me when he abruptly stepped back and said in utter surprise, "Stary! Your hands!"

Snapped out of my warrior moment, I incongruously looked at my fists to notice that they were glowing the brightest and prettiest form of yellow I had ever laid my eyes on. The brightness and warmth reflected off my skin for a few seconds before it vanished, leaving me dazed and breathless.

"This is great!" Umbra yelled with glee, jumping up and down like a frog on a sugar rush, allowing his strong limbs to fly in the air almost like a cheerleader. "That means you're tapping into your full spirit powers, the ones you have to use to take the evil out of the murderer. All you needed was real determination and confidence."

I was taken aback by Umbra's response. I knew I could never do it without Umbra not being scared to hurt my feelings, without his reassurance, honesty or, unknowingly to him, the kindness he gave to me and the bond of love I felt for him. I flipped my hair and spun to face him. I hoped he would see how truly important he was and how I needed him, how I cared for him. "Thank you so much Umbra."

He reddened a little, dropping his gaze before his silky, chocolate-like voice replied, "You're welcome."

We made it back in plenty of time, about another hour before my time was up. I safely got into my flesh body with no problems. I was correct however; I had gotten so mad that I was bleeding a little and had a lot of cuts on my hands. As I watched Umbra float by the wall, I remembered how beautiful the stars were and how enjoyable floating was. Yet, guilt ran up my spine at that moment. Sure it was fun . . . when one gets to choose when.

"You know, Stary?" Umbra said in a raised matter-of-fact tone. "It's unbelievable that the murderer could have got me in outer space and with my unusual super powers. In all cases I know, murderers have been . . . human."

I nodded, seeing his concern. "That black liquid that hurt Chloe didn't seem like an ability a human could have."

"Ah, yeah. I did see that after Chloe and Cally were in the nurse's office and you went back to class. I felt . . . sickeningly dark vibes and came back. I have no idea what that black liquid was. It could mean the murderer's blood is heartless and they are more powerful and evil than before . . ." His voice got darker, more focused.

I was about to say something when I saw the sun reflecting off Umbra, blinding me. As I tried to regain my composure, Maren flew through the door, looking ragged but still delicate.

Maren glanced at us both once and smiled kindly with a little sigh of relief. "I have been tracking all night and the trail is very weak and not targeted near Stary." I looked lost for it sounded good, but it sure didn't mean the murderer was gone. Umbra opened one eye and shrugged, allowing a fun loving smile to brush on his calm, fond face.

Maren took one step closer to me, allowing the lovely sunrays to hit her golden hair just right. "It means that they spent so much energy scaring you Stary that they are somewhat weakened and will have to hide out for a while. I give it about a week at the least."

I sank into my bed and tossed my hair back as I smiled. What a relief! I could finally get some sleep, get ahead of the murderer's trail, and maybe be normal for a week, hanging out with my friends and family. And what perfect timing with the spring dance only five days away and I had a date with my dream guy. I looked at them and thanked them with my eyes before covering them from the blinding sunshine; I was beat. A plan of action would come soon, but at that point, I begged God to let me feel like a normal girl.

THE RIDGED GRASS OF PLANTERSVILLE BEGAN TO SHINE WITH glorious splendor as I walked to the main lobby with my best friends, reflecting on my last week. The air was warm and delightful, pulsing an enchanting fragrance throughout the school and the wind circled us like a gentle flowering vine. Although it had been partly cloudy for the first three days, it was a perfect 78 degrees, enough to make the Grim Reaper smile with pleasure. The weather cleared up slightly and made grand promises for tomorrow, the tomorrow I already loved so.

Maren and Umbra were still guarding me close by, but as far as the energy flow department went, nothing was happening, so they had time to rest and even played cards once in the corner of the school. Maren was just as thrilled as I was for the dance and my date with Credence. However, Umbra looked uneasy and sickly, almost the color of an exquisite green apple. When he saw me, his lips would tighten and his eyes were locked in apprehension. I never did understand the reasoning.

Worrying about what to wear to the dance or how to celebrate our first spring pep rally didn't cloud the dark fear that hung from my heart that the murderer or Barbara caused. I was worried they were watching nearby, waiting to attack. For some reason, I thought about these unpleasant thoughts during gym, probably because I was no good at sports and we were starting gymnastics. How they expected a long-legged, clumsy freak like me to be graceful on a front flip, I had no idea!

While trying to perform my routine, I allowed the suppressed thoughts to flip in my mind: Barbara had been extremely weak and pale all week and even odder, she didn't talk at all. Maren had pinned the trail to inside the school, but the location had vanished. Umbra seemed dazed, unable to focus on anything, and Credence seemed just as excited about the dance as I did.

Every time he mentioned it, I got a stupid grin on my face and couldn't talk in proper sentences. Credence . . . he chuckled at me and always left with a promising wave. It was after he was gone that worried me, because I felt a stab in my chest, a painful punch of guilt. Its wound was equal to the amount of joy I got from seeing Credence being so sweet to me.

The comfort of allowing these difficult thoughts form, letting them take new, enlightening shapes as the feelings sent tingling vibes cascading through my body became a unique thrill. I guess one truly cannot run away from their problems forever.

"Stary! Come here for a second."

I looked for the source of the voice. I knew that in-control voice too well; it was Coach Loyal. Confused, I blinked to see that not only was I standing there swinging my arms stupidly, but I was blocking the warm-up mats. Embarrassed, I ran to the corner to get off them, nearly tripping on my way to Coach.

"Yes Coach Loyal?" I was in full attention.

She gave me a glare, one of disappointment, which cut me just as deep as the others. I gulped, waiting for her to collect her phrase, bending my head down a little to look more noticeably into her glass blue eyes.

I had known Coach Loyal most of my life. Her husband was one of my father's best friends and the only person on the planet that could make him act childish in public. Her daughter was a year older than me and her son a year younger. The three of us went to daycare together and were good friends and she had always liked my parents. I supposed that was why I was the only student she called by their first name, making me seem like a teacher's pet, but that was an odd conclusion since I was so terrible at gym!

Finally, to break the ice, she sighed crisply and gave me a sympathetic smile. She said to me softly, "Stary, I understand being so tall makes it hard for you to do gymnastics, but I know you can do it. Since you don't like this sport, you don't focus on the final mission, the goal. You only worry about getting it done. That would be okay . . . if it wasn't messing you up on your landing. You can do good cartwheels, cartwheel-flips, somersaults, kips, and you're a wiz at the balance beam. Front flips are scary, but you need to focus. You are in control, not gravity."

I found that humorous since I knew Mrs. Shell would have disagreed full-heartedly, but I nodded. "Stare at the corner wall and focus, dream of that area, and tackle all the things in the way and then you can get to your destination." With a small smile and final pat on my shoulder, she stood back.

Buzzing in my head like wildfire, the flame she created filled and lit up my heart, inspiring and comforting me. Focused on the final point and tackling anything negative in your way . . . It was the only way I could be victorious in doing a flip or defeating the murderer. Umbra was right that sometimes, you cannot be nice to let good win and God would understand if I had to do something less than perfect; he gave me the job. With that drive, I ran, positioned myself, and landed my first, almost perfect, front flip landing.

I was racing, running with all my might to beat the speed of time. Faster, faster, even faster, allowing not even one breath to catch up with my pulsing body in fear it would slow me down. At the end of the tunnel, I saw her bleeding, struggling to stay in one piece and almost allowing the force to control her being.

"Maren!" I screeched, unable to get my hand to reach her no matter how clearly I could see her sickened face. The black hole, the force I had felt earlier, was taking her, destroying my little glimmer of hope. Maren was leaving me and Umbra was nowhere to be found. My tears hit my cheeks and my ears rang like I stood next to a bomb going off. I saw the final second she looked at me with trembling eyes.

"MAREN!" My voice pierced the sound barrier of my sanity. I snapped out of my state with wide eyes to see that all I was witnessing was my mind's doing and my body would not let me move a nanometer.

"Stary," a voice spoke my name with gentleness. It sounded like it wanted me to follow it out of the empty space the black hole left that was so white now it was about to blind me. My body was stuck, unable to move. I felt like I was someone's puppet. "Stary!"

"Whoa . . . What?" I finally heard my cracking voice. I looked up to see that Credence was leaning on my desk with a worried look. He gave me a comforting, sly smile once I noticed he was there. I did a double take to look around and saw I was in homeroom. Chloe looked at me with huge saucers and Barbara wasn't moving in the back. I gulped and looked again at Credence, embarrassed and unable to remember anything no matter how long I held my head in my left palm.

"Are you all right, Stary? Did I say something wrong?" Credence asked full of so much sorrow that I was expecting a gray rain cloud to be over his head like in a cartoon.

"Oh! No, not at all Credence! I'm very sorry. I was having a weird daydream that took away all of my focus. Again, I . . . I'm sorry . . ." I lowered my head and looked at the desk. It was covered in my sweat, which looked like ice beads. That vision must have really affected me.

He smiled and nudged his head toward me, telling me not to worry. I grinned back, filled with relief. "So . . . what were we talking about?"

"The dance. I was asking what time to meet you here. 7 o'clock good?"

"Sounds great!" I said with too much spunk that it made me blush and him laugh. I was able to catch a glance from Chloe. She gave me a thumbs up and her blessing. Barbara was still not moving at her desk, almost like a dark circle was around her. I was trapped under her spell again, staring at her motionless appearance until Mrs. Nodeon woke me up.

"Come on class. It's time for the freshmen meeting in the gym." We all did as we were told like good little robots and marched to the dreaded meeting, complaining. I waited for Chloe, but she pushed me into

Credence, painfully jabbing my shoulder while informing me she wanted to sit with Lisa, adding a wink.

I was about to protest when Credence approved bashfully. "I'm sort of glad she left. I really wanted to sit by you . . . if that's okay . . ."

I almost leaped to the ceiling with joy, but caught myself and instead nodded. He motioned for me to hook my arm through his like a prince and I did with a curtsy. I was the luckiest girl in the world at that moment. Yet, the daydream made me realize I couldn't get too comfortable. If I did, that was when my world would come crashing down.

Upon entering the very stuffy gym, I caught sight of Umbra and Maren at the top of the bleachers where the seniors normally sat. Seeing them brightened my mood, easing my mind from the terrible vision. Before I knew it, Credence had led me through the crowd to the freshmen section, the prince leading a frightened princess.

Credence's friends howled from the top row, hooting for him to hurry to their spot. I stared upward, skeptical and surprised. The very sweet and calm Credence had friends who acted like truck driving monkeys?! Wonders never cease! I became shy all over again. Credence grinned at them, giving an awkward wave, but refused their offer and led me to the seventh row, toward the middle. It was tight there, but I was so relieved because I was scared of the top row. Maybe Credence knew that . . . but as I was about to ask, I caught sight of Umbra stretching his arms behind his head. It made him look so normal and . . . *appealing*.

I gulped and he noticed me. He grinned tenderly before straightening up, mouthing to me, "You would have fallen off and embarrassed yourself again . . ."

I pouted, arching my eyebrows, and mouthed back. "At least I would do it in style, mister . . ." and he snorted before my eyes were forced to gaze at the seniors asking us to stand to sing the school song.

I loved how the world groaned when music was involved, but I loved singing; it was my only passion in school. Opening my mouth, allowing the melody to escape my lips to create meaning, warming hearts . . . What was better than that? Of course, most students wouldn't have seen it from my point of view. Maybe I also felt more soulful about singing because of the lovely, shimmering song I heard in my head when I was with the one I cared for . . . I blinked before allowing the thought to surface. Only about sixty-two of us from choir knew the words, so it was real soft, but I smiled and sang my soprano part as Credence stood there, admiring me with matchless eyes.

As we sat and the seniors talked way too loud about how awesome their last year had been, Credence leaned close to me and whispered, "You have a beautiful voice Stary . . . You should sing at the talent show on Monday." Just as he said that, like clockwork, the seniors told our class about the talent show to end our spring prep celebration.

Nervous to no end, I rapidly shook my head and reddened at the unexpected compliment. "That's sweet of you to say Credence, but I'm not that good although I really enjoy choir. Plus, I'm way too shy to sing alone!"

I began to shake, shutting my eyes tightly, again like that scared, alone child. I hated being afraid. I could help defeat a murderer, but I was so scared of disappointing or losing people. I was too dependent for my own good, no matter how mature or strong-willed I tried to be. I thought of Umbra, hiding his ache, his talent in the band room due to hurt. Maybe we weren't so different . . .

Then, I felt a loving wind reach my ear and move my soul, telling me I would become myself and be able to show myself someday, to not rush that treasured quest. Surprised, I tilted my head up to see Credence smiling at me, his face glowing alone in the darkness covering him.

He had his hand gently placed on my shoulder blade and whispered, "I wish you would, but I know you will let your talent show . . . ha, someday. It's so cute how shy you are Miss Stary Moon and why I like being with you . . ." His words and his touch were reassuring and reached me like a melody.

I could not express the ecstasy I was feeling, so I smiled sweetly back, patting his hands in my own as I thanked him silently before turning to listen to the rest of the meeting. I looked over to the other side of the gym and grinned as Umbra nodded, his face encouraging. Credence may have been my prince, but Umbra was my support. I had that smile stuck on my face for another twenty minutes, listening to the seniors' instruction without another needed word.

Being the day of the dance, the halls were chaotic with papers, screaming, and stupid, reckless acts, but I somehow was able to avoid all of the annoying distractions to achieve my personal journey, my own sin before leaving the school with my father for the weekend. On a mission, completely focused, I did a sharp turn into the cafeteria and into the girl's bathroom. I had to read the message Umbra and Maren left for the murderer. I knew it was none of my business and I had promised, but maybe there was a clue, a hint that could trigger something in my mind. The pulling force was too strong to ignore, a vortex too deadly to let slip away just by a word promise to my spirit friends.

"I'm sorry . . . ," I whispered before entering the dwelling that would never leave my soul.

I barely stepped both my feet into the room when I heard a moaning, a terrible sound not meant for human hearts to memorize or ears to know. Someone was in pain or trouble or both. The restroom was dim and it took a moment for my eyes to adjust to catch sight of what was making that noise: Barbara.

She was breathing like mad, hunched over, looking like she was unable to see me. With her pallor, I would have thought she was a ghost, a spirit losing its glow. With her hair in ridged curling rags around her thinning face, I got to look into her eyes; black, pure black, so dark that I felt like I was blind, falling into the depths of Satan's sanctuary. She tried to reach the sink, but ran hard into the wall, banging, allowing another powerful wail to escape her burned lips.

The sight . . . it was not what I ever wanted, but I couldn't allow my number one suspect to get away nor could I have let my peer leave in such dire pain. "Barbara," I said gently, taking a timid step closer, reaching my arms out to her. She was shaking like a little, wet kitten that had been abandoned in a downpour. An innocent creature . . . the thought grabbed my soul back at a revelation. Barbara was scared and needed help. Maybe none of this was her fault. I took a deep breath to allow myself to think.

"Barbara . . . I'm here to help," I said. I was almost able to touch her when she flew at me, a mutant bird, staring into my eyes although I could see nothing of her in her irises. The stall door swung back and forth, the only normal sound I had to hold onto my sanity with.

"I didn't do anything! Get off my back!" she yelled and then suddenly, stormed off like an injured race horse—fast, stubborn, but still needing aid. I turned as fast as I could, running a few steps out of the bathroom to follow her, but she vanished. My eyes scanned everywhere, but nothing. How or why she could have disappeared after looking like that was beyond my understanding, but there was nothing to be done. The look, the lethal look she gave me . . . My heartbeat actually stopped cold.

Barbara was so ill . . . There was no way she could have been a heartless killer having that kind of reaction when she saw me. It was a look of guilt. It's like a split soul, two halves . . . I slapped myself. There was no easy answer and I didn't have much time to check the message.

I went into the stall with the ectoplasm energy. It was practically faded into nothing, but I was able to find the response Umbra and Maren had left:

Dear messenger. We know you are here; there are positive and negative spirit energies everywhere in this school. However, please understand that we must be cautious. There is a lot at stake for everyone, even those who have nothing personally to do with this fight. I hope our sides will cross one day, but not on the battlefield.

I dreaded to read the answer. I was so weak and numb inside; my bones shook, their vibrations the only thing my mind could focus on. I read the short, shaky message below:

I agree.

It was so crooked and unstable that it almost fooled me to be someone else's. But, it was new. Brand new.

The murderer was losing herself and fast. I could tell from the weak energy of the ectoplasm message even though it was fresh. Umbra told me in one of our training sessions that the stronger the spirit user, the stronger pull and feeling their ectoplasm would be. If this was so, that most likely explained why they were able to hide their trail, but there haven't been any attacks on us in about a week.

What was also true from feeling this new message was that I couldn't feel a difference between Barbara and the murderer anymore, even if the aura was weak. I wanted to fall to the floor and hug myself, allow tears to wash my chilled body. I wasn't ready to deal with this yet. I kicked the bathroom door and with no emotion, walked to my father's room, hiding my current fear that was drumming at full volume inside me, praying the dance would allow me one more night as a teenager before it vanished forever by my hand.

Getting ready for a social gathering was more of a nightmare than I could have imagined. I was ready by 4:30 and the dance didn't start until 7:00 or later, depending on the status of the football game beforehand (which I knew Credence would be attending). Should I dress up fully? Semi? What really is semi-formal anyway? Or be completely comfortable? And if comfy: to look cute, innocent, cool, naughty . . . I wanted to punch something!

I decided on a mixture of all the above. I chose my favorite and most comfy pair of blue jeans with my white tennis shoes with pieces of candy all over them. As for the top, I picked a black, snug t-shirt with a pink heart on it, covered in fake glitter. White, angelic wings came out of the heart, spreading across my chest. I just hoped my look would make Credence happy.

I was lucky that I never wore make-up. That would have taken more time, energy, and screams that would have injured my vocal chords. I had only been to three dances and this one was my first with an official date, especially being Credence Horton. Staring at myself in the mirror at 6:25, I decided that I was going to look cute but cool at the same time. I only wished I was prettier like Maren. She was so graceful, lovely, and elegant . . . and I was . . . . so blah.

After combing a wave into my hair to my liking, making sure I smelled nice, and that I had enough jewelry on, I took a final breath before stepping into my darkened bedroom where Maren and Umbra were waiting to give me words of encouragement. I knew Maren was going to be over-the-top sweet, but I wasn't sure what Umbra would say. For some strange reason, it bugged me that he approved of what I looked like as much as Credence did. Timidly, like a little lamb ready to go into the wasteland where ten hungry lions waited, I turned to hear my friends' opinions.

Maren, who had her back facing me, twirled on point on her dainty feet like a little ballerina and gave me the most exquisite smile one could imagine. She ran up to me and flung her slender arms around my neck more tightly than I expected. "STARY! You look beautiful!" I rolled my eyes; I knew she was going to say that.

It was not until I could see over cute Maren's yapping blonde head that I remembered Umbra was there. He stared at me, his mouth half-opened, and the most appealing slight curl on his cheeks, hiding a smile. He looked like he forgot how to speak or that maybe he was mute. A thought occurred to me then: Maren never got to do anything like dress up and he probably would have loved to take her to a dance. Umbra really loved her. My heart sank twenty thousand leagues and it was not until Maren whimpered that I realized my head lowered with it.

"Stary, are you all right dearest?" She bit her lip.

I nodded eagerly to not worry her and gave her a fitting smile. Maren and Umbra would have had fun at the dance. Maybe they could hide in the back and come with me . . .

"We are staying here. You deserve a special date with Credence."

I blinked, amazed. Maren must have been part telepathic or spirits could read minds . . . I hoped it was the first one.

She squeezed my hands one last time and then turned her head to look at the boy hiding in the background. "Umbra! Please get over here and tell Stary how nice she looks before she has to leave."

We both gulped, almost at the same time, not really sure what to do, say, or think. Not in any hurry, he strode over in a way that almost made my mouth water and bones melt. About three feet from us, he stopped in his tracks and tilted his head, gazing at me with a gorgeous smile that made my heart hammer in a rush.

"She does look nice," he stated, flipping his bangs at the last word. Why did he have to be so attractive when I was so excited about dating my dream guy? I blame Dr. Rowe!

Maren stepped back then to join him with a pretty and motherly looking grin on her face. She patted my shoulders, gave me a sweet wave, and closed her eyes. She added one final statement of advice, "Have fun."

Ready, I nodded and beamed like a little second grader going to an amusement park. "I will!" I promised with much flare. Maren then nudged Umbra forward to me, who had his face locked on the cranberry-colored carpet. I thought I saw her mouth "tell her," but it was hard to see with the lack of lighting.

He took two baby steps forward and lifted his head to show me his big brown eyes that looked stricken, sad, and pained . . . all the feelings aimed at me, affecting my fragile heart. He took a breath before warning me: "Just . . . just be careful Stary . . . Please . . ."

I had an abnormal yearning to hold him in my arms and to never let him go, to spend the rest of my life with him if he promised to never give me that sad look again. It took all my strength to fight my urge because for some reason, I knew he wasn't talking about the murderer. I tilted my head a bit to gaze at his pitiful tanned face before answering and promising in my kindest and softest tone, "I will," with a smile to match.

I heard my dad yelling it was time to go, signaling me to wave goodbye to my friends. I left before my heart could give in to its desires—the ugly duckling hugging for eternity the beautiful, caring, and mysterious black swan.

Alone, isolated at the social event of the semester, I scanned around the room, allowing the quick flashes and twinkling of the lights to burn my wandering eyes. It only took a minute to observe the inches of the dance floor, the tiny food station, and the boring white ticket booth. Watching the other students dance wildly and enjoying themselves made me feel like I was a worm with no right to be in their presence.

I sighed at my failed attempt to find Credence and began to play with the fake flower and balloon arrangement, twirling it flirtatiously with my finger. Credence was late. I knew why. The football game at that point was going in its third overtime and he was stuck there for forty-five extra minutes according to my coral-toned watch.

I knew it wasn't his fault and I knew I wasn't the only one waiting, but I felt so alone. Chloe was scared of being rejected to a dance, Lauren and Rin thought they were stupid, and Mark's father, being a minister, thought it could lead to "other things." Other than my friends, I was an outsider, a goody two-shoes to be blunt. My mind was rushing past judgments of important things such as school, life, and spirits and then focused on Credence, on dances, on romance. I should be happier than this. I was on a date, or would be soon, with my dream guy! Why wasn't I more excited? Why did I feel a little guilty?

As if God had been kind and answered my prayers, a large group of people came in talking loudly with gold plastic footballs in hand and black paint on their cheeks. There, somehow, I saw his skinny self laughing with a buddy, looking around for me after paying for his ticket. I ran to him because I didn't want to get separated from him again, almost tripping over a chair on the way like an idiot. I waved and said his name, tapping his shoulder. He looked a little surprised, but it faded into a comfortable glow of light on his face.

"I'm sorry I'm late. The game was really long!"

"I heard!" I said with too much zing. "My dad and I listened to it on the radio before I came in here and I heard the final score a few minutes ago when the king announced it. I can't believe after all that we lost! Three overtimes and we lost! I was so mad for the game making you late that I punched the radio behind my table! The chaperons weren't too thrilled with that."

Credence looked funny after I said that, like I did something illegal. I wasn't sure why I got that look . . . Was I too excited? But, I knew Credence didn't really like football; he only went to be with some friends. At last, he broke the cursing silence spell. "You *hit* the radio? Why?"

It sounded like he questioned my sanity. I gulped, ready to be honest with him, not scared of waiting anymore. "Because . . . I really wanted to be here with you . . ." I slid my feet on the floor, creating a pattern, pleading he understood how much this date meant to me.

To my dismay, he didn't react the way I dreamed. His eyes were locked on the table, wide, like he was a frog pinned to a tray and I had a knife, ready to cut him open. He took a deep breath and in a distant monotone said, "I'm sorry you got so upset . . . but, don't hit anymore radios okay?"

I nodded and was about to apologize when he leaned cutely on the table, did a one-eighty turn on his heels, and waved like a madman with a cheesy grin on his face. "There's my buddy Ernie! I went to the game with him. Come on, let's go sit by him." I was going to answer that we could for a little bit, but he ran off, leaving me to use all my might to push through the crowd to find him. By the time I got there, they were laughing while I was panting for life.

"You look a little tired there, girlie," Ernie said in a teasing tone. It wasn't mean per se, but I still felt the jab. Credence was a friend of his? I remembered seeing him in Spanish, talking to Foils a few times. Out of all the boys in the back row, he was the nicest sadly. I supposed anyone who liked Foils was not a favorite of mine, but I swallowed and fixed my hair before playing along with his banter.

"Yeah well, I didn't get the note that I had to race through crowds to reach my date," I said overly sweet, giving an almost blinding smile to Ernie. Credence seemed to jump a little at the word date. Was he nervous about that? I mean, he asked me and all my friends knew. Boys are strange! I just felt like he wasn't connecting with me.

Credence took a sharp breath and looked from me to Ernie before leaning his palm on the table and using the other hand to show me off like I was choice meat. "Ernie, this is my history teacher's daughter. She's my date tonight."

Ernie gasped and rolled into a fit of crackling laughter. "You're dating your history teacher's daughter? The old man, right? Dude! Is he trying to kill you or are you doing it for bonus points?"

Old man? I hated when people compared my dad to the other freshmen history teacher, Mr. Ivan, who was twenty-four and nice. Everyone assumed he was a better teacher due to his age and his looks. My father had always worked hard at his job. And Credence was snickering at the rude comment. He told me he loved my dad. And why didn't he say my name? I do own one, but maybe because my father was old, it didn't deserve to be used in public!

Credence sat down sloppily and added to Ernie's comments in a scornful tone. "I think he likes me and all. He seems to. And good idea about the bonus points!" He remembered I was there, that I was alive, breathing, and hearing perfectly well.

He smiled amiably at me. "Stary, please sit down. You can—"

I gave a tight half smile and said coldly, "No thank you. I don't feel like sitting." The truth was I didn't want to be close to him at the moment.

"Stary, please. You're making me nervous standing behind me. Sit by me. You *are* my date for this evening." His tone was pleasant, but had some sarcasm in it, some poison added to the sweet apple. I slid a little to the right so I was not directly behind him to prove my point. He frowned, his eyes narrowing, a look I hated on him, but I wasn't ready to sit.

Ernie began to laugh hard, picking on his supposed chum. "Man, pal! She sure knows how to work you."

Credence glared at me. I sighed a little and leaned on the back of the chair, about to sit down due to guilt when Ernie added, "Oh, a slow song! Why don't you ask her to dance Credence? You two will look very cute as dancing lovebirds."

Credence shook his head with embarrassment. "Nah, probably not . . . I'm not good at dancing and everyone will look . . ."

I looked at him, stunned. He was nervous? We danced at the wedding practice and he looked a little scared, but eager to be with me. I knew we were alone other than the DJ, but . . . why was he being so shy?

I smiled a little at him, leaning down to look deeply into his eyes. "Yeah Credence. I'd really like to dance with you . . ." I sounded sincere, a splash of begging in my voice.

Ernie kept urging Credence on with waves of his chubby hand. Finally, Credence ducked his head on the table and grabbed my wrist for only a second. I thought he was going to hold my hand, but he only did it to warn me to follow him to the dance floor, behind a pillar no less. As I passed it, my pace slowed and I could almost feel Umbra's pulse inside it, echoing our memories out into my soul. For some reason, I wanted to be with him. Credence must have gotten tired of waiting for he came back and grabbed my arm, pulling me along like a cheap train on its last hard working wheel.

There, he stood in his pose and forced a smiled. I slowly wrapped both my arms around his neck like before, but the warmth, the thrill, the magic was gone and all I felt was a painful longing and awkwardness. It was hurtful to be hidden behind the pillar like Credence was ashamed of me. It was hurtful to look into his eyes due to how clumsy I was stepping on his shoes and giggling nervously. It was hurtful that when I did look at him, his face was only staring at the top of my head if I was lucky and his smiles were like a dog showing teeth.

What was wrong with me? What was wrong with him? What was wrong with us? I leaned my head on his shoulder for a moment, scaring Credence into a chill fit. I didn't do it that time for love, but to hold in frustration and despair. I knew I was not a prized date, but it was too much.

Once my face was hidden between his neck and shoulder, a row of claps and joyous yells were overflowing my ears. Dazed, I glanced around at Credence to see one of his fists in the air, smiling and joining in the fun, which, again, was not like the reserved boy I fell for. Then, a line of yellow and red light hit my eyes. I looked up to see the king and queen in the school colors, wearing their crowns in full show-offing glory, holding their microphones like celebrities.

"Okay guys. The dance is about half over. So now, if anyone wants to make an announcement that is school acceptable, come on up and show your spirit!" I was amazed by how everyone was either hissing about how lame the idea was or how delighted they were to be noticed. There was no middle emotion as I was frozen still to find myself in all the mess.

Out of thin air, I felt a light and pleasant breeze flowing, a scarf of silk over my shoulder blade. Bewildered, I blinked and turned to gaze into Credence's warm face that sparkled enchantingly in the dancing colored spotlights. He looked like the Credence I wanted to be with, to want me. He grinned sweetly and said something that made my heart sing and that tingled every ounce of my body: "Stary, I like you. I really like you a lot . . ."

I was over elated although his timing was so random. Maybe that was why he was acting so abnormal and why his friends were teasing, making him question his loyalty. I shouldn't have given him a hard time with the stupid chair. I wanted to embrace him, tell him in a romantic and somewhat corny way how being around him caused me panic attacks and tied my guts in knots and how I treasured it.

I tried hard to form my feelings into less than a paragraph, but Credence beat me to the punch line while stroking my cheek so gently that it made me choke on my own breath. "I want to know how you feel Stary . . . I want the whole world to know so please . . . will you announce it?" His request shattered my soul. I was too shy to do such a thing, no matter how much I cared for Credence Horton.

Before I knew it, he began to beg, making my heart melt, but my legs were unable to move on their own, making Credence push me gently up by the stage stairway. Horrified, I was then in full awareness, but the king smiled at me, signed my name on a list, and told me to wait while three popular jock-type guys were in front of me.

The crowd by the stage was so compact that I wasn't sure where my date was. All I saw were shadows. The shadows made me think of Umbra. I was about to make a large decision that if I agreed to it, I would have to give up the part of my heart that Umbra had. I never had a chance with him; I was only a partner, only a human, only a girl. That thought made me shake worse than the bliss of Credence's confession.

Before I was emotionally ready, I heard the king say my name and give me a kind wave for me to come onto the stage in the center of the spotlight between him and the queen. I took a diffident breath and was going to whisper a goodbye to Umbra, but I couldn't let him go no matter how selfish I was being. I closed my eyes for a quick second, focused all my energy on Umbra and whispered honestly, "Wait for me Umbra . . ."

At an as even of a pace my stressed and nervous body could handle, I smiled, shook the royal couple's hands, and grabbed the mic after hearing a few cheers, but many gasps that I was doing something so bold. I said hello to the crowd of a select few of my peers in a shaky voice. I swallowed hard, thinking how to word everything so Credence's heart would get it and the world wouldn't get bored with me. I wanted to look directly at Credence so, again, I scanned for him in the sea of students. However, I could not find him no matter how hard I tried, depressing me, sinking me into a downward spiral.

I started my sentence to calm me down a little. "I wanted to give a special thanks to someone and tell them that . . ." Out of the ocean, I heard in front of me some wicked sounds, noises that pierced my ears worse than Barbara's screams of terror when I found her in the bathroom. There, pointing at me and sounding like a menacing pack of wolves, were some guys from Credence's Spanish class group, including Ernie. However, the bitter sounding laugh that traumatized me most was on the side, joining and butting in with them was Foils! In horror, the whole night dawned on me in slow motion, burning my insides whole. I couldn't feel the king tapping me hard on the shoulder at all although I could see him. Then I heard their mocking voices sing over and over:

"Twinkle, Twinkle little star, look how stupid you really are!"

There it was. The hurt. Like when parents give their child a box of candy, expecting them to be irresponsible with it and the innocent youth crams it in their mouth and then feels so sick, they are immobilized, the parents saying mockingly, "I told you so." I could see the risk, but the craving was so sweet that I ignored it. But . . . I was sick because he broke my heart; he offered me the deadly sweets.

In a blind trance, I looked around the corner for Credence and there, leaning sexily on the wall, he was. His eyes had a glimmer to them, a mean, taunting look appeared to ridicule and break me into pieces. Under his arm was a pretty blonde girl flirting with him. She looked at me like I was the scum of the planet and compared to her beauty, I was. Credence gave me a dismissive wave that destroyed my soul. In terror, unable to stand the raging heat of humiliation, the cracking of my chest, or the laughing cutting my eardrums, I dropped the mic, creating a banshee screech that trailed me as I fled.

There was only one place that was safe and my legs knew where to go. The night covered my sorrow in a cool blanket, the stars dully shining to comfort me, but they knew it was impossible. I was fooled, no, I was foiled! Maybe Credence never cared about me, maybe he used me . . . The worst part was I didn't know why. Soon, I was at my healing destination.

The white gazebo was my favorite place to think. It was so peaceful, beautiful, and full of life with its purple, white, and yellow flowers surrounding the gazebo in a field of protection. I came here to reflect and to create words for poems I wrote to express my inner thoughts my lips never could. Now, it was the place where I tried to forget the events that haunted me.

The moon was almost full, looking like inviting milk in the cup of the sky, smiling and frowning along with me. I allowed my tears to escape for I knew my sister moon and brother stars would not judge me like my fellow human beings. Life had some harsh turns.

"Stary . . ." A quiet, timid, but in control voice tapped my delicate ears, carrying a message into my soul; he was here. I didn't have to look up to see him because for some unique reason, I knew he was watching me, protecting me in secret like he always had. I was able to glance at his reflection by turning my head slightly. I had never seen such sad and sorry eyes on the divine black swan called Umbra.

"I'm sorry for spying Stary. But, that jerk . . . you don't deserve him . . . You deserve the world." He spoke in a voice that even in my darkest hour made my heartbeat increase.

The moonlight spilled on the crown of my head as I leaned down and gave a fake smile. In a bitter whisper, choking to stay alive due to the tears attacking the inside of my throat, I answered, "Thanks Umbra, but . . . I don't feel like talking right now . . ." The night became clear and silent, so much so that a butterfly's flapping wing could have been heard. My hair was moved by a gentle breeze, sticking to my face like a picture frame, making me feel like a lost, unwanted goddess.

Suddenly, I saw a graceful hand, warm and welcoming, in front of me. Surprised, I gazed up to see Umbra looking like a mysterious and eye-catching prince, more stunning with the wind whipping the spikes and bangs of his hair. He had a very introverted, kind smile and an appealing rose-colored tint to his tan cheeks.

I was locked onto his lovingness, his tender compassion, but his question blew my pain away: "Stary . . . although I've never done this and I doubt I'm any good, but . . . may I have this dance?"

Smiling quietly, I brushed away my bitter tears and allowed my body to be filled with warm sweetness, better than any nectar in the universe. I was happy to be with my number one and then, I could see why I couldn't whisper goodbye to Umbra; it was because I needed him more than I needed any guy in my lifetime. I not only needed him, but I wanted to spend time with him.

Slowly, standing and trying to look as attractive as I could in my messed up state, I accepted his invite full of love. "I'd love to very much Umbra . . ." He grabbed my hand with benevolence, lifted me like a princess, the princess I was in my dream, unlike what I expected from my ex-date whose name I could not recall. On the glossy deck below us, I could see my smile brightly turned into a mile long train of light more grand than my brother stars.

Together, we amorously danced under the blissful night in my dwelling. I could never describe in a million years how wonderful I felt, how breathtaking Umbra looked or how beautiful he looked looking at me, like I was someone special. The night hid us, as if the world was our own private house and I had nothing to fear since that feeling was perfect, just right, as we twirled in circles in our own dance.

18

THE HEAVENS SEEMED TO BE PRAYING FOR MY SAFETY, apologizing for my sorrows with the refreshing tears known as rain. The angels boosted my spirits with the shining rays of the sun that shone vigorously and a beautiful clear sky while it rained; a devil kissing his wife, mocking me with irony. However . . . my heart was soaring, rumbling louder than a 747 taking off. My smile was larger than the vast universe, my attitude lighter than air, bouncing, and my eyes sparkled at a greater carat than the biggest diamond every time I looked at myself in the mirror.

As I entered school Monday morning, I felt like all eyes were on me as if I had just walked onto a stage and I was the star, the Stary star. This made it easier to get my personal point across. For every hurtful person in this world, there was one to make up for all the pain.

I walked about two steps before Chloe appeared on my right and Rin and Lauren on my left. In my mind, the four of us, walking in step with each other, could do anything, but right now I felt like we were ready to accept an Oscar.

I told them everything. Chloe was the first person to know followed by Lauren and Rin. They all reacted in their own way, but their loyalty to me never wavered. They were the light that shot through the veils of darkness of this situation.

Chloe was the first to shatter the silence. "I *cannot* believe Credence did that to you! And with stupid, jerk face Foils? I swear . . . the next time I see him in homeroom, I'm going to strangle him with my bare hands."

I sighed and gave Chloe a gentle smile. "Chloe, it's okay, really. Yeah, I was hurt for a while, but I'm truthfully fine with it. Things happen for a reason, right?"

I knew what Chloe was thinking by how her mouth was opening and closing like a fish on land. Her words were fusing together as she tried to speak.

"Stary, it is *not* 'okay'!" She added mocking air quotes around 'okay.' "You cannot defend Credence for what he did. Why are you being so nice? It's . . . it's . . . unbearable! Please . . . I want to destroy him and we'll all help, right girls?"

Rin looked amused and pumped, breathing fire under her breath the whole time with a red face. Softly, she gazed up at me to answer Chloe's war cry. "Yeah . . . I'm going to punch him in the face so hard that his supposed 'innocence' will spill onto the floor like fish guts! And Lauren . . . well, since she's a third degree black belt, she can do a triple front flip, twirl him in the air with a seven foot high kick, and slam him in the wall, bones first!"

Lauren looked at Rin like she created stupidity. "What am I, a Power Ranger?"

I was about to comment, when I heard a delicate whisper about four feet behind me, "What is that . . . ?"

The good mood I was trying to partly contain exploded and I laughed vociferously, stopping for a moment to fling the rolls of laughter off my side. It did help control my vibrating ribs as I wiped my silly tears away. Maren was the one who asked that question and I was giggling because she was just too endearing.

The whole weekend, although I knew I should have been sad and mad, I couldn't be. I couldn't stop staring at my hands, feeling Umbra's incredible touch tingling through the core of my body. I couldn't stop imagining his perfect face, looking only at me with gorgeous eyes that for a while seemed to be made to only admire me. I couldn't stop my urges of wanting to trace the outline of his flawless face to make sure he was real, to get closer to him, and tell him that I—

"STARY! Are you with us? What are you laughing at?" Chloe was thumping my shoulder. I nodded and thanked my friends for their concern and told them that they had nothing to worry about. Rin and Lauren shrugged at the same time to tell me they understood.

A few more steps and I waved to depart from Rin and Lauren, getting ready for first hour. I was then ready to motion Chloe to go, but instead of her bubbly personality and rewarding grin I got most mornings from her, she grabbed my wrist and dragged me back to the corner to face her, almost making me trip.

"Stary . . . I hope I'm not being too pushy or nosy because I know I tend to do that, but . . . I'm just so upset because none of us saw this coming and I care about you so much. You're too innocent and usually have the best judge of character even if it's hidden deep inside. Yet . . . I know you're, to some extent, hurting. Is it . . . well . . . Stary, do you still have feelings for Credence?"

I was taken aback by her cheerless tone, her honest clarity, and her devoted nature. I sighed with a little tight smile spreading awkwardly across my cheeks, unable to look her in the eyes, but I nodded. No matter what Credence did to me and no matter how I felt about Umbra, I could not deny that I still did have some feelings for Credence. How could I not with all the time and commitment I gave so that the supposed relationship could have a chance to blossom?

"Thank you Chloe for your concern. You truly are my best friend and I can't live without you. Yeah, the pain still hurts, but I'll keep these memories, let these feelings grow, and learn from them like they're buried treasure. I'll never say I wish I never had them. I'm pumped Chloe! I'm ready to take life by the horns and see what destiny has in store for me."

Tears began to build in her eyes and she sprang back to life to give me a bear hug. I smiled again and patted her back, thanking her and loving her.

She hopped back to her spot by me on the floor and made a sound that I could not describe or imitate; it sounded like a toddler giggling with Pop Rocks in their mouth. "You're so lucky Stary and brave, knowing when you're in love and not chickening out by denying it! It's . . . amazing . . ." I caught her at the end of her phrase looking down at the floor and then blushing.

I roared with laughter inside, thinking and knowing that Chloe was picturing and talking about Mark. If only she could understand . . . but then we parted ways and left with our new words of wisdom and new goals. For me, I was ready to come to truce with my emotions.

The day was normal, and I was on top of cloud nine, if that was possible. All I could think about was Umbra and I dancing in the streaming moonlight. The sensation poured inside me but was it true or close like Credence had been? I didn't want to analyze that at the moment due to being scared of opening old wounds. I just wanted to continue living my life, aiding Maren and Umbra no matter what it took, and engage in a social life with a new light.

During homeroom, we entered the gym for the singing talent show the seniors were hosting followed by an ice cream social in the lunchroom. Once I entered, Mr. Wave came up to me and told me to get prepared because my name was on the singing list! Well, there went my happy mood! Robert Frost was right: nothing gold can stay.

I didn't recall signing up to sing, but I might have been so overwhelmed by Credence telling me how much my voice appealed to him, I joined the line up in "lover mode." I told Mr. Wave I really wasn't psychologically ready to sing in front of the whole school and staff. He smiled, seeing how much I was shaking and told me if I wanted to sing, to find him. He nudged my shoulder before walking off. I let out a long breath of relief, allowing the short lapse of fear to escape and the feelings of Umbra to fill up my being again.

With a whistle in my heart and a bold smile pinned to my face, I was about to skip away from the stage area and sit with my friends, seeing Mark waving at me in the sixth row, when I felt a tap. Overjoyed that I could finally see Umbra since my dreamy, fateful night, I excitedly turned to see instead the masked villain himself: Credence.

With him was a smile that seemed it was not fazed by any harm he caused me. That grin was like a steak knife stabbing plastic wrap as a joke. In a state of panic, I jerked away from him, holding my hands against my hammering heartbeat. I wanted to run into a blur, to never be near his sight again, the place where his face mocked me, but I couldn't move. I felt his twinkling eyes pulling me in with a force greater than all my positive being. It was similar to Darth Vader pulling an enemy in with the Force.

"Hi Stary," he said casually, looking down straight afterward, kicking his feet like an embarrassed horse, creating a small whirling dust storm. He looked up at me again, his eyes dancing to see me. Horrified that I still found that puppy look appealing, I turned away, creating my own dust storm colliding with his as I tried to make a break for it. But he stopped me by firmly grabbing my left wrist.

He looked at me with glassy eyes, about to break down. "Stary! I know you're mad at me, but please, let me explain." He pulled me in, sliding my sneakers across the floor only a few inches before I fought, the squeak blasting across the front row. I shook my head fiercely, moisture droplets blurring my vision, wanting to scream before I did something I regretted.

He was stronger than his boyish exterior implied. I was soon shaking madly, only a few inches from him as he held me tightly, forcing me to gaze only at him. "I'm begging here Stary! I'm begging for forgiveness!"

My mouth was burning, my eyes were stinging worse than a thousand bee stings, and I had an urge to rip my face off. An evil yearning grew into cruel and delightful images of ringing his cute little neck that almost took over my vibrating hands.

I couldn't contain my boiling blood. "How can you ask me that? How could you have hurt me, Credence? I have always liked you, trusted you, and you allowed Foils and his friends to laugh at me, making me go on stage when you know I'm terrified of crowds and that blonde girl! You were flirting with her right in front of me when I was your date! You didn't even treat me like a person in front of your friends. You didn't even go after me! And you didn't defend my father either when Ernie bashed him. How can you stand there and ask for such a crazy thing?! Do you know how much *pain* you caused me?"

Credence looked haunted by my fury. He allowed my wrists to slip a little from his sweaty hold, but he continued to grip me, tracing his finger across my lower arm and sending a small chill down my spine. He took a deep breath.

"I have no idea what you're talking about with Foils and his friends. I *hate* him! He's such a jerk and I would never hang out with him! I've known Ernie since fourth grade, which is why I'm still friends with him. And I do like your dad a lot. And that girl was my sister Tina. She wanted to make me leave and I had only been there for an hour due to the football game. I was trying to convince her, but she was arguing, which was why I waved at you, meaning to wait."

He paused and blushed, silently staring at the ground. I pondered what he said. He never did acknowledge Foils or his gang there and since I knew Ernie hung with Foils sometimes, I guess my mind assumed Credence was in on that. The way he was acting didn't aid my suspicions either. I had heard about his sister. She was blonde and beautiful, but super protective of her darling little brother. I guess I only saw blonde, pretty, and leaning by Credence in the semi-darkness. My heart began to hammer again, yearning to forgive him.

He continued. "The reason I acted like that was because I was shy, I mean *really* shy. I've always wanted to go on a date with you, but when the game became late, I got more nervous and soon, my brain was a haze to just remember to speak to you! I saw Ernie and all the wrong things came out. I'm real sorry Stary . . . Star." He gave me a small breathtaking smile that made the metal lock I placed on my heart for him melt more.

Out of nowhere, he brushed my cheek and looked passionately into my eyes, making me forget how to breathe. "Stary, I like you. I wanted to know if you still felt that way about me and the stage announcement would have made me the happiest guy in school! And I really think you should sing because you are a beautiful singer, no lie there."

Credence made me blush so warmly that I bet the whole school felt the heat. He gave a stunning smile and grabbed my wrists again to lock me into an embrace so strong that the world stopped for a moment. He whispered, his lips against my silky hair, "I just want to know how you feel . . ."

I was still a sucker for that angelic look of his; he was my major high school crush, maybe more. Yet . . . I could see Umbra in the background, looking worriedly toward our hidden public scene. My heart was pounding, sending pleasurable pressure into my brain, but who was it for: Credence or Umbra? I couldn't deny the fact that I still had feelings for Credence, so I had to at least try.

"Credence . . . I . . ." I was about to tell him what my begging heart was screaming when Mr. Wave yelled at everyone to sit down and prepare to watch the singing contest. I was humiliated and my face must have showed it because Credence laughed a little.

Then, like a fairy tale, his gentle lips touched my right cheek, the one facing the stage so no one would see. The sweet moisture of his majestic lips cooled my blazing body, but fueled my burning desire. He beamed afterwards, a little embarrassed, and leaned his forehead on mine before whispering, "Please sing Stary. Your heartfelt voice will make everyone happy, including me. I want to know your feelings."

With one last glowing smile and a light tug on my shirt, he turned to sit in the front row with Ernie and Kendal, sitting tall with pride like I was already his girl.

Mark signaled to me with a confused expression. I pointed at Credence with a smile, gave an okay sign, hugging myself a little. Mark raised one thin eyebrow but nodded towards the girls as he moved to the edge of the second row, his eyes glued on Credence. He showed me an incredible smile of his own that made my knees weak for a second and I mouthed "thank you" to him since I knew he was protecting me just like he always had as my knight in silver armor.

Ready to approach a new chapter in my life, I slowly turned to sign-up for my chance to figure out who my heart belonged to. As I told Mr. Wave, Umbra gazed at me from behind the curtains of the stage with dazzling eyes, eyes reflecting the pure beauty of darkness. He gave me a playful sneer, tightening his fist, and mouthing "good luck" before vanishing, more than likely to be with Maren. Yet, seeing Umbra disappear made me see that soon, he would forever be in happiness . . . without me. Maybe, then, I should move on too, no matter how loudly my heart was screaming no.

Mr. Wave tapped me because I stole his pencil (we had a writing tool relationship apparently) and to tell me to get in line with the other singers. I was the second to last to perform, so until my turn drew too near to turn back, I sat with my choir director, Mrs. Wave, whom I adored. She was surprised I was singing alone in front of the whole school, but thrilled people would hear my "shy, but sweet and moving voice," according to her. I nodded with a small smile, feeling like a robot on auto, crying in fear inside, and mentally shouting: *Why am I doing this?* as I tugged on my cascading hair.

Some enchanting voices hit my ears and some destroyed my eardrums worse than the murderer's vibe, but as I began to get used to the habit of my knees shaking like a roller coaster about to break, Mr. Wave signaled me to stand on the sideline—I was next. My roller coaster car was plummeting to the ground in slow motion. I knew I should get over my fear since I brought it upon myself over the boy I was crazy for but my heart was racing more than I ever imagined. My blood was pumping, burning as it flowed into my pleading chest.

"Stary? Are you listening to me, hon?" Mr. Wave's booming voice sent lightning into my bloodstream.

"Ye-Yes?" My eyes grew wide, my arms tugging on the deep velvet curtain for dear life, giving him a smile like I was caught in some kind of criminal act.

He gestured me to the CD list sitting on top of the stereo system, asking me to pick a song. His serious look proved to me how close my spotlight was shining on me, my fresh dawn.

I wanted to show Credence how I felt. Thumbing through the list, I finally found a CD with only versions of Disney songs. Feeling younger and peppier, I skimmed through it and found one that made a connection and met my approval, the calling as powerful as the murderer's. I wanted my voice, my inner voice, to be heard, the meaning to be appreciated with my own unique tenderness. More than anything, I wanted Credence to understand my words to answer his pulsing question.

Mr. Wave went on the stage, announcing my name to the dazed looking students. I heard no sound for a few seconds, but then I heard a few little gasps popping in the back of the wall where the teachers stood to monitor. I can bet my dad's face was frozen! Feeling like my legs were replaced with metal poles, I awkwardly approached Mr. Wave across the black and gold painted stage.

Before I made it to the center, I heard some whistles from the front row: it was Credence's friends (Foils and his gang were sadly next to them, but they were ignoring each other), but I didn't see Credence himself. Nevertheless, after the annoying whistling, I heard Mark clap loudly and cheering me on, calling me his girl. This caused Chloe, Rin, and Lauren to clap noisily away. Soon, the whole school was clapping for me, my own name echoing in my ear over and over again.

The one voice I heard beyond all others was a soft and gentle one that made my back tingle. It was from the left side of the curtains. He was hiding like a wolf, beautiful and deadly. His stare was piercing, but enchanting. I smiled over my shoulder as prettily as I could, allowing my teeth to be the sparkling light that melted the alarm in the eyes of Umbra. I looked out into the standing crowd then and took a deep breath in order to face the world and tell Credence I liked him.

"Thank you. I will be singing 'True to Your Heart,' by Raven-Symoné. I want to dedicate the words of this song to someone special to me."

I grinned to the group and allowed the mic to slide into a comfortable, but tight grip, ready to spread the emotions I had been hiding into the vastness of the gymnasium. The music began to play.

I was shy at first, but once I allowed the music to fill my soul, I warmed up, forgetting where I was and how many people were there. I focused on who I was. I was Stary Moon, singing a confession to Credence Horton and my thanks to all the people I loved in my life from my family to friends to my spirit partners. I didn't care about perfection but warmth, and my peers seemed to sway in a positive response, making my heart soar in delight. I could feel Credence's vibe although his face was hidden in the midst of faces.

My body began to lose its nervousness and I rocked back and forth in a basic rhythm. Slowly, I began extending my arm toward the audience. I wanted to find Credence in the front row and touch him, brush my fingers against his to feel the static, and send a quick sensation down him like he did to me. I could not locate him, but I saw a mass of people moving to the music and even the teachers were bobbing their heads in the back.

Nothing else mattered at that moment as the gorgeous sun shone over me, reflecting my honesty even more than I could hope, adding purity to the lyrics. With this honesty, I admitted something. I wouldn't have been strong, knowledgeable, or understanding if not for Umbra being in my life; he was always protecting me. Even now. With a turn of my head, allowing my hair to fall over my shoulders, I thanked him by looking at him on the last sentence of the verse, pointing to him.

His beautiful dark eyes lit like candle fire and his cheeks gained a lovely velvety texture to them as he gasped. He showed me a smile more amazing than any carat of any gemstone for a moment. I looked back into the crowd so they wouldn't get concerned although looking at Umbra was easy and so enjoyable. Tearing my eyes from him was one of the most difficult things I had ever done.

With singing the word "light" with the required intensity, I thought of Umbra, screaming in the band room about the light he saw everywhere on his path to destruction. I shifted my eyes a little to notice him leaning on the post, his fingers grazed over the curtain , the ones that sent a thrill in me hours after our one second impact. But Umbra and I could never be. I knew that in my heart, but the power of emotions always seemed to ignore all the important, life changing details. I supposed the Lord liked being ironic sometimes. But I had Credence, the enjoyment of singing, and the magic of music.

As the last line drew near, I flew my hand high into the air and belted, allowing my natural, fast-paced vibrato to shine, making the crowd scream deafeningly with glee. I heard laughter as pure sweet sugar behind me, but for some reason, it turned sour the second my heart absorbed its power. Surprised, I blinked before continuing my plea, still looking for my bronze head of hair, shining within my eyes. I was planning to reach out my hand to Credence on the last line, showing the world I chose him.

It was time: my glory, my finest hour, my body sick with worry that something would go horribly wrong. When will people learn to never question the good fortune fate could bring? Those thoughts only proved I was still human, still a teenager, still a mortal. Overwhelmed with fear, I prepared myself with the vibrations of the stage, the hum of the fake gym lights, the radiant gust from the air vents, and the tap from behind the stage . . . tapping? I also heard a squeak like from a pulley. An urge to run filled the void my heart made for my true love, a warning siren shrieking in my head, but I ignored the calls, allowing my mind to think of them as only unsettling nerves that my worried confidence created, to tell him when he listened to his heart, it was going to lead him to—

"AHHHHH! HELP! GET OFF!"

It all happened before I could think of blinking, similar to getting hit by a flying car from the side. Credence was bleeding right in front of me after soaring through the air. He landed so hard on the wooden flooring of the stage that the force cracked some of the wood paneling. Horrified, I saw his bruised cheek, his blood-stained teeth, and busted mouth, dripping with a line of blood so thick and lush that a vampire would have gone insane. The back of Credence's leg was also banged up with an ugly colored knot and his legs were irritated with raw red marks. It was sickening and I was more than likely to blame. How did I know? Umbra was the one on top of him, beating the soul out of my Credence.

Umbra's enraged voice, full of sulfur, shattered my feelings, destroyed my moment in the sun, and drowned out my music—on the CD and inside me.

"How *dare* you try to hurt Stary you sick, twisted bastard?! I'm going to beat the hell out of you for this!" His shouts reverberated through the room, but the last few chords of my background accomplishment only forced me to feel the turning of my stomach and the pounding thoughts rising in my head. Before I sorted my emotions, I had to stop Umbra from hurting Credence. Or at least from slaughtering him.

The mic slipped from my swaying hand as I sprinted towards them, but I felt hot, boiling like a volcano with fresh lava being formed. The heat made my ears ring from the madness of the chaotic situation. As I stopped short of their fight, my mind raced, trying to absorb the horrid sight. I could see Umbra making contact with Credence's body and creating wounds. This meant that Umbra had made his muscles solid just to beat Credence to a pulp. This also meant I could drag Umbra off Credence like he was any other human.

I pounced, painfully digging my nails like claws on top of Umbra's back as I grabbed his neck by the collar. I tried three times to lift him up, but his fury and weight pulled me down, almost into a tripping spell. I took some cool air into my body that hit my aching lungs with a bizarre force, but it gave me the strength to get Umbra off Credence and stop him from punching any other part of Credence's priceless face that he hadn't already rearranged.

Umbra's eyes were as vast as space, raging with a spark that took me back for a moment like I was looking at a monster. It must have been part of his programming: the reaction, the glare, showing no mercy . . . Umbra was not only dead, but not even human and was meant to be a fighter. Umbra needed to remember to control himself no matter how noble he thought he was being.

"Umbra! What the heck are you doing? How can you beat up Credence in front of everyone? He's human! He can't defend himself and how can you embar—"

I paused, cutting off my draconic fury. I forgot where I was and that Umbra did not exist to my peers and professors. I was alone.

Someone was carrying Credence off the stage, my golden shield called music was done, and I was gazing at a crowd of over 1200 people with huge doe-like eyes. I felt like a freaky bug that everyone wanted to step on. The teachers seemed surprised that my voice could even reach them without a microphone. In those heated moments of agony, I realized the truth: being different was not acceptable.

I gulped, my head spinning to come up with an excuse, but my basic genetic needs from the dawn of time were screaming again: "*Danger, run!*

You cannot beat this enemy. RUN!" I wanted to flee, but I was shaking more than I ever had before. The floor was going to cave under me.

All around me, I heard the whispers: "Umbra?", "What's Stary talking about?", "What's with Credence?", "She's talking to herself," and the most heart wrenching: "Freak!" Vomit was rising in my throat. I had never been so humiliated in my entire life. There was nothing I could do. My mind had shut down and my body wanted to exterminate itself. Vanishing was the only thing I could do to save any ounce of my sanity.

I closed my eyes tightly, not wanting to see the faces, the mocking stares of the students, the concerned look on my friends, or my dad's shadowed expression. I didn't think either; I simply failed. Why couldn't I just disappear? Not even Umbra's calm breathing next to me could repair any of the damage.

An odd noise hit my numb ears. A light boom and a puff of something blended into the atmosphere, yet my eyes were full of tears, immortalizing my broken self for the world to see. A rush of warmth, a fan of comfort ran over my cheeks that whipped my hair at the speed of lightning. There, making footprints as pure white as a bride's first dress and the same texture as grounded chalk, was Umbra, covered in what looked like flour. He must have opened one of the sacks that supported the stage. His whole body was covered. Every inch, every crack was temporarily stained in white powder.

He nodded at me. Why was he doing that? Why was he revealing himself, risking the murderer to see him and Maren and even me, humiliating himself in the eyes of my weak species? A very tiny crease indented his smooth cheeks, a percent of a smile, and his eyes were grave looking; sunken and gray. He looked . . . sad, ashamed, and maybe hurt.

To my surprise, he raised his hands next to his ears, positioned them in a reaching spread, and wiggled them like worms. Then, one little word passed from his lips: "Boo!" he yelled, sounding scary and lame as it echoed in circles.

My peers screamed and began to run around like chickens with their heads cut off, looking extremely stupid. The teachers wailed and pushed the students out the door in a frenzy. In about four minutes, *every* single person in the gym was gone from the intimidating white ghost.

I was in a blank daze, frozen in my spot like a statue of mockery only remembered to make others feel better, but left alone with no other meaning or purpose. I began to shake again, worse than a tremor and my heart absorbed all the hatred in the world and made me its puppet to express it. Spinning on my heels, I stared Umbra down, trying to push the anger back no matter how much I didn't want to. He was bent down, chuckling, delight in his oblique eyes.

"Ha, ha, ha! God . . . humans are so easy to scare. Ha!" The pure delight in his slick voice, no care for me or remorse of what he had done made me sick.

I allowed the flood gate in my eyes to break into a million pieces, sinking, rotting to the sea of my soul. "Umbra! How could you *do* this? Why would you beat up Credence in front of everyone? Do you just hate me?"

He was paralyzed, making his blank eyes fuel into a new emotion I could not determine, but I didn't care. His voice was foreign and it made me despise his attitude even more. "What in heaven's name are you talking about? How can I hate you? How can you stand there and accuse me of that? I beat him up for *you*!"

"Beating up the boy I love is helping me?"

"Pfft! *Lo-love*? You don't love him!" He looked at me like I stabbed him with fifty thousand sharpened penknives. He was yelling just as loud as I was, his voice hoarse.

"How can you tell me to feel? It's not like *you* have feelings! You never wanted me involved in this!"

"Stary, bloody shut the he—heck up and listen to me!" The pause to not cuss in front of me gave him a moment to calm his Zen a tad, his arms slapping his hips and stopping so he could breathe. "Credence was trying to hurt you. He doesn't love you, doesn't want you. He's a creep using your delicate heart like a sick game. He doesn't even know you or ever will . . ."

"And *you* do?" I threw my arms up in the air. Spit began coating my words in heartlessness. "The first day you came here, you hated me, shattered my confidence. Do you think I knew what I was doing, that I was planning on helping you and Maren?! I wanted to help, but I was terrified and you never *flippin'* cared! You don't care about me! You're just mad that you could never help her yourself. All the kindness you gave me was fake to suffice Maren and to get me to go along with working with you.

"You don't know *anything*! How would you know what love is when you were never human, when you never even tried to have compassion? How could you *freaking* humiliate me? All you care about is yourself you manic creep! *I hate you!*"

The last words were venom dripping off my tongue through my clenched teeth. It felt like a demon had possessed my core. I started to pant. I knew what I said and my heart regretted some of it, but I was upset seeing Credence hurt by Umbra's hands when Umbra was lying. He only wanted a fight and destroying one of the boys I cared for most was perfect revenge. I couldn't believe I ever thought I liked him or had an attachment to him. The demon in my ear vanished, satisfied with my work.

I looked at him squarely in the eyes. He looked like he was about to explode at me and his bite was way worse than my bark. I didn't blame him for fighting back, but I was standing firm, fists tightened. He had to learn to treat humans better, to be more than a program. He didn't realize my life was ruined more due to his mistake.

He began to quiver like a rabid dog. His eyes locked onto mine, full of hatred.

"You don't want to believe me? You want to stay with that idiot and screw the rest of your life up? Fine! I'll never see you again if that's what you want! Have fun ruining your life, Stary Moon!"

Before I could react, he was down the steps and running at rapid speed toward the door, leaving a trail of flour footprints behind. Most had fallen off his body.

The world seemed to turn in reverse, the sensation making me sway and twirl in an unstable state, but my body was lifeless. All I knew how to do was breathe. My nostrils flared, my breathing became controlled, my mind became more human, but I was still furious. The sunrays that once warmed my heart when I was on my perfect planet of singing made my heart ache for a pleasant memory I couldn't feel. When it became blinding, intense, I looked over my shoulder. The light was too beautiful to be purely sunshine.

Maren was five inches behind me. Seeing her pale and pretty face melted my anger and I was able to be Stary again with her company. I prayed to God to not leave me alone; I didn't want to lose Stary ever again. I . . . I wanted to know how that demon was able to mutate my essence.

"Maren . . . ," I choked out in a tone quieter than a whisper, knowing she could hear me. "Umbra hurt Credence for no reason . . . He's really hurt, blood and all. I . . . I didn't want to yell, but . . . life is so . . . precious and . . . to humiliate me like that! He . . . he needs to understand better, try harder to be human . . . He needs to open his heart up." Being with Maren made me not only feel breakable, but guilty, like she was all the goodness in the world and I had to prove to the universe I was not a fiend by nature.

For the first time since I had met her, Maren's china doll face was emotionless, a blank slate washed over with waves of so many emotions that she seemed to give up on caring. And the way her eyes stared at me, all dull and vacant . . . It looked like she had given up on me.

Her voice was monotonous, distant and final. "Stary . . . you need to learn to not only open your eyes, but learn how to use them." It shattered me into pieces to hear that and before I knew it, she had vanished, more than likely to track down Umbra.

I shivered in fear. I was confused, lost, a freak according to my peers now, and a horrible person. Umbra wasn't the monster. I was. I hated myself at that moment. I was still angry, but I never gave him a chance to explain. Like with signing up for the singing contest and the dance announcement. Credence was charming and had used it against me, though I seriously doubted he had meant to. My extreme crush on him seemed to clean my brain, hush my heart, and send my hormones into an unbelievable form of madness. If Maren was upset and disappointed, then I really messed up. Humans mess up to learn, but I destroyed my life more than Umbra meant to in the selfless act he thought he was doing.

If I ever sensed that demon again, the demon that made me not give someone a chance to explain their situation, the demon that caused me to react without thinking, I would pour acid on him and snuff out his existence. I knew my anger made me explode, but I felt like a lost form of myself, a mind-controlled droid.

My muscles ached, screaming in pain, but I ignored it and listened to the heart hammering inside my chest. I had the chance to live, the honor of having them in my life, and I was going to try to make things right no matter how much I liked Credence. Credence was alive and well and he would be waiting for me. I tracked Maren's trail and used my spirit impulses in the air to find the wave of my friends . . . if I could still call them that.

A painful clap echoed through the darkened senior hallway. It was empty since everyone, after the ghost attack, went to the lunchroom for free ice cream sundaes. I stopped to glance out the rusty door that led to the old inner courtyard. The clouds were gray and it was pouring rain. The storm came out of nowhere. I supposed God was showing his feelings toward me.

I lowered my head. "I don't blame you," I whispered until a lovely ring, a familiar melody of words caught the attention of my ears.

"She did not mean to say those things Umbra . . ." Like a dog happily hearing his master's call, I ran with all my little strength, the old me fully aware of the horror I had caused. I had to reach them.

I only had to go about eight feet and turn sharply left, almost falling, to where the foreign language and old history wing split on the sky blue chipped stairway. Two feet beyond that was a chained lock, red paint falling off it like blood in the snowy night of a battlefield. Behind that was a door outside to the track and football field. There, I saw Maren with her back turned. Her hair was a mess of tangles and knots, damaged by the raindrops I knew she couldn't feel, but she continued to reason with Umbra for me. Ashamed, I pinned myself to the hard block pillar that opened to the stairwell.

"I know what she said, Maren!" Umbra's voice shook the whole wall, making me, by survival impulse, hold on for dear life until my fingertips were white. I cocked my head a few inches to get a better look. All I saw, sitting against the landing on the second floor was a strip of wavy, oil black hair, decorated with rain drops that looked like diamonds were embedded on his handsome head.

"Dang it! Why?" It sounded like he was crying, pleading in distress to God himself. "I can't feel the rain. I've always wanted to feel the rain, to wash away my pains and sorrow so I don't have to *feel* weak or force girly tears out of my body . . . Why is it I never get what I want? I know I don't deserve one thing, but why can't I do anything?! I was created to be flawless and use my own programming as I pleased . . . but still I . . . Gragh! Why can't I do anything right?!"

He was holding his head, clenching his hair like it was his only connection to being whole. What had I done to him? I wanted to run to him, to allow him to hit me as much as he wanted. Even if I lost my own life, at least I could have been with him, if I deserved that treatment. But he had morals and I didn't believe him. I still knew Credence didn't do anything, but I doubted his heart. Umbra had always had one and a beautiful one at that.

Maren straightened her back. "Umbra . . . Stary was only confused. I did not see anything happen with Credence either and she likes him very much, but she did not mean to get so angry and shout at you. I know she feels awful. You need to let her come talk to you . . ."

"Yes she did, Maren! But, it doesn't matter. I mess everything up. I always screw everything up! It's . . . it's better if I never existed. I just want to be forgotten!"

Before Maren could rebut, Umbra flew away to another part of the top floor, a shorter landing that could only fit him with his knees pressed against his broad chest, his t-shirt soaked to the core. His wet body was heaving up and down. Umbra was allowing his emotions to break in silence, to flow. He was doing the motions of crying although no drops escaped his childlike eyes.

Maren had left with her head down in defeat, drowned to the bone. She took the long way inside, missing my presence, although I hid just in case. She was heading toward the math wing in the newer part of the building. Maren carried herself like she was on an internal mission of her own.

My legs lost all feeling and it felt like half a dozen needles were being stabbed into them. Slowly, giving up all hope of entering a world of light since I never deserved happiness again, I slid down the wall, allowing the static to destroy my straight, delicate hair, it forming it into a bird's nest. My eyes were locked on Umbra's light, trembling figure. I forced my body to feel the despair I caused. How I wished his pain could be trapped forever inside my soul and he could be freed! I cried like an insane maniac, angry at every ounce that was me, wishing every part I hated about myself would drown.

After about fifteen minutes, I couldn't breathe and I was about to upchuck all over the place. I had to cough and clench my hands to the wall to subside my utter discomfort. I wiped my weak eyes with the outer part of my hand and bent down, holding my face, gluing them into my locked knees. Terror was shaking me. But I couldn't deny it any further; I had to talk to Umbra.

Dizzily, I grabbed a slick stone in the middle of the wall to pull myself up on my rubbery legs. With teary vision, and fright almost as strong as death, I faced the beautiful creature and the doomed fate that was meant to only destroy us.

I propped the door open that led outside to where Umbra was, but I noticed he was on top of the building and there was no way from where I was to get to him. There was a small window on the roof of the building. I shut the door and ran upstairs to the old history wing, trying to find the window. It took an eternity to find it. It was hidden behind a bookshelf in the hall. After grunting to move the bookshelf, I found the rusted window. Thank goodness it was easy to open, but I had to crawl to get through it and outside. The rain was so frigid that it not only chilled me in mere seconds, it cut my skin on contact.

There! He was in clear sight now. All I had to do was hop on the landing two feet in front of me to the other side of the roof. I leaped the two feet gap, landing hard on my heels. I was lucky for the adrenaline because that was one of the scariest things I had ever done!

I was sideways but still behind him, seeing his priceless body breathing, staring forward blankly at the world like he was trying to figure it all out. I knew once I opened my mouth, I would shatter his peace and force the rage to return, but I could not end things with this outcome.

"Um-Umbr-Umbra . . ." My voice was thick and alien. Was it *me* even talking? I gulped, matching the static sound of the clouds bumping each other in an unknown war like Umbra and I.

When I called his name, he stared at me, like he yearned for me to hold him, like he was waiting for me to return, and like he was deeply insulted and he wanted to kill me with his bare hands, painfully and slowly. He was only responding naturally and I was shaking from the cold and nerves so much that I probably didn't sound or look like Stary. One thing was sure; our relationship, no matter what it was, would forever be changed if it continued.

I had to begin, but where? I wanted to scream, punch myself, cry in distress, and just vanish from horror all at once. I choked, trying to control the chaos that built into my brain. This chaos pushed my heart into an unhurriedly and fatal black hole that made my stomach into a pit where it fell deep and deeper into spikes. "Umbra . . . Umbra . . . I . . . I'm . . . I'm so . . . I'm so sor—"

As it was foretold, Umbra lost to his lunacy. "I *get* it Stary! You *have* to come up here to sink me lower, if that's even possible. Well, you win! I'll admit it: I'm not worthy to be in your presence, so *I must be lower than the lowest scum of human ever created*!" He pointed angrily at me at that last part, making me widen my eyes a tad and take a tiny step back. I was the lowest scum on the Earth.

"You will have your wish princess. So, stay damned well away from me!" He grunted and let out a puff of air my way, allowing me to see the damage I caused in his eyes. Again, like he did to Maren, he flew off, farther away where I could not see him at all.

I was twisted backward, alone, stuck on a slippery rooftop. The rain fell harder, the sky hitting my soul with large thunder and streaks of lightning, shocking my essence as the static crackled my eardrums to the point of no return. My nerves were shot and all the mad shaking I had done in the last hour probably cut a year off my life, but I deserved it. I deserved all the wrath, all the pain. I had lost all feeling; even numbness was too good for me. I had destroyed my soul beyond a timeless amount of any repair; my life was gone.

That thought made me see that all I wanted to do was get soaked by the tears of heaven and melt away into no memory, no scarring mark on anyone I pained, but I was too big a coward to leave the amazing thing called life. I had been trying to figure out the meaning of life, the tricks to it, how to deal with its events, its emotions. I now realized that the only thing I needed to know and would know about life is that I wanted to live it, even if I wasn't worthy. I also knew that no amount of gifts, money, ice cream, awards, music, friends, family, or Credence could ever restore my heart, find my feelings, or answer my ultimate question: Would I ever be able to forget Umbra and the feelings he gave me?

"No . . . ," I whispered to myself. My message was light and crisp as it clashed with the roars of thunder. I hoped somehow Umbra would hear me through his heart. "This lowly scum doesn't deserve an amazing creation like you . . ." The vastness of the universe seemed to have a glitch in them, a mission of their own as the heavens cried louder and heavier, the angels showing how ashamed they were of me. I learned on this day that crying and the rain were the same thing. With this new fact implanted, I carefully turned to go back inside to a world where I could never turn back what I had done.

19

SQUEAKING DOWN THE CORRIDORS NEAR MY FATHER'S ROOM, I allowed my walking to ram into the harsh speeds of reality. I was a blur, an invisible speck, doomed to the curse I saw in front of me—a confusion of colors and angry sounds. I supposed the colors and sounds were all people I was bumping into, not abiding the warnings they gave me. My vision was fuzzy, like I had been drunk to the core for ten days straight.

A trail of tears my body wasn't able to express followed behind me. My aching body knew where to turn to reach my hidden, desired location. Dazed, I opened the door that weighed a ton against my boney body and stood up straight, despite feeling spineless, to see my father and Mrs. Shell drinking soda and discussing something. I only looked at them, not really allowing their images to sink in my pupils.

I was about to grab my ancient hoodie to cover myself in its warmth, but did it really matter? I was soaked to my veins and no amount of heat would have made me feel warm for a long while. Still, I did as my body told me and grabbed it. Off in the distance, I heard my father's call.

"Stary!"

Like a puppet being controlled by the strings of a fate that couldn't be changed, I turned my head towards my father's call.

"Stary, babe, you're wet! You're wet to the bone. Honey, what happened? Did you go outside? How did you get outside anyway?"

He sounded as frantic as when the stuff in his room began to melt. He had his hands on my shoulders, but I didn't feel anything other than more pressure, more guilt that I hurt someone else in my life. I guess that was the destiny of the Spirit Warrior.

I wanted to answer, but my voice was gone, vanished into the depths of despair, too calm from no emotion. When I tried to form meaningful words, my voice choked and my throat swelled up like a thousand pin needles were lodged forever inside me. My voice was what got me in trouble in the first place; now it was too afraid to come out.

"Sorry . . ." was all I managed. It was too dark to be light, but too light to be dark. It was nothing, merely a monotone. I couldn't even look into my father's sapphire eyes for the sparkle and shine in them would have made my heart break more.

My eyes were trapped on the dark rings on the floor. I heard Daddy sigh and caught in my peripheral him turning towards Mrs. Shell for a moment and then back at me.

"We were talking about you being on stage. I was shocked to see you up there since you're so timid, but I'm very proud. You were splendid! Too bad that 'ghost' thing came and ruined it. I guess you knew them, huh?"

My eyes popped out for a moment and I felt a sparkle of relief inside me that my dad wasn't worried about my blow up or belief in the lame "ghost."

Mrs. Shell's usual hoarse voice was sweet and crisp in the day air. "Your voice was simply beautiful Stary. All of us teachers were amazed."

I only stood there like a zombie, thinking that I should respond back. It was then I understood why puppets wanted their freedom so passionately.

"Thank you . . ." It came out like before, programmed words implanted in human brains at birth. My eyes were locked on the dancing dark shapes on the floor, me wanting to touch them, but also not worthy of moving into their dark world.

"Stary! What have I told you about not looking at a person when they're speaking to you?"

I should have remembered that rule. We've had numerous discussions on it before, but I knew my eyes would terrify my father. But because the string had been pulled, I slowly lifted my head into his line of sight.

My father gasped, but tried to contain the expression on his handsome aged face. I knew what he was seeing; I could see myself in the window right behind him. My eyes were blank, completely, utterly blank. In the midst of my irises, the far foreshadowing background of my lake colored eyes, I saw sadness. Tears trapped, lost in a void in my soul, but they were still struggling to come out. It made my heartbeat skip a little faster, but my face was not going to give in to the charm of sorrow.

"Stary, stay right there. I'm going to go get you a towel."

Before I could turn or decline, he ran into the blinding glare of the hallway.

A crackle filled my ears from the far corner of the room. It took me a moment to identify and absorb its strength. It was a voice, an odd voice, but gentle, calling to me until I allowed my eyes to focus and see Mrs. Shell speaking to me. "Stary, why don't you come sit by me?"

I allowed my eyes to drown in the image of Mrs. Shell smiling at me by the same window where I thought Umbra had emotions. How cruel I was to him, not knowing the pain and anguish he went through. I should have learned more about him; I never honestly tried hard enough to. Still, the unknown master of my body made me obey and I strolled to my science teacher.

Mrs. Shell was gazing out the window, deep in a peaceful train of thought, her eyes streaming like she was trying to figure it all out like

Umbra. The devotion and kindness in her eyes was strange, hard to read, but it made me want to start feeling the power of thought and I allowed some rays of the sun peeking behind the clouds to grace my eyes with life.

"Nature is amazing Stary. It is truly wonderful in many ways that we will never be able to capture or figure out. Because of this, we are jealous and that makes us the vainest of creatures, no matter how smart we are. We have to accept our natural gifts and use them to benefit everyone. Nature is our friend, our life, not merely a resource."

I was lost, completely overcome. Her words, her feelings, were *not* what I expected. They were so pure and beautiful—honest. It opened up the gate, allowing some of my emotions to flow freely inside my heart, swelling it up. I felt as though the sun was my own personal spotlight although it was hidden by clouds.

I needed to use my gift, my natural ability. But why did I deserve something as wonderful and important as the title of Spirit Warrior? I lowered my head down in shame. How could I have been so hopeful when I did something so terrible? When I failed at my life's mission?

Mrs. Shell must have felt my distress. I saw the outline of a smile spread across her thin cheeks. She patted my hand like I was made of glass. I gazed up to see the twinkle in her glasses. "Stary, hon . . . I've known you since you were small and after what you did today, I have no doubt of what you can do. Your light is bright enough to stand on its own."

My light? Alone? Those words should have stabbed my heart with irony, but the way they intermingled sent chills down my spine and flashbacks into my mind. I stared, amazed, at Mrs. Shell. Why did that trigger a memory? Why did that not scare me? Why did it make me want to try my hardest to succeed when I had already failed my destiny? Why did I feel a connection with Maren and Umbra at those words? What did they mean?

"Stary!" My dad rushed into the room, shattering my train of thought for a moment. All my emotions went dormant inside me and I could only stare at him, lost. I knew my dad and Mrs. Shell were there at least and that gave me hope as he came behind me to wash my jokingly radiant, water stained hair.

Mrs. Shell had a small smile on her face but looked more concerned about me as I slowly stood up, needing the aid of a nearby metal chair like an elderly person. Before I turned to face my dad, I gave a tight smile to Mrs. Shell and a nod to thank her for her compassion and insight. She seemed to understand for her unease streamed into the sky and enhanced her face into a pretty, yet timid look.

My dad decided I needed to go to Spanish although I had fifteen minutes left before the ice cream social ended. I didn't argue and did as I was told. Before I departed, I allowed my father to nudge me out the door into a slow moving future where my strings tied me down more than my body could bear.

Although my body was sliding across the hallway, my arms kept swinging behind me as I walked ahead, as if it was telling me if I didn't turn back now, I would break at any moment. The air, the piercing air I was breathing was thick, seeming to have a life of its own. Where had I inhaled this torment before?

Having a few minutes before class started, my legs led me to the lunchroom to see the damage done by the ice cream party I missed. But what did ice cream matter? I was too cold and sour to even deserve to watch it melt into a useless puddle.

Clacking on the steps, I made my way to the side hall attached to the cafeteria. I couldn't see any of my peers, but I heard laughter, bittersweet laughter. It made me feel hollow and haunted my mind. I continued. I was about three feet from being visible when I heard a shout that cracked my skull.

"You creep! How dare you! How could you do that to Stary? She did nothing to you! How can you be so cruel?!" The shout sent my mind in a flashback and this voice had the same velvety texture, the same anger, the same intensity. But, it wasn't Umbra this time. It was Mark.

I pinned myself, gripping the wall as if it was the only stable thing holding my soul intact. With caution, I tilted my head and shifted my eyes to gaze at the verbal fight. Mark was circled by about fifteen spectators behind him, pointing his finger at Credence. Credence was across from him in their human ring. Behind him stood Foils and his gang, all mocking Mark's ire.

Smugly, his tone rich, Credence spoke. "I have no idea what you are talking about . . ."

"*I saw you!*" Mark's voice was fierce and violent, a lion on the hunt and Credence was clearly his prey. "I saw you trying to lower a sandbag backstage while Stary was singing. You snuck out of the audience close to the start of her song. I didn't trust you. Why do you think I moved? How could you think about hurting someone Credence, especially someone like Stary? I thought you were better than that! Explain yourself *now*!"

My breath caught for a second in the back of my throat. Mark was saying that about Credence as well? Come to think of it . . . I never did see him while I was singing and I did hear a squeaking noise around the end of the song. Was Umbra right? Was Credence after me?

I looked at Credence, the beautiful golden angel my heart wanted to sing to. He had been wrapped up and cleaned of his wounds, but overall looked well. His face was shining in my eyes even then when my emotions were locked in the dungeon of horrors. However . . . something in Mark's words, his hurtful cry, made it hard to doubt his loyalty to me.

Before I could think of another question, two of Foils's bigger boys grabbed my sweet knight by the collar, lifting him a foot off the ground. I gasped, but swallowed it, making my throat ragged. Like when Foils had grabbed me, Mark was thrown backward about four feet, making a loud slap across the floor, shaking my world for a few seconds. I wanted to save him, my dear best friend, but my feet were screaming *no* and my eyes were glued to the show. Oh, why were teachers away when major things happened? Bullies were too clever!

Mark pulled himself up on his elbows in a pacing, jabbing style to dart into Credence's blackened eyes. Credence just gave him a nasty smirk that was new on him. Foils had that same look, but it fit him. I had never known him to have *any* other look about him. Mark struggled to get up as Foils addressed the crowd.

"We hate Stary's dad. He yelled at me the first day of class because I talked slang to him and talked all hour. I guess the old dinosaur can't be social." He gave a short, bitter laugh. "We had to get revenge on a Moon and since Mr. Moon himself is untouchable, sweet, naïve, and stupid little Stary, the daughter of the horrid teacher, was the perfect target."

He paused, licking his lips, watching Mark struggle to stand up. His eyes were like a snake who was watching a mouse die gradually and excruciatingly. "Credence wanted to join our crew. At first, I wasn't sure he was capable, but he's a good actor and the whole world can see Stary has a major crush on our handsome agent here. So, his test to join us was to humiliate Stary. That's what the plan at the dance was, but that didn't work out quite like we wanted . . ."

My ears rang viciously as what was left of my body was ripping in two by the ironic turns of fate. The holder of my strings was trying to steal what little sanity I had left, choking me with my own source of life. Credence . . . used me? He never liked me? And worse . . . he tried to physically hurt me to join Foils's awful gang. My insides were floating in a dark sea of sadness, drowning, and I was thrown in by the supposed keeper of my heart. Credence was the puppet master that I needed to escape from. He was the demon who possessed me, poisoned my mind with sweetened drugs, burning out my emotional system. It was all Credence . . .

Credence looked straight at the audience that formed behind Mark, getting their attention like he had a hypnotic power. They were shocked by his change as well. His head was cutely tilted, once again a puppy. However, I would describe his glare like that of a homicidal guard dog.

"Yeah . . . it's all true. I mean, Stary is kind of cute and all, but she is super annoying and way too peppy for her own good. It was nice to know I had that sort of effect on girls. Messing with her was so much fun. And I do owe her, Shorty. She was my ticket."

"WHY YOU AS—"

"Stop, Mark." I couldn't take it anymore. My emotions were fusing, combining into a whirlpool of confusion. It was worse than not having them at all. I don't remember how I got to Mark. As I approached, the Earth halted and everyone's eyes were focused on me, not cheering or mocking, but just observing like human nature was made to do.

Mark looked surprised, his eyes twinkling like grass after a refreshing spell of rain. I helped him up, my gallant knight, and placed my hand on his shoulder, giving him a small, reassuring smile. He took in this new, braver me and nodded, allowing me to show this new pulsing power that was inside me.

Rage. That was it. That was the emotion pushing out of me, flowing into every river in my blood stream. I felt like every tiny sound around me was intensified one hundred times, but my world was silent, eerie silent. Foils and his gang were in a laughing fit until I stomped toward them with struts so heavy that their eyes almost landed on the ground. Credence halted as well, surprised to see me, but his eyes showed no fear. His eyes were beautiful, sparkling like onyx gems, but at that moment and for the rest of my life, that look made me sick.

I was never going to be Credence's victim again.

Finally, in a voice like a coy crow, Credence asked dumbly, "You heard?"

Did I hear? I wanted to laugh maliciously and smack him to the floor, but instead, I smiled. It twisted on its own across my face like pointed vines. The sharpness of this smirk was almost too much to bear, so I closed my eyes and took a deep breath.

"Yes, I heard. And it's okay cutie. I still want to be with you Credence. After all . . . you did steal my heart." I added a little girlish giggle at the end and jumped toward Credence. I added too much enthusiasm to the last sentence, which left even Foils speechless and impressed by Credence's supposed "talent" of being a lady killer. Credence looked baffled, but after a moment, glad of what he had done.

"Well . . . this is unexpected. But, you are cute Stary. I might let you be with me for a while." Our audience was watching us so intently, almost like our words were going to complete their lives.

I smiled again. It coming from someplace dark inside my mind.

I could feel Mark's eyes behind me, wanting to yell, '*What are you thinking Stary?* That's just it. I had no idea. The power burning inside me was controlling me, but I knew it needed to so I could burn away my ties to Credence Horton.

Credence continued as he nonchalantly brushed his fingers over my edgy hands. "No hard feelings, right?"

At that, my hair began to rise at every end, pulling toward the lighting force of heaven. My throat burned with brimstone and my ears were on fire, worse than the core of the Earth. Stings of moisture were attacking my eyes, wanting to escape their fury as my hands shook, only wanting to destroy the black evil in front of me, the hurtful human touching me.

I took in a deep breath, allowing fruition and anger to engulf me for a few moments. I turned away, unable to look Credence in his soul stealing irises, but Credence's hands were still brushing mine. Although they were cold, it made me feel like fire was burning off my flesh.

The breaking point was made. So softly and calmly, I said, "I agree." I barely heard my own voice what with it being trapped under lock and key for so long, but it was being released. The harsh heat in my body was melting the metal that was trapping me with unemotion. I heard a little chuckle from Credence that brought more tension to my dying pools of vision. My strings were officially cut; his horrible laugh was the blade.

Before I could stop myself, I turned to face Credence, released my hand violently out of his, and slammed it hard against his lower chest. It was like the time I tapped the Ping-Pong ball. Credence went flying backward, soaring with a powerful force ten feet away from me, and landed hard in a mustard plastic chair. He was lucky the ice cream table was there to stop his journey.

Everyone gasped and became silent. Amazed exclamations were popping up everywhere in the airspace like fireflies. I coolly walked past Foils and his crew. They were too scared to even approach the weak, stupid daughter of Mr. Moon. The lights where I walked under began to flicker frantically and my hair was sliding down from the electric current the universe sent me.

Credence was struggling to get up and he looked at me like I was a monster, begging for mercy. It was too late for pity. My strings faded in the abyss of his void heart. I smacked his demon essence into the mantel of Earth mentally, the demon dripping sickeningly like an ink blot being sucked into the depths of a carpet.

Then, an idea struck me. I picked up a left over sundae with every kind of sauce and topping known to man on it and an opened carton of milk and slammed it onto Credence's bronze, autumn-toned hair. His head was a sticky, melted collage.

I bent down to his eye level and wiped some of the whipped cream that landed on his nose with my pinky, giving him the final honor of hearing my voice: "Don't *ever* talk to me again *sweetie*," I said as I licked the whip cream off.

The voices of my peers rose behind me, mocking Credence and cheering for me. I took a step back and shared a quick glance with Mark. I allowed a waiver of a flame to enter my soul as a thank you to my beloved friend before staring down Credence once more.

Credence's eyes rounded. He tried to get words out, but they came out as incoherent sounds. I took a step back to spit the sweet topping that had touched the devil's helper's face on the ground then stormed off to Spanish.

I stomped down the stairs, my steps feeling like lead, making crashing noises worse than Godzilla ever could have hoped. My body was so enraged I could almost see steam in front of my nose. All I could do was mumble under my fiery breath, my breath burning like sulfur so strong I felt it stain my teeth.

"That stupid Credence! He had to destroy everything!"

I had to pause often for the burning in my lungs made it hard to breathe and I would growl like a mountain lion with each resting beat. Every locker I passed flew open with an amazing gust as I became my own personal tornado. The voices of the memories possessing them were frightened. The lights above flickered and crackled with static and bolts of lightning when I walked by. I even made a dent in the floor! This was a new side of my powers! I supposed it was a warning to the world: do not make Spirit Warriors angry!

I wanted to curl in a ball and cry. I wanted to be set free and allow my wholesome, honest feelings to come out of the darkness. I stopped in the middle of the hallway, panting like crazy to try to become myself. My shoulders heaved so much that I was surprised they were still intact.

After a minute, I was able to get the breathing pattern of a person who just finished a marathon. I looked at the damage I caused. All of the lockers were hanging by their bolts. The lights were dimmed. There were black shoe marks I created that left the tile burning. Gazing at my fury, I felt guilty, irrational.

I turned around to face the skylight in the center of the ceiling and prayed to the Lord: "God, I'm not sorry for what I did, but I'm sorry I enjoyed it so much."

After saying that, I felt calmer and was able to think clearly again. It was like I was being lifted up into the clouds and the normal Stary was almost completely inside my being again. I smiled to myself to welcome her and promised to never lose all of her again. The sun began to peek out again, but only through the skylight. It was warm like the feeling of love. A dawning revelation seeped into my mind . . . Umbra was right all along.

I closed my eyes, remembering Maren told me to use them. The warmth of love: pure, true, and powerful love was still inside me, just as strong as ever. It was never for Credence. I was never fully in love with Credence; it was an attraction. It was Umbra that picked me up when I fell. It was Umbra who helped me with my Spirit Warrior abilities. It was Umbra who made me strong, who made me think. It was Umbra who pulled my heartstrings. It was Umbra who formed that melody that now played in my heart. It was Umbra who I was in love with.

I knew deep down that I had been in love with Umbra for a long time now, but I subconsciously refused to let it surface. I needed a normal love, a mortal love, a safe love, and I thought I convinced myself that was Credence. Umbra was the star I knew I could never reach. But that did not stop me. Umbra's love was quiet, starting at the center of my soul and becoming a part of me. Credence was fast, outside my body. It fizzled before it reached my being. How can I reject a love that is as a part of me as my lungs, my soul, my mind? I was a fool to try!

I covered my mouth and lowered my head. Tears wanted to escape from me, happiness and sorrow, washing away the burned marks of hatred that I could barely recall. Umbra was right about Credence. He wanted to protect me and what did I do to him? How could I have been so terrible? And Maren must have known my feelings the whole time. Did that mean she accepted my love for Umbra? But it was impossible for us to be together after the damage I caused.

My heart sank, not even trying to float out of the ocean my insides formed. *Let it drown,* I thought. I didn't deserve such a sweet, beautiful love even if God destroyed all the trials we were meant to face to become a couple: Umbra was dead while I was alive. Umbra was half machine and I was human. Umbra was created, but I was born.

I lifted my head and noticed that no one was in the hallway. My watch said I had a minute to get to Spanish. Amazing how much time it took to realize what turns life could throw. Though class wasn't too far, my destiny was light years away.

I wanted to dissolve into a puddle and allow my body to deteriorate. The spot where I was standing was where I saw Umbra last with tearstained cheeks and passionate fury.

As I reached for the shiny silver knob to Spanish, I heard a scream. It was high-pitched, in painful distress, the sound faint and light like an illusion, but I heard it, pulsing inside my eardrums and floating into my mind like a feather. My head jerked backward from where I had just come. Where? Why? Who?

"*Stary, ¿Cómo está?*"

Shocked, I turned to see Señorita behind me with her loving heart-shaped face, gazing at me confusedly. I was not sure how to respond. I wanted to dash off to find the person in distress, wondering why no one else had heard it when they sounded like they were in so much harm. I listened again, but it was gone, vanished into the air.

Chills went up my back, sliding like worms as I shook from fright. Something was coming. Something was going to get me. I had to remember how to breathe. Señorita patted my shoulder and led me to my seat. The feeling, the movement inside me, would not cease. All I could do was lock my chest tight to stop myself from crying out like a mad woman.

I could see my teacher's lips moving, telling us to study our chapter list of words, but nothing was surfacing. I knew some of my classmates worried about me because I felt their eyes on me, but I could not stop my shaking or the shudders running up my spine.

I knew I hadn't imagined that scream. I couldn't imagine something so awful even when I felt so bad about Umbra . . . Umbra. His voice was still as enchanting as it passed my lips and mind. However, that was the problem. I wanted him back. I wanted to smile at him and tell him everything, but that dream was easier said than done.

Will the earthquake inside me ever halt? It was aching. I felt so helpless, so weak. It was like I was watching my lover kiss a prettier girl in front of me in a pouring rainstorm, and I was too petrified to stop it.

Well . . . like my daddy said, "If no one will give you a chance, give yourself one."

I grabbed my throbbing heart that was weighted down with the richness of sorrow. My index finger slid over the doodles I just did, allowing some of the lead to stain my skin. There was a cloud with sparkles in it, some angel wings and a heart. I grinned for a moment at the heart. It was loopy and childish, but it was honest. That heart glued a smile onto my face

"Umbra," I whispered so gently that I doubted the lightest breeze could have found it.

On my desk, I saw Umbra's prince-like face, his hair bouncing. A smile spread across the image, flowing like a river and it was brighter than all the fireflies ever created. His eyes were shining, saying my name softly to pleasure my ears. I knew Umbra was never really like that, but my heart was yearning it in my mind, forcing me to view and enjoy the beauty that would never be. I must have finally gone crazy. Where were the men in white coats?

Looking at Umbra appearing so solemn and innocent made me think of a beautiful passage from one of my favorite Shakespeare plays, *Romeo and Juliet.* Juliet tells how she wants her Romeo, her Romeo so fine that if he were cut up into little stars, he could even make the heavens more beautiful. A night sky so breathtaking that the entire world would be in love with the night after Juliet died . . .

Die . . . A rush of unbearable discomfort hit my brain like an ax. True, Umbra would be beautiful in the stars, but why was I thinking the word "die" and so terrified by it? Umbra was—and Maren too—already dead. I knew that, but was there something I was missing? Was it me that was afraid of dying? Probably, but I couldn't get that wave of intensity out of myself.

Perhaps thinking more rationally would allow me to calm down again. I turned my head to see everyone working on a puzzle with the new terms on them that somehow magically zapped itself on my desk. But I couldn't even start it.

I had to stop being concerned about myself drowning in the sadness I deserved for hurting Umbra when there were two people I loved that needed me. Even if they hated me, I would complete my mission not merely for them or for my honorable Lord, but for everyone who had suffered, everyone who had been a victim and everyone who wanted to give up. I was determined.

After deciding, my fate seemed clearer. My body rang more beautifully than a silver bell, warming my body with some sort of power. Wait . . . that ring, that warmth, that surge of might. I knew I had felt it before. It was more powerful of course, but I had felt it before. My body seemed to be glowing? It was dim, but comforting like a nightlight to a scared child. My power, my Spirit Warrior powers . . . they were coursing through me.

Maybe I was capable and had some natural abilities to give to the world like Mrs. Shell said. Maybe I was strong enough if I believed in my might . . .

A sense of shock and amazement hit me all at once, making me gasp ever so slightly out loud. I stared at my desk blankly again. I saw Umbra's loving face grinning at me in the reflection of the desktop. Again, I slid my hand across the smooth surface of the desk, hoping to gain an answer to all the confusion compressing me

SNAP!

The sound echoed across the room, sending currents pulsing through my bloodstream. That snap and the ripples it caused . . . I'd heard them before. Yet, that snap was unique. I felt cold to the nucleus of all my cells. Ice shards seemed to form on my heart like frost sticking to a window in the winter time.

Excruciatingly, I opened my eyes to feel the snake. The black monster-like snake that almost took Maren away from me was now in front of my eyes, sliding across my mind. It was taunting me, forcing me to be locked in fear by its existence and feel its vibes stabbing my skin. But, as quickly as it came, it vanished, seeming to go out the door. The snake brought me back to reality, but as it left, it became something different; it was a line, a current of pure darkness. It was trying to lead me somewhere. It was coming to get me . . .

I screamed. My eyes were locked onto my desktop. My mental image of Umbra was still there, but a black fog was surrounding it, appearing out of the blue. It was thicker than the night. His smiling face didn't move, but in a speck of madness, Umbra vanished before my eyes, leaving nothing behind.

However, I did get to see his eyes before he was taken. Panic was all that was in them. My mind was running, screaming for Umbra to come back, begging with all my power for him to return. My fingers were ghost white from squeezing the desk, hoping he would come back from my sheer physical force and willpower.

"AHHHHHHH!" That scream. It wasn't the same, high-pitched one I heard earlier. It was low, deep-toned, rich. It was just as painful sounding as the first scream I heard earlier in the hallway. A mere illusion? I was lying to myself. I knew deep down in the hollow depths of my heart that it wasn't. Someone was—

Bump-bump!

Wait . . . my arm. I realized my arm was pounding loudly, my veins responding to my over active heartbeat. I felt it, another pulse, crashing and colliding with my own, fighting to support itself. It was declining rapidly, suffering with every mere second. I knew that warmth, that doomed desire. My powers were connecting us and saying his name in my head. It was Umbra.

Umbra's pulse, his life force was—No! Tears welled in my eyes, but I dared not let them fall like rain. I pleaded to the Lord in my head to allow me to be strong, to allow me to hold on to Umbra. *He can have my heartbeat if it means keeping him safe!* I prayed.

But my cries were not answered. His face was in my eyes for a few precious moments. It was scared and strained with overflowing, unimaginable pain. His eyes were glowing gold, but they were struggling, tormented to continue to fight on. Umbra was battling something and he was losing. His voice was barely recognizable, his own breath choking his being. All he could do was focus on standing and trying to stay together. As he gritted his teeth, about to fall, my mental TV connection with him died and I was unable to receive anything.

"*No!*" I screamed out loud, so loud that I felt the high windows shake, rattling the glass, scaring my peers. The pulse, the images, the current . . . it was all too much. I would not sit there anymore. I would not allow that murderer or so called evil destroy him.

With tears falling down my cheeks, I ran out the door, startled, not worried about my peers' whispers. However, I only got a few inches out the door before Señorita grabbed my wrist, making me halt to gaze down at her. I never did things like this. I knew that was the worrisome question crossing her mind as I looked into her milk chocolate eyes. I broke free without a problem, but instead of retreating, I grabbed her hands as tightly as I could. I was so shaky that I was scared I would drop them.

"*¡Señorita, por favor!* Please . . . this is an emergency and I can't give you any details, but please . . . You have to let me go. Just trust me!" I was shouting, allowing the last of my tears to slip on the ground before the feeling of courage consumed me, filling my insides.

I was about to explain more until she surprised me by giving me a comforting, beaming smile and dropped my hands to my sides. With a velvet tone, she told me kindly, "Just go," and pointed toward the stairs.

I bowed my head and ran without a thank you or a second thought. It was important. It was my destiny. It was why my friends needed me. I had no idea where I was going. My legs were being controlled by my feelings and none of the blurred visions I passed were clicking, but my light was ready to stand on its own. No matter what it took or what happened to me, I would complete my fate until my last breath.

20

NOTHINGNESS, EMPTINESS . . . IT WAS ALL THAT MY BEATING heart could feel, my eyes could see, my ears could hear, and my mind could know. Once I reached my destination, I stopped to catch my breath and analyze my surroundings. The lunchroom was as bare as the trees in January after an ice storm. The walls seemed to glow more than usual, brighter than the most blinding snow. It was hard to believe that less than a half hour ago, I was pushing Credence into the table. Scanning the room, my burning eyes picked up what I wanted to witness: Umbra.

He seemed to be pretty banged up. His tan skin looked like it had been burnt with hot coals as scars spread across his arms and face like the stars marking their territory. His clothes had more holes than a police academy dummy and his breath was loud and harsh, worse than anything I had ever heard. However, he struggled to stand with sharp eyes. "You bitch! I refuse to allow you to touch Stary!"

His scream was so passionate and fiery that it made my heart stop and head spin. After all I had done to him, he was still protecting me. But from what? He was in the far corner of the lunchroom, but there was a pillar blocking my view of his enemy. I focused more on the left side of the pillar and saw a dark, ink black figure. It was still, appearing to stare Umbra down. Without warning and with a quickness I could not follow, it flung its shape at Umbra, ramming him hard into the tile floor and then the form sank into the ground, vanishing.

A bolt of panic hit me hard, almost knocking me over. The attacker was probably still there, but I didn't care. I had to help Umbra. He was lying face down on the ground, unable to move, not even groaning or tensing his muscles like before.

"Umbra!" I screamed and ran to him with lightning fast motions, reaching his limp body.

"UMBRA! Umbra, please, wake up . . ." It was difficult to contain my salty dewdrops from forming in my eyes, but I had to focus my energy on keeping Umbra with me. Slowly, he fluttered his delicate eyelashes, exposing his beautiful chocolate eyes.

With a weak tilt of his head, he gazed confused at me, but the look was gentle. "Star . . . y . . . ? *AH* . . . !" His chest heaved. It sounded like a large rock was crushing his air supply.

"Shhhhh . . . ," I told him. I knew he was going to protest me being there, but I wasn't leaving. I tried to give him a reassuring smile although my vision was becoming misty, tears wanting to break free. I hoped my expression would tell him how sorry I was.

"We need to get you up first and then out of here right *now*. Don't move too much okay? I'll help you."

He slid a little on his knees, struggling, allowing me to hold him. A wry smile crossed his priceless face, his honey-toned eyes staring straight into mine, made my heart hammer even in our desperate situation. "Stary . . . you need to be careful. The murderer is still here." His voice was weak and breathy, but he sounded more determined than I would have ever dreamed.

"That's correct." A voice, cold and twisted, popped like a firecracker in the atmosphere but lingered like the smoke left behind. As Umbra was able to almost stand, I felt someone behind me. Swiftly, I turned my head towards the lunchroom's side entrance by the restrooms where I first entered and there she was. Out of the women's bathroom came the opponent I was destined to fight: Barbara.

I gulped and planted my feet firmly on the ground, trying to hide my hurt. However, Barbara looked gravely ill. I could feel the power of the ultimate evil, true hatred encircling her presence, but my heart was telling me she was not up for the battle and that she couldn't be my enemy. Her face reminded me of flakes of fresh, unstained snow, her hands whiter than sugar. She was hardly able to stand with her wobbly legs. Her bruised eyes didn't look at me. Her fingers clasped her chest as she took short breaths. Breathing seemed to take up all of her strength. I took a step forward, hoping to maybe reason with her, but the snake of sin appeared again, transforming behind Barbara in the form of a slick hand.

It wrapped around Barbara's throat and pinched her tight flesh in a vital vein marking her swan-like neck. Barbara fell down like a rag doll out of a chair. The black liquid creature was gone as soon as it had appeared.

"Barbara!" I ran toward her and tried to hold her upright, but she wouldn't make a sound. The whole room was hollow and trapped the sounds within its walls where not even a breath could have been detected.

A boot, black with red outlining, was only inches from my hand as I rocked Barbara like an infant. Steadily, I looked up to feel the dark aura pulling me painfully to stare into the eyes of the murderer and no matter how hard I tried, I could not contain my shock. It was Cally Sun!

Sweet, smart, and adorable Cally was standing there in dark clothing with a red whip that looked like a large laser pointer at the end, the color as crimson as rich blood. Her eyes were blacker than night and as blank as a child's slate. Sets of crossing lines were under each of her eyes, giving her stare a robotic look, a robot that was programmed for a horrid mission. Her smirk and glare was so piercing, so cruel that I knew it would haunt my dreams forever. I knew I wasn't in a nightmare.

I carefully placed Barbara on the cool ground and stood to look Cally in the eyes, my heart more surprised than frightened. I knew that would change. "Cally," I whispered so softly that I doubted she could hear me, but her devilish smile told me she did and that she found my youthful personality deliciously delightful.

With a fast movement of her palm, fragments flew, aimed behind me. Barbara glowed in a deep red light and then evaporated into thousands of circles into the sky, leaving blood-spotted dust behind. "Barbara! NO!" I cried petrified, but I didn't make it to her in time and she was nothing more than a memory, lying there as a speck in my mind.

"Welcome, Stary, to the start of your own personal hell."

I stood tall to glare at Cally or the evil using Cally. I didn't care if this was some sort of trick. I just knew I had to protect Umbra and figure out what was going on, every ounce of the truth. I had a responsibility as the Spirit Warrior to understand.

"What should I call you?" I knew that was an idiotic question, but maybe the evil destroyer would explain to me who I was truly facing.

With a light laugh under her breath, she responded, "You can call me whatever you like. It does not matter. I would prefer The Sealer of Your Demise, but I will grant you some freedom."

"Barbara . . . Where is she?" I sounded like a little mouse trying to sound tough, preparing myself to fight a thousand knights with a tiny toothpick sword.

"Oh, that girl I just sent away you mean? I did not need her anymore. She was taking up space, but she did prove to be very useful." She flipped her red hair to spread it across the black planes of her shoulders. It looked like fire blazing on a deep lake. "She was weak physically to begin with, but a strong, nasty will lived inside her. It took me longer than I wanted to track you once I sensed your partners over there seeking your aid. It is nice to be able to track the souls you destroyed and you can interact with them like when they lived. However, you were unpleasantly a concern to me. I knew I had to stop you with my bare hands, but they hid you well." She pointed at Umbra, who was holding his throbbing arm in place and moving himself away from the pillar as she continued.

"Once I finally located you, I knew you would be easy to target, but I needed reassurance. I noticed a beautiful hatred forming in your pure heart, an anger building for that girl you called Barbara. The day before I entered your classroom for the first time, I stole her aura and it was easy to manipulate it to my will. Since you had such a strong dislike for her and her personality was not shocked to the events happening, I allowed her to lead my trail while sweet little me became a victim, taking you further away from the truth. Her energy was a good source to absorb after I used mine to warn you, using your loved ones as bait. She did try to resist me once, that day you came into the bathroom to read the newest ectoplasm message that, yes, *I* wrote, just like the others before it. It was only a fluke, your presence of light messing up my channeling abilities to control her, but after she ran away from you, I regained control. It was just simply enjoyable to see you suffer through another person, to mess with your innocent little soul . . . Miss Stary . . ."

It was her, the murderer, who really did hurt my friends. It was because of her doing that Rin's ankle broke, that Credence's eyes got banged up, that Allen's shoes melted, that Chloe fainted, that Lauren got cut, that Mark's cheek got scraped, and that my daddy almost got burned. It was the murderer who attacked Maren with that snake—Maren! I couldn't feel her presence.

"Where's Maren?!" I screamed at her, my eyes narrowing in disgust.

"Hmmmmm . . . it took you long enough to recall. You sure are a mighty Spirit Warrior, huh Miss Stary?"

"*Where is she?*" I yelled, making my vocal chords vibrate and break like the strings of an overused guitar.

The murderer seemed to be taken aback a bit, but she cocked her head like a killer German shepherd and pointed upward toward the pillar where I found Umbra. I had to bend my head far back, but I gazed at the horrific sight of Maren, chained to the wall in navy-colored jail chains, her face full of panic and fear.

"Maren!" I called and she looked down in fright. Her eyes swirled like a maniac at the sound I created.

She shrieked, full of terror as she tried to struggle free. "Stary!" Her tone had no maturity, none of the lady-like graces I was used to and loved. It was consumed with fear of losing to the darkness of nothing.

Maren must have been the angelic high-pitched scream I heard earlier. The last time I saw her . . . she was alone in the hallway after failing to comfort Umbra, walking to the hall toward the cafeteria. Cally must have got her after everyone cleared out when my outburst at Credence ended. Umbra must have decided to battle alone, responding to her distress cry, nobler than I did, but Cally was too much for even him.

"The demon," I whispered, almost inaudibly.

Cally cocked her head to one side, looking lovely and lethal. "Demon . . . ? Ah, yes. You are referring to my smaller dark essence form. Your connection to your partners was too powerful for me to get a good advantage, which also made it a weakness. So, I made a special essence out of parts of my soul."

I gulped, pushing back a revolting heave.

She played with her lacy fingers, tracing patterns in the air. She was lost in her own impressive story. "However, this one had a catch, unlike my shape shifting essence—the snake essence I sent to scare you and Maren. Your heart was too pure, so you had to be in a heightened emotion in order for him to . . . assist you. I assume you can get the rest, my dear . . ." She ended with Lucifer's smile, the one I saw in the clouds in the alleyway when I encountered a possessed Barbara. It seemed like the dark follower was learning a lot from the fallen angel.

So, it was my own fault Umbra was so hurt. Those were my own words stabbing him like daggers; Cally had added poison to the tips. I had never felt so angry and ashamed in my life. That was why I could not regain my emotions until I heard Credence speak. The dark feeling I got when I saw Umbra beating up Credence, the way I overreacted . . . it was the fault of that dark spawn of darkness. This ink blot demon locked my soul away, separating me more from Maren and Umbra . . .

Umbra was next to me then, still holding his body intact from all the scratches his skin had. He was shaking and his breath was staggered. He looked about as bad as Barbara. But I knew he wouldn't give up.

"None of that matters now." His voice was hoarse, but authoritative. His words stopped my gears from reeling and all my thoughts became guesses on what Umbra would say next.

He took a step in front of me, struggling to even pick up his feet. By heartfelt instinct, I reached out to aid him, but he turned his enraged face towards the demon human, the mortal sergeant of Satan's army.

"Release Maren . . . now!" His breath caught and he began coughing. Umbra grabbed his throat. Maybe something was lodged in the back of his throat? His body flung forward about half a foot before both of our hands grabbed his waist at the same time. His eyes were tightly closed. Ectoplasm oozed out of his cuts. It was sickening to look at, but I refused to leave him.

"You better be careful there dark hero. You appear to be close to death, are you not?" Cally cruelly mocked, her eyes black and shining with a demonic glow.

As I held Umbra, he slid farther and landed on his knees. Umbra used one of his hands to prop himself up on the chilling tile for support and the other to cover his lips. He was coughing in between breaths of air so painful sounding that it made my lungs want to stop working from the sheer noise. As I wrapped my hands tighter around his hips, I noticed how I could practically see through him again like when we first met. His image flickered with each cough and breath. His body felt more like dissolvable warm fog in my hand. Umbra couldn't be disappearing. He couldn't be *dying*.

I darted my eyes at Cally, making her cackle for a second. "What are you talking about? Umbra can't die. I mean, he's already . . . dead . . ." The word was so heart wrenching to say that moisture hit the corner of my eyes, but I ignored them to hold onto Umbra.

Cally laughed twistedly again, so loud and burning that I felt like I would rather have an eternity of nails on a blackboard than a moment of that hateful cackle. "You did not tell her anything, did you robust combatant? You see dear, if a spirit gets hurt badly enough, their life force vanishes and becomes little pieces in the wind, meaning they can never be reborn or go to heaven. They become nothing, like they never existed. The living soon forgets about them."

"*Stop it!*" Umbra screamed, pushing my arms off him. Although he was on all fours, he glared so heatedly at Cally that she had to take a step back. His jet-colored bangs were in his eyes. His panting was so awful that I had no idea how he could even use his madly shaking arms to hold his body up. "Don't tell her things like that. She doesn't . . . need to worry about it!"

"It's true?" I whispered quieter than a leaf floating off an autumn tree. My surprise was enough to turn Umbra's anger at Cally into soft, pleading eyes toward me. His gorgeous eyes shone to comfort me, full of concern, but we both knew it wouldn't work. I quaked as the thought raced around my brain. I glanced up for a moment at the startled Maren, who hid her face from me by staring at the floor. It was true. When we die, we have to worry about keeping another life intact before entering eternal happiness?

"It . . . can't be true, Umbra. Please . . . it can't be true. It's . . . not right . . ." I did not mean to question God, but I was just in so much shock.

Umbra moaned, trying to tilt his head up. His eyes pleaded with me to forgive him. Tears welled in my eyes, able to steadily break free. Cally watched in amusement, laughing shortly a few times and staring straight at the depressed Umbra. "Wow Umbra . . . you really have no confidence in your Spirit Warrior, do you?"

"SHUT UP! I . . . I . . ." He glanced with doe-shaped eyes between me and the murderer, moisture forming, but the tears would not fall. His hands curled into fists. He screamed with all his passion, all his might, "*I did it to protect her!*"

I snapped out of my sorrowful state to see Umbra, the one I hurt, still continuing to suffer after what I did, wanting to help me. After the outburst, Umbra fell forward again, this time as motionless as a statue, his face pained from failure to be strong.

"*No!*" I cried in agony, grabbing Umbra to roll him on his tense back. His eyes were forever locked away in the dark abyss of defeat.

"His will, no matter how glorious, cannot withhold his decaying body anymore. That is one beauty when you allow your already darkened heart to be empowered by Lucifer; you can kill anything, even the souls of the lives you have already taken. And only I was able to do this to your partner Umbra. You are both welcome for this rare experience," Cally informed me, her face triumphant.

I leaned my body on top of his to shield him from any cheap attacks Cally might strike against him. More tears flowed from my eyes, my sobs louder and more devastating than a hurricane. Cally took a few clicking steps toward us, her whip forming static as she walked. In a rush, I glanced into her eyes, all the light swelling in my being.

She stopped and allowed me to speak. "Please Cally . . . please stop this. I . . . I can't stand to see Umbra or Maren get hurt. I know I'm a horrible Spirit Warrior, but . . . I have to protect them. I really don't want to fight you. I *know* you're good. All those times I talked to you . . . I refuse to accept it was all an act. I'll give you whatever you want. I'll help you in any way I can, but please . . . can't we stop fighting? I don't understand. *Why are you doing this? Why are you like this?*" My voice cracked and tears formed a puddle the size of an ocean beneath my limp body. I could hear sweet Maren whisper my name in distress from above, guiding me still. I had to do something.

"Parents. My parents made me this way," was all Cally said.

21

HER VOICE WAS HARSH, BUT THERE WAS A SPRINKLE OF SORROW and humanity in it. Her parents? Her parents made her into a killing machine? Parents were supposed to love their child, support their child, let their child grow. How could parents hurt Cally so much, wound her so deeply? My mind couldn't wrap around the unpleasant thought.

Cally pulled me in with her gripping, yet quiet tone, taking me back into the past of her former self. "My parents, the adults who created me and were meant to love me, never did. I was lucky if my father would even look at me when I asked him a question. I was in heaven if my mother ever showed me something other than a frown or glare. When I was about seven, my father left and my mother was so angry, blaming it on me entirely that she abused me to no end. I still have the marks, bruises, and scars to this day, which is why I always wear long sleeves. I almost got thrown into the lit fireplace once. I would have died if I had not grabbed the screen and pretended to faint."

My breath caught into a mothball-sized sting in the middle of my vocal chords. An abusive parent and neglect? I could see and understand the pain Cally herself had to endure. She went on with her mind-boggling tale:

"The madness went on for years, nothing but continuous hitting. I separated myself from the other kids' perfect worlds. I was smart, however. Studying and learning allowed me happiness, a form of joy no one could destroy for me. When I was around ten, after moving about thirty times since my father's departure, I met a wonderful old woman who lived in the trailer next to our own. My mom decided to get a job at a nail salon, so that woman watched me after school. She gave me food, sweet treats, read me stories, helped me with school work, and taught me how to dance. She let me enjoy life, vent my problems, and cry for no reason. She . . . gave me love."

The murderer, no Cally, had to pause at the last part, almost choking on tears that I could tell were forming in her throat. If she wasn't so unpredictable right at that point, if I wasn't holding my weakening love in my arms, I would have gladly held her to soothe her. To be hurt so much . . . it was unbearable to listen to let alone imagine experiencing.

"One night, a few days after my eleventh birthday, I went over like any other day, but that sweet old woman who insisted I call her grandma due to her not having any granddaughters, threw me a surprise party. It was a real party with cake, games, gifts, and decorations. I was smiling from ear to ear and felt such a thrill that I forgot to look for my mom.

"That was the golden rule at my house. I had to look for my mom's headlights and be in the house to open the door, no questions, no speaking. If I went hungry, that was my own fault. I think I was about ten minutes late, but I didn't notice until she barged in the door. She was so red, so engulfed with anger, but seeing the party, all the colors and love . . . she lost it. She grabbed my arms, banging my head against the frame a dozen times. My sweet grandma tried to stop her, threatened to call the police, but my mom had no soul to feel bad. I knew my mom threw me against the wall again and I was barely able to stand and she . . . she just . . ."

Cally paused. When I heard the crack in her voice, the malevolence in the room seemed to disappear by a touch, my chills lessen. Perhaps the murderer's spirit was losing some of its dark power. Cally's youthful heart was recalling the love she felt for her grandmother.

At that point, I heard a moan underneath me and then the room slowly lit up. Umbra opened his eyes but groaned in pain, tilting his head like he was spinning, losing his mind. Shocked, I looked at him, his faultless eyes gracing me, the expression on his face told me he wanted me to tell him that he was all right. I nodded, trying not to create more sobs. He was able to prop himself on his elbows and face Cally, who's aura was red with hatred again.

I mused, no, more like hoped, she would let out all of her sadness to escape her nightmare, but instead her anger for her mother seemed to overflow into a burning rage. Umbra and I had to duck from the electric current pulsing through the air and thank goodness Maren was able to evade it as well.

"My horrible mother killed her, the only human who ever loved me and made me feel the emotions of joy. My mother slugged my arm and forced me home, locking me in my room for days with no food, telling me to not tell anyone. All I could do was sit in the darkness, holding my head and rock back and forth in madness. After about three months of that, my anger was the only thing building and I had nowhere or no way to release it, no person to vent to . . . It consumed me and took my heart. Cally Sun has not existed since she was eleven years old. Sure, the process was slow at first right after the killing, but one extremely dark, lightless night, it happened . . . My soul split. The pain was terrible, but the velvet voice inside was strong and led me, took over me."

Lucifer. The name kept ringing in my ears like a siren.

"I left my bedroom, disobeying my mother and making her very angry, but she did not have much time to react. I killed her the same way she killed my beloved grandmother. At first, I was horrified at what I had done, but when I saw the lake of blood, the power I had, what I could actually do . . . I loved the power. More and more, the dark power controlled me. I should know; I *am* the darkness residing in Cally's heart!"

Umbra and I locked expressions, sharing the same insight. So, the darkness talking to us, the evil creating all the madness, the person taunting us in full view, was not all there was to Cally Sun. The Cally that knew love was hidden inside her own tainted heart, scared to no end while darkness continued to, in a way, host her body.

As if Cally had the power to read my thoughts, she smiled like the Grinch and replied, "Murderer souls need a body to do their actions, right? I practically have had control of her body since that night. The good part of Cally is about to disappear into oblivion, allowing me the full use and graces of her body . . . How kind. It may not be the strongest or prettiest, but it will be good enough to destroy the cruel world that hurt us. She has suffered enough."

"How dare you!" I snapped, not realizing exactly what I was doing, but if Cally was inside the murderer, if there was even a spot of a chance she could hear me . . . I had to reach for her and bring her out of obscurity. "If you're saying Cally is still inside you, then that means that I must have talked to Cally, the good, kind Cally at school at some point. You were weak at one point, correct? I know I talked to her a few times then! I like Cally. I want to be her friend. Cally, please hear me calling you: Stary Moon is here and I'm ready to be your friend!"

The dark, heart shattering cackle came out of the murderer's poison-stained lips once more, cutting my head open like a jack hammer. Umbra was pained as well, shutting his eyes toward me for a moment, but he brushed his fingers across my arm, nodding towards me like we made a silent agreement. If only I had time, if only I had the words to tell him how I would be nothing but a weak human without him. However, my mission required me to focus on saving Umbra, Maren, and Cally, not love them.

"Stary, I know murderers are inhumanly cruel and strong, but the unfortunate thing is, they are born from doubting or violent hearts that cannot allow their anger to be expressed. Why do you think your beloved Lord allows you to be angry? All murderers started out as good humans and even with the evil controlling them, the good side and the bad side have to share one body, God and Lucifer, like the rise and fall of the sun are a part of the sun itself until the strongest wins over, the prize being the horizon expressing their colors. Since the beginning of time there have always been murderers." The murderer may have had all the facts, but she was lacking the drive to do anything. If she was as madly evil as she looked, then she wouldn't have been giving me all that valued information or she was just really arrogant.

She went on, sighing. "Later, I ran off and soon found my father, destroying him as well. Being a scholarly student, I had always admired the machines of the Angriff Squad and knew they secretly used them for wars and tormenting causes, which pleased my new dark tastes. They were impressed by my quick relaxes, my skills, and violent ways, but hesitant since I was not yet twelve and the minimum age to be a killing agent is fifteen. So, I got a picture of one of their backstabbing agents and found him hiding within a few hours when they had spent months tracking him. When your soul splits into light and dark, you seem to have almost super villain powers by just imagining what you want done. I destroyed him with no trouble with him begging for forgiveness in front of the administration. They were delighted and made me a top agent on the spot. My first major assignment was Dr. Rowe. I had heard of this brilliant inventor and his machines that could greatly revolutionize the whole Angriff Squad and their secret plans for domination. But he was still too stubborn and stuck on that 'being good' crap. Well . . . I am sure you know what happened to him. He was worth a lot in my bank account . . ."

At Cally's last beyond cruel sentence, Maren gasped and tears rushed down her eyes like a cracked dam flooding the town of her heart.

I wanted to smack the murderer so hard for destroying Maren's family for thrill and money after all she had lost already, all out of her young control. Umbra was engulfed with fury, almost able to stand, looking better than he had in a while. Cally smirked, as if entertained by Umbra's struggle and Maren and Umbra's bond being broken by her.

Sickeningly, she licked the handle of her blood-toned whip and added the most hateful sentence to ever have been formed: "Maren was just a bonus . . ."

"*You monster!*" Umbra screamed so loudly that a herd of charging elephants would have gone unnoticed. His face was so tight that I wasn't sure if he could ever fix it. Maren gasped again, yet her face was still beautiful in the hidden sun peeking through the sunroof.

The murderer placed the whip to her side and groaned. "My mission was to murder Dr. Rowe and grab all his experiments, especially the ultimate living creation that had such power. We wanted to use the power of 198145 to clone and cause chaos to all mankind. But . . ." She pointed fiercely at Maren, chained to the wall like a pretty princess. "That stupid girl had to ruin it and send the vital experiment down to the depths of Earth! She brought her own death and then I could not track Umbra because I had no idea what it looked like."

Maren allowed wrath for the first time to form on her sweet face as she glared coldly at Cally. "I had to save Umbra. I am the one who named him and we will be best friends and family for eternity. I would gladly sacrifice myself again and again before allowing a witch like you and your horrid Angriff Squad to use him or any of my grandfather's beneficial creations. You think I was stupid to what you were after? I would never let your hands stain Umbra!"

Umbra and I mouthed her name at the same time, staring at her determined and truthful face. Her passion, her love, her well-mannered and tranquil nature allowed her to achieve anything, no matter the cost. I gave her a proud and reassuring smile and she blushed a bit, giving me a weak, but embarrassed smile of her own.

Cally was cross that we were not shaken by her intimidation. Bluntly, with a hot coal voice, she told more of her story. "Your little plan was wasteful, dear Maren, for soon, I will have taken your precious Umbra's life as well. I was the one who reactivated the living device, the metal beast, on Dr. Rowe's moon base after Umbra decided to help mankind instead of using his powers for a beneficial purpose. I was planning on getting only the Mighty One for I figured I could capture the ultimate living form and twist his mind and heart into hatred again. I almost succeeded in doing so. However, Umbra used his last ounce of the power to save his new companion by pushing him out of the way before the explosion I created hit him. The force knocked the weakened Umbra backwards where he burned into the blazes of the sun."

Umbra, who I could tell by the spiteful way his eyes flickered, was possessed with rage over what Cally did to him after he changed and helped save the world. Yet, his tone surprised me; it was calm. "I always wanted to know what that explosion I saw behind me was before I was sent into a spiral into the sun. I always wanted to know how I died."

Umbra turned to me and in his gruff, professor voice, told me, "Stary, do you remember the first day you met Maren and I and Maren told you her backstory? Do you recall that Maren told you that there was a prototype for the ultimate living being before I was created, one that was so dangerous and obsessed with power that it had to be locked away?"

My body shook as I stared at Umbra's level gaze. I knew what was coming next.

Umbra turned his hateful gaze towards Cally. "I'm not sure how you got into our secret area and unlocked the storage unit Dr. Rowe created. So, you got my prototype program up and running again and used it to destroy me? How clever of you . . . However . . . you will pay greatly for what you have done."

Cally narrowed one of her eyes to scan my skinny body over, making me feel timid. "You are that confident in your puny Spirit Warrior?"

Umbra smiled and took my breath away for a second. His hand patted my shoulder as my eyes locked on her stance. "My Spirit Warrior, no . . . this wonderful human girl named Stary can do anything and I have no doubt in my mind that she will defeat you. Plus, she has me and Maren here and we will *never* leave her!"

Umbra . . . he truly was my prince. I grabbed his arm tightly to allow him to feel my readiness. He was a little surprised, but when I nodded with a wry smile, he smiled again with fierce eyes and together, we stood Cally down.

The whole room became swallowed up in a sinister aura so vile that I had to recall how to breathe. Cally's hair was standing almost on its own, her hunter's eyes about ready to eat us, especially me, alive. Umbra and I stood our ground, prepared to save our world that we held dear.

"I will *not* let you in my way, Stary Moon!" Cally screamed. In a flash, she charged at me with driving fury and before I could blink halfway, I landed hard on the ground, two feet away. I grabbed a metal chair leg on the way, holding onto it like a life force. The frail Umbra struggled to stay afloat from the madness of the blast.

The twinge in my spine, the knot digging into my flesh like a knife, the sizzling pop on my beat up arms . . . It was worse than I had ever imagined. So . . . this is what death feels like? The thought was as weak as I felt. I knew I wasn't dying, but if the fighting continued to be that tough . . . I had no idea how I could protect Umbra or Maren. It took a lifetime to stand, me relying on the cracked seat of the chair for support, but Cally was almost to me then.

I took in a sharp breath, but groaned in tear jerking agony. The rush was too much. My eyes were a little hazy, but the dark circles around Cally's pupils were detailed, her expression showing me she was ready to strike me down with a flick of her wrist.

Umbra was still on the ground, clawing across the tile, gritting his teeth. Yet, the purple bruise tone around his divine eyes allowed me to know there was no chance of him regaining his composure anytime soon if I wanted to keep him safe.

Cally took her shot. She grabbed my fingers tightly, pulling them backward in a swift motion. With no hint of strain, Cally lifted me about two feet in the air by that arm and flung me backward. I was somehow able to slightly catch myself with my palms, but my torso took the blow. I screamed, hearing the sound of a bone shattering and feeling the edge of my right rib. My right palm was heavily cut, a huge gaping hole exposed to show dark, rich blood outlining the iris-shaped mark, a constant reminder of my failure and it felt like a gunshot wound. Cally was stronger than I imagined. Somehow, by a miracle by my savior, I was able to stand, but my humanly instincts told me something different—run.

I ran. Not fast or gracefully due to the countless number of knots and bruises on my legs, all the sizes of eggs, but enough to confuse Cally for a few moments. My survival tactics were controlling me, making me run in zigzag patterns across the black-marked lunchroom floor. I was a coward or at least that was what I wanted her to think. I knew I could never outrun her speed forever, but I had to concentrate on a plan. There must have been a way to save Cally Sun and release Umbra and Maren from their hardships. I had to protect them at any cost.

A red light blinded my eyes, making me stop to see the splendor of the explosion inches from my glowing face. I moved my eyes to notice Cally tapping her leather boots behind me, the tip of her crimson-stained whip pointed toward the outer edges of the wall. The smoking glory was made for me and I barely evaded it. I took a painful gasp of air, my lungs about to cave in. I continued to run for my existence.

There was a gap in my breathing pattern that felt so sickening that it would take years to get rid of the waste that built up in my throat. I spun around while I ran, feeling the peculiar thrill surging through my delicate bloodstream, the rich liquid drowning my discomfort to numbness. As I made my first lopsided lap around the lunchroom, one of the red flashes came close to my head, burning my scalp a little. I lifted my shaky hand to feel the side of my head. A strange oozing substance was on my hand from the wound and although my vision was blurred, the room engulfed in a chaotic haze, I continued to run. My rib rocked, the bone sliding and twisting worse than a mechanical bull gone loose. Still, I continued to run.

I stopped behind the pillar that Umbra had crawled his way to so I could check on him. His golden eyes were shining dimly in the abyss of the dark shielding created by the ceiling. He gazed concernedly at me. I ran past him, fire torching the roof of my mouth to no end. I held my chest tightly to slow my rapid rush, darting my eyes left and right to look for Cally.

I couldn't swallow. My spit was so thick that it made me choke, almost vomit. I couldn't consume the alternate world. But my pondering was soon over. Cally pressed her elbow roughly into the middle of my spine, making me fall forward hard. I slid on my cheek. My skin tingled into a burning sensation that I could have lived without.

Slowly, I got on my hands, my hair a wreck, its tips dipping into the river of blood streaming down my pale cheek. My arms were as badly scraped as my knees from the newest blow, making finding an inch of undamaged skin impossible to locate. I gazed, scared for my life, at Cally. She was ready to hit me with her whip, tossing it into the air, but my mind hit me with an idea and I dodged the attack by a half of a second by crawling under her legs.

When Cally mentioned that following her evil side and allowing the power of murders become a part of her gave her super powers, she was not lying or joking! This had to be the reason why serial killers were so hard to track! Pin missiles flew down like birds diving from heaven, suicide attacks so fast that Superman would have lost the fight. But by a hopeful prayer, I did a two foot leap over a knocked over lunch table and pinned myself to it, gripping the metal pegs like a large shield for a knight. True, a few sharp missiles hit my legs and the red eerie glow was beyond painful, blood dripping like a dagger cutting through melted metal, but I dared not worry about the scars. I kept my brave face on to think of a chance to attack Cally back.

I could hear the snapping of the sweet smelling shards of finished lumber and see the paint chipping into an ash-covered snow storm, but I had to hold on. My body was weak and I was shocked I could even move at all, but once I thought that, my legs grew woozy. I had to press my head on to the cool rusted bolts on the back legs for equanimity.

I couldn't doubt anything. I had to live. I had to protect them, but my powers weren't kicking in. After all I was forced to witness with Umbra fainting and Maren being a prisoner . . . Why couldn't I save them when it was time? Maybe destiny calls us at the wrong time. Maybe I was being too selfish because deep down, I was terrified beyond words, terrified of dying. No . . . I couldn't touch Cally as a spirit so I knew I was meant to live to aid my friends, but how?

A bomb crashed my ears louder than thunder. I ducked just in time to see that the top half of the table had finally broken off thanks to the murderer's wrathful blows. It smashed into the wall toward the stairs with such a force that my teeth felt like they were breaking into a thousand pieces to become dust in the sky. How close it had been to slicing my head . . .

The metal leg I was using as a fort bent into a right angle in the crash, going right above my knee with authoritative success, making me wail higher than a police car's siren. My tears turned into grunts of pain. A substantial amount of blood stormed out like heavy rain onto the tile.

Still, I couldn't stay there or I was sure to become missing in obscurity. I could hear Cally moan and Umbra groan in the background.

Running was much more difficult with my knee completely deformed and me tripping every other step I tried to take. I'd be hospitalized and paralyzed at this rate, but the powers of light must have been protecting me like darkness was strengthening her. But how much longer did I have to fight? A plan was not formulating either. Hatching a scheme was harder when one was so concerned on escaping a personal heck and my spirit powers were still asleep, refusing to awaken. I had to—

I hit the floor again, with a gargantuan echo that filled all the corners of the cafeteria. Shaking, I was able to lean on my arms enough to face Cally and felt my cut on my cheek had been reopened, staining my cheek in red.

"You are such a little coward for running hon . . . You think you can stop me? I never tire and you are at your wit's end."

I panted, trying to find anything on the tile I could grip to pull myself up with. Cally was still about five feet away, taking her time to approach, savoring my death like a holiday. "Oh, by the way, I have an audience for you. They have much enjoyed the suffering you have caused yourself." She pointed to the opposite corner from where I entered, her eggplant-toned fingernail shining.

Sweat dripped in my eyes, stinging my sight until I realized what I was witnessing was correct, but my brain didn't want to compute. It was Chloe and her business class staring at me in dread. Chloe looked at me in horror and utter disbelief while she held onto Barbara like it would make the world explode if she didn't. I exhaled, relieved to see Barbara alive and in my sight. She still wasn't moving and her body looked colder and blacker than a spider. A clear shield blocked them from the lunchroom, putting all of them out of harm's way. But for how long?

I cocked my head toward her, crawling on my screaming-in-distress hands. "Chloe!" I cried as loud as my tired voice could reach, but she made no response. I saw her breathing and staring into my eyes like heaven's dome was caving in on top of me, but she didn't react.

"Chloe!" I wailed once more due to stress, but she was only locked onto my face. Chloe and the others could not hear me. They were in a fish tank created from the world's most potent glass and I was the freak being watched to no end.

"She cannot hear you. None of them can. They are here to be entertained, although our battle has frozen their senses; a pathetic human trait, making them easy prey. And once you are long gone . . . I am going after them next. They will be my reward for getting rid of my one true, weak obstacle." Cally slid the tip of her tongue along her knuckles as I gazed helplessly at her, her words not connecting to the meaning of her phrase.

Chloe . . . Barbara . . . She was going to kill them after me? But they had nothing to do with this. They had no clue what was going on, no mission to prove! I refused to let them die because of me. The people I loved most shall live their lives to the fullest like it was meant to be by my grand Lord as long as I was here.

"*No!* I won't let you hurt anyone else!" I screamed, tears escaping like a dripping, broken faucet as I dug my fingernails into the tile, allowing the dust and blood to mix under them to get a grip.

Cally halted her victorious march, looking at me with those deadly robot eyes again, but then she smiled in a small way, looking more heartless than ever.

"I'm sorry!" I wailed, piercing the air. It made the murderer freeze into a pose of a dauntless martyr. The sobs were wedged inside my heart, but I knew they were twinkling in the fullness of my eyes. "I'm so sorry for what happened to you. No one deserves that and I know revenge is tempting. But is it worth it? What you're doing . . . it's too much. Do you feel any better? Cally, please stop this. Spare everyone. There are good people in the world and I want to be one you can trust. JUST STOP CALLY AND DON'T HURT ANYONE ELSE!"

I shivered in chilling madness, unable to see if I could do any good. I allowed a pointed breath to attack my lungs. I gazed into her face, holding on to hope and refusing to give up.

Suddenly, I saw it. It was quick, but a flicker of dazzling light full of question and concern was in her eyes. I let that image swell into my soul and it gave me enough confidence to stand on my wobbly feet, ignoring the throbbing of my exposed knee and probably fractured rib. My arms dangled like string at my aching sides.

The light that was a glowing yellow, bathing the red of Cally's hair into an elegant orange of a sunset turned into a light blue fire. Her hands began to create enough static that it seemed it could drown out nuclear explosives. The heat, the intensity of the burning heat from the current was blazing to the core and so out of control that Umbra had to duck in cover multiple times while Maren's chains seemed to absorb the blows. Chloe and the group seemed to be screaming, but thank goodness the glass force field bounced the bolts back in our direction.

"I refuse to let you interfere Stary. Cally is dying, fading into the dark abyss for all eternity and beyond. She is almost a speck of nothing and soon, you will join her." Her whip cracked the floor and dented it with a black mark in the shape of a snake. The contact created smoke that filled my nostrils, making my breathing worse than I could have ever imagined. The snake must have been her main form of hatred, her essence, a symbol of never turning to the light. It fit.

I ran as far away from the danger zone as I physically was capable, which wasn't much. I dodged an attack of laser fire, missed flying debris, and avoided everything I could. My legs felt like I had run sixty miles with iron shackles on that squeezed the life out of me.

Once I passed the wall where the glass force field entrance was for the fourth time, I had to stop for my cough was so violent that I was about to puke if I didn't rest for a second. I thought my lungs were about to explode. I had to stay calm somehow or my powers would never come.

"I am getting bored of this," Cally said, aggravated. A beautiful blue orb with many spirals and clouded circles forming inside its delicate design was in her clawed hand, her royal-colored fingernails positioning it for its purpose. In a flash, the ball hit the back of my legs that were trying to start moving again near the wall, knocking me over in a heartbeat like I was the Berlin wall.

I caught myself on the floor in frenzy without getting hurt, but as I tried to get up, I froze . . . literally. I couldn't move my body! I struggled, moaning like a princess in distress, but nothing was working. More frightened than ever, I glanced at the murderer.

With a devilish grin, she answered my dazed expression. "That was a freezing orb that I created with Cally's own life energy. It will freeze you for about ten seconds, which is more than enough time for me to eliminate you. The hunt was fun and I admit that you are more determined than your weak little body lets on, but it is time to end this." She pretended to wrap her fingers along my neck from a foot away and choke the life force out of me. I felt the pain and groaned. I felt faint. I understood why Yoda cautioned the Force.

"I will say goodbye here to you, Miss Spirit Warrior. Enjoy hell for me Stary Moon." The murderer's voice was so evil that I could feel my heart absorbing her poison, ringing my hope out of me with a bend of her pinky.

She was now inches from my face. I was locked onto her blank, pitiless eyes that were blacker than night.

So . . . this is what death looks like? This is what death feels like? My heart went out to who had suffered before their entry to heaven.

She sharpened the end of her whip until it was smoother than King Arthur's righteous sword. I allowed one breath to exhale my body before I looked her full on and gave a smile to my beloved Maren and my darling Umbra. I tried to tell them how deeply sorry I was and to tell them to stop looking at me with their twisted faces of agony, that meeting them was so precious to me, that I loved them, but my mouth could not form the words. I nodded at Chloe, praying she would be able to escape and let everyone I cared know they would always be in my heart.

I focused my gaze on my foe, the keeper of my fate, blocking out the rest of the world. There was just me and Cally. Cally raised her arm a foot above my head. It was over . . .

"STARY! NO!"

It was all too quick. There was a dark figure that jumped in front of me, clashing with the whip's sinister powers that made a confusing ray of blinding white light and a terrifying pitch blackness. I stayed there frozen in astonishment and dread. I could have sworn I saw the face of the savior, the knight who saved me and his smile was tiny, but more beautiful, yet hurtful than anything I had ever seen.

As soon as it came, the radiant flash battle was over and I only heard panting. I saw Cally hunched a little, huffing for air. Her shoulders were shaking worse than the whole school in an earthquake. And there, lying on the ground was my hero, my prince . . . Umbra.

"*No!*" I wailed, cutting the sky worse than a steak knife. The spell was off my legs and I somehow hobbled past Cally at lightning speed, not caring about the pain eating my body alive or the murderer hitting me full on. I had to go to him . . . Why would he do such a reckless thing when he was just as near death as I was? Where did he come from?

Umbra . . . please be okay, I prayed with all my heart, begging to God with all my being like Maren was probably doing.

"Umbra!" His head slammed into the corner of the other wall where the lunch menu was listed. Fear. That was the only emotion that would fit what I felt as I looked at the horrible shape Umbra was in. My heart was screaming and my brain was in shock, refusing to process and accept what my eyes were seeing.

"Umbra, please open your eyes . . . UMBRA!" I shook him, but massaged his shoulders, cradling them in tenderness. My gentle lighthearted Umbra wasn't replying to my pleas . . .

A whimper hit my ears and I gasped, gazing to see Umbra struggling to open his eyes a third of the way. But, still, he continued to fight and amazingly, he smiled sweetly at me, but even that seemed quite painful for him. His lips began to quiver. A weak cough came out of his mouth, but he managed to form words and produced his velvet, gorgeous voice for me as I held him closer to my lap.

"I'm sorry I wasn't much help to you, but I'm so glad I got to know you. I . . . I need to tell you something though. It may be silly and pointless, but I need to. Stary . . . I . . ."

And he was gone. His voice, his pupils, his breathing, his precious glow . . . everything was gone. All that was in front of me was a husk of the man who stole my heart. Tears flowed from my eyes, not stopping for anything and I would never let them.

Umbra . . . my rival, my partner, my friend, my love . . . They all vanished away from me forever. I heard Maren crying above me and Cally called him a moron. The shock was slowly approaching my being, attacking me from every angle in every way.

I grabbed his left wrist tighter in my hand hoping to restart his spirit body by any means necessary, but I felt a tickling sensation wrapping around my fingertips like ivy vines. Surprised, I looked to see Umbra's arm was transforming into white speckles the size of confetti or baby angel feathers. They then lifted into the sky like little fireflies glowing white. But in a snap, they faded and blew into the wind, blending with its invisible grave, and his arm was no longer there.

Umbra was . . . dead. No . . . my heart was being stabbed with a million long blades. *No* . . . my body was so weak that I was about to black out with the touch of a sunray hitting my head. NO . . . the visions in my head, the memories flooding me like rushing waters and the feelings poked my skin until it was decaying beyond repair. The agony . . . the tears . . . it was worse than the physical pain I was feeling. My body felt like it was being ripped by the stems, an angel pulling at one end and a devil at the other.

I stared at that priceless face, the person I wanted to tell so many things to, learn so many things about, confess numerous things to . . . My emotions would never reach him. I rocked myself frantically, allowing the resentment to devour me, the mourning to swallow me whole and leave me bare. Umbra . . . Umbra . . . my Umbra. No, no, no . . . "*Nooooooooooooo!*" I screamed and cried so loudly that I made the entire ceiling shake.

A pulse, a driving force so mighty was controlling me. It felt sinful, but I knew in my soul it was not evil or awful like Cally's. It was regret, confidence, and acceptance. I was the Spirit Warrior. I would not focus on energy, but allow it to flow to me, to awaken me. I would open the door to my destiny and close the door of Cally's suffering. I would listen to that song that played in my heart that became a comfort to me when Umbra was near. He was my melody, my duet, my vibrations I lived by, and he always had been since I first gazed at him. I was ready to gain that all back and avenge what I held dear.

Infuriated, I glared at Cally. It was the most enraged I had ever been, but also the most set I ever had been. "You hurt Umbra . . . Umbra! I *won't* let him go!" I screamed again and a beautiful vibrating harmony that would have blended with any song was created in my tightened fist. A miniature white dwarf star with blazing rays was peeking through the gaps of my closed fingers, the warmth and magic entering my heart.

An alto-toned mocking entered my ears as I was focusing on the shining glowing flakes forming in my hands. I gazed up from my scowl, my eyes narrowing in rage toward the murderer who stole my life from me; I had nothing left to lose.

"That is too rich! Ha, ha, ha! You want to get nasty for a machine that was already dead . . . ha, ha! How pathetic! Like weak little you can do anything now . . . ha!" Cally sounded amused.

I refused to lose my focus. I scanned the room, looking for something as Cally was in her laughing fit. I needed to conduct a plan to touch her with the energy pounding in my palms. Then, I noticed it; the back corner of the lunchroom catty-corner from Cally. It was nothing special, but it hit me. The reason I couldn't beat Cally was because I was too nervous about messing up and being engulfed by multiple emotions.

Coach Loyal's voice entered my ears, soft and full of wisdom: *Stare at the corner wall and focus, dream of that area and tackle all the things in the way and then you can get to your destination.*

Saving everyone was my destination and the murderer was the evil obstacle I had to tackle. I allowed my eyes to swell up the image of the wall, ready to only stare at that corner as I made my move.

In control, I pointed my hands in a heavy, rigid swinging motion. The light crawled up my arms, absorbing into my skin, becoming a part of me, strengthening me with the goodness of light. Cally was still crackling maliciously so the timing was perfect; it was my only chance.

I could hear inspiring words flowing into my heart, words from the past Spirit Warriors. "Hold on to what if. Take that what if."

The light inside me grew, filling me with warmth and courage. It radiated through my bloodstream, numbing my injuries. Knowledge poured into me. I knew what to do. I ran forward, preparing my body to bend forward. The thrill, the temporary loss of gravity, the suspension in the air was ideal like an angel racing a 747 in the clouds. I did a perfect front flip, my body only looking at the wall as I allowed the light to invade my body with delight.

I heard Maren gasp from her chained prison, saying something that sounded like: "The aura of the ultimate Spirit Warrior."

My whole body began to glow a pure bright white, humming enchantingly like a flute and harp doing the world's most glorious duet. After three full, flawless front flips, I was at the corner wall and bounced off it, looking like a skateboarder in the air about to land a flip. I then landed on my feet to start another round of front flips.

At least all I had to do was avoid Cally reaching me with my new method. By the appearance on her face as I flew two feet above her head, my Spirit Warrior powers fueling my heightened abilities, I could tell she wasn't prepared in the least. I twirled gracefully in midair, my hair spinning around my neck like a ribbon. No matter how tired I knew I was or how hurt I sensed I was, the feelings never reached me. It continued for a countless amount of time: doing flips, jumping at the speed of sound around Cally, and her turning in fury for a chance to break my neck with a tap of her wrist. We looked like a funky dance of yin-and-yang colored light.

I ever so slowly got so into it that I taunted her a little, pausing with her out of breath reaction once to smile bitterly, adding in a dark tone, "You can't catch what you can't see."

Finally, bathing in a precious spotlight, I got my chance. I dug my fingernails deeply in the burning flesh of her side, the spot that my light was telling me I could release the evil from her with the spell of the Spirit Warriors. The look on Cally's face was crushed, horrified that I was able to kidnap her away from the murderer's clenching effect. But Cally . . . I gasped for the sense of humanity reached inside me, pulling my heartstrings for a time period. My fingers slipped a tad yet still kept their composure to block the murderer from escaping.

Cally . . . the sweet young girl was still glowing, breathing inside the murderer who used her body as a shell. I knew Cally was in a sense the murderer, but also not. She truly had two people inside her, both named Cally. My Cally was hiding in the back of her leaking heart, ready to give up. I didn't want to kill her. Maren once told me that once the evil was released that the good soul would be able to return . . . if it was strong enough. Water stung my eyes, tickling my eyelashes like dewdrops on a lotus blossom thinking Cally might not live. Another innocent life could be gone because I wasn't strong enough.

My glow began to dim . . . *No!* I had to keep it burning. I pressed my hands harder above the murderer's hips, but the quivering of my arms made Cally glance up, full of mocking joy.

"Please . . ." A faint whisper more pure and elegant than a white song bird caught my ears in delight attention, away from my doubt. It stopped the murderer from her dark, confident thrill ride. I adjusted my neck to gaze up at an angel glowing in a wholesome bright light but looking dimmer by each trivial moment. Above the murderer's head was Cally's being, her true, gentle, birth soul . . . or what was left of it.

Her eyes were intense, water petals flowing on her cheeks. Her hair whipped around like it was made of fire. Her forming smile mouthed, "thank you, my friend," and she crossed her heart after she said it.

"I have hurt so many people and I would rather be dead; it would cause me less pain. Please Miss Stary . . . DO IT!"

I stopped the choking balls forming in my throat, swallowing the need to cry for her. I had the drive in me as if Cally was flowing inside me. We would win. Together.

While evil Cally's mouth was agape and foaming from sheer surprise that Cally was alive, I charged my hands into her sides like she was made of water. She fought back, scratching my arm, clawing my wrists. I stared her down. I refused to lose. My aura entered her body like a sword and I chanted the spell my heart knew from memory although my mind didn't:

O malum unum cum tenebrarum repletus, sinos vestri ops flow in mihi et servatis esse. Ad mei impero tollis in caeli. Sum spiritus bellator et per vires Dei . . .

The last word, the final influential sound my lips made . . . it was frozen on the warmth of my face. The pride, the accomplishment . . . I had to make sure I didn't fail. I glanced at Umbra, lying like a perfect doll, his arm slowly disappearing into dust, but my love would never fade away. My eyes found Maren's next, my angel, my guardian, the missing fragment of my soul, showing me her beauty with a lighthearted face. I then looked at Chloe, staring in confusion, but allowing her praise of me to shine brighter than the moon. I then locked my gaze in front of me at Cally, my friend, and placed her gentle palm on top of mine. The blazing glow of her affection aided me in the final quest to vanquish the murderer. I had to protect them.

"*Solvo te!*" I yelled with all my being, tilting my head all the way back toward the gate of heaven. The evil light and light evil swirled in a whirlwind upward to the sky. The true Cally smiled one last time, mouthing, "thank you," before she vanished into a speck of light to the highest of the universe's clouds.

Evil Cally fought back with all her might, slapping the side of my face with her edged, eggplant-toned fingernails with a blazing force harder than steel against my flesh. The blood poured out like a waterfall and created a trail along my slender neck. Flying out of her shoulders were white and black swirls, twisting into the atmosphere like a clashing funnel. With each swirl spitting out at lightning speed, the host inside Cally's body was weakening, her hits on my sore cheek bone becoming less aggressive and soon, she was on her knees.

My hands refused to release themselves from her body . . . I had to completely get the darkness out no matter how much energy I needed to keep my light aglow. After a few minutes of intense concentration, little paper birds of black and white danced in the tornado we created. The murderer fell forward with a large, painful sounding thud, landing on her face with her hair spread across the floor.

Her body was limp and turned blacker by the second, starting with her head. Her hair looked like it was being attacked by heartless crows. The radiance of her pulsing evil skin was flashing like a declining heartbeat. Her self was disappearing into God's deciding hands.

Gasping, my hands did a free fall to my hips, slapping them intensely with a gusting force. My right knee twisted into an unbelievable and most uncomfortable motion that made standing closer impossible. Blood was coming out of my body like there was no tomorrow and in spots I didn't recall getting hit, staining the floor in a deep pattern.

I supposed I used too much energy and in an adrenaline rush, I felt the pain later at double the normal effect. The light from my activated Spirit Warrior powers were dimming into a smolder. Although they did not stop the pain or injuries themselves, I could feel that this light from God was what was keeping me alive from these wounds. Yet, none of that mattered for a powerful pulling control made me run to my lost love although my eyes said I was fooling myself, but there was something . . . He was moved over to the center pillar where he was at the start of the battle.

"Umbra!" I screamed out of breath while running towards him. Tripping every step of the way, my trashed body didn't stop me because Umbra was laying there on the white tile, a dark swan on speckled snow, and the pieces of his arm were returning into their rightful place like a puzzle. As I got closer, I noticed his stunning deep as the core of the cosmos brown eyes were opened as I adjusted to the dazzling hues of the lights fluttering above us.

"Umbra!" I called again, that time more delicate because my breath was failing me. As he heard my call, he carefully lifted his head up to see me stupidly running and tripping toward him. A solemn look of confusion, peace, and warmth stretched on the vast universe of his glorious face, his spirit living face. At last, I reached him, sliding hard on my knees to get as close to him without falling. The sting from the pain may not have been worth it and I was pretty sure I heard the side of my jeans rip.

I bent down, placing my nails into the material of my jeans to not fall for Umbra was hardly able to prop himself up. Umbra blinked very slow like he was trying to figure out what was happening and to get used to the light entering his eyes.

"Umbra . . . ," I whispered, about five inches from his princely face. It made me feel like I was his wife waking him up from a peaceful nap. That thought made my face flush, but thank goodness Umbra mumbled and then showed me his nearly stable eyes.

Although he was still weak, his breathtaking eyes said everything he needed to: "Congratulations. You looked idiotic tripping towards me. I'm sorry I scared you. I forgive you for the Credence thing; I'll eliminate him later. And thank you."

He allowed me the honor of seeing his warm smile. It was so beautiful that I knew all the stars in heaven would not have been close to its worth and I knew that the fluttering butterflies his look gave me would never fade. Shaking, his hand lifted to my smooth cheek and stroked it lightly, my veins burning with intensity. I wanted to hide under a rock with how embarrassed I was, but I also wanted the power to stop time and replay the act for all eternity.

His enchanting lips began to form moisture, making them healthy and vibrant again. His elbows tucked underneath his body a little, making me lean back by impulse to give him room. Though he was still trembling, his hand stayed on my cheek, but then he brushed it with his palm in delicate motions, making me feel special. My heart felt like it would explode.

"Stary . . . ," he said in the sweetest and softest tone I had ever heard from his deep, soul-jerking voice. The gaze he gave me, the melting smile he saved for me was more than anything I could ever ask for. He was safe. All the people I loved were safe and I could live with that forever.

"You did it . . ." Those simple, magical words broke what I was containing inside me loose.

"OH!" I cried and flung my arms around Umbra; his eyes grew three times their expected size.

I hugged his broad chest, feeling the glow of his skin, the lovely sound of his ghostly heartbeat, and the happiness inside him. He was free and I was home. There was no way to describe that comfort, that warmth, that magic. Umbra's arms . . . It was like Dr. Rowe made them just for me. Tears flowed from my eyes, cooling the feverish heat between us. But for once, they were tears of the everlasting joy despite the fact of how worn out I was.

"Ouch . . ." I heard above me, quickly looking to see Umbra's face was leaning hard on the edge of the pillar, his eyes shut and face tense. I must have been too excited to realize how bad he was injured. I felt very stupid.

Blushing madly, I loosened my grip a hair and slid back a foot so he could scoot closer away from the pillar. "Oh . . . I'm sorry . . . ," I squeaked with embarrassment as I covered my mouth as my face became redder, red enough to be seen in the tile.

Umbra held his side, fixing his position to get more comfortable. He groaned a little, but tried to give me a satisfied, manly stare. "It's okay . . . I suppose some men are babies when girls tackle them . . ."

My mind grinned with pleasure at the rude comment. That was without a doubt Umbra!

For a second, I dug my head into his shirt, whispering into his chest where his heart would have been, hoping it would ring inside him. My sobbing blended into a harmony with my truthful words. "I would be lost if anything happened to you . . ." I heard Umbra gasp deeply, his temperature climbing like a rocket.

I looked up at him and was about to let go completely when he placed his strong hands over my wrists and pushed me forward, making me land face first into his chest again. That made me redder than a cardinal, having my lips only a few centimeters away from his flawless skin. I glanced up for a moment to see him staring down at me, his eyes narrow and challenging. His face seemed to be red as well. It appeared to be he was trying to be sexy. I blushed harder and concentrated on his breathing, soothing me to the bone, not ready to be prey again.

Comfortable again, I hugged him tightly, still being careful, praying my feelings would reach his loving and beautiful heart. He moved his right hand off my waist and began to smooth my untamed jungle of hair, breathing onto my skin to send goose egg size chills up my spine.

"Stary . . ." he whispered again, the same as before. Umbra was just right and I felt perfect being in his arms, even though I felt like I was not allowed.

I laid there for a few more counts of a beat, memorizing everything about the blissful occasion, the little flower that bloomed in the ash of a destroyed world. I noticed Umbra had a smell to him . . . It reminded me of lumber. I supposed it rubbed off on him from fighting. I nudged my body upward a little bit to allow the stirring feeling to swell me. Sadly, I bumped Umbra's nose and immediately went back to my original spot, feeling busted.

I could see him gazing at me through my hair and his face, his priceless face, was focused, but kind; the most handsome look ever born. He wanted something. He was bending his face down to mine, his cheeks flushed. My heartbeat was so loud that I could hear nothing else and all I could do was gaze at Umbra's hypnotizing whirlpools called eyes. The song that was a part of me, the song that was now telling me it was created from my love from Umbra, was beating into madness, the pressure of the moment too much for it. I didn't need it to tell me how I felt anymore and I had Umbra's heartbeat and breathing to be my comfort song for the rest of time. The person you're meant for is the one you're willing to change for but don't have to. We accepted each other, faults, differences, and all. We wouldn't be in this state if that wasn't true.

I didn't deserve him near me like that. His gorgeous lips were drawing nearer to mine. It wasn't the time or the place no matter how weak in the knees he made me feel, no matter how much I craved for a moment like that, no matter how much . . . I loved him. He held me tighter but bent my back more so my face was tilted upward to stare at him, my lips about three inches away from him. Umbra and I were opposites, but a force was pulling us like magnets . . .

"I do not mean to be rude, but could someone get me down . . . please?" A harp-like hum hit our ears. Something was speaking to us, something pretty and familiar: *Maren!*

Panicked, Umbra and I let go instantly, me almost ramming him into the pillar again. I stood up in a rush, running to the side to see Maren, grinning and blushing a little. Had she seen? Did she know? That didn't matter; I had to get her down! My mind felt like it was frothing . . . Then an idea hit me like a tool box cracking my skull. I could use my spirit powers. I had more energy. I thought of the dazzling grace of the light inside me and in mere seconds, my hands were glowing brightly again and I jumped up to the pillar where Maren was at.

On autopilot, my hand looped under the center where a heart-shaped, ink-colored lock was. It was covered in off gold snakes with large fangs, apparently binding the chain mess together. I closed my eyes and allowed magic to fill my being, the feeling projecting itself into my hands.

"*Solvo*," I whispered gently and the chains fell to the ground of the platform then disappeared into the darkness.

Maren was overwhelmed with delight and jumped up to hug me close. "THANK YOU STARY! Are you okay? I did not hurt you more did I, love? Look at your cuts . . . Oh gracious!" she said like a child getting candy for the first time; her hyper tone the same, but her mood ever changing like the wind. I tried to calm her down by waving my hands and allowing her to look me over from head to toe.

Her eyes then turned enthralling like a princess. "I thank you from the bottom of my heart Stary, my darling friend . . ."

I hugged her warmly back. Sweet Maren . . .

I would be lost without you too, my heart whispered, feeling she would get the message. We both looked at each other and giggled, holding hands as we floated down to Umbra, who was now able to stand on his own and was dusting his pant leg off.

While Maren went sprinting off to embrace Umbra, I heard the shattering of glass in the distance behind me and a group of confused voices. I whirled around to see Chloe and her class all there, looking around frantically. Chloe was the only one on the ground, blinking fast and gazing at Barbara in her arms. A wave of panic showed on her face.

"Chloe!" I called with a grin on my face, my heart racing. Relief, utter, faithful, and soothing relief was all I was feeling as I looked at my peers. Thank the Lord no one was hurt.

I reached her, my pain getting to be familiar in the components of my body. Chloe glanced at my face, looking up at my shoulders before it dawned on her that this whole situation was real.

"Stary! What happened? I have no *clue* how I got here, but . . . never mind that! LOOK AT YOU! You're bleeding everywhere and I *hate* blood! What happened?" Her beautiful river-colored eyes were overflowing with fret, but I had to smile at her.

However, I hadn't thought of getting my injuries checked out, let alone explaining them. I hated lying because it made me feel rotten and I was horrible at it, but I couldn't exactly tell them the truth especially since my classmates didn't recall any of the sights they had witnessed (not that I was complaining there).

I giggled nervously as I rubbed the back of head. "Oh, you know me. I just had another clumsy moment, except this time it was a bit more major . . ." I chuckled nervously.

Chloe looked at me with hardly any emotion, blank, totally lost. I had seen that look when we had to write in English class. I glanced down at Barbara and nudged my head to get Chloe on a new topic. It worked too well. She flipped out again. "OH! Barbara! I have no idea how she got here. Stary, Barbara's, I mean . . . will she be okay?"

I bent down. Chloe caught sight of my exposed knee in horror, but I focused on Barbara so she didn't say anything. I checked her pulse; it was a little slow, but still close enough to the safety zone from what my mother, who was a nurse, taught me. Her skin was still as pale as paper, her lips cracked, and her eyes glued shut. However, I had a good vibe that she was going to be fine after a good rest. Hopefully, she would never recall anything and she would return to the normal, snotty Barbara we all "adored." I brushed a dark brown curled bang from out of her eyes and took off her glasses, placing them in her jacket pocket.

I looked up, grinning at Chloe to ask her for a favor. "Chloe, could you please take Barbara to the nurse? I know she'll be fine after a good rest, but she does need to be looked at right away. Maybe nicely ask one of the older guys to help you."

Surprised by my take control attitude, Chloe nodded with her mouth opened like a tunnel for a toy train set and asked two of the more athletic junior boys to carry Barbara. As she was leaving, Chloe looked at me with worried and heart pulling eyes that made me feel guilty for lying. I smiled, giving her a powerful fist pose, and mouthing, "thank you," to my best friend. She walked to me swiftly, tracing her fingers carefully in the inside of my hand to make sure not to touch my cuts and beamed, giving my hand a gentle squeeze. Her eyes that pierced me told me to get checked out later. Before I could react, she went skipping off to aid Barbara.

I knew then I was truly blessed. I glanced back to see a smugly smiling Umbra with his healing arm around Maren's tiny shoulder. She was smiling as brightly as a new day. I looked farther back to see the murderer, almost nonexistent, and Cally's body so faded that the spell was only spitting out baby pill size specks of black evil.

Maren and Umbra looked back at the murderer as well, the reason our fates were intermingled and our lives and afterlives forever changed. Without gazing at us, Maren tranquilly said, "This chapter of our lives is almost complete . . ."

So engulfed by the grace of our words, I didn't realize right away that it wasn't only an end to all the hurting evil, but the end of our story. Umbra and I looked at each other at the same time, his eyes huge. Fear entered my heart and the sea of sorrow buried was rising, soon to flood and sink me again. I was locked onto his gaze that was reading the same emotions I was. It was too late. Umbra and I . . . would never see each other again.

The bell for fourth hour homeroom started to ring, but I stood there, locked in dread. Had it been only forty minutes since I darted to save Umbra? I knew I wasn't going to class since Mrs. Nodeon would send me to the nurse due to all my outrageous injuries and I was sure Umbra and Maren had a lot to prepare before going to heaven. I ducked my head down, not caring if anyone was coming. The bell continued to ring, sending the horrid echoes in my heart: *Time's up.*

22

THE NIGHT AIR WAS CRISP AND CLEAR, LEAVING A CLEAN FEELING. The stars shone, winking their praise as we stood under them, their comforting, glowing blanket guiding us into eternity. The moon was half-clouded, reflecting my feelings on Maren and Umbra's departure. The night itself was beautiful, pure, like all the negative energy in the world was gone. It made me feel blessed like the feeling one gets hearing a baby's first laugh. A light breeze grazed my cheeks, chilling me to the core although my skin was scorching. The only thing out of place was the decaying red-like colored farm that was behind us, about twenty-five feet, I presumed.

"Maren . . . ?" I asked.

She was twirling in the grass like a ballerina, humming some happy melody, on occasion singing "dreams come true."

"I'm a little confused on why we're here at this spot." The question was legit for it was around nine at night. Umbra and Maren told me to ask my parents if I could sleep over at Chloe's and they accepted with blank stares, not questioning my injuries. I remember eyeballing Maren and Umbra suspiciously after my parents' zombie-like agreement, but they dragged me away before I could ponder it.

Maren blinked a few times, leaning her ears towards me to make sure she wasn't imagining me speaking. Cutely, she spun on her heels with her pale, fragile fingers behind her back and answered, "Because Stary, once the murderer is gone, we get to go to heaven, but the gate opens in the spot where we took our last breath and since spirits cannot keep their forms in space for more than a day, we have to be directly under our location."

She pointed upward to the moon and the cluster of stars by them. I was curious if God had told them. It amazed me how fate had brought us together in my hometown of Plantersville.

"My grandfather's ship had top notch security. Once Cally came in, the alarms sounded. I am sure as soon as they possibly could have, the director of Grandfather's Hoshi Project sent troops to see what was happening. For a reason I do not know, Cally took my body and buried me deep within your school. So, this field we are standing on is directly under where I died and east of your school, like the rising sun, where I was buried.

Umbra and I are partners, so he will go with me here. This is where we must await the gate into our heaven."

I nodded and stepped backward, right in line with Umbra, who had his arms crossed in his signature pose and was looking off into the unknown distance of the field. Although we were about six feet apart, I felt like the moon could fit in the distance between us. Umbra didn't want to talk to me, but I knew he wasn't upset with me. I felt sorrow pulsing from him, but my heart was shattering so loudly that my feelings were probably incorrect.

I glanced once at his stone set face as he observed the planet he had once fought to live on and also fought to forever leave. His eyes were as black as coal again, glassed over with a super thin layer of honey brown. I felt friction. Maybe Umbra noticed it too because he glared at me questionably. I jerked my eyes away, staring in the opposite direction.

While Maren continued to dance in the bathing glows of the moon that created the rightful spotlight for the princess, I recalled the rest of the afternoon after I defeated Cally.

The bell had rang when Maren and Umbra had to go on their way to heal Umbra's wounds. I had stood there, my mouth zipped shut with imaginary glue. Maren had been sparkling and smiling with full glory, but Umbra had looked confused and depressed. Maren had to drag him around like an old blanket.

I didn't remember moving, but I ended up in Mrs. Nodeon's room after all and had the honor of everyone staring at me like I was an experiment gone wrong. Poor Mrs. Nodean shrilled so loudly, the tower of books by her desk almost collapsed!

I was huffing by the time I got to the nurse, leaning on the icy doorframe to comfort my blazing skin. She was in a panic, screaming for someone to call 911 as she ran around her office. As I struggled to reassure her, I saw a hand behind the nurse's head, an ectoplasm hand. It went inside the back of her head. She froze, her eyes becoming glassy. When the hand disappeared through the wall, the nurse smiled wide at me and in a sugary voice, told me, "There is no need to call 911 Stary. I apologize for overacting. I will do the best I can to fix you up here babe."

I stood there, stunned. As she led me in the office, I saw Umbra leaning against the wall in the corner, his arms crossed. He waved his hand at me, winked, then flew through the wall. My mind began to reel, thinking Umbra just went into my nurse's mind like he did with mine! Before I could fret over it, the nurse grabbed my arm and let me lean on her.

Barbara had been in the only bed, sleeping, so I had been taken care of in a rolling chair. She fixed my knee first, trying to hide her disgusted expression, but she wrapped it tightly in a white cover and told me I would probably have to wait six weeks for all the skin to grow back.

Right after she had put rubbing alcohol on the many cuts on my leg, my dad came barging in the door like a madman escaping from prison. His humble breath buzzed like a ward of bees. He looked at me from head to toe, his eyes becoming whiter and I was scared he would need the chair more than me.

First, he had bombarded me with questions, mostly about how I was feeling, but then he asked the question I had been dreading: "How did this happen?" For my classmates, saying I fell big time was perfect, but it wasn't going to cut it for my daddy. As the nurse smoothed my cracked elbows with some sort of glossy lotion, I told him I was in the bathroom, getting ready to wash my hands when there was a small puddle of water in front of it that I didn't see in time and I slipped, banged my knee against the pipe, and slid forward into the wall, body first. He looked at me amazed and angry at the same time, but later when he asked my Spanish teacher, she backed up my tale and gave me a secret wink. I was so lucky I went to her.

During the battle and walking up to homeroom, I didn't feel the pain that much. Now, as I was being treated, I felt it a lot! My knee was wrapped so tightly that I saw it pulsing up and down to break loose. The white bandage over my knee had to be changed twice because it was soaking the blood into a lake that reminded me of an old Japanese horror film. By the third one, it was slowing down quite a bit. My back was killing me with sharpness. I could barely bend a third of the way down, but I argued this, telling everyone that I was never able to touch my toes anyway. My eyes were twitching, vibrating worse than a seismic activity. It felt like I stayed up for three days straight, staring at the lights of a computer screen. I was fortunate that my rib was not broken, but it needed to be closely monitored.

All of my many cuts (I lost count after about 32) stung from the alcohol like hornets were injected into each mark just for me. The oddest thing was on the left side of my forehead. I had a huge red and puffy knot that hurt insanely every time I blinked. I had to put ice and warm water on it off and on for nearly a half hour to make the swelling go down. Of course, I had to go to the doctor right after school as well and watch my mom hyperventilate from distress. My dad refused to leave me and tried hard to calm me down although I was fine and I had to stroke his hand numerous times to reassure him. He rewarded me with a shy smile every time. I was just so grateful I could hold his hand and see my mother's face still . . .

"I cannot believe we are almost there!"

I snapped back into reality, hearing Maren's childlike and beautiful sweet voice blending into the air. I wanted to answer, but all I could do was smile. It was swallowed by the depths of my despair and the power of Maren's larger-than-life grin. My hands were locked behind my aching back, my fingers tangling with each other to form a chain to contain my exploding emotions.

I could only stare at the ground, the blades of grass swaying in perfect harmony, seeming to slow their growing, stopping time in their movements. I could see Umbra looking forward, but not really seeing anything in the cosmic space circling us. How handsome he was. I caught sight of him rubbing his left arm, his eyes flickering with confusion. He set his eyes on Maren and automatically turned around.

"Man! Why does my arm tingle so much? Strange! I swear it's shorter too," he said, his voice angry.

My face heated up like the wick of a lit oil lamp and Maren smiled coyly, hiding her knowledge like I did. Maren whispered to me before she and Umbra left school that he wouldn't remember anything that happened to him when he started disappearing into the wind. Still, I was so embarrassed that he noticed.

Suddenly, a strong wind began to blow, its delightful whispers landing in our hair. A bright golden light soared across the dazzling universe above like a comet. It flashed from the size of the sun into tiny, twirling stars with lovely shines that belonged solely to them. The children of hope that graced the world at night spun in circles, forming a line to where Maren was, directly under the moon.

Maren lifted her china doll white hands to the heavens, allowing the stardust to slip through her slender fingers like rainfall. With a focused face that formed a caring smile, Maren nodded, making her gorgeous eyes sparkle more. At her gesture, the stars scattered a few more feet above, forming two groups, each with six in them.

Then, the two groups each did a darling dance, forming a rapid circle of golden thread it seemed. They were humming a piercing song that echoed inside my hollow soul. Quickly and without warning, a bright light bathed in white glory came from each of the groups for only a mere second and then they were replaced by two flawless, beautiful crowns.

My mind was stuck on the wonders of the heavenly world and how much Maren and Umbra deserved them. I was happy for them, thrilled, but my selfish earthly attachments didn't want to let these two amazing people I had grown to love in just the past month go. Maren turned to face Umbra and I. We were frozen in our positions as her dress spun in an ocean wave of wonder.

She lifted her finger up like a teacher and explained, more than likely for my benefit. "When we wear the crowns, the gates to heaven will open above us, and we will get the ability to fly that high. I suppose they are like a key card here. Once we are at the gate, we will be greeted by the attendant of the Angel Counsel and given wings. Later, once we step through the gate, the crowns will become our halos. That is what the angels working in purgatory told us before we were allowed to track down our murderer."

I took a small step forward, my mouth slightly agape, to get a better look at those splendors called crowns. They looked like they were made of solid gold, the kind that could never be damaged unless burned. They shone brighter than the morning sun scorching on the hottest day of the year and they were beautifully engraved with a pair of detailed angel wings. The points at the top were simple, but made to perfection, having six on each crown, and a small sphere on top of each tip. Once Maren and Umbra wore their fitting creations of the stars, they would disappear out of my life forever and be granted eternal happiness.

I stepped back, unable to look into Umbra's heart grabbing eyes. Maren's expression changed as she gazed at me with her crystal wonders. I smiled as warmly as I could, plastering the feeling on my face as I nudged at the crowns to tell her how beautiful I thought they were. Maren's face wrinkled up slightly and her eyes looked misty. She ran, flinging her delicate arms around me. The hug felt like it lasted forever.

"Thank you so much for everything Stary. You are so wonderful and I will solemnly miss you. Please continue to shine and not forget me."

Maren . . . my angel, one of my best friends, my sister . . . My dear, sweet Maren. I hugged her tightly back, smoothing her hair to calm her cracked voice. I didn't want to let her kind spirit be trapped in sorrow like mine when she was jubilant to move on to her rightful place.

I whispered full of pure honesty into our embrace. "Maren, you are the best friend I have ever had or could have ever asked for. I could never forget you and I'm glad I could help. Promise to be happy like you deserve to be up in heaven." There was so much more I wanted to say to her, to both of them, but my heart was breaking because I knew the end was near and I could never speak that many words in a thousand life times.

Maren let go of me, her tears disappearing into the thrilling sky as she beamed so beautifully that the crowns could never compare. I could feel Umbra's eyes on me then, touched by my treatment toward his dear Maren. Yet, I only turned a centimeter before he noticed and turned away. Time seemed to freeze as Maren stood at the line between us, pondering how it could be so thick when nothing was really there.

Maren walked toward the direction where Umbra was and pushed him hard in the shoulder, ramming him with a jab of her fist. "I will go retrieve the crowns," Maren said as she skipped and partway floated to the spotlight.

I was shocked beyond belief she did that and Umbra couldn't control his clumsy movement as he bumped shoulders with mine. Our blades touched, static forming between them, but like the same magnets, they bounced off each other. We both just stayed there, embarrassed.

It was over. My destiny was complete, my fate as a Spirit Warrior done. Maren was in the sky, almost in reach of the crowns and Umbra was jiggling his feet like he needed to go, the aura of heaven too strong to ignore much longer. I tilted my head in his direction, wanting more than anything to look him in the face. I was craving to tell him all the feelings that were overflowing into my heart. But all I could do was stare at the lush, dumb grass.

"Goodbye . . . ," I whispered so softly that I wasn't sure even a fairy could hear my sorrowful words. The wind picked up, a piece of his hair brushing his face. Umbra stood up straighter but did not respond.

I leaned my head up to stare at Umbra one last time, no matter how much it hurt my destroyed heart. Dirt was circling our feet like magic, swirling up into the air. I was able to somewhat look at his profile, but he turned away from me out of the blue. I was caught, silent, as rushing streams of tears dampened my cheeks. I must have looked utterly stupid and horrible. Umbra only looked at me with fiery eyes, melting our connection to each other even further.

As fast as I could, I turned around to face my shadow so he couldn't stare at me any longer, so I couldn't burden him any more with my presence. Invisible strings were keeping me in my spot. I could still feel his eyes tracing the outline of my head, the lines of silk that made up my hair. In a second, I heard his feet shuffling, moving away from me for all time. The world was slowing down with him.

I couldn't let it end like this! No matter how hard it was, no matter how much agony I had to go through for the rest of my breathing life, I had to show Umbra how I felt. He was and always was going to be my first precious love.

Without realizing what I was doing or thinking, I reached Umbra, grabbed his shoulders to make him halt, spun him around to gaze only at me, and threw my arms tightly around him to land my lips on his. With all my passion, I told him I loved him through my first kiss.

And the world just stopped. I felt the ground shattering below me and felt like I was floating to heaven myself. All that was able to keep me grounded was him, my Umbra. And at the same time, he was making me insane with over-the-brim happiness. I knew I shocked him for his eyes were massive in size, but soon, he adjusted and kissed me back with the same tenderness. I then closed my eyes, relaxing that he was accepting me.

Kissing a spirit was interesting. I could breathe through our kiss and I didn't feel his lips, just the pressure of warm air. But, it was full of Umbra's feelings. His kiss told me everything: that he accepted me, that he wanted to be with me, but was heartbroken he had to leave and . . . he loved me too, just as much.

Time picked up again. I had to destroy my perfect world, shatter my heart by releasing my lips from his and let Umbra find eternal peace. However, when I let go and began to turn away, he grabbed me so fast that I got dizzy.

His hands were firm on my back and I was unable to escape his embrace. I was forced to look into his unfathomable eyes, burning with fire and what looked like anger. His eyes were calling my name, speaking to me in an unknown tongue, and they whispered in his grand voice, '*How dare you think you can leave me?*' He pushed me into him hard, kissing me lovingly, refusing to let go.

I was surprised but only for a few milliseconds before I let the feeling of our own personal planet engulf me. It tingled my body. I wasn't sure how long we were kissing sincerely and passionately, perhaps for many minutes, but I could and would do it forever. It was my first kiss with my true love and although it was different from most girls, I wouldn't dream of it being any other way. I was ready to give up everything to be with Umbra.

It was like all the sourness of the real world turned sweet and all the evil became pure in the game called life. Umbra . . . he was my healer, my strength, my weakness; he was a part of me. No embarrassment hit me, no feelings of regret or nervousness, but joy filled my body that was glowing for only Umbra as we continued to kiss. I could see his peaceful, striking face in my mind although my eyes were sealed in his tenderness; we were truly, deeply, madly connected.

Please Lord, let this feeling last forever, I pleaded. Lord . . . God . . . Umbra had to leave soon. The fear made me grab the back of his priceless head tighter, my fingers trembling as they wrapped a few of Umbra's darling curls around them to keep the threads that bonded us together.

A small golden light hit my closed eyelids from above Umbra's head, sending my senses into alert. I swore I heard a crisp sounding sigh within the light's glory. I supposed it was a sign from our divine God that he had to go. I forced myself not to cry by pressing my lips harder against his.

I felt his lips curl up into a smile as we kissed and he stroked my cheek, kissing me so sweetly and warmly that I almost fainted in his arms from the heat. I stopped my fear. I was in his arms at that point and in my heart, no, my whole self, knew I would always love Umbra. He would take a part of my heart with him. In a few seconds, I would let go and release him into his eternal paradise.

The passion, the adoring and indescribable love in my kiss was getting warmer and it almost made me blush from the fire. It felt like Umbra was blushing too, so much that it was merging into my cheeks . . . Wait. I had never *felt* Umbra blush like that. It almost felt . . . alive. I rubbed away the thought and traced Umbra's face so I could forever feel the blaze and brilliance of the moment.

My hand felt the smoothness of his cheeks right away . . . That was also odd. True, I could feel Umbra and Maren, but it felt more like rubbery gel and my fingers took a few seconds to adjust to find the surface. The glow from Umbra's face was still locked onto my lips and they were burning up, almost like a fever. My lips started to quiver as I felt pressure. It was tender, soft, and elegant, but it was real pressure on my own lips and I could no longer breathe.

Struggling for air and to beat Umbra's deity-like strength, I somehow found a way to push myself away from him. I had to lean my hands on his chest for support as his arms still braced my back. I only allowed myself to catch my breath for an instant before gazing up, wide-eyed in wonder at a confused and somewhat hurt Umbra.

His face . . . his face was . . . real! It had real flesh. The magic was spreading downward to his shoulders like refreshing snowfall.

By a miracle, I found the might to stand up straight. "Um-Umb-Umbra! Your face!"

Puzzled, he tilted his head to look at me, not sure if I was mocking him or honestly shocked. Hesitantly, he lifted his fingers to feel his cheeks and instantly, his eyes widened. Umbra stroked every corner on his perfect face.

He tried to form words, but everything was coming out as funny sounds or short breaths. He was acting like he was in a foreign world and unable to find comfort when it was right in front of him. I supposed he was having trouble feeling his face like I used to. He looked at me in amazement, but then a firefly ball of light, like the ones at our gnome friend's house, circled Umbra's arms, tangling them in a spider web of dazzling wonder. His fingers began to form flesh as well. Umbra was locked on the transformation crawling up him like an ant army.

The golden light above us was blinding and flickering between sky blue, pure white, and flawless gold. The fireballs of light then circled around his feet like the wings of Hermes's shoes and lifted him directly into the transformed large egg-shaped formation of splendor in the sky. My eyes sparkled with astonishment. Was Umbra leaving me? It sure looked like it with the fantastic phenomenon I was witnessing. But all I could do was absorb the enchantment of the lights' dancing spell as Umbra's head leaned back, his eyes closing, appearing to be in a sudden but peaceful slumber.

A beautiful humming was escaping the creation, soothing my ears. The egg began to turn, blazes of dodge blue flames whipping the air like streamers that covered the night, blending with the loveliness of the stars. Abruptly, the light parted like a sea, looking like fluttering wings, and branched out behind a sleeping Umbra, lowering him to the ground before vanishing like feathers in the breeze of heaven.

I ran to Umbra's side. He was standing there, staring at his fingertips and down to his genuine looking pant legs. I stopped dead in my tracks once I got a few inches from him, engrossed in the same expression, swallowing the fear I once had.

"Umbra! Are you okay?" I asked, pausing for a moment to catch my breath and get a good look at him. It was Umbra all right with the exact same handsome and gallant looks, but he was a . . . human! He coughed, holding his chest as I smiled slowly—lungs! Umbra had to breathe so not only was he human, but he became a live one at that!

Umbra stared at his hands again, smoothing his oil black hair and feeling the point of his spikes he formed on the back of his neck. He then gazed at me, his eyes in a trance, but sparkling with pure excitement of the unknown. "Stary . . . I'm . . ."

With a large smile controlling my face, I stiffened so I wouldn't cry from joy for him. "You're human . . . ," I breathed.

Umbra nodded confidently, his mouth open as he looked around, like he was holding the wonder in his brown eyes for the first time. Finally, after allowing the wind to brush the edges of his hair, he turned to me suavely. "But . . . how?"

A breathtaking giggle reached our ears at the same time and we turned to see Maren floating toward us, her smile tender and engaging. She closed her eyes once she reached us. Her hands were tucked neatly behind her dress like she was a child not wanting to contain a secret of something they had accomplished. "You look very good like that Umbra."

Umbra parted his legs farther apart, digging them into the ground for solid support. He blocked me from reaching Maren, but I could still see her glowing face fine . . . wait. Her glow. The outer blue line she and Umbra had to show they had the same murderer . . . it was flickering like a dying light bulb.

Umbra, in a thick but controlled voice, asked, "Maren, what did you do?"

Maren smiled again, purring for a mere moment before answering, "I saw you two kissing right before I was in reach of the crowns. My heart sank at the sight. Your shine was so dazzling and it would soon be crushed. So I looked at both crowns and an idea crossed my mind: if one crown has all the might to send a spirit to heaven, combining the power of both must have the power of a miracle. So I placed the crowns on top of each other, whispered my wish to make you human, and threw them above you."

Her voice was so wholesome and caring, not having any regret at all that it made my heart sink. I made her do such a risky and rash thing. I wanted to embrace her, but Umbra was so appalled that he was having a fit, his arms flinging around like an enraged crow. His voice did so many different frequencies that I thought my ears would explode.

"But . . . what? Maren! You . . . you . . . you can't do that! I mean . . . no one has ever combined the power of two crowns or made a spirit human again. It . . . it . . . could be . . . forbidden! You could get in trouble. And now . . . you . . ." Umbra's voice became soft and gentle as he hid his face in distress. "Now . . . you won't be able to go to heaven and you'll be stuck here for eternity . . ."

"NO!" I cried, flinging myself forward, trying to reach Maren, but Umbra blocked me. I looked at her with heartrending eyes, squeezing my fist to contain my hurt. I wanted Umbra with me more than anything, but not like that.

"I don't want you to be a wandering spirit because of me!" I screamed in anguish, my shoulders heaving.

Maren patted my hand and smiled tenderly, telling me it was all right. I stepped back, hugging my aching chest tightly to control the panic building inside me. Maren, who deserved to be an angel more than anyone, was never going to be one because of the selfish spell of love.

She lowered Umbra's arm, pressing it downward like he was a stuck machine. "I had to do it. Umbra found something here that he would have never found in heaven: love. And I will gladly walk on Earth for eternity as long as I see that happiness." She nudged toward me and I became as red as a cherry.

Umbra shook madly, worse than any volcano, his eyes darting at the ground, fists pounding into his pants. "Why . . . why don't you ever . . . think about yourself . . . ?" He questioned, dampness and pain building in his luscious eyes.

Her fists pounded into her sides as she answered Umbra's question with fixed eyes. "I *was* thinking of myself!"

Umbra snapped out of his regretful state and gazed up into Maren's shaking pools of water. She crossed her arms like Umbra usually did, trying to act all cool as she groaned to look tough, her flute-like voice becoming rugged. "If we were in heaven, you would be sad without Stary and I do not think I could stare at your pitiful face for all eternity. Plus, when Stary enters heaven, she might have moved on away from you and then you would never recover." She then opened one eye to see Umbra's childlike face, looking like he just saw the zoo for the first time. My words were locked inside as I felt Maren's loving vibe, touched by her amazing graces.

A zoom echoed across the sky, breaking the sound barrier, swallowing a hole into the cosmos. A long cloud came overhead, the length of about six mansions. It was black, but lovely shaped, looking almost invisible to the mortal eye in the night sky. Thunder was trapped inside the cloud, the waves bouncing off every inch like a drum. Small clumps of light lined the inner edges of the vast creation like lightning sizzling in its own personal room. A roaring rhythm entered my ears, rumbling my heart. I could have sworn that it sounded like Maren's name.

Maren replied, looking astonished. Her face tightened a little in unexpected fright. She bent down on one knee, full of devotion, looking like she was proposing. She gazed up at the cloud with love, praise, and respect. "Sa-Sav-Savior . . ."

Savior? I noticed a shuffling movement beside me from the corner of my eyes. I cocked my head to see Umbra bending down as well in the same adoring and elegant position as Maren. He arched his hand handsomely in front of his stomach and closed his eyes like he was a knight ready to receive a blessing from his king before going off to battle. Could it be?

"My Lord," Umbra whispered, smooth and full of faith. Lord? Lord as in *the* Lord, my Savior, my God? The bewilderment I was feeling, the shock scattered through my body, and the honor that was reaching my brain was overpowering. I was in the presence of the Lord. I couldn't believe it! I supposed that was a privilege of being a Spirit Warrior. Umbra nudged me with his elbow hard, nodding toward the ground. It took a second to register, but I nodded in realization and kneeled like Umbra and Maren.

"Please stand Maren, my daughter." A voice with the power of thunder and the glory of hope filled the night as he spoke. Maren stood, but Umbra and I stayed still, lowering our heads to not intrude on their conversation, but we still watched in admiration. Since the cloud was directly over Maren's head, a wind graced her stringy blonde hair, making me see the Lord wanted to speak to her.

"Maren Crystal Rowe, I have not seen any one of my children in a long time be so compassionate and loving towards others not only in his or her life on Earth but also in his or her afterlife. I am truly touched by your commitment to your friends, your love, and your faith in me."

Maren's face was bashful, the color of a red rose. He continued his praise of her, "I have an offer for you Maren, my child. I understand you cannot grant entry into my kingdom due to you giving up your crown for two people you hold dearly in your heart and you know that we follow the rules to the letter in heaven. However . . . your kindness is too pure and inspirational to ignore. So, I will give you an entryway on my cloud if you join the Angel Counsel."

Maren gasped, her hands covering her mouth in shock. Her eyes were moving to the swaying of God's silver wind of opportunity. I tilted my head an inch to the left, trying to hide my confusion and curiosity, but my beloved sensed it, holding my hand with his free hand. He knew what I wanted.

Umbra answered my question in a hushed voice, "The Angel Counsel is like a government system that helps the Lord with maintaining the rules and they're in charge of different categories. The most loyal and kind hearted of His people get seated in the counsel if they want and can stay there as long as they want. It is an unbelievable honor and if Maren accepts, she will be one of the youngest angels in the counsel."

What an astounding honor! Tears welled in my eyes and glowing respect hummed in my heart. Maren not only got to go to heaven after all, but got a grand position that she deserved. I knew she would succeed beyond expectations.

Umbra and I stood up as Maren stood up straighter as well, her eyes swallowing her face, cheeks blazing like a campfire. Maren began to tremble like she was wet from a shower and stuck in a winter snowstorm. I could see the gears in her mind were wheeling at an immeasurable rate.

Dazed and wide-eyed, she bent down in a bow from her waist so deep that I was surprised at how she was able to keep her balance. "My Lord . . . I am most honored and delighted by your beyond generous offer, but I . . . I am not sure I am worth that much to heaven to make such impacts as to helping your children . . ."

"No Maren. Don't say that, please!" I said in dismay at Maren doubting herself. I knew those feelings too well: the lack of confidence, the fear of failing before you tried, and the fright of losing something so dear to you because you're not strong enough. Still, the influence everyone can have on others, the gifts and talents they can spread to help the world was a feeling a million times brighter than no confidence.

I walked up halfway between her and Umbra, the wind blowing dark swirls around me backwards, allowing my hair to flow like an elegant waterfall. I motioned my hands toward Maren, who glanced to look at me like she was stunned and lost. Her eyes were dull with shame.

I bowed lowly to the cloud that held my Father in heaven, averting my eyes away in profound respect, the bell of thunder ringing in my ear. After a few moments, I felt a comforting wave from my Lord and stood up straight, nervous, but proud to be his child.

"My Lord . . . please forgive my intrusion, but I must tell Maren the honest truth. Maren . . . you are one of the most loving people I have ever met and so knowledgeable. Please, believe me. You are talented and I know you can be an amazing addition to the Angel Counsel and the entire world. We, the living, need your guidance and heaven needs your gentle touch. Maren, you are my best friend and the finest person in my life and I will miss you terribly, but I couldn't stand in the way of this chance, nor could Umbra. I love you, so please, for yourself, me, Umbra, our God, and for the benefit of mankind . . . follow your Lord and be on the Angel Counsel."

The holler of thunder silenced into a low but warm hum that soothed my soul. It felt like God himself was listening to my words. Maren twirled to gaze at me with tearstained cheeks, her eyes twinkling the most stunning dodge blue like tiny whirlpools swirling on the beach of her reflective, overwhelmed heart. Maren whispered my name into the wind in a sorrowful voice. Umbra was at my side then, poking me adoringly in the shoulder, nodding with a sweet toothless smile that extended for miles to Maren.

Maren inhaled a deep breath. She turned to face the Lord and answered his generous offer. "There is nothing more that I would love to do, my Lord, than to serve you on the Angel Counsel and aid you to the best of my abilities."

A smile stretched over my face. Happiness overwhelmed me and a squeak came out of my mouth. To add to the humiliation, I clapped my hands as I jumped a hair off the ground. Umbra laughed hardily, clasping Maren's tender hands as she giggled with pleasure.

Again, thunder cracked the sound wave of the endless night sky and God threw a lightning bolt downward inside His sanctuary, making it look like a nod of approval. "I am honored by your heart Maren. I will give you a few moments to say goodbye." Maren nodded with a smile prettier than any rare gem, but God continued in a command that made me perk up with a slight adrenaline rush.

"Stary, my chosen child. You must remember you are my Spirit Warrior with the pure heart, with the abilities to take evil out of my suffering children I sadly cannot help. Cally is here with me by the way, so please do not fret anymore. She is safe, happier, and thanks you. I know you are young, but I chose wisely and am very proud. However, do not forget your inner will and your mission to aid all of my children left behind on my Earth. You have a huge responsibility now with Umbra. Young Umbra, you must not forget your duty in this new, revived life as well.

Continue to live and grow. Remember your past, live in the present, and reach for the future for me."

Umbra and I bowed sincerely to our Lord, taking his words to full heart, replying with, "We gladly will," in sync, blushing a tad as we rose. Even God had a hint of low laughter at our connection. The thunder and lightning cracked the air like a smoking firecracker, popping the clear night into a small haze, meaning it was time for our goodbyes.

Maren went to Umbra first, their relationship flourishing like a cherry blossom tree, so beautiful that my heart melted. They honestly did love each other and I knew moving on would be hard on both of them; they were the only family the other had. Still . . . their love for each other was so magical that the living would forever be jealous of its clarity.

She hugged him closely, embracing him as if they could travel together to the end of the universe with only their content spirits as fuel. Umbra's smile was so lighthearted that I thought I could peel it off his exquisite face and keep it in my pocket. Although there was so much to say, they knew each other well enough to hardly need words; that was devotion and ultimate friendship to inspire.

Maren stood up on her tip toes, leaning on Umbra's warm chest. She sweetly kissed his cheek, making him blush in an adorable shade of pale pink, feeling her enchantment. Then she stepped down on her silk slippers and beamed, saying amiably, "You better take care of Stary . . . my brother."

Again, Umbra's living cheeks flushed. Those treasured words made their relationship known to the world—Umbra was in Maren's heart and that he cherished it as much as he loved her. Umbra smiled full of admiration and grabbed her hands like a knight, stroking them as he lifted them like they were the cleanest of air to his soft lips, placing a chivalrous peck on the top of each smooth surface of her hands.

He grabbed her into another hug and kissed her forehead before letting go and adding with the same smile, "I will, Sis."

Maren made a small curtsy like a proper lady to Umbra before stepping in a hopping motion in front of me. I cared for Maren and knew I had no time to tell her every little yearning in my soul, but I hoped I could make her remember me and how much of an impact she would always have in my life; we would always be beloved, treasured friends. Maren grabbed my hands firmly, swaying them in a movement a mother uses to rock a scared babe, back and forth, making a rhythm for her departing words.

"Stary, my dear, please always be you, the Stary Moon I love with all my heart, and never forget how special you are to me and everyone."

My heart was about to burst from a nuclear explosion of intense heat from her adorable affection for me and I couldn't stand it any longer. I embraced her hard.

"Oh Maren . . . ," I cried, tears dripping out of my eyes like a leak in a water balloon. I securely squeezed my slender arms around her swan-like neck. She giggled and hugged me with the equal amount of emotion.

She smoothed the frizzy, loose hairs at the crown of my head, and whispered into my scalp, "Awwwww, Stary." She let go gingerly, allowing me to see the longing she held to stay by my side. But then she poked my nose with a light tap, spreading fairy dust joy inside my body, and added in an adorable pixie voice, "You are so cute!" Before I could react, she grabbed my shoulders and placed a light, but loving peck on my cheek, shocking me to the end of the country. She snickered again as I gasped and then she turned her back away from us, walking forward into her new life.

Maren floated like a pure maiden, my human curiosity lost in her otherworldly charm and beauty. The fireflies that changed Umbra returned and weaved under her feet, lifting her slowly into the golden light that was then shining out of God's home cloud. The world around us was spinning into a vortex of unparalleled loveliness and Maren was the core of its existence.

Before she completely vanished into the sky, she turned around to us with lowering, saddened eyes, but her smile was brighter than life itself and she gave us a final parting wave. We returned her tenderness. And then . . . Maren was gone into the beyond comparison haven of the afterlife, forever an angel.

Umbra and I stood there, almost shoulder to shoulder, engulfed by the power of the music of the night disappearing as God's gifts and cloud got sucked into the vortex of the atmosphere. We weren't feeling sad or happy, but content, okay to live and face the world. The changes we had to face would be fine . . . as long as we were together.

I grabbed Umbra's hand, feeling the pressure rising in his veins of everything that had happened. Mine began to climb as well. We turned to face each other at the same time, friction sparking between us. I was trapped to stare hopelessly into his dazzling honey brown eyes and flawless beauty that still amazed me. My arms were crossed to hold my beating, hammering heart from being released from the cage known as my chest.

With quivering movements, I released them lightly to my sides to ask Umbra a life changing question, acting extremely shy, "Do I have to tell you or do you already know?"

With a twisted smile and arms edging the outline of his hips, he cocked his head to gaze more at my ocean eyes. He gave me an irresistible sideway and evil smile, tauntingly stating, "I don't know. Humans are pretty stupid, especially boys I hear . . ." He added a heart throbbing wink and placed his finger under his chin like a detective with a hidden agenda, making him look so meltingly cute that I wanted to collapse.

I laughed my normal, sweet laugh, feeling so comfortable and natural with Umbra that I knew I could live in that comfortable love for eternity. I tilted my head to focus more into his breathtaking eyes, eyes that shone like candles of true romance floating to their destiny on a river.

In my most heartfelt tone, I told him the words I had been going insane to tell him: "I love you."

Umbra sighed, sounding like he was also a bit relieved I was able to choke out the meaningful words. This made me giggle like Maren by his nervous reaction. He responded to his heart's plea: "I love you too."

The moment was perfect and we knew it, feeling the driving force as we listened to its cry to calm our desires. Warmly, we embraced under the stars, my siblings shining and laughing with embarrassing ecstasy of our love. Umbra grabbed my shoulders and twirled me like a princess until I stopped into his firm majesty of a chest, the arrow of love burning and shining to the world in our smiles, the smiles created just to complete the other. Then, in the vast sky, a comet soared above our heads, encircling us with twinkling magnificence. It left a trail of comet dust dazzling the sky with the new light of Umbra's love and mine.

We both paused, but still held each other, not wanting to let go for our needs were too great. I looked closer to see a wishing star, blazing in wonder. It was Maren, a sign from her. Looking into each other's eyes made us both know it.

A soft glow like a lamp entered my soul, the star telling me to make a wish, but neither Umbra nor I needed it; our greatest wish had already come true. Instead, I prayed hard in my mind that Maren and Cally would be content and Umbra and I would be happy throughout the vastness of eternity, but I knew God was kind and merciful and with the help of our love and will, my prayer would always be reachable.

23

SITTING IN FRONT OF PRINCIPAL SEA'S OFFICE WAS BORING. IT made my mind blur from looking at all his numerous golden awards, all melting together as the dates became fuzzy. To entertain myself, I swayed my feet back and forth in a comforting momentum, trying not to whack the polished floor with my long model-like legs. I sighed, placing my hands in my lap then pinned my ears to the imitation brick wall, but I couldn't hear anything anymore.

As I was turning my head to pretend to stare at the secretary typing away at the speed of light, the door cracked open making me jump like a dolphin out of water and hold my heart intact. I glanced up and then happily ran to my love's side, grabbing his hand so we could discuss what happened down the hallway of Plantersville High School.

"*So* . . . how did he take it? What did he say?" I asked Umbra cutely for the silence of his impassive face was killing me. I leaned on his shoulder, giving him a puppy-eyed look as irresistibly as I could, intertwining our fingers even more so he could not escape.

He blushed, trying to contain his laughter at my humorous expression, but he failed. Umbra let it out, charming me with his heartfelt eyes that flickered with delight. He sighed and looked forward while talking.

"Everything went fine. He was impressed and utterly shocked at my test scores. I told him my name was Umbra, but he looked at me like I was in a motorcycle gang or something and said he would not accept that as a real name. As a result, I had to make one up . . ." He blushed redder than a tomato and groaned "Stupid" under his breath with clenched teeth.

I nudged him again, not letting him get away. "And . . . ?"

"I . . . I told him my name was . . . Gary . . ." He bit his lip so hard that I thought white blood would come out.

I tried to hold it in: the bulging pain of laughter climbing up my body, pushing my throat to the limit, and the tingling on my tongue. Umbra rolled his eyes at me with an annoyed grin, hitting me in the head and I lost it. The laughter made me halt my journey in the school corridors and grab my quivering sides, trying hard to keep my respect and dignity. I heard Umbra laugh a little as well as he rubbed my shoulder.

When I was finally able to breathe after a few seconds of madness as my male peers gawked at me with weird eyes and the females were drooling over Umbra like he was all the money on the planet, I asked him, "Ga-Ga-Gary? How did you . . . think of . . . that?"

Umbra helped me stand up straight as I looked into his brimming eyes. He rammed his hands hard into his jean pockets while he explained. "I panicked! He kept glaring at me with those black eyes and glossy glasses and I'm not used to panic Stary. I eliminate my embarrassment before I can panic. It's how I'm programmed. I just . . . I noticed his pencil said 'Gary' on it and he had a large, yellow box with the name 'Gary's Pencil Company' on it, so . . . it slipped out of my mouth and he looked at me oddly, but bought it and wrote it down on the stupid paper!"

I chuckled again by how flustered he was and how adorable it made him seem. I covered my mouth to control my laughter; it was not nice for a girlfriend to laugh at her boyfriend too much. "Well . . . I'll still call you Umbra," I said sweetly, but partly mocking him.

He rolled his eyes in disapproval, glaring at me like an angry vampire bat. "I will *never* be known as Gary!"

Placing my hands behind my back, I smiled up at him and looked kindly, curious to learn more about the meeting. "So . . . what did you pick as your last name?"

Umbra's mood darkened as he lowered the arm he had placed in the air to playfully hit me on the back of the head again. His breath became uneven as his eyes narrowed to the ground. I was worried, sizzling with concern, but Umbra refused to let me feel that way. He lifted his head up high to the heavens and answered, "Rowe . . . in honor of Maren."

I was taken aback, but not at all surprised. Their bond would live on forever and everyone needed to remember its might.

"The principal asked me why it sounded familiar until it hit him and he did ask, but . . . I couldn't answer him. I only ducked my head down. I didn't mean to. My body took over. But he was . . . kind about it and didn't talk about it any longer. I suppose he's . . . not a bad man after all."

I beamed at Umbra. "Maren . . . would be real happy you did that Umbra. And . . . I'm proud. Besides . . . you *are* a Rowe. That is the family you belong to and always will, just like I will always be a Moon."

He looked at me like a muse, telling him all the words he needed to find his inspiration to move on. I giggled, mimicking Maren and tossed Umbra's bouncy curls in my fingers before rubbing his head softly like a puppy, which he actually lowered his head to allow me to do. "You're a good boy Umbra," I said.

His look was surprising. I expected him to be annoyed, but his face glowed like a child discovering an extra Christmas gift after they thought all the joy was over. I blushed at his care for me that burned from his eyes into mine, making my hand dangle down. He refused to let it. He grabbed my hand, placed a small, but heart throbbing kiss on it, and tightened it inside his own hand. I smiled and he motioned for us to continue our quest down the hall, fitting together.

I saw Chloe in the corner of the business wing talking to the recovered and normal Barbara as we were closing in on the lunchroom. She looked stunned, but I gave her my most happy grin and waved at my dear friend. She waved back like a zombie, her mouth flabbergasted as she gazed at Umbra. I knew I needed to form a story to tell her before third hour history.

Walking was still a little difficult with my banged-up knee, but I was moving much more effectively than I ever imagined by that point. Even the doctors were amazed at how fast I was healing. I was sure my Lord had something to do with it, but it would still take some time. Still, Umbra slowed his steps for me, which I knew was hard for him with his need for speed, but it made my heart elated.

As we grew nearer to the steps, I had to continue my twenty questions session. "Have you found a place to stay yet? You know you can't stay with me . . ."

He laughed like a lumberjack, tilting his head far back, his hair waving with each shake of his body before replying, "I would love to live with you, but I don't think your dad could handle it. Or you, for that matter . . ."

He grabbed my cheek, making me jerk and step on my bad toe in the progress. I blushed like wildfire as he whispered with darting, cruel eyes, "I'm an animal sometimes and with you and me alone in the same room . . . Who knows what could happen? Anything is possible . . ."

My voice began to squeak like a church mouse and my body rocked like it was a rocket about to launch. I never thought of that! Oh my goodness . . . My mind was going a million different directions, tugging on all my emotional strings.

Umbra looked away to allow me to breathe before answering, "Yeah . . . I found an apartment not too far from here. It hasn't been rented in a while due to rats or something. It's rather tiny, but it's free. The landlady and her two sons probably won't mind if I 'borrow' it."

My embarrassment attack began to cease and I laughed simply at Umbra's criminal attitude. Some things never changed. I supposed it was all right as long as no one knew.

Umbra and I took a few more steps before he stopped, almost lunging me forward. I gazed at his pleased expression that was focused on the sunlight in the center of the cafeteria. A strong ray of bathing gold was streaming down from the solar squares, looking warm and inviting.

Umbra did a double take between me and the glass panel, lost and about pushed to the limit. "Stary . . . Could I have a moment?"

I frowned at him and gave him cold eyes, placing one of my hands on my hip, disappointing him. When he turned away, I smirked and pushed him forward with my free hand, almost making him lose his balance. When he glanced back confused, I grinned and answered, "You don't even have to ask. Go on!"

Umbra's smile turned pure and full of so much thrill that I was amazed he was breathing. He hugged me before he went off. I could hear his pounding heartbeat, his beautiful, living heartbeat. It was the melody I would forever need to stay sensible. It was the most glorious sound my ears could ever know. He went to the final step, mouthing he loved me, and ran into the sunlight. No one was around. He started spinning around. I leaned on the pillar, shaking my head at how silly he was and how lucky I was he was that way.

As I glanced at my true love, my heart was at ease, but I couldn't keep my focus. I motioned my eyes around to the side, the images of my battle with Cally fluttering madly in my brain. Her soul . . . her lovely soul was forever gone. *God speed to her.* Still . . . I knew it was the right thing for everyone and although it was not the best ending, it was the fated ending.

I sighed and looked forward in Umbra's direction, but glanced at the wall. Something in my bones was calling me, vibrating insanely, pulsing like a current. Some force was telling me my Spirit Warrior powers would be needed again . . . and soon.

I wasn't surprised. My Lord told me that as well. I wasn't sure what I could do, but I was willing to give it my all and ready to do the job destiny gave to only me. I would learn everything I could about being a Spirit Warrior, blessed by the chance to help the world with my powers unlike the others who had been destined before me. At that second, I felt like I could do anything. I was not alone and I had my darling who would never leave me as I would never lose him.

Umbra came running up to me, looking finished and satisfied with his adventure in feeling the wonderment of the sun's uplifting rays. A smile lit his face that was even brighter than the roof's tinted glow. He was perfect, made for me, and I knew I didn't deserve him, but I would care for him more than any other person ever could dream of.

I grinned shyly to welcome him back, but he caught me off guard. He cheerfully jumped up to the top step, lifted me up into the air like a princess, and spun me around in the sky as we both laughed. Together, we gave in to the soaring of our hearts.

At the end of the third spin, he smiled and made my lips flawlessly land on his in a larger-than-the-universe, more-romantic-than-words kiss. It made me weak in the knees, but I knew I could wrap myself around him for support and stay forever in his arms. I loved him and he loved me; that was all I needed to be strong. I was worried about what was to come, but like my God said, I needed to live in the present. I wouldn't mind at all if this happy moment with my true love, my Umbra, lasted forever. Right then, other than being with him . . . nothing else mattered.

Hello everyone. My name is Morgan Straughan Comnick and I want to thank you so much for reading my first novel. I have been working on this book off and on since the end of my freshman year of high school thanks to the inspiring words of my English teacher, Mr. Banger, my love for supernatural/ghost stories and romance books, which started in the ninth grade, and my connection I have had to spirits for as LONG as I can remember. I hope you enjoyed *Spirit Vision*; it means so much to me.

There are so many people I have to thank:

- My parents, for loving me all these years, making me the person I am today, giving me this chance along with my brothers for being my drive to do my best.

- My family, for helping me grow up into a proper person. Sissy says thanks!

- The in-laws, my Comnick family, for always giving me smiles when I mention a new project.

- My friends (Marissa, Kristen, Sarah, Jennifer, Nathan B., Tabby, Evan, and many more) for caring deeply about me and my work, making me strive to become half as talented as they praised me.

- My classmates for making high school a living, amazing place and experiencing it with me. GO KNIGHTS!

- My writer buddies (Danny and Jamie) who not only experienced every agonizing step with me but allowed me to vent, grunt, and smile from joy over the whole process. I hope to make more author friends in the years to come.

- My darling, my true love, the other half of my soul, my own Umbra, Derrick, who makes me soar and sparks romance in me every day.

- My teachers, who made me go through all of the hard work of learning to make it feel so rewarding later in life.

- I especially want to thank Mrs. Sue Bauche, my high school choir director, who recently passed away. She gave me confidence in myself and taught me the power of music and trying my best along with giving me more love and laughter than I can count. I know she is on the Angel Counsel with Maren and will help her "Bauche babies" still.

- My co-workers for accepting my crazy costumes, weird voices, random holidays of the day, and still clap for me when I update them on my author projects. They are the best cheerleaders anyone could have. FMS and CFK rock!

- My students. You guys teach me every day and make me try harder to change the world, so I can help you and make you shine. You all have made such an impact in my life.

- Farmington, my hometown, who has given me a wonderful, magical, and safe place I want to call home for the rest of my life. Plantersville is based on you!

- I want to thank one of my favorite video game series, *Sonic the Hedgehog* and the band Crush 40 for inspiring me to create powerful character relations and to "hold on to what if." You rock Sonic Team!

- Everyone who has written a book; you guys make me see it IS possible and how wonderful it is to hold the fruits of your labor, the craft of your imagination!

- My publishing company, Paper Crane Books, and all its authors, for being my light to guide my dream and who teach me so much about the world of writing.

- My grand publisher, friend, and fellow *otaku*, Sheenah, for keeping me sane, pushing me, and making me laugh with our nerdy conversations.

- My artist, my adorable friend Suzy for making my characters come to life and encouraging me in everything I do.

- To all the *otakus* out there! Japanese culture is out there and hanging out with you guys gives me the energy to do the impossible! I especially want to thank my web siblings from my *Cardcaptor Sakura* website days; thanks to you, I was able to embrace my inner nerd, one of the best choices of my life!

- Of course, I thank my Lord for all He has given me and for my church family at All Saints for showing me my faith, helping me whenever I fall, and for all the fantastic pot lucks we are known for!

- Finally, I want to thank YOU, my fans and loyal readers, for their compassion in giving my work a chance; it makes me overjoyed.

Thank you once again dear reader. We will meet again soon, in the pages of a book. TTFN: Ta-ta for now!

With love,
Morgan

VISION

Questions and Answers

When I got permission from my publisher to announce my book, I did it in a big way over the intercom at school. I was really nervous, but it was fun and everyone was so supportive. Most authors include excerpts from their next books or something extra with theirs. I wanted to do that as well. I decided to ask all the students at the school I work at to write down a question for me about my book, the writing process, and so forth after they heard the synopsis. I mean, this book IS for their age group; I wanted to know what they thought! I got hundreds of questions back and went through every single one. In this Q & A, here are what I thought were the best questions and the two most commonly asked ones. All of them were fantastic and I want to thank the students of Farmington Middle School and High School for their support. Guys, this whole section is dedicated to you! Thank you from the bottom of my heart! You rock!

The cover for this section was made by a very talented young lady and student of mine, Ms. Jennifer Preston. All credit belongs to her.

What inspired you to write a book?

I remember writing stories in second grade at my grandma's house, even drawing pictures for them (although I am not a good artist). My imagination was always on. I even spent most of my recess time drawing story ideas with a twig in the sand or dirt in the shade! In school, we really started writing in 6th grade. My language teacher, Mrs. Horton, read my first essay out loud, describing my 8th birthday party and she cheered, dubbing me the Queen of Details for the rest of the year! I had so much fun writing after that. Once I hit 9th grade, we were required to write several papers. My communication arts teacher and my dad's co-teacher, Mr. Banger, informed me I would make a fantastic book character for HIS future book, where I laughed, but it triggered the question within me, "Why can't I write one?" He worked us hard, but he made me care about my bad spelling and grammar at the time, giving me this goal to be a writer. I took a writing class with him the next year to improve even more. The question nagged me until I began to find inspiration everywhere and soon, *Spirit*

Vision was born. By the way, Mr. Banger became a character in my book . . . Pay attention to Mr. Tin; that is how Mr. Banger acted!

What is with the names?

HA! I always liked unique names, but names you could still pronounce. So, I will tell you how the main characters got their names:

Stary Moon—I was sitting in the car after school one day, a week after I decided to try writing a book, waiting with my dad to pick up Miles from elementary school. He came out of the building and handed me his backpack. Bored, I looked in it and found a class book. I flipped through it and it had a picture of all the students in my brother's class with their pictures. I stopped when I saw a girl named "Starry." I asked my dad if that was a real name and he said he guessed it was. I fell in love with that name because I was obsessed with stars at the time due to my love for *Cardcaptor Sakura*, where Sakura uses a star wand. A few days later, I was looking at the sky, again in the car, and was trying to find a good last name for Stary. As I leaned on my window, I glanced up at the moon and it clicked. Stary Moon. I started chuckling, but I knew that it was the right name for her.

Umbra—I wanted a name that was cool, dark, but not evil. I thought about Shade, but that seemed too close to Shadow from *Sonic the Hedgehog* to me. I started studying Latin and I found, in science, the name Umbra. Well, there you go!

Maren Rowe—Maren reminds me of a beach with her refreshing energy. I was looking up baby names and I came across Maren, which means "star of the sea." Well, not only did I get my ocean, but I found a name that connected her to Stary! I wanted a sophisticated name for her and her grandfather and for some reason, I wanted it to start with an R. I had a friend with the name Rowe and it fit!

Chloe Dew—Chloe is based on my best friend Marissa. She told me she wanted to name her future daughter Chloe. She got the name for now.

Rin Fortune—Rin was the nickname for my dear friend Erin.

Lauren Flower—Lauren is the name of Kristen's, one of best friends, sister. I gave my character Lauren all of Kristen's looks and personalities, but I named her Lauren since I was friends with both of them!

Mark Steel—Mark is based on my close guy friend Mikey. Mark sounded similar plus pairing it with the last name Steel sounded cool!

Cally Sun—I just got my first cat at the time, Callie, and since my dogs were already in the story as dogs, I honored Callie this way (along with all my cats now). Sun is to represent the opposite of Stary, who is Moon.

Credence Horton—Until the first edits, Credence's name was really Sure, but it confused my publisher so after much research, I went back to Latin and found Credence, which means something is okay, close to the word sure. The reason I named him Sure in the first place was my sixth grade language arts teacher that I mentioned earlier had a new baby nephew that year and he was named Sure. She loved the name. I thought it was so unique and since I wanted to thank her for her inspiration in my writing, I named Stary's love interest Sure Horton for this teacher, Mrs. Horton. Now, he is Credence Horton, but the thanks is still there. Credence is also said to be a name of light, which is opposite of Umbra's . . . Hmmm . . .

The teachers all have a play on their real names or their personalities. A challenge to my class of 2007 who went to Farmington High School is to see if they can figure out who is who!

How was the experience (of writing)? — asked from BR

I have loved to write since I was in elementary school, but writing something this massive was scary at first. I was not sure I could do it and I knew all my mistakes in spelling and grammar would shine in a book more than a poem or my other fun writings. However, once I started, I fell in love with the characters and got sucked into the world I had created. The world was guiding me to write its story! There were challenges of course, such as writer's block or wording a section just right, but overall, it was a powerful experience that I would not trade for anything. Now that I know what to expect, I cannot WAIT to do it again!

What kind of things help your wonderful book? — asked from CC

First off, you are one of my favorite students for calling my book wonderful before it is even ready for publication! Thank you! To answer your question, I like having background noise, such as the TV on quietly or music playing. Having a beat or noise helps get the writing juices flowing. I also get inspiration from reading other books. I love to read anyway and it is neat to see what other authors are doing when it comes to word uses. Oddly enough, a lot of my inspiration comes from dreams I have or when I am taking a walk. When those ideas come, I write them down right away so I do not forget!

Is this story about your life? — asked from TW

Yes and no. Most of the characters in the book are based on people I know, including all the teachers; I just made their personalities fit the world of *Spirit Vision.* Plantersville is supposed to be Farmington and the high school is ours (go Knights!). This is because I love my hometown and I was 15 when I started this, so high school was sort of my life. Some of the normal events in this book are true or loosely true; all the spirit warrior stuff is fiction. Although, in the chapter Stary tells Umbra about the few ghost experiences she had growing up, those three events actually did happen to me! How unique is that?!

Would Christians or people who believe in God even like the book since its talking about God? — asked from EW

I have thought about this since I started this book. My answer is that a book is meant to entertain. I believe in God, but do I believe in all the spirit warrior stuff I wrote about? Not necessarily. Do I believe it is not possible? Not necessarily either. I wrote this book because I created this world and I wanted to share it with others. If you remember this is a work of fiction and can separate it from the real world like any other book, then I hope you will find something you will enjoy about it. There is love, friendships, growing up, social issues, high school humor, and more to it than God and spirits. I wrote this to share and if you learn something from it, I will let that be your choice on your own personal journey.

How did you find a publisher? — asked from MZ

A great place to start with this is talk to other authors. I had a college professor who wrote a young adult book so I went to her first. She told me to subscribe to *Writer's Digest* magazine and go to Agent Query's website (http://www.agentquery.com/default.aspx) once I wrote a query letter to find an agent. I tried many, many, MANY companies and got just as many rejections, each more positive about how good my work was than the last until I found Paper Crane Books. If you believe in your work, do research, read about writing, and never give up. It took me four years, but I finally found a company who believed in me and *Spirit Vision*!

How many drafts did you have?

HA! I went through seven full edits (adding elements, changing chapters, and so on) and more than I can count readings! Many new authors do more than this!

Do you think I will like your book?

Well, I sure hope you will, fine middle schooler of mine!

In the book, was the teacher your dad? Because I know your dad is a teacher.

Oh! A student who listens! Yes, Stary's dad is her teacher just like my dad was my freshmen history teacher and their relationship is almost identical to ours. I had to include my family in my story!

What inspired you to write this book about God and the battles Stary faces? — asked from MD

My goal was to write a story about spirits. I was into books about helping ghosts and forbidden relationships between humans and ghosts when I was in early high school. They were popular then like teens with super natural powers are now. But, when you talk about spirits, God and death go with it. My goal was to try to explain these things that cannot be explained in my own way. Like I stated above, I may not believe them myself, but it fit into the story. As for the battles she faces, I wanted to make them as fantastical and believable as possible for her situation. I drew inspiration from songs, dreams, and mostly, my own imagination.

How did you pick a topic and stayed on it for a long time? I always get off track. — asked from AG

I know that is hard for you guys! I had to take several breaks in my work; it was not ten straight years. I had high school work to do, a steady boyfriend when I turned 16 (who is now my hubby), college, and life. There was one time where I went 18 months without touching my work because I could not write a good transition paragraph for these two critical parts! In the start of college, I got this urge to work again on the project and I finished over half of it in a year! I was not going to give up on myself and what I was passionate about!

When you think of Stary Moon, what kind of person do you see, based on personality and relationship? — asked from KM

I based Stary on myself, but braver (like when she tells Umbra off from time to time; I could NEVER do that). I wanted a girl who was shy to show the world who she truly was, but would never change herself for any one. Someone who was kind and had a unique way of looking at people and relationships, which helped her understand spirits. Someone who believed in growth, love, that good and bad could have a balance, and who was innocent in mind, but wise in soul. Plus, it was fun to give her all my obsessions and nostalgias, such as anime, *Power Rangers*, singing, and so on. She is me, yet she is her own person. Does that makes sense?

How did you come up with the title? — asked from KS

I knew I wanted the word spirit in the title, but I was going back and forth on what word should be paired with it. I was actually in the bathroom during lunch, in the early stages of handwriting ideas for the book. The whole scene with Stary and Maren finding the spirit writing came when I was staring at the wall and I saw someone write something in white marker. It was hard to see and I thought, "I want Stary to be able to read spirit writing!" But, then I was not sure how she, a living human, could. Then, as I was washing my hands, I facepalmed myself mentally and said "Duh! She's the Spirit Warrior! She'd have spirit vision . . ." I kept saying spirit vision to myself, watching my expressions in the mirror. The name was so right that I knew it was my title! So, the title, *Spirit Vision*, was born in a bathroom!

What inspired the topic of your book? Was it hard for you to tie in religion and past lives? — asked from MS

Like I said earlier, I liked books about ghosts and their relationships with humans. I also was obsessed with *Sonic Adventure 2* for the GameCube at the time, which inspired Maren and Umbra's past. Religion was a little hard at first, but like I said earlier, this is a work of fiction and I can separate it from reality. The concept of past lives has always interested me so I knew I wanted to work that into my series as well.

What made you decide to make your character a freshman? — asked from CC

Two reasons: One, I was a freshman when I wrote this, so I had the view point of a freshman girl down. Two, I wanted to make *Spirit Vision* a series and starting all of them as freshmen made that much easier timeline wise.

Is this the genre you usually write about? — asked from NH

Funnily, I am not a fan of suspense, mystery, or horror books or movies and yet I have been told I am good at writing them! HA! No, I will not limit myself to just paranormal books. I have plans for several other books that I hope I can write someday. Before I started writing *Spirit Vision*, I mostly wrote poems or short stories that were set in the past, but had normal situations. Yet, many of them had sort of a . . . twisted twist. Maybe I'll publish them one day?

What is Lucifer's origin? — asked from MK

Lucifer, according to most research I have done, is a fallen angel. He did work for God until he realized he was beautiful, intelligent, and powerful. He became prideful and chose to sin in this way, not being controlled or forced by another force. He thought he could have the same power as God. This made him fall and later, he claimed another name: Satan. There are several different versions of the story, but Lucifer falling and in our minds, becoming Satan are pretty consistent. Since I gave Stary the power of light that were gifted to her by God, but it was her will to use them, I did the same with the murderer and Satan/Lucifer. Lucifer did not make the murderer kill Maren or Umbra; the thought was there and he just saw his chance to enhance it and let the murderer do what they wanted, what they chose.

About the Author

Educator of young minds by day, super nerdy savior of justice and cute things by night, Morgan Straughan Comnick has a love for turning the normal into something special without losing its essence. Morgan draws from real life experiences and her ongoing imagination to spark her writing. In her spare time, she enjoys doing goofy voices, traveling to new worlds by turning pages, humming child-like songs, and forcing people to smile with her "bubbliness." It is Morgan's mission in life to spread the amazement of otaku/Japanese culture to the world and to stop bullying; she knows everyone shines brightly.

To learn more, visit her at her website: morganscomnick.com

Made in the USA
Monee, IL
19 March 2020